D0501386

# THE

## PATH
### OF
## NAMES

## ARI GOELMAN

ARTHUR A. LEVINE BOOKS *An Imprint of Scholastic Inc.*

Library of Congress Cataloging-in-Publication Data

Goelman, Ari.
The path of names / by Ari Goelman. — 1st ed.
p. cm.
Summary: Thirteen-year-old Dahlia's reluctance about attending Camp Arava changes to wonder as strange things begin to happen, and soon she is connecting with David Schank, a student of the kabbala, and the maze he built at the camp in the 1930s.
ISBN 978-0-545-47430-6 (hardcover : alk. paper) — ISBN 978-0-545-47431-3 (paperback) — ISBN 978-0-545-54014-8 (e-book) 1. Magic — Juvenile fiction. 2. Magic tricks — Juvenile fiction. 3. Jews — United States — Juvenile fiction. 4. Cabala — Juvenile fiction. 5. Labyrinths — Juvenile fiction. 6. Camps — Juvenile fiction. 7. Brothers and sisters — Juvenile fiction. [1. Magic — Fiction. 2. Magic tricks — Fiction. 3. Jews — United States — Fiction. 4. Cabala — Fiction. 5. Labyrinths — Fiction. 6. Camps — Fiction. 7. Brothers and sisters — Fiction.] I. Title.
PZ7.G5537Pat 2013
813.6 — dc23
2012030554

10 9 8 7 6 5 4 3 2 1          13 14 15 16 17
Printed in the U.S.A.    23
First edition, May 2013

FOR MY SWEETHEARTS:
J, E, M & D.

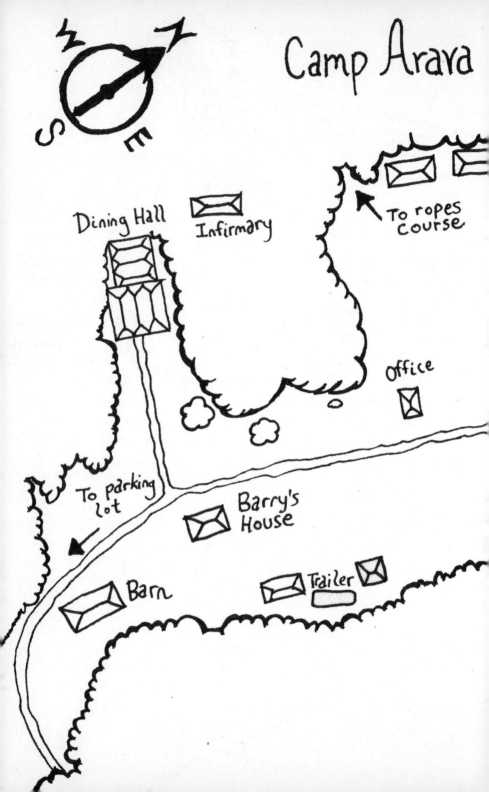

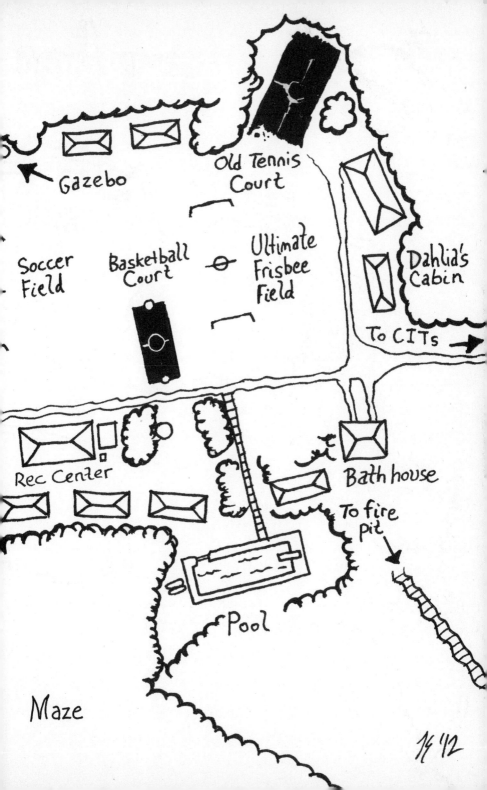

"The whole Torah is comprised of the Names of God, for the letters of the words separate themselves into divine Names when divided in a different manner. . . . In this way they write the Great Name."

**— RABBI MOSES BEN NACHMAN** (1194–1270)

"Religion is just magic, but with more words."

**— BERNIE CLOUD** (1887–1946)
(BORN LEIB YAAKOV GABBAI)

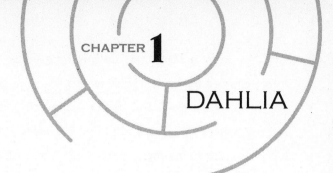

# CHAPTER 1

# DAHLIA

**D**ahlia stared out the car window and thought about Harry Houdini. She knew at least eight ways that Houdini had escaped from a straitjacket, including two escapes that he had performed underwater.

None of them did her any good. Her parents didn't have her in a straitjacket. In fact, although her father had easy access to straitjackets at the hospital where he worked, he refused to bring one home. Which was annoying, as it was impossible to learn to escape from a straitjacket without having one to practice with.

*Three weeks*, she thought again. Three weeks at this stupid camp. She'd probably be the only person there who liked math or magic tricks. Even the ride up was ugly, with the little highway taking them past a seemingly endless strip mall. Costco, Best Buy, McDonald's, Acme Fresh Market.

"Dahlia," her mother said. "Will you stop sighing like that? It's not the end of the world."

"Oh. I'm so sorry. Were my sighs bothering you?" Dahlia said. "Here's an idea — why don't you make me go to summer camp, so I won't be around to bother you so much with my *awful* sighs? Oh wait. I forgot. That's exactly what you're doing."

1

"No one's making you do anything," her father said. "You freely entered into a deal with us. To wit: You go to Camp Arava for three weeks now, and we let you go to your magic camp in August, where I presume you'll get even better at such important life skills as drawing pigeons from hats and avoiding the sun."

Dahlia shook her head. It was blackmail, plain and simple. They knew how badly she wanted to go to magic camp. "If you want to get rid of me for July, why couldn't you just send me back to math camp?"

Her mother kept her gaze trained out the window. "Nobody wants to get rid of you. We just think it won't hurt you to meet some Jewish kids."

"Plus it's a way for you and your brother to spend time together," her father put in, glancing in the rearview mirror and turning right onto a smaller road. The strip malls receded behind them, giving way to fields of green, waist-high cornstalks.

"Who says I want to spend time with Tom?" It had been years since Dahlia would have been excited to spend three weeks with her brother — years of Tom teasing her every time she got 100 percent on a math test or tried to show him a new trick shuffle. Neither of her parents bothered responding. Dahlia dug a quarter out of her pocket and started rolling it over her knuckles. It was an important move in coin magic, and she still wasn't very good at it.

After a few minutes, her father turned left onto a gravel road. Dahlia's stomach tightened. They were almost there. Sure enough, a moment later they drove across the bridge spanning the little creek that skirted the camp.

She remembered throwing rocks off the bridge three years ago, the last time she had let her parents drag her up for visiting day. After that, she had flat-out refused to go anywhere near the camp. Until now.

She was thirteen years old now. Thirteen was too old to be afraid of . . . whatever it was that had happened. Which was nothing. There was no way lightning had really struck her. It had been a perfectly sunny day, and Tom had been, like, two feet away, close enough to make fun of her for whatever look he'd seen on her face. And Tom hadn't felt anything, so it couldn't have really been lightning. Still, thinking about it, especially now that she was back at the camp, was making her skin prickle.

Dahlia pushed the memory away and looked around. When she and her parents had come up for visiting day, they'd always left the car in the small lot next to the creek. Today, though, they drove past the parking lot and straight up the gravel road into the center of the camp.

Each cabin had a handful of cars parked in front of it, with parents and campers moving in and out, carrying trunks, duffel bags, audio speakers, and whatever else the kids had brought to camp. Her father maneuvered their minivan around the periphery of the central sports field, pulling up in front of a double cabin next to the bathrooms. He turned off the engine and said, "Here we are: Tzrif Grofeet. *Tzrif* means 'bunk.' You're going to learn a lot of Hebrew without even knowing it."

"And you say magic camp is useless," Dahlia said. She glanced at the cabin, automatically checking that it had a lightning rod.

Two girls about her age were talking in the grassy area beside the cabin. They were both wearing tank tops and skinny jeans. The one with wavy brown hair said something, and the other one — taller with curly, sun-streaked hair — laughed.

Dahlia was wearing a faded T-shirt her grandfather had given her that said CUTIE $\pi$ and old cutoff jean shorts. Her stomach turned again. Three weeks was a long time to spend living with other kids her own age. Seventh grade was bad enough, but at least she could go home in the afternoon and hang out with other magicians online. At home she didn't have anyone checking if she was wearing the right pajamas to bed or something. She bet she'd be the only one in her bunk who even wore glasses.

"I changed my mind," she said abruptly, hating the quiver in her voice. "I don't want to stay here. Forget our deal."

"Dahlia." Her mother had a bit of a quiver in her own voice. "You cannot spend the summer practicing magic tricks and playing *Guitar Hero*."

"The Wii is good exercise."

"Only compared to sleeping," her father said.

Her mother spoke before Dahlia could answer. "Honey, we really believe you'll have a good time."

"Well, I don't!"

"You know the deal," her mother said. "Just try it for one week. Tom has promised to get you to a phone next Sunday. If you want to come home then, fine."

"If you let me bring my cell, Tom wouldn't have to . . ." Dahlia let her voice trail off.

Something was *shimmering* in front of the cabin. It was like the heat shimmer you see on a very hot day at the beach, or when you're looking past a hot stove. But it wasn't that hot out. And — she squinted, blinked, and squinted again — it wasn't just a shimmer. There was a person there. Two people. Little girls.

"Campers aren't allowed to bring cell phones," her father said. "They detract from the sense of community they're trying to build here."

"Uh-huh," Dahlia said distractedly. She blinked again. Yeah. Definitely two little girls, though it was hard to make out the details through the shimmer. One looked to be about ten, and the other even younger. Probably dropping off their big sister at camp.

Dahlia opened the car door and stepped out. What was making that shimmer?

The older of the two girls seemed to notice Dahlia looking at them, and she grabbed the other girl's hand. She took a step away from Dahlia, toward the cabin, dragging the smaller girl with her. Then another step. Then another.

Straight through the cabin's wall.

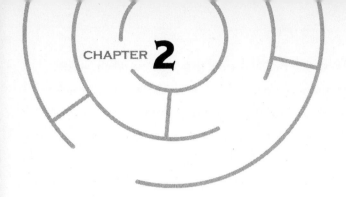

# CHAPTER 2

**D**ahlia stared at where the little girls had been standing. The shimmer in the air had disappeared as soon as they had. She rubbed her eyes.

"Sweetie, please." Her mother got out of the car next to her. "It's just one week."

"I'm not crying," Dahlia said. "Did you see that?"

"What?" Her father yawned. "Looks like a pretty typical first day of camp. Hey, do you see Brad? Tom said Brad was going to be one of your counselors."

Dahlia walked toward the cabin. The little girls were definitely gone. What a great magic trick. How had they done it?

The cabin walls were solid brown planks of weathered wood below a gray-shingled roof. Not the kind of thing that would have a concealed entrance, although she rapped on the walls a few times just to be sure they weren't hollow. The building had two doors, each with wooden stairs leading up to it, as the cabin was raised a few feet above the ground — but the little girls had been standing squarely between the two doors, several yards from either one of them. Dahlia supposed they could have ducked under the cabin, but she'd been looking straight at them, and they hadn't seemed to duck or crawl. Still, she squatted and peered beneath the cabin, just to check. Nothing.

"Um. What are you doing?" An unfamiliar girl's voice interrupted her. Dahlia quickly straightened and found that the two tank-top girls had walked over. The one who had spoken was about Dahlia's height, slim and tanned, with wavy brown hair. Her friend was taller, with curly hair cascading around her face in perfectly formed ringlets.

"Just looking at the cabin. I saw these little girls —" Dahlia hesitated. Were the tank-top girls in on the trick? They didn't seem like the type. "I saw these little girls standing over here."

"You saw little girls under the cabin?" If she was in on the trick, the wavy-haired girl was a really good actress. She seemed disbelieving without being particularly curious.

"No," Dahlia said, flushing a little. "They were standing in front of the cabin. I was just wondering where they went."

"Oh," the girl said, obviously losing whatever tiny amount of interest she had mustered. "Anyway, you're new, right?" She sketched a small wave with her hand. "I'm Chelsea. This is Michal."

Dahlia remembered Tom mentioning Michal as one of her bunkmates-to-be. She had a feeling he just knew her because she was pretty: tall and curvy, with big brown eyes. "Hi," she said. "I'm Dahlia." She glanced back at her parents. Her father was standing at the back of the minivan, wrestling her duffel bag to his shoulder. "I better give my dad a hand."

"Don't let us keep you," Chelsea said, giving her a transparently fake smile.

Dahlia walked back to the car.

"What do you got in here?" her father said, struggling under the weight of her duffel. "Gold bricks?"

"That's really funny," Dahlia said. "Ask your wife." The only things she had packed for herself were a few books and the props for a handful of magic tricks. She'd figured her parents could pack the rest, if they were so desperate for her to go to camp.

"Squirt!" She turned to see Tom jogging toward them from the sports field. "Hi, Mom! Hi, Dad! I thought I saw your car." He gave Dahlia a bear hug, lifting her off the ground for a moment before she jerked out of his grasp.

"Don't call me Squirt," Dahlia hissed, conscious of Chelsea and Michal still standing by the cabin.

"Why not?" Tom said. "What, have you adopted some stage name for your magic act?"

"Don't be a jerk, Tom," their father said. He handed Tom her duffel, which Tom hefted to his shoulder as though it were filled with pillows. Dahlia suddenly wished she *had* packed gold bricks. Or just the regular kind of bricks. Something heavier than clothes and with more pointed edges.

Tom walked toward the cabin, and Dahlia followed him. He waved at Chelsea and Michal as he climbed the stairs to the cabin door.

"Hi, Tom," Chelsea said.

"Hey, Chelsea, Michal," Tom said. "This is my sister, Squ — Dahlia. Dahlia, Chelsea and Michal."

"We met," Chelsea said. "Dahlia was inspecting the cabin for little girls."

Tom shot Dahlia a quick sidelong glance but didn't say anything. He maneuvered the duffel through the door.

"You didn't tell us you were Tom's sister," Chelsea said. It seemed like she was about to say something else when she noticed a red Mercedes SUV pulling up in front of the cabin. "Hey!" she said with real excitement. "There's Lisa's car!"

Dahlia watched as Chelsea and Michal ran toward the Mercedes. *Dahlia was inspecting the cabin for little girls.* Great. She'd been in camp for two minutes and already given the mean girls a reason to make fun of her.

"They seem nice," her father said, coming up behind her with another suitcase.

Dahlia went up the stairs to the cabin. It smelled familiar from visiting Tom all those years: the musty scent of old wood, mingled with the smells of clean laundry and dirty shoes and nylon sleeping bags. She had sort of liked the smell when they visited Tom, but the girls' bunk smelled different, more girly. Had someone really brought perfume to a summer camp?

There were eight bunk beds and one single bed arranged around the room. Two more girls her age were sitting on beds in the back corner, unpacking their luggage. Dahlia felt a little better when she saw them — neither was dressed any more fashionably than she was. One was wearing a tie-dyed T-shirt and blue jeans, and the other was dressed all in black: black T-shirt, black jeans, and black sneakers.

Tom nodded to the other side of the room, where an open door led to a much smaller room. "That's where your counselors sleep."

Dahlia counted the beds in the main room again to make sure she hadn't miscounted. "Seventeen kids sleep in a room this size?"

"You're lucky," Tom said. "Last year we had to jam twenty-four in here." He put her duffel down in the center of the room. "So where do you want to sleep? Most people like the bottom, but I'd go for the top. That way people won't sit on your bed and get your sheets dirty."

"Fine. I don't care." Dahlia wasn't particularly surprised to find that the little girls she'd seen weren't in the cabin. Because, of course, they hadn't really walked through the wall.

Tom picked up her duffel and put it on top of a bunk bed against the back wall. The girl in the tie-dyed T-shirt leapt up as Tom walked by. "Hi, Tom!" She gave him a hug.

"Hi, Sarah," Tom said. "This is my sister, Dahlia."

Sarah beamed at Dahlia. She had long, curly hair that went to the middle of her back, kept out of her face with a bright blue head-band. "We're neighbors!" she announced. "Me and Hayley have our bed right next to you." She indicated the bunk bed next to the one on which Tom had put Dahlia's duffel. The top bed was already made up with slightly faded yellow sheets and an unzipped sleeping bag as a blanket. "Hayley's not here yet, but we share a bunk bed every year, because Hayley likes the bottom and I like the top. Hayley's afraid of rolling off the bed."

"Hi," Dahlia said. "Um. Nice to meet you." She walked over to the bed Tom had selected. The springs of the bed were so loose that the weight of the duffel bag was enough to make the mattress sag several inches below the frame. She pulled the duffel onto the floor, but it didn't make the bed look any more inviting. "So you've been here before?"

"Yeah!" Sarah said. "This is my fifth summer! I started when I was eight, but then I took a few years off before coming back when I was eleven. Now I'm addicted! This year I'm finally getting to stay for second session too. How about you?"

Ha. There was no way Dahlia was staying for more than three weeks. "Nope," she said, trying not to sound too happy about it. "I'm definitely leaving after first session."

"That's okay," Sarah said sympathetically. "There are lots of people who only come for one session. Maybe next year you'll get to stay for the whole six weeks."

"Yeah. Maybe. So . . . do people play a lot of tricks on each other here?" Dahlia asked.

Sarah nodded enthusiastically. "Tons. Last year we came back from the hike, and every single piece of furniture in the cabin had been turned upside down. Even the bunk beds!"

"What about more like, um, magic tricks?"

Sarah looked blank. "You mean like card tricks?" she said.

"She means magic tricks," Tom said. He was smiling like it was the funniest thing he'd ever heard. "Dahlia's really into magic tricks. If you need someone to cut a rope and then put it back together exactly the way it was, she's your girl."

"You showed me that trick," Dahlia said. "You can't show me a trick and then make fun of me for knowing it."

"I'm not making fun of you," Tom said. "And anyway, I showed you that trick when I was, like, ten."

"You showed me that trick when *I* was ten," Dahlia said. "You were sixteen. Three years ago." It had been one of the last tricks Tom had showed her.

"C'mon, Tom." Her father took Tom's arm. "Give me a hand with the rest of Dahlia's bags. Let the girls get to know each other." He led her brother out of the bunk.

"I don't know if this counts as magic," Sarah said. "But last year Rafe and Benjy figured out a way to get Max's trunk to the top of the flagpole. It was really funny. The first ladder the counselors got wasn't long enough, and we ended up having to do flag raising while his trunk was still up there." She looked thoughtful. "I don't know how they got the trunk down in the end. I think Barry had a taller ladder —"

"Um, excuse me," the other girl interrupted. She was sitting a few yards from Sarah, on the one single bed in the bunk. In addition to her black clothing, her hair was dyed black and she was wearing black eye shadow. "When do they give us our food back?" To Dahlia, she said, "I'm Eileen. I haven't been here before either."

"Oh — you can't have food in the bunk!" Sarah exclaimed. "It might attract mice or rats! The counselors keep it in a storage room and give it back to us throughout the summer."

"But when?" Eileen said. "I'm hungry."

Sarah shrugged. "I guess it will be a surprise! They're great about surprises around here."

Eileen reached into her trunk, pushed aside some clothes, and pulled out a Mr. Goodbar. "I hate surprises," she said.

There was a moment of silence. Sarah stood. "Hey, do you guys want me to show you around?"

12

"Sure," Dahlia said. She closed her trunk. She'd unpack later. It would give her something to do when everyone who'd been here before was hugging and being excited to see one another. She thought of the girls walking through the wall and cheered up a little. At least one other person in the camp was into magic tricks.

They walked out of the cabin, and Dahlia saw her parents were talking to Nicole and Brad. Sarah grinned. "That's Nicole. She was our counselor last year. She and your brother —"

"I know," Dahlia quickly interrupted. "Is she with us this year?"

"I don't think so," Sarah said. "I think she's with the older girls."

Nicole caught Dahlia's eye. "Hey, Dahlia!" she called. "I haven't seen you in ages. Ha-ha!" She said this as though she and Dahlia had ever had any interaction aside from a handful of awkward hellos.

"Ha-ha," Dahlia said.

Brad nodded at her and raised one hand. His hair was a little longer than the last time she'd seen him — probably a year ago at Tom's high school graduation party — but otherwise he looked exactly the same. He and Tom had been best friends since Tom's first year at camp. "Hey, Dahlia. So how'd they finally convince you to come to camp?"

"Handcuffs," Dahlia said. "Threats. Ha-ha."

Dahlia's father put his arm around her and kissed the top of her head. "Watch it, punk. Brad's your counselor now."

"Ha-ha," Dahlia said. She leaned into her father a little.

"It's okay," Brad said. "I've already warned the other counselors that she's a bad seed." He pointed at the next cabin over. "I'm in there if you need anything. Don't worry. You'll love Alyssa."

13

"Everyone loves Alyssa," Nicole said.

"Ready to go?" her father said to her mother.

Her mother stepped closer to Dahlia. "Do you want me to help you unpack, sweetheart?" Her lips were trembling, and it looked like *she* was on the verge of tears, despite this being entirely her doing.

Dahlia shook her head. "You can go." It took an effort to keep her own voice steady.

Her mother hugged Dahlia. "Oh, sweetheart. You'll see. It'll be fun."

Dahlia returned the hug. "It'll be fun," she repeated, not so much because she believed it, but because she didn't want her mother to cry. This all felt much harder than going to math camp. Math camp had only been one week, and it had been full of people like her.

"Sarah, you'll show Dahlia around, right?" Nicole said too loudly, obviously for Dahlia's parents' benefit.

"That's what I was doing! Her and Eileen!" Sarah walked away, and Dahlia trailed after her, giving her parents a final wave as they got back in their minivan.

Dahlia and the other girls made it about twenty feet when another minivan — a battered gray Toyota — pulled up. Sarah shrieked when she saw a short, redheaded girl climbing out of the car. The girl looked at Sarah and immediately returned her shriek. They ran toward each other and hugged.

After a few more shrieks, Sarah seized the newcomer's arm and turned her toward Dahlia and Eileen. "Hayley, this is Dahlia, and this is Eileen. Dahlia and Eileen, this is Hayley."

"Hi," Dahlia said.

Hayley's glasses were so thick and so smudged with dirt that Dahlia could barely see her eyes behind them. "I can't believe we're finally here!"

"I know!" Sarah said.

More cars pulled up, more girls, more shrieks. By lunchtime, all seventeen beds on Dahlia's side of the cabin had been taken.

"Wow!" Sarah said. "There are a lot of new girls this year. You two plus another ten that I counted. That's, like, half new girls."

"Actually it's closer to a third — 35.3 percent," Dahlia said. Sarah gave her a funny look, and Dahlia quickly added, "I mean, assuming that there are seventeen girls on the other side too, and rounding to the nearest tenth of a percent." She hadn't seen the other side of the cabin yet — you weren't supposed to walk through the counselors' little room, and otherwise you had to walk all the way around to the other door.

"Neat!" Sarah said. "Do you do other math tricks? There's this guy in my class who knows pi to, like, one hundred digits."

Dahlia was about to say that knowing pi wasn't a math trick, it was just memorization, when she noticed one of the girls she hadn't met rolling her eyes. She flushed a little and said, "Math trick? I totally made that up. You're right. It must be, like, half new girls."

Sarah laughed. "Oh! You totally had me! Good one!"

Almost against her will, Dahlia smiled back at Sarah.

There were first-day activities. Stupid name games and introductions. After the second name game (say your name and an animal with the same first letter as your name), she had memorized everyone's name in her age group and was bored. After another three name games, it was time for flag lowering, then dinner.

She found herself walking to dinner with one of her counselors — a skinny girl named Alyssa. The sun was low behind the trees to their right, and the sky was rapidly turning a darker blue. The gnats had fled the evening coolness, and the air smelled faintly of honeysuckle from the bushes growing off to the side of the rec center.

"What a nice night," Alyssa said.

"Yeah," Dahlia said.

They heard singing coming from the direction of the dining hall, and Alyssa quickened her pace until they were almost jogging. "Darn. I didn't realize how late we were. They can't let the kids in until there's a counselor at every table." As they approached the dining hall, Dahlia saw that all the campers were clustered on the porch, with the crowd spilling down the stairs. Alyssa touched Dahlia's shoulder. "See you later — you have to wait out here."

She left her alone at the back of the crowded porch and squeezed through the press of kids around the door. "Sorry. Sorry. Coming through."

Dahlia cast around for someone she knew. She saw Chelsea, Michal, and their friend Lisa sitting on the porch railing surrounded by half a dozen older boys. She shoved her hands in her pockets and kept looking. Finally, on the other side of the porch, she caught a glimpse of Sarah and some of the other girls standing near one of the doors. Sarah was enthusiastically singing the predinner song while Hayley and Eileen were talking a few feet away.

Dahlia hesitated. She couldn't believe she had to stay at the camp for a whole week. Twenty-one meals with people she didn't know and didn't have anything in common with. She took a deep breath and walked toward Sarah and the others.

"Hey, Dahlia!" Sarah said. Hayley waved at her and even Eileen managed a faint smile, almost immediately replaced by her habitual scowl.

"Finally," Eileen said as the doors to the dining hall opened. There was a momentary pause as the entire camp tried to squeeze through the two doors at the same moment. Then the logjam broke and the dining hall started filling up with campers.

"Hey," Sarah said. "Do you want to sit with your brother?"

"No!" Dahlia saw Alyssa sitting at an empty table at the far end of the room. "Let's go sit with Alyssa." She led the other girls toward Alyssa's table, moving quickly enough that there was no time to discuss it.

They were just sitting down when Sarah motioned to someone behind Dahlia. "Rafe, Benjy! Over here."

Two boys from their age group walked over to their table.

"Hey, Rafe," Sarah said. "Dahlia's the one who was asking about tricks."

Rafe stood next to Dahlia. He was a short kid with braces and disheveled brown hair. "Great!" he said, speaking loudly into her ear, so he could be heard over the singing. "Benjy and I are doing one tonight. Do you want to help?"

On her other side, Sarah started singing a different Hebrew song and took Dahlia's hand. Glancing around, Dahlia saw that all the kids were holding hands as they sang the new song. Rafe took

Dahlia's hand for a moment, then dropped it as the song ended and they sat down.

A bowl of salad — just iceberg lettuce and tomatoes — was already on the table, along with a pitcher of dark red juice. She was surprised at how hungry she felt. Their table was right next to the entrance to the kitchen, so she could see the plastic serving carts laden with spaghetti and meatballs being pushed out of the kitchen.

"What kind of trick?" Dahlia said.

Rafe lowered his voice. "Benjy and me are going to put Jell-O mix in the spigots of all the bathroom sinks. So in the morning, the water will run red and purple, and taste weird when people try to brush their teeth and wash their faces. Maybe in the shower-heads too. If you want to help, you could do the girls' bathroom."

Next to him, Benjy grinned. He was taller than Rafe, and darker, with straight brown hair cut very short. "We brought the Jell-O mix from home."

"I knew it," Eileen said triumphantly. "I knew no one would give all their food to the counselors."

Rafe shot a quick glance at Alyssa, but she was still standing, chatting with the counselor at the table behind her. "So, are you in?"

"No," Dahlia said. "Definitely not. I was actually asking Sarah if she knew anyone who was into *magic* tricks."

An older camper dropped a platter filled with spaghetti and meatballs in front of Sarah. She ladled a few spoonfuls onto her plate and passed the platter to Dahlia.

"Magic tricks?" Rafe looked interested. "Like what?"

Dahlia filled her plate with spaghetti. She tried to keep her voice casual. "I don't know. Like making it look like someone walked through walls or something."

"Huh," Rafe said. "Do you know how to do that?"

"Um. Kind of. I mean, I know how it works when people do that in a stage show. But I can't figure out how someone could have done that trick outside in the middle of the camp."

Rafe stared at her. "Wait. When did someone do that trick at camp?"

Dahlia looked back at her plate and shoveled some spaghetti in her mouth. "Today. Do you know anyone who's into that kind of thing?"

Benjy snapped his fingers and nodded. "What about what's-his-name?" He elbowed Rafe. "You know — the little kid who's always trying to pull a rabbit out of his hat. I mean for his bonfire act."

"Josh Goldman," Rafe said. "But he could barely get the rabbit trick right. And I don't think he's back this summer." He shook his head and turned back to Dahlia. "What did you see, exactly?"

Dahlia pretended to have to think about it for a few seconds. "Um. Two little kids — girls, I think. They were standing outside our bunk, and then it looked like they walked right through the front wall of the cabin."

Rafe grinned, like Dahlia was telling him a joke. "What did the girls look like?"

"I don't know. Little girls. The older one was probably around ten. The little one was . . ." Rafe and Benjy were both grinning now, and Dahlia let her voice taper off. "What?"

"Nothing," Rafe said. "Go on. Tell us what they looked like."

Dahlia didn't say anything, and after a moment, Benjy said, "Sorry. You have a great straight face. It's just that your brother was the one who told us the McMasters story when *he* was a counselor in training. We sort of expect it from your family."

"So," Rafe said. "What did the walking-through-walls girls look like?"

"Forget it," Dahlia said. "It's no big deal. It's really not such a complicated trick."

"Really?" Rafe said. "I thought you said you couldn't figure out how someone could have done it. I mean, in the middle of the camp."

Dahlia noticed that Alyssa and the other girls were listening now, and she felt herself blushing. Stupid fair skin. Fine. In a magic trick when you wanted people to forget about something, you directed their attention somewhere else. Magic was all about misdirection. Dahlia eyed the saltshaker. It was an old trick, but that didn't make it bad. "Nah. I was just wondering where the girls had stowed the salt."

She forced herself to smile, a big smile like she had practiced in front of the mirror while she did magic tricks. People relaxed a little — watched a little less carefully — if they thought the magician was having a good time.

Rafe wrinkled his forehead. "Salt? What? What are you talking about?"

Dahlia shrugged while she thought through the trick's patter. It was an easy trick, but that just made the patter more important. "Everyone knows you can make things go through walls if you have enough salt."

"What are you talking about?" Now Rafe was smiling too, like he knew it was a trick, but he wanted to see it. Good. That was the best kind of audience.

She nodded at the saltshaker. "You want to see? Pass the salt." Taking the salt, she pulled a quarter from her pocket and put it on the table, then covered it with the saltshaker. "I'm going to use the salt in this shaker to make this coin go through the table."

"Awesome!" Sarah said. "I love magic tricks."

Dahlia unfolded her paper napkin and used it to cover the saltshaker, which was sitting on top of the coin. Then she hit the napkin-covered saltshaker with her hand. "There."

She picked up the napkin-covered saltshaker. While they were looking at the coin, which was still on the table, she slipped the saltshaker onto her lap. The whole table was watching now. Even some of the kids from the next table over.

Dahlia pretended to be surprised that the coin was still there. "Okay. Sometimes it takes a few tries."

She put the napkin over the coin — holding the napkin in the same shape, so it looked like it was still covering the saltshaker. She gave the napkin a light tap with her other hand. Then she picked up the napkin to show that the coin was still there. "Shoot. One more try."

She pushed the napkin and coin farther from herself, so they were in the center of the table. She brought her hand up high and smacked it down, flattening the napkin at the same moment that she let the saltshaker drop from her lap.

Sarah heard the saltshaker hit the wooden floor and glanced down. "Oh my God! How did you do that?"

21

"That would be a great bonfire act," Hayley said. "I can totally help you if you don't want to do it by yourself."

Rafe snatched the napkin from her hand, revealing the coin still on the table. Dahlia reached down, picked the saltshaker off the floor, and put it on the table.

"That was great," Benjy said admiringly. "Much cooler than where I thought you were going. I thought for sure it was going to be something about McMasters and the missing girls."

"What missing girls?" Dahlia said. It was probably just from eating too many of the meatballs, but she suddenly felt sick to her stomach.

Rafe rolled his eyes. "Just a stupid story about how every few years girls go missing from the camp. I mean, it's obviously not true, but every year the CITs" — he saw the look of confusion on Dahlia's face and explained — "the counselors in training, every year the CITs scare the little kids with some version of the story."

Dahlia was about to ask for more details when there was a burst of applause from the next table over. She turned to see Chelsea and Lisa with some of the other girls, all looking at her and chanting, "Go, Squirt, go! Go, Squirt, go! Go, Squirt, go!"

Dahlia scowled down at her plate. Alyssa abruptly stood and went to talk to the counselor at the next table. The chanting stopped a few moments later.

"Squirt?" Rafe said.

"A stupid nickname my brother used to call me," Dahlia said, without looking up. Her face felt hot. She waited for Rafe to make some stupid joke about it, about her blushing or her nickname or whatever.

22

Instead he said, "Old nicknames are so annoying. Especially the ones you get from your family. I have two older brothers and they . . ."

She missed the rest of what Rafe said. *Older brothers . . .* Of course. That was the answer to the mystery of the little girls. There wasn't another person in camp who was interested in magic tricks. It was just Tom being a jerk.

She scanned the other tables until she saw him a few tables behind her, his head looming above the little campers he was sitting with. He was wearing a tank top, no doubt so everyone could see his biceps, and laughing at something. Dahlia stood and stalked toward him. She heard Alyssa calling after her, but she ignored her. "Tom!" she said.

He broke into a broad smile. "Hey, Sq — Dahlia," he said, registering her scowl. "I'm sorry about the Squirt thing. Don't worry. They'll forget about it by tomorrow."

"We'll see. Did you —" She paused, suddenly aware that all the people at his table were listening to her. "It wasn't funny."

"I said I was sorry," he said, sounding annoyed. Then, looking around, "Campers aren't supposed to leave their tables in the middle of the meal."

"I want to talk to you . . . alone." Dahlia felt so mad her stomach hurt. He was supposed to be making camp easier for her, not harder.

"You have to sit back down," he said. "Let's catch up after dinner."

Dahlia glared at him for a few more seconds before stalking back to her table.

"Everything all right, Dahlia?" Alyssa asked.

"Sure." Dahlia looked down at her plate and covered her remaining meatball with some spaghetti sauce.

"We were just talking about the evening activity," Sarah said enthusiastically. "They do this thing where they give you a list of weird facts and then you wander around the camp, asking counselors questions and trying to match each fact with a counselor."

"The thing is," Hayley put in, "you can only ask yes or no questions."

"That's so lame," Eileen said. "And this spaghetti sucks."

Alyssa gave Eileen a sympathetic smile. "It'll be easy for you, Dahlia. At least to guess the fact that matches Tom. And you'll probably know Brad's and Nicole's too, because of Tom."

"Uh-huh," Dahlia said.

"Why do you always use the same one for Barry?" Hayley asked Alyssa.

"Barry's the camp's caretaker," Alyssa told Dahlia and Eileen.

"All the other counselors come up with a new fact for themselves every year," Hayley said, "so campers who were here before don't have an advantage. But Barry's fact is always that he doesn't have a belly button."

"Is that even possible?" Eileen said.

"Who knows?" Rafe said. "You never see him with his shirt off."

"Or his hat," Benjy said. "He might not have a forehead either. Now *that* would be a strange fact."

"It probably started as a joke," Alyssa said in a placating tone. "Barry doesn't come to camp activities, and anyway, everyone's too scared of him to actually ask him for a strange fact. Some

24

counselor sometime probably thought it was funny to make up a random fact for him. It just stuck."

Dahlia turned back to her food, still thinking about Tom. She wasn't sure why it made her so mad. He knew she loved magic tricks, so he had tried to make her first day special. At least, that's what he was going to say.

# CHAPTER 3

**A**s it happened, Tom denied it all. "I don't know what you're talking about," he said.

The evening activity had just ended, and Tom and Dahlia were sitting on one of the half-log benches next to the dining hall. Around them, campers were still making their way back to their bunks and tents.

"Look," he said. "I was busy with my new campers all day. And anyway, I haven't been into magic for years."

"Oh right," Dahlia said. "I forgot. You haven't been into magic since you were ten. Just let me know if there's anything else you want to change about your past."

Tom sighed. "Okay. So maybe I was thirteen when I taught you that stupid rope trick. The point is, I have no idea how to make two girls disappear."

"They didn't disappear. They walked through the wall," Dahlia said in a low voice.

"My mistake."

"It's a totally different effect."

Dahlia could barely see Tom's shrug, with the fading sunlight shrouded by the trees. She turned away to watch a handful of the counselors in training straggling up the road, carrying free-standing shelves back to their tents. Behind them, across the road, there was a little white house. She heard the front door of the house open, and a man stepped outside. He was a tall guy, wearing a baseball cap, and slightly stooped with age. It was hard to tell in the dim light, but he seemed to be staring straight at Dahlia.

"Who's that?" she said.

Tom turned to follow her gaze. "That's the camp caretaker, Barry. Why's he staring at us?"

Without thinking about it, Dahlia stood and started walking toward Barry.

"Where are you going?" Tom said. Dahlia kept walking toward the yard, and Tom darted after her. "Hey. Kids aren't allowed into Barry's yard. Seriously. Even counselors aren't allowed to knock on his door after working hours. He gets really mad."

Dahlia ignored Tom. She wasn't sure why, but she wanted to get a better look at the caretaker. She came up to the white picket fence that surrounded the house. The baseball hat was pulled low over Barry's face, so she couldn't see his eyes, but she had the impression he was glaring at her. "Hi," she said.

Barry didn't say anything. Dahlia put her hand on the metal handle of the little wooden gate, and she heard a low, very angry growl. A shadow unfolded itself from the darkness to one side of the house's door, and bounded toward her, barking. Tom grabbed her arm and pulled her a few feet back from the gate.

The dog barking seemed to shake Barry out of his trance. He slapped his thigh, and the large black dog slowly backed toward him, still growling furiously at Dahlia.

"What are *you* doing back here?" Barry said to Dahlia angrily. "Stay away from me!" He didn't wait for a response. Instead, he opened the screen door, let his dog bound inside, then stepped inside after it. The screen door slammed shut behind him, and the dog and he vanished into the darkness within. Barry didn't have a single light on inside his house. Dahlia stared at the windows, waiting for a hall light to come on, a reading lamp . . . some sign of where the caretaker had gone. But the house remained dark.

"Whoa," Tom said. "Barry doesn't like anyone. But he *really* doesn't like you."

"I noticed." Dahlia frowned at the darkened window. Was he walking around in the darkness? Watching them from just inside?

"He must think he remembers you from last summer," Tom said. He was still holding Dahlia's arm, and he gently pulled her down the road, away from Barry's house. "Why would you walk up to his house, anyway? He's, like, the one person in camp you have to leave alone. Even the camp directors don't mess with Barry."

"I . . ." Dahlia hesitated. "I don't know." The thing is, it felt like she remembered him from somewhere too. There had been something familiar about Barry's voice and the way he stood there.

"Don't worry about it," Tom said. "Just stay out of his way." He glanced at his watch. "All right. I have to get back to my bunk to start my kids getting ready for bed, and you should be back around your cabin too." He reached out and tried to ruffle Dahlia's hair, but she leaned away. "Come on. I'll walk you back to your bunk."

"I'll walk *you* back to *your* bunk. I'm not the one who's scared of the caretaker."

Tom frowned, and for a moment she thought she'd see a little of his old temper, but then he just rolled his eyes. "Yeah. I'm terrified. Come on."

As Dahlia and Tom ambled toward the distant lights of the bunks, she wrapped her arms around herself against the evening chill. Once they were through the grove of trees, she could hear the shrieks and laughter of the younger kids running through the nearest sports field, now almost completely dark.

"Okay," Tom said, heading toward the cabin where he lived with his campers. "I'll see you tomorrow."

"So long." Dahlia made herself walk back to the bunk slowly, just to prove how not-scared she was. Still, she flinched when a pair of fireflies suddenly arose from the grass in front of her. She shivered a little. It was amazing how much you could hear from the middle of the field. She heard crickets and the voices of campers in the distance, and someone playing guitar in the far-off area where the counselors in training lived. Against the light of the nearest cabins, she could make out the flickering silhouettes of Tom's campers playing in the darkness.

It was a relief when she got back to the noise and other people in the bunk. Hayley and Sarah were deep in a discussion about the counselor scavenger hunt that evening, still wondering which counselor had ridden a horse in nothing but their underwear and which counselor had performed with a New York City ballet company.

"Was it Nicole?" Hayley said when she saw Dahlia. "I mean the one who rode the horse in her underwear?"

"No way," Dahlia said. "Nicole doesn't even like big dogs."

"You could like horses, even if you don't like big dogs," Sarah said.

Dahlia shrugged. "I guess."

"All right, girls," Alyssa called from the little counselors' room. "Last chance to brush your teeth before lights-out."

Dahlia walked over to the big communal bathroom with Hayley and Sarah. She brushed her teeth and washed her face, still thinking about the caretaker glaring at her. *What are you doing back here?*

A few minutes later, lying in her bed, she found it was just as uncomfortable as it looked. She thought she would have a hard time going to sleep, but she drifted off seconds after the light went out.

**S**eventy-two years and two months before Dahlia arrived at summer camp, David Schank waited to be called into the office of Reb Isaac Ben Yisachar. He checked his watch, thrust it into his pocket, then checked it again.

As usual, Reb Isaac's outer study was full. The couches were mostly filled with the Rebbe's older followers, sharing some food after the morning prayers, but there also were a few other yeshiva students like David, and even a handful of secular strangers, beardless and hatless, come to ask the famous Rebbe for advice.

"Well, well. If it isn't the boy wonder. What are *you* doing here?" One of the other yeshiva students, a guy called Jacob, shoved in beside David on the couch. He offered David a small silver flask. "Drink?"

David took the bottle and brought it to his lips. He'd been too nervous to eat breakfast this morning, and the drink hit his stomach hard. Still, it made him feel a little steadier. "Thanks," he said.

"Why are you here?" Jacob asked.

David shrugged. "Rav Shlomo told me the Rebbe wanted to see me." Shlomo was the senior teacher at the yeshiva.

"No kidding?" Jacob stroked the patchy beard covering his

chin. "Me, I've been waiting for months to see the Rebbe, so I can tell my mother the *Rebbe* says it's okay that I go to City College. That I don't have a good brain for Torah study, anyway. But you, he summons." He took a swig from the flask. "Now why would the Rebbe distract the best student in his yeshiva from Torah study? Even for a morning?"

"I don't know," David said. He took another, smaller sip to avoid saying more. It was true that he didn't know for certain, but he had two very definite ideas, neither of which he wanted to tell Jacob.

Jacob took the flask back and looked at David speculatively. "Well. Let's see. You must be what — sixteen, seventeen?"

"Seventeen," David said absently, twisting his right sidelock between his thumb and forefinger. Had someone seen him leaving the magic show on Broadway? It had been his first one in weeks. The performer had been good, with a few tricks David couldn't for the life of him figure out. But his patter had been full of references to spirits and false gods, so attending his performance was obviously forbidden to any Jew, let alone a senior student at the Yebavner yeshiva.

"Seventeen is plenty old enough to get engaged," Jacob said. "Maybe the Rebbe has found you a match. My father was married by the time he was our age." He frowned thoughtfully. "Esther Chover is looking for a husband."

"The widow?" Esther Chover was one of the old women who pinched little boys after shul and told them to keep quieter during services. She had a long, pointed chin and downy hair covering her upper lip.

"She's a little old, but she has enough money that you'd never need to leave the study house."

"She's twice my age!" David said. "Three times, maybe. He can't really want me to . . ." He saw Jacob chuckling, and he stopped talking. "You're a schmuck," he said.

Jacob shook his head, still laughing. "As though the Yebavner Rebbe doesn't have better things to do than play matchmaker for the likes of us."

David shook his head, his own smile fading. Easy for Jacob to joke about meeting the Rebbe. Jacob's family had been Yebavners for generations. Jacob's grandparents had followed the Rebbe's father when he was the obscure leader of the tiny Jewish community in Yebavneh, Poland. Jacob and his parents had been on the same boat as Reb Isaac himself when the Rebbe led the community from Poland to New York City.

David had been nothing — a scrawny kid running after the Lafayette Street gang, the only thing going for him a good head for calculating the odds on the latest horse race. Then his mother had somehow convinced the Rebbe to take David into his yeshiva. Later, after she died, the Yebavners had found David a place to live and made sure he never went hungry. He had to work twice as hard as everyone else just to show the Rebbe he hadn't made a mistake.

After a few minutes, a serving girl came by with herring and crackers. Finally, the inner door opened, and Rav Velvel — the Rebbe's son-in-law — gestured for David to stand. Velvel firmly grasped David's shoulders and kissed first one cheek, then the other. "David," he said in his clear, precise Yiddish. "Come with me."

Jacob winked at David. "Good luck."

"So long," David said, trying and failing to return Jacob's smile.

Velvel guided him through the main dining room, past the entrance of the kitchen, and down another corridor. A door stood open, and Velvel motioned David into a small room.

The Rebbe sat on a low couch next to an open window. He held a thick book in his lap, but he was staring out the window, fingers plucking at the strands of his full gray beard. He was formally dressed in a long overcoat of black silk with velvet piping around the wrists.

He rose as David entered. "David," he said. He folded his arms around David. He smelled of alcohol and cigarette smoke. It always surprised David that such a great man would smell so ordinary. "Peace be upon you. Thank you for coming."

· David flushed. The greatest rebbe in the United States, maybe in the whole world, was thanking him for coming. His overcoat alone was worth more than all of David's possessions put together. "Thank *you*, Rebbe."

"Come." Clutching his arm, the Rebbe brought him to the couch and gestured for him to sit down. David sat, feeling as though at any moment he would wake up from a dream. Just him and the Rebbe, alone except for Rav Velvel. He had studied at the yeshiva for eight years, and this was his first personal audience with the Rebbe.

Another serving girl came in with a tray of caviar, fine table crackers, and a decanter of whiskey. David took only a cracker, hoping it would settle his stomach.

The Rebbe favored him with a small, distracted smile, then took a sip of whiskey. "You have discovered something, something important, correct?"

"I . . . I . . ." David squirmed in his seat, suddenly terrified of his own impudence. Who was he to discover the most sacred and hidden name of the divine? It was ridiculous that he had even day-dreamed the discovery. "Nothing worthy of your time, Gidolin. Great Ones."

"Don't lie," Velvel roared suddenly. "You are talking to the Seer of New York City. His foresight has saved our people from horrors of which you can only dream, and you dare —"

Reb Isaac raised a finger and Velvel immediately stopped talking. "He's not lying, Velvel. He's being humble." He motioned to David. "Go on. You can tell us. You *must* tell us."

David stammered. "I — I — I believe a holy name has come to me, Reb."

Suddenly, the room felt very quiet. The Rebbe motioned to Velvel. Velvel immediately shooed the serving girl out of the room, closed the door, and stood before it. Reb Isaac rubbed his hand over his face. "It is as I feared."

"Perhaps not," Velvel said. His face seemed calm, but he didn't look at the Rebbe. "It could be a different divine name. There are many names of God hidden in the Torah. It could be he has discovered one of the other names and had it in his mind when he went to the godless magic show last week and —"

They knew about the magic show. David started to stand. "Rebbe, I didn't. I'd never defile the name — I mean, I had not yet discovered the name when I —"

The Rebbe waved his protests away. "The performance you saw last week is nothing, David. A very small vice in the scheme of things."

Velvel continued, "All this is assuming he actually discovered a hidden name at all. He could simply be mistaken. Or he —"

"Enough, Velvel," the Rebbe said gently. He turned to David. "Please. Say the name."

David took a deep breath and pronounced the 72nd name.

Reb Isaac regarded him seriously. "Once more, please," he said.

David repeated it.

Reb Isaac glanced at Velvel. Velvel shrugged. "The first time I heard a sudden trill of a bird outside, the second time something crashed in the kitchen."

"Ah. And I heard the sound of prayers from downstairs." The Rebbe sighed. "The 72nd name. What other name would hide itself in such a sublime style? How I hoped I was mistaken." His sharp eyes fixed on David. "How? How did it come to you?"

"Yesterday, I was finishing my afternoon prayer, standing in the small classroom on the third floor." David looked away from the Rebbe's keen gaze. "I was in the middle of the Amidah, and the name emerged in my mind." He hesitated. How could he describe that moment? The power that had filled him. The desire to teach the name to everyone.

"The name *emerged* in your mind," Velvel repeated. "Generations of sages pray for this precise revelation, and it simply *emerges* in your mind. Why should the most sublime name of the Lord reveal itself to you?"

"Well," David said. He didn't understand the anger in Velvel's voice. "I've been reflecting on the 72nd name for months. I believe that it is precisely three hundred and sixty years since it revealed itself to the Maharal of Prague. Three hundred and sixty is — ah — five multiplied by seventy-two, of course. I further believe that every seventy-two years, the name weakens the boundary between this world and the world-to-come, and so by focusing my —"

"How very clever of you," Velvel interrupted. "Did you consider in your 'reflections' that scholars are explicitly prohibited from the study of kabbala until the age of forty? As are men who are not married — both prohibitions that most emphatically apply to you. Unless . . ." He paused and raised his eyebrows. "Wait. Have you been married and I didn't hear? Have you miraculously aged a few decades since your last birthday?"

"No." David stared at the carpet between his feet. Of course he was aware of the prohibitions, but he assumed his success would be all the more impressive given his young age.

"The study of kabbala is not a parlor game," Velvel said harshly. "It is solely for the purpose of reassembling the fragmented light of the divine. Bad enough that you ignore —"

"Velvel. Enough. Stop taking it out on the boy." The Rebbe turned to David. "Have you told anyone else of your discovery?"

David shook his head. "No one."

"All right. There's someone you should meet." He gestured to Velvel. "Take David to meet our guest."

Velvel hesitated.

"He should see with his own eyes." The Rebbe's gaze was steady on Velvel. "Be prepared. I am sorry to lay this responsibility solely on you, but the fewer of us who know, the better."

David cleared his throat. What was going on? He had rediscovered the 72nd name of God. The very number seventy-two was magical — eighteen, the number of life in the Hebrew alphabet, multiplied by four, the number of letters in God's proper name YHWH, which only the high priest of the Israelites had been permitted to say aloud, and that, only on the most holy day of the year. The 72nd name was the name Moses had used to split the Red Sea, the name that sages had used to create golems, to slay demons, to exorcise evil spirits. With it, the Rebbe could protect not just the Yebavner community, but all the Jews still left in Europe. Where were the congratulations? Where was the celebration?

The Rebbe picked up a sheaf of papers from a small side table and tucked them inside the book he had been holding when David entered the room. He handed the book to David, and David read the cover.

### The Path of Names
### by Reb Isaac Ben Yisachar

"Rebbe," he said, awed. A whole book of the Rebbe's thoughts.

"You're giving that to him?" Velvel obviously disapproved.

The Rebbe looked at Velvel bleakly. "And what else is it good for now?" He turned to David. "Half of the pages in this book have been left blank for the English translation. In the days to come, you may find it useful to have something to concentrate on that is not the most sublime name."

"Rebbe," David said again. To be one of the first to see the Rebbe's work, and then to be trusted with the translation . . . It was an enormous honor. "I don't understand."

"It will become more clear shortly," the Rebbe said. He rubbed his eyes with one hand, then pinched the bridge of his nose between his thumb and forefinger. "Take the book. May it bring you joy."

"Rebbe?" David said. "Are you well?"

"Go," the Rebbe said. "We — you — don't have much time."

He motioned to Velvel, and Velvel grasped David's elbow. "Come with me."

"Rebbe?" David looked to Reb Isaac, not understanding. Shouldn't they at least drink a toast to the Rebbe's book?

The Rebbe met his eyes. "Go with Rav Velvel. He speaks with my voice on this matter." He hesitated. "I'm sorry."

"You're sorry?" David said, growing even more bewildered. What the devil did the Rebbe have to be sorry for?

The Rebbe turned away from David and looked back out the window. Velvel's grip on David's arm tightened. "Come with me," he said again. "There's someone you should meet."

After a moment, David let himself be drawn from the Rebbe's study. He followed Velvel deeper into the private passages of the house. The halls were lavishly appointed, covered with gilded golden wallpaper and paintings every few yards. It was totally quiet, except for the occasional giggle of the Rebbe's daughters in the distance.

Velvel led him down several flights of increasingly narrow stairs. A serving girl passed them carrying an armload of linen, and a cat brushed by David's ankles. After the third flight of stairs, they came to an open door to the street. Outside, a man standing next to a cart full of vegetables was engaged in a low-voiced but heated argument with two or three women from the Rebbe's household. Velvel paused for a moment as one of the women glanced over at them, then he led David down yet another set of stairs.

As they walked into a dimly lit storeroom, David reluctantly gave up the hope that Velvel was taking him somewhere to celebrate. They picked their way past burlap bags of flour and crates of wine. At the back of the storeroom, there was another staircase leading down.

Velvel continued descending. After a moment, so did David. These stairs were broader than the previous ones, and were made of stone rather than wood. The room at the bottom of the stairs was unfinished and smelled of dirt and rock. In the dim light of a single lightbulb, David could make out little more than a few benches placed along the walls. Velvel walked to the far wall, and David saw a safe set into the plaster. Velvel spun the dials.

"What are we doing here?" David said. "I thought the Rebbe wanted me to meet someone."

"He does." Velvel opened the safe's door, reached inside, and flipped a switch. "Many years ago, the cellar of the house that used to stand here was a stop on the Underground Railroad. We have our own uses for it."

Velvel stepped back, placed both hands on the wall around the safe, and pushed. With a creak of hinges, a small door swung open, revealing yet another set of stone stairs leading down.

"Rav Velvel. What's going on?" David said.

Velvel indicated the opening. "Go on."

David stepped up to the threshold. What was the Rebbe hiding down here? With only the single bulb behind him for light, he could make out nothing below. He took a cautious step down and hesitated. It was so dark, he had to feel for the next step with his foot before continuing down the stairs.

He was about to turn back to Velvel and request a light when he heard something below him. It sounded like a groan.

"Hello?" he said.

A hoarse voice said. "Help me. Please."

The door clicked closed behind him, and the darkness was complete.

# CHAPTER 5

# DAHLIA

**I**n Dahlia's dream, she was sitting in a room with two Orthodox Jews. Not just a little Orthodox, but really Orthodox — black hats, black coats, big Santa Claus beards. They were both looking at her, encouraging her to say some kind of magic word. She opened her mouth, both frightened and proud of the word she was about to say, and a man's voice emerged.

"Good morning, Camp Arava! Flag raising is in forty-five minutes."

The Beatles' song "Good Day Sunshine" started playing loudly from the loudspeaker mounted on the cabin wall. Dahlia threw her arm over her face and squinted against the morning sun. It took her a second or two to remember where she was. Right. The second day of camp. Six more days and she could go home.

What a weird dream. Why would she dream about being an ultra-Orthodox Jew? She'd never even met an ultra-Orthodox Jew before. Being at a Jewish camp must really have her subconscious freaked out.

She rolled over and closed her eyes, but the music was too loud to even pretend to go back to sleep. She opened her eyes and sat up. In the next bunk bed over, she saw Lisa pull her comforter over her head.

The screen door slammed shut and Sarah and Hayley came into the room, already showered and carrying their toiletry buckets. Sarah beamed at Dahlia. "Good morning! Hey, did you help Rafe and Benjy? My shower was green this morning."

"Mine was purple," Hayley said with distaste. "I had to let it run for ten minutes to get the Jell-O out of the showerhead."

Dahlia half waved at Sarah and Hayley, then rubbed her eyes. For a moment, she felt a distinct urge for a cup of coffee. Which was weird, as she never drank coffee. She pushed her blankets off and climbed down from her bunk bed. Grabbing her towel and toiletries from her cubby, she slipped out the screen door.

Outside it was a bright morning, still so early that the grass was moist with dew. By the time she was showered and changed, the bathrooms were crowded and there was a line of girls waiting to get in. She walked back to the bunk and dropped off her toiletries. About half the girls in the cabin were still in bed. Alyssa and their other counselor, Selena, bustled out of the small room where they slept and flicked the lights on.

"Wakey, wakey," Selena said in a falsetto. "Let's go, girls."

Chelsea opened one eye and glared at Selena. "That voice is so annoying. Could you please just pour water on us or something?"

"Speaking of water," Alyssa said. "If you want a shower before breakfast, that window of opportunity is just about to close."

That was enough to get Chelsea and Lisa up. Yawning, Lisa

pushed past Dahlia and nudged Michal, who hadn't stirred throughout the exchange. "Come on," she said.

Michal yawned and stretched, then obediently sat up. "Why didn't they make an announcement?" she asked sleepily.

"Come on," Chelsea said. She and Lisa walked out the door, with Michal straggling behind them. None of them so much as looked at Dahlia.

"How did you sleep?" Alyssa asked her in a cheery tone.

"Fine," Dahlia said.

"Great! This morning we're picking work groups." Alyssa glanced around the cabin. Everyone was awake except Eileen, who had turned toward the wall with a pillow pulled over her head. Alyssa stepped toward her and nudged the frame of her bed with her sneaker. She sang, "Come on, Eileen. Oh, come on, Eileen. At this moment —"

Eileen bolted upright. "I'm up. Please don't sing that song to me. Nineteen million times is enough."

Twenty minutes later, all the campers and all the counselors in the camp stood in a large unwieldy circle around the flagpole. After everyone quieted down, the head of the camp, a short guy with a goatee, said, "Good morning, Camp Arava!"

"Good morning, Aaron!" the crowd shouted back.

Dahlia stood there wishing they would just hurry it up. Her odd desire for coffee had given way to a more general hunger for food. Any food. Which was *also* weird, because she hardly ever ate breakfast at home. Now, though, she couldn't wait for breakfast, or at least a piece of fruit. Something. She hoped Aaron wouldn't talk too long.

44

"So. Last night someone put Jell-O powder in the bathroom showerheads." Aaron waited for the smattering of laughter to pass. "That wasted both food and a lot of water. And there's still a lot to be cleaned up. Who's going to clean the bathroom?"

A few campers in Dahlia's age group cast sidelong glances at Rafe and Benjy.

"Aside from Rafe and Benjy," Aaron added, "who have already generously volunteered to spend their free time for the rest of the week cleaning the bathrooms."

Rafe muttered something, staring sourly at the ground in front of him.

"Of course, the real answer," Aaron continued, "is Anaf Briut — the bathroom cleanup work group!"

For some reason, there was scattered applause throughout the camp. "Yay!" someone shouted. "Go, Briut!"

Three counselors ran up to the flagpole, holding plungers and mops. This began a series of skits aimed at introducing campers to the various work groups they could choose. After a few minutes of standing, Dahlia sat on the patchy grass like most of the other campers.

There were about two dozen work groups to choose from. She could sign up to serve breakfast to the camp every day or paint the inside walls of the barn or clean the rec center or any other random chore she could think of. There was a "lumberjack" work group, which, as far as Dahlia could tell, would spend the whole week gathering deadwood and preparing for the Saturday night bonfire. This seemed like an awful lot of work for something that probably lasted about an hour, but maybe she was missing something.

She was trying to decide which would be worse, cleaning the bathrooms or feeding the chickens, when Tom and Brad ran through the crowd of campers and jumped onto the low stone platform around the flagpole. Tom was wearing a red blanket tied around his neck as a cape, and Brad was wearing a cheap plastic Batman mask.

"Wow, Batman," Tom said, shading his eyes with his right hand and pretending to examine something in the distance. "This maze sure is cool."

"Yeah, Superman, who'd have thought that Camp Arava would have an English hedge maze in the middle of the woods?"

"With real juniper bushes! And to think, no one had used it for years before that work group pruned back all those bushes and made it usable."

"What a great work group," Brad said. "Those guys were the real heroes."

Tom turned to face the campers. "Be a hero with Anaf Maze! There's an old maze in the woods that hasn't been used for decades. In our work group, we're going to clear it out."

Brad punched the air. "Pow. Kazaam. Yipes."

Rafe leaned over Eileen and Hayley to tap Dahlia's shoulder. "Your brother's totally got the best work group," he said loudly.

Dahlia rolled her eyes, but she had to admit that if it wasn't Tom's work group, she would have joined it for sure. A real hedge maze, like in Harry Potter. Who, she wondered, would have put an English hedge maze in middle-of-nowhere Pennsylvania?

One more skit followed Tom's. Then every camper got a little slip of paper and had to mark their top three choices for a work group. Dahlia made the breakfast work group her first choice, mostly because she was so hungry and they got to eat before the rest of the camp. For her second choice she selected painting, because that was the work group Alyssa was leading. She didn't give a third choice, figuring that would make it more likely to get one of her first two.

Finally, the counselors collected the papers from all the campers, and the campers were allowed to race to breakfast. It was still only nine a.m., but Dahlia was so hungry that she ate three of the doughy pancakes before realizing quite how bad they were. Then she ate another two anyway, smothered with enough fake maple syrup that she couldn't taste them.

After breakfast, Aaron read out the work groups, speaking so quickly that he managed to get through two hundred campers in less than ten minutes. Dahlia was in Alyssa's painting group, along with Chelsea and Michal and half a dozen kids she didn't know from other age groups.

Alyssa was getting the group organized outside the entrance to the dining hall when Tom led his maze work group past them. Tom's group was almost all boys, most of them younger than Dahlia.

"All the boys who didn't get into lumberjacks," Chelsea said to Michal. Who, of course, giggled.

Dahlia watched as Tom's group walked up to the road, then turned right to head down to the woods. As the last of them walked past the caretaker's house, she saw Barry step out of his front door. He was wearing his baseball cap pulled low over his face again, but from what Dahlia could see, he was frowning as he watched the kids walk into the woods.

"Okay, guys," Alyssa said loudly. "Everyone in a circle in the grass here." Dahlia made a point of sitting where she could keep an eye on Barry. For the moment, he seemed content to just stand in his front yard, sipping his coffee and staring into the woods where Tom had led his work group.

It turned out that the paints Alyssa had ordered hadn't arrived yet, so they ended up playing name games to get to know the other people in the work group. While they were playing, Dahlia counted that she had memorized the names of forty-seven people since arriving the day before. At this rate, she would have the entire camp memorized in something like four and a quarter days.

A small crash from Barry's yard caught Dahlia's attention. She glanced over and saw Barry stomping angrily out of his front gate, almost running in his strange, stiff-legged gait. His coffee mug lay in pieces where he had dropped it on the redbrick path leading to his front door. He headed down toward the barn, climbed onto his little tractor, and drove into the woods.

Down the same dirt road that Tom had led the kids.

"**O**uch. Ow. Ouch," Tom said. He tossed the remains of a blackberry bush onto the pile near the maze's entrance. Canvas work gloves were just not enough protection for pulling up blackberry bushes. He needed a leather suit. Or plate mail.

"Um. Excuse me, Counselor Tom." Tom looked up to find Mitchell Atkins, one of the new kids in his bunk, peering earnestly at him. Mitchell was a skinny kid whose blue eyes had this kind of tic where his eyeballs vibrated slightly from left to right. His friend, Jaden, stood a few inches behind him.

"Hi, Mitchell. You don't have to call me 'Counselor Tom' when the other Tom isn't around," Tom said.

"Oh. Okay. Can me and Jaden go back to our cabin?"

Jaden pushed the haze of blond hair out of his face and said something to Mitchell too quietly for Tom to hear. Jaden's voice seemed to have two volumes: too soft to hear, and shouting.

"Yeah," Mitchell said, apparently in response to whatever Jaden had said. "There aren't enough gloves for everyone, so there's nothing for us to do."

Tom glanced at his watch. Another fifteen minutes to kill.

"Why don't you guys pick blackberries? Bring back what you find and we'll all have a snack when work period is done."

The two boys immediately brightened up and ran past Tom. They were soon out of sight, squeezing through gaps in the not-yet-pruned plants as they made their way farther into the maze.

Tom looked around. Clearing the maze was easier than he'd thought it would be. It hadn't been used for God knew how long, but by tomorrow they'd already be clearing its second circuit. Oddly, the juniper bushes themselves seemed to barely need trimming. Most of the work was pulling up the other plants that had grown in the pathways over the years.

He heard the *put-put* of the tractor's motor approaching on a nearby trail. He wondered what Barry was doing all the way out here. The sound grew closer and closer until it stopped just down the hill from the maze. The motor stayed running, though, filling the hillside with the smell of diesel.

*Someone should really tell Barry to turn off the tractor when he isn't using it*, Tom thought. Then he saw Barry limping up the hill toward him, a cigarette clenched between his teeth. *Yeah, right. No one even told Barry not to smoke around the kids.*

"Hi, Barry," Nat Larson said brightly as he carried an armful of blackberry bush past the caretaker.

Barry raised a hand in what could have been a wave. "Kids aren't allowed down here," he said.

"They're with counselors," Tom said. "We're clearing the maze."

Barry looked at him, smoke curling up from the cigarette at the side of his mouth. It was hard to read his face under the shadow of his baseball cap and the large sunglasses he wore. "You. You're the one who was bothering Tramp last night."

Another rule broken — scolding a counselor in front of kids. The staff was supposed to do that stuff in private. "No, I wasn't," Tom said. "One of the new campers didn't know your yard was off-limits. I was just letting her know."

Barry blew air through his lips. It could have been a sigh of acceptance. It could have been an exhale of cigarette smoke. "Anyway. No kids in the maze."

"What?" Tom said. "Why?"

"Dangerous down here. Copperheads. Worse."

"I keep the kids away from the creek." Tom wondered if there were any copperheads left in these woods anyway. In eight years at camp, the worst he had ever seen was a garter snake, and he and Nicole used to hang out by the creek all the time when they were counselors in training. That was how he'd come across the maze in the first place.

Barry walked past him into the first circuit, where Rafe Anderson and a handful of other kids were clearing the bramble. "The creek ain't so bad. I git the rocks down there sprayed for snakes. This bush, though . . . Tons of snakes in this kind of bush. Raccoons too."

Hannah Vogt gave a little shriek and backed away from the bush she'd been clearing. Barry kept walking until he passed all the kids except Mitchell and Jaden, who were out of sight within the maze.

Tom followed the handyman through the first circuit of the maze. They stood facing the uncleared bramble together. "But I thought copperheads liked the water."

"Copperheads don't *like* anything," Barry said. "They don't have pref-er-en-ces" — he drawled out the word — "that you'd notice." He turned and looked back at Tom. "We got a tree bench that could use repairing. Why don't you do something useful with these kids, 'stead of putting them —"

In the distance, they heard Jaden shout, "Stop throwing blackberries, Mitchell."

Barry spun to face the heavier underbrush farther in the maze. Tom had never seen him move so quickly. "How many kids you got in there?" Barry hissed.

Tom felt a vague stirring of unease. "Two. Two boys."

"Call them back. Right now." Barry was staring into the maze, his whole body focused and tense. His lips were pursed and white, his cigarette evidently forgotten, smoke still drifting from its lit end.

"Jaden, Mitchell!" Tom raised his voice. "Come on back."

There was a moment of silence. Then Tom heard the breaking twigs and complaints of two small boys picking their way through a tangle of blackberry bushes. Mitchell emerged a few yards away from them. His forearm was bleeding from a few small scratches, and his lips were purple with blackberry juice. In one hand he held his baseball cap, half filled with blackberries. Before Tom could say anything, Mitchell burst out, "I wasn't throwing ripe berries. They were totally green, and we're going to chop down the bushes before they ripen, anyway."

Jaden emerged behind him, his empty hands covered with blackberry juice and scratches. "I didn't find any berries!" he shouted. "No berries!"

"Yes, he did," Mitchell said. "He just —"

Barry interrupted, "You kids see anything in the maze?"

Mitchell nodded. "Blackberries. Some other bushes, I didn't know the name."

Tom was pretty sure Barry relaxed a bit, although his face didn't change expression. "Get these kids out of the maze," he said to Tom.

"This is our work group," Jaden shouted.

"Yeah!" Mitchell shouted, and laughed.

"Not anymore," Barry said. He kept his eyes trained on Tom. "You make sure these kids don't come back here," he said. "Not for work groups. Not for anything. You hear me?"

Tom hesitated. He felt like a camper getting scolded for going into the woods without a counselor. But it was genuinely freaky seeing Barry this unnerved. Maybe there really were poisonous snakes in the maze. "Tell you what," Tom said. "We'll make sure that the counselors are always the first ones into the uncleared part of the maze, and we'll make sure all the kids wear their hiking boots before they're allowed down here with us. How does that sound?"

Barry stepped closer until his dangling cigarette was just a few inches from Tom's forehead. The smoke made Tom's eyes water. "Tell *you* what," Barry said softly. "You'll cancel this work group right now, or I'll let the camp committee know you're endangering campers, and they'll cancel it for you. How does *that* sound?"

From outside the maze, Brad called, "Hey, Tom, what's up?"

"Ah . . ." Tom said, stepping back from Barry. "Change of plans. Meet me at the entrance."

The kids had mostly stopped working by now, with the exception of Nat. Nat was grimacing as he tried to cut through a small sapling that was clearly too big for the gardening shears he was using.

"Okay, folks," Tom said loudly. "We're changing things up. C'mon out to the entrance. Nat, this means you too. And point the shears at the ground, please. At the ground!"

Brad was waiting at the entrance with the older kids. Tom quickly told him what had happened, minus the threat to call the camp committee and the general Barry freakiness.

"Where's the tree bench that needs repairing?" Brad asked Barry.

"In front of bunk five."

*Bunk five.* Barry had been at the camp longer than anyone, but he still refused to use the Hebrew names of the cabins. "Which bunk is that?" Tom asked.

"Next to the bathrooms. To the right." Barry turned, took a few steps, and paused. It was hard to tell, but again Tom thought Barry looked relieved. His thin lips seemed slightly closer to a smile than usual. Or at least, his frown was less pronounced. "Let me know if you need any more saws or wood for the tree bench. I got plenty of extra below the barn."

"Thanks." Tom didn't dare to make his tone too sarcastic. There was something about Barry — maybe just that he had been the caretaker since before Tom was born. Or maybe something else entirely. Whatever it was, everyone knew you didn't mess with Barry.

Barry nodded and trudged away, head bent against a wind that wasn't there.

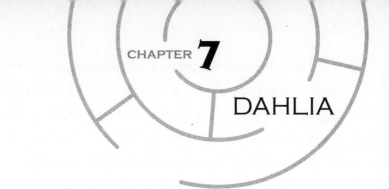

# CHAPTER 7

# DAHLIA

**D**ahlia was relieved when she saw Tom leading his work group up the road. She wasn't sure what she'd been worried about. It was just that Barry had seemed so mad, and he'd driven off in the same direction that Tom had gone.

Alyssa saw Tom's group approaching as well, and said, "Okay, guys. We'll end early today too. Hopefully our paints will be here tomorrow, and we can get started." Alyssa stood and walked down the hill toward Tom.

Dahlia went the other direction, back toward her cabin. Most work groups were still going on. Some kids were sweeping the porches of the rec center. An older boy walked past her, carrying a big package of toilet paper and a plunger.

The cabin was empty and dark. She went to her bed and took out her book on sleight of hand. Tricks like the saltshaker one were fine, but she really needed to get better at sleight of hand before going to magic camp in August. Right now, she was no good at hiding anything bigger than a silver dollar in the palm of her hand. She put down the book and picked up a pen someone had left on their cubby. All she had to do was hold the pen hidden in the crease of her palm while the back of her hand faced the imaginary audience. She took the pen in her right hand, and waving her left hand over her right, she tried to palm it.

And tried.

And tried.

She was picking up the pen from the floor for the tenth or eleventh time when she realized she wasn't alone. A young girl stood on the other side of the bunk, just in front of the counselors' room.

"Oh," Dahlia said. "Hi."

The little girl looked down shyly. She seemed to be about ten, maybe even nine. She was wearing an old-fashioned ankle-length denim skirt and a ruffled white blouse. The girl must have been in the counselors' room when Dahlia came inside, because Dahlia was sure she hadn't heard the outside door open.

"Hey," Dahlia said. She took a step toward the girl. "You're the one who did the trick yesterday, right? Where you walked through the wall? How'd you do that?"

The little girl shrugged.

"Is your sister in this bunk or something?"

The girl glanced at Abby Simkin's bed.

"You're Abby's sis —"

Dahlia stopped talking. Another girl was sitting on Abby's bed, one who looked even younger than the first. Maybe just six or seven. Definitely too young to be at sleepaway camp. The girls had to be sisters. They both had blonde, curly hair, and they were both overdressed for the heat, with the littler one wearing a long-sleeved, orange dress.

"Aren't you guys hot?" Dahlia asked. She didn't understand

how parents could send these little babies away for three weeks at a time. They didn't even know how to dress themselves.

The older one cocked her head, then glanced at her sister. The littler girl walked over to Dahlia. She mimed holding the pen, then held her hands together in a beseeching gesture.

"Um, okay," Dahlia said. Maybe they were deaf-mutes or something and couldn't hear her or speak. "Sure. Then maybe you can show me how you walked through the wall." She held the pen in the fingers of her left hand, then pretended to take it into her right hand while actually letting it drop into the palm of her left hand. Once again she fumbled the palming action, although this time she managed to catch the pen before it fell.

The two girls collapsed into silent giggles, and Dahlia smiled too. Oddly, she still didn't hear the tiniest sound coming from them. Even someone who couldn't talk would make some sound when they laughed, wouldn't they?

Then, abruptly, both of the girls stopped laughing and looked toward the back of the bunk. Dahlia followed their gaze and saw — or, for a moment, she thought she saw — the barest outline of a man's figure walking toward the girls.

She blinked. There was no man there, just the trembling shadows cast by one of the big trees outside the cabin. But the girls were still staring toward the back corner of the cabin. The older girl took a few steps away from the shadows, obviously frightened by something.

The younger girl seemed to be more puzzled than scared. Glancing back and forth between the shadows and Dahlia, she slowly mouthed the words, "He . . . knows . . . you."

She was pointing at Dahlia to emphasize the word *you*, when she abruptly spun around, one arm craned above her head. She appeared to struggle to pull her arm down.

Dahlia stepped toward her. "Who knows me? Are you okay?" Was she having some kind of fit?

The younger girl tripped toward the cabin's front wall, one arm still lifted awkwardly over her head. But even as she staggered away, she kept her head turned to face Dahlia. "How . . ." Her lips moved too fast for Dahlia to have any idea what she was asking.

"How what?" Dahlia said. "Who knows me?"

The little girl half walked, half fell through the front wall of the cabin, still staring at Dahlia.

Dahlia looked around. The older girl was already gone. She realized what the younger girl's exit had looked like. Not a fit at all. More like someone tall was standing next to her, clutching her arm and dragging her through the wall.

Which was plainly impossible. Not just that the girl had gone through the solid wall. But that there had been some almost-but-not-quite invisible man in the cabin who could drag two little girls around with him.

Dahlia's face felt hot, her mouth dry. "Oh, come on," she said loudly, trying to keep her voice from shaking. "A good trick should be for lots of people, not just for making one person feel stupid. And you shouldn't repeat the same effect either."

Footsteps on the front stairs. The cabin door opened and shut with a loud bang as Chelsea and Michal came in. Chelsea looked around. "Who were you talking to?" She glanced toward the counselors' room.

Dahlia didn't bother answering. How stupid did they think she was? At the same time, she felt almost relieved. For a second there she had almost believed . . .

"Oh, right," she said. "So you just *happen* to show up just after them again?"

"Um. Crazy often?" Chelsea said.

"Come on," Dahlia said. "I know it's a trick. How do you do it?" She walked over to the wall the girls had appeared to pass through. Like all the walls in the cabin, it was covered with graffiti.

*Neil Bernstein, Sofim 2006–7*
*Toby 2006*
*Briana and Justine — BFF*

And so on. No mirrors, no doors. Just a solid wall. She rapped on it with her right fist. It sounded the same wherever she knocked on it, and anyway, it wasn't thick enough for a secret compartment. She looked around — there *had* to be something.

"You're such a freak," Chelsea said. She turned away from Dahlia and went over to the bunk bed that she shared with Lisa. She had hung a sheet from the upper bunk so her lower bunk was hidden from view. She pulled the sheet aside and tossed her sweatshirt on her bed.

Dahlia followed her. "Are they your little sisters?" she said.

"Who?" Chelsea said. "What are you talking about?"

"Are the little girls who were just in here your sisters?"

"How would I know who was just in here?" Chelsea said, brushing past Dahlia on her way to the door. "And anyway, I don't have any sisters."

Michal gave Dahlia a hesitant smile and hurried out the door after Chelsea. As they walked away, Dahlia heard Chelsea's voice through the screen. "I honestly don't think she could be any weirder. I mean, she's like the . . ."

Dahlia didn't hear the rest of the sentence, but Michal's laugh carried back to the bunk.

She walked over to her bed and sat down on the edge of the bottom bunk. Who would drag a little girl away so brutally? The girl had seemed so scared when she was pulled through the wall.

*Stop it*, she thought. No one had really passed through a wall. It was a trick, it *had* to be a trick, and here she was thinking about the girls like they were ghosts or something.

*Ghosts.* Dahlia dug through her trunk and started looking for her book on Houdini. Houdini had spent half his life searching for evidence of an afterlife, and he hadn't found it. Then for years after his death, his wife had held séances on the anniversary of his death, praying for some sign of life after death. She'd never seen a thing.

Dahlia found the Houdini book and started paging through it, reading about all the fake ghosts Houdini had exposed. There had been fake knocking, books floating on tiny, almost-invisible wires — all sorts of tricks that con men used to convince people that their loved ones were trying to get in touch with them. The only communication from dead people that Houdini hadn't completely debunked was what he called "spoken words to the young."

He'd come across three verifiable cases where little kids had known things about dead people that they shouldn't have had any way of knowing. Houdini thought maybe certain rare children somehow had the ability to hear spirits, but he had never proven this theory to his own satisfaction. And in any case, Dahlia hadn't *heard* a thing from the little girls.

A few minutes later, Eileen trudged up the stairs. "What a crappy camp," she announced. "What kind of morning activity is a work group?"

"Yeah," Dahlia said, not really paying attention.

Eileen came over and sat on the bed next to her. "But you must have really wanted to come, with your brother here and all. I mean, he's so cool, right?"

It took Dahlia a second to even remember what Eileen was talking about. She shook her head. "He's okay. I actually wanted to go to math camp."

"What? That's even worse. At least here we don't have to do schoolwork."

"I went for a week last summer, and it was fun." *And there weren't any scared little girls walking through the walls at math camp.*

In the distance, a bell rang twice. The loudspeaker in the cabin came on. "Attention, attention. Work group is now over. You have half an hour to wash up. Thank you."

Eileen looked at Dahlia. "Did you understand what that announcement said?"

"Sure. Work is over. We have half an hour to wash up."

"I think that's so unfair to make the announcements in Hebrew when only, like, a quarter of the camp speaks Hebrew."

"That wasn't Hebrew," Dahlia said absently. "I don't speak Hebrew."

"What was it, then?"

Dahlia looked up. "English," she said. "That was just regular English. Maybe you didn't hear the speaker right."

Eileen shook her head. "That was not English," she said. "I might not be good with languages, but I know English."

The door opened. Lisa stood in the doorway, took off her sneakers, and threw them in the dirt in front of the cabin. Her pants were covered with brown streaks. "Stupid . . . freaking . . . pig," she said. "Why the heck does a Jewish camp have a pig?" She padded across the room, grabbed her towel, and turned back toward the door.

"Was that announcement in Hebrew or English?" Eileen asked quickly.

"Hebrew." Lisa walked out the door just as Sarah and two other girls walked in, but Dahlia could hear her voice clearly through the screens. "All announcements are in Hebrew here."

Hearing the tail end of what Lisa was saying, Sarah said, "Don't worry — once you learn a handful of words, the announcements are easy."

Eileen cast Dahlia a triumphant look. Dahlia narrowed her eyes. She was sure she'd heard English. The announcement that had woken her up this morning had been English too. Good morning or whatever.

"So what's next?" Dahlia asked. If she was going crazy and had just imagined that she heard English, then she wouldn't have gotten the translation right.

Nikki, a plump girl from the other side of the bunk, said, "Washing up. Then we're supposed to meet in front of our bunks."

"Don't worry," Sarah said again. "You'll figure out the words in no time!"

"I'm not worried," Dahlia said. "About that."

So she wasn't going crazy. Or even if she was, there was also something really weird going on. Understanding Hebrew and seeing . . . girls walking through walls. She grimaced. Ghosts. She didn't believe in ghosts. She closed the Houdini book with a snap and put it back in her trunk. There had to be some trick. Next time she saw the girls, she'd touch them and see for herself if they were solid. Or if they were ghosts, she'd somehow document their visits and be the first person to prove that ghosts were real.

She found herself smiling for a few seconds. Just until she remembered the little girl's face as she was dragged through the wall.

The rest of the morning was activities with their age group. First, the counselors divided them into groups of six, and they had a scavenger hunt where they had to run around the camp gathering items. The items were all pretty easy to find: a sock from the lost and found — which, remarkably, was already full on the second day of camp; a baseball from the sports shed; and so on. Dahlia was sure her team finished the hunt first, but the counselors insisted it was a tie.

After the scavenger hunt, the whole group came back together and played more games in front of the boys' cabin. Throughout the morning, the counselors — especially an Israeli guy named Ofer — occasionally used Hebrew, and Dahlia was reassured to find she didn't understand any of it.

Lunch was okay — a kind of casserole with mushrooms and meat. Again, Dahlia was so hungry she was almost done before she realized it wasn't very good. Oddly, she wasn't the only one. Everyone at her table seemed to eat a full plate of the stuff.

The campers on server duty were still clearing dishes when another round of counselor skits began, this one about the different special-interest clubs you could join. There was a swimming club led by the lifeguard; a Jewish mysticism club led by Peter, a bearded counselor with several Asian characters tattooed on each of his muscular biceps; a nature club led by two of the Israeli counselors; a comedy improv club led by Tom's friend Brad; and more of the like. Dahlia wasn't really interested in any of the clubs, and after the first few skits, she stopped paying attention. As the skits were finishing up, a camper dropped a pile of slips at every table. Dahlia glumly read over the list.

"What are you going to do?" she asked Eileen, who happened to be sitting next to her.

Eileen seemed surprised at the question. "Music appreciation. I mean, isn't that what everyone's going to want? The girl who's leading it was wearing a signed Joanna Newsom T-shirt!" It was the first time Dahlia had heard Eileen sound at all enthusiastic about anything. "And did you hear? She said she has, like, four thousand hours in her iTunes library!"

Dahlia looked across the table. Sarah nodded sympathetically. "I know," she said. "It's hard to decide when they all sound so good, right?"

Before Dahlia could answer, Chelsea stopped by and dropped a box of pens on the table. She caught Dahlia's eye and asked, "So, did they have a club that was — um — *unique* enough for you?" She smirked. "Hard to imagine."

Dahlia looked back at the list of clubs without saying anything. In her nasty way, Chelsea was right. None of the clubs interested Dahlia at all. When the counselor at their table collected the slips where you were supposed to write your choice of club, Dahlia tucked her still-blank slip into the middle of the pile. She'd just take club period off.

# CHAPTER 8

**D**ahlia sat on the tree bench in front of her cabin. She held an acorn in her left hand, displayed it to her nonexistent audience, then pretended to take it into her right hand while actually dropping it into the palm of her left hand. The acorn was small enough that it was easy not to drop it, but she wasn't sure she would really fool anybody. She found herself wishing the ghosts would come back, if only to give her an audience.

There it was again. She was thinking about the little girls like they were real ghosts. Shoot. The truth was, she was starting to believe they *were* real ghosts.

She had hung around the cabin for much of the afternoon in hopes of seeing them again, but there was always someone else around and the little girls hadn't returned. Eventually, she'd given up and gone out to sit on the tree bench where it was cooler. Now that everyone had to go to their club, she would have the cabin to herself, and maybe the girls would show up again.

Finally, Alyssa came out of the cabin with the last camper left, a quiet Israeli girl named Irit. Dahlia hopped off the tree bench. She had one foot on the steps leading up to the cabin door when Alyssa's voice stopped her.

"What's *your* club, Dahlia?"

Dahlia's heart sank, but she decided to play innocent. "I didn't join one," she said airily. "What about you?"

"It's my free period," Alyssa said.

"Oh. Me too, I guess."

Alyssa laughed. "No. If you don't choose a club, they assign you one. Campers can't have a free period during clubs."

"Well, I didn't like any of the clubs," Dahlia said. She showed Alyssa the acorn, then palmed it as she seemed to put in the other hand. She held out both fists. "Tell you what. If you can tell me which hand the acorn's in, I'll go to the club."

Alyssa pulled a folded piece of paper from her pocket. "Let's see which club they gave you." She scanned the list. "Here you are. You're in Peter's club about Jewish mysticism, which is meeting . . . right over there." She pointed to the little gazebo. Dahlia followed her gaze and groaned. Peter was there with three campers sitting around him. He was wearing a tank top, no doubt so everyone got a clear view of his tattooed biceps. Alyssa squeezed her shoulder. "You'll like it — it's all about numbers and codes and magic and stuff."

Dahlia left her fists extended before her. "Go on. Guess."

Alyssa tapped the top of her left hand. Shoot. Dahlia opened it, showing her the acorn.

"Nice try," Alyssa said. "If it makes you feel any better, you would have had to go to your club anyway."

Dahlia kept practicing the sleight as she walked back toward the gazebo. It was hard because it was so simple. You had to direct the other person's attention to the wrong hand, which meant you had to direct your own attention to the wrong hand, all while hiding the item in the palm of the other hand.

Peter smiled at her as she approached. "Hey, Dahlia. Come on down for the first meeting of Club Kabbala."

Dahlia paused, hopeful that Alyssa had sent her to the wrong club. "Whoops. I'm meant to go to the club about Jewish mysticism." The three other campers in the gazebo were Rafe, a counselor in training named Wanda Sorkin, and a little dark kid whose name she didn't know.

"No, no," Peter said. "You're in the right place. Kabbala is just the Hebrew word for Jewish mysticism. Jewish meditation. Jewish *magic*." He lowered his voice and grinned when he said "magic."

Dahlia wondered if it was too late to switch clubs.

"Sit," Peter said. "Make yourself comfortable." He waited for Dahlia to sit. "So. Welcome to Club Kabbala." He glanced down at a few pieces of paper he had arrayed around him. "Let me start by saying that you all are in the most important club."

He waited a few seconds for the reaction he seemed to think this was going to get. No one said anything, although Wanda Sorkin did smile at him.

Peter smiled back at Wanda. "See, religious Jews think that kabbala is the one way to get the world back to how God intended it." He nodded along with his words. "They think that by meditating on kabbala, we can reassemble all the light and goodness that scattered when God made the world." He nodded again.

Dahlia yawned. What they really needed was a nap club. Maybe she could pretend she was sick.

Peter tapped one of the books sitting next to him. "Anyway. Today we're going to talk about the tenth sefira of kabbala — Malchut. 'Kingdom' in English. Then we're going to meditate on —"

"What's a sefira?" Rafe interrupted.

Peter glanced back at his notes. "The simplest translation is number. Um. You can also think of the sefira as gates from the divine to the rest of the world."

"What?" Rafe narrowed his eyes. "What does that mean? If they're numbers, how are they gates? And you just said Malchut meant 'kingdom' — that's not a number."

Dahlia didn't get why Rafe cared. Who expected religion to make sense?

"It's complicated," Peter said. "There are ten sefirot, and the idea is that they're the ten emanations. . . ." He said the word slowly, like he was sounding it out. "I think it's like they're the ten different ways that God is perceived in this world."

"Wait," Dahlia said, intrigued despite herself. "There are ten numbers you can use to perceive God? What are they?"

Peter glanced back at the sheet of paper in front of him. "The tenth sefira, and the one that is most accessible to human consciousness, is Malchut — that means 'kingdom,' like I said. The ninth sefira is Yesod — that means 'foundation.' Then there's Hod. That means 'splendor.' Then —"

"Those aren't numbers," Dahlia said, losing interest.

"Okay, okay." Peter smiled and looked around at the group. "Let's not sweat the details. I want to lead us in a chant."

He took a deep breath. "Okay, so everyone take a deep breath into their stomachs, and on the exhale, say 'Oooommm.' " He was sitting in a weird cross-legged position, and when he chanted, he closed his eyes. After a moment, Wanda and the little kid did it too, although the little kid kept sneaking glances at Peter as if to make sure he was doing it right.

Rafe stared past Peter, watching the Frisbee game in the field beyond them. There were about thirty people on the field, running back and forth with no strategy that Dahlia could see. Peter took a deep breath. "Again," he said, not opening his eyes, and he, Wanda, and the little kid did another long "Oooommm."

Dahlia took a deep breath and gave a tentative "Om" of her own. Rafe quickly followed suit. She gave him a sidelong glance, but he didn't seem to be making fun of her. After a second, she closed her eyes as well.

Between the breeze and the shade, it was pleasantly warm in the gazebo, as opposed to the stifling heat in the cabin. Dahlia sleepily wondered if she could lie back and have a nap while Peter and the rest chanted.

"Malchut," Peter said.

He said something more after that, but Dahlia wasn't paying attention. Something had shifted in her head when Peter said that word. She felt a surge of energy dart up her spine. Nonsense syllables ran through her head. *Malchutyesodhodnetzach* . . .

She took another deep breath, trying to clear her mind, and for a second she wasn't there at all. She was sitting at a small table, her back to a busy street full of cars and people's voices. She had a thick book open on the table in front of her and was sketching in it. She was hungry and scared.

The page in front of her was blank except for her sketch, but the page facing it was covered with printed Hebrew writing. She was supposed to be using the blank page on the left to write the English translation, but instead, she was drawing a maze, scribbling Hebrew letters around the margin. Anything to keep from thinking about . . .

Rafe nudged her. She opened her eyes. No table. No sketchbook or ghosts or traffic noises. Just the buzz of insects and the shouts of the campers playing on the sports field. She rubbed her eyes. Just when she thought the day could not get weirder . . . She could still see the image of the maze in front of her.

"Whoa," Rafe said. "You were really into that."

"I'm hungry," she said. As she said it, she realized how ravenous she was. She couldn't possibly make it to dinner without a snack. "Is there somewhere —"

"Shh!" Wanda said. She nodded toward Peter, who was in the middle of saying something.

". . . When you meditate on Malchut, you're supposed to try picturing a castle. Each sefira has a symbol, and the castle is meant to be —"

"Wait. What's a sefira again?" the little kid said.

Peter sighed and glanced down at his notes. "Look. It's like a gate. A pathway between the source and the rest of the world. The idea is that you use meditation to work your way through the sefirot and connect to the source."

"When you say 'source,' you mean God, right?" Dahlia said with distaste. She wished she had signed up for music appreciation.

Anything would be better than this. Meditating on castles and talking about God . . .

"Exactly," Peter said. "The sefirot are like different aspects of God."

Dahlia yawned again. Next he'd be saying how lightning happened because "God" was mad that someone was eating milk and meat together.

"Anyway, we're going to meditate on them a little more before we do massages."

"Massages?" Rafe said with real alarm.

"When do we do the stuff with numbers?" Dahlia asked.

Peter furrowed his brow. "Oh yeah. Sure. Gematria. I'm, um, not so good with the math. I *think* the idea is that every Hebrew letter has a number paired with it, so you can add up the numbers for all the letters in a word, and that sort of gives you the number for the word. So, um, take the Hebrew word for 'life' — *chai*. In Hebrew, you spell that with two letters: chet and yod. Chet is the eighth letter in the Hebrew alphabet, so the number for chet is eight. Yod is the tenth letter, so the number for yod is ten. Add them together and you get eighteen, which is the number for life."

"That's it?" Dahlia said with disgust. "That's Jewish numerology? A basic alphanumeric code?"

"No, no. It gets much more complicated." He looked down and shuffled through his notes. "There's another word for life — *chaim* — which is worth sixty-eight, and it only has two more letters than *chai*. The thing is, once you get past yod, the letters start going by tens. The letters after yod are worth twenty, then thirty, then forty. God knows why."

Dahlia blinked. "Isn't that just because there are ten digits in a decimal system?" Peter looked blank, and she tried to explain. "You don't need any letter to be eleven or twelve or whatever, because you can use different combinations of the first ten letters to get you every number between eleven and nineteen. The next number you need after ten is twenty, because there's no letter with a zero value, right?"

"Oh. Right," Peter said.

"Although I guess you could just use two tens next to each other to make twenty," Dahlia said, more to herself than to Peter. "Anyway, who cares? How could it mean anything that the Hebrew word for life translates to sixty-eight? So do tons of other Hebrew words. Like — I don't know — 'maze' and 'nothingness' and —"

Dahlia paused. How had she known that? For a moment, she had known the Hebrew words for "maze" and "nothingness" and added up their numbers in her head. She felt suddenly like she was suffocating, despite being outside.

"That's right," Peter said agreeably. "The idea is that words with equivalent numbers are the same on some higher, metaphysical level."

Dahlia stood up and stepped off the gazebo. "I'm quitting this club."

Rafe stood up. "Me too."

"Dudes," Peter said, still smiling. "You have to go to a club. You can't just quit."

"We can go to sports," Rafe said.

Dahlia looked at the books next to Peter. *Kabbala for Dummies. Zen and the Art of Motorcycle Maintenance. The Tao of Pooh.* "Those aren't even Jewish," she said. Then her eyes came to the last one, a thick, dark-red hardback with no title on the spine. The hairs on the back of her neck lifted, and she shivered, despite the heat.

She stepped back toward Peter, leaned down, and pulled the book she had seen out of the pile. The red binding felt like real leather. The book's front cover was blank, but on its back cover there were some Hebrew letters in calligraphied golden writing. Of course. She remembered from her Bat Mitzvah that you read Hebrew right to left. So what she'd thought was the back cover would actually be the front cover.

When she opened the cover, the title page had four Hebrew words and the sketch of a tree. On the facing page, someone had handwritten in small, neat English letters, *The Path of Names*.

"Pretty cool, eh?" Peter said. "I found it in the camp library. About half of it is translated. Check it out." He flipped open the book at random, and Dahlia saw that each page had Hebrew printing on one side and handwritten English on the other side. "If you want, you can read this instead of doing massages." He looked at Wanda and she smiled at him again.

The little kid frowned. "I want to go to sports," he said.

"No problem, Russell," Peter said, not looking at him. "You go."

The little kid ran off to join the crowd of campers chasing the Frisbee around the field. Dahlia picked the book up and walked over to the tree bench where she'd been sitting before.

Rafe fell in with her as she walked. "That was awesome," he said. "You totally got us a free period. What a crappy club."

"Why were you in it?" Dahlia said absently. She perched on the edge of the tree bench and opened the book. She turned a few pages, not bothering to read the cramped writing of the translation. The Hebrew writing meant nothing to her, which was vaguely reassuring. She could pick out the letters if she tried, but the weird fluency that had come over her earlier was gone.

"I didn't sign up for it." Rafe sat next to her. "I didn't sign up for any club, so they probably put me there because they needed more people in it. And anyway, first I went to the Prank Club, but that was all little kids, and the counselor was just planning stupid stuff, like running through flag raising and spraying people with shaving cream."

Dahlia nodded, not really listening as she paged through the book. After the first few chapters, the translator seemed to lose interest in translating. At first it was just a sketch or two in the margins of the translations, but by the fifth chapter, the translator had given up altogether and covered the pages with drawings and diagrams. There was a faded sketch in gray pencil of people walking on a crowded sidewalk; a sketch of a cup of coffee steaming on a saucer. Mostly, though, there were mazes. Page after page of different mazes.

"Huh," Rafe said, looking over her shoulder. "Seems like buddy got bored with translating."

"I guess so." Dahlia turned the page and froze, looking at one more sketched picture of a maze. It was exactly the same sketch she had imagined a few minutes ago, right down to the Hebrew notations around the margins.

She turned back to the title page. *The Path of Names*. She carefully flipped the page. The next page was filled with Hebrew letters. Glancing over to the facing translation, she read:

THE PATH OF NAMES

BY REB ISAAC BEN YISACHAR

DICTATED TO REB VELVEL BEN ELIEZER

NEW YORK, 1941

And then in very small letters at the bottom of the page:
*Translated by David Schank.*

**D**avid knew an instant of complete panic in the pitch blackness of the hidden chamber. "Velvel!" he said, his voice little more than a whisper. "Let me out! Velvel!" Why had the Rebbe betrayed him?

"Calm down," Velvel hissed. Only then did David realize that Velvel was standing one step above him. "I had to get the door closed before this one could make himself heard. This chamber is soundproof when the door's closed."

"Help me!" Again, a man's voice from below them.

A flashlight clicked on in Velvel's hands. "Silence," he said in his heavily accented English.

The flashlight illuminated a small chamber containing little more than a bed and a man. The man was lying on his side on the bed, hands and feet bound to each other and to the metal frame. He was a thin, blond man, unshaven. "Please help me," he said to David, squinting against the flashlight. He spoke in English with no trace of an accent. "These people are fanatics."

"This is who you're looking for," Velvel told the man in his own halting English. Switching back to Yiddish, he told David, "The Rebbe had a vision last night that this one was sniffing after you. We picked him up in the middle of the night outside your building."

The man was staring at David, his nostrils inflating and contracting like he was trying to get his smell. "Oh," he said. "Yes. Say it," he said to David. "Tell me the magic word."

Velvel ignored the man. "Reb Isaac wanted you to see him before you left."

"Left?" David said.

"You are leaving," Velvel said. He walked down the stairs and approached the man. In English, he said, "Tell again why you look for him?"

The man tried to look innocent, even while staring at David with naked hunger, unmistakable despite the flashlight's dim light. "To learn from you. My master is fond of magic words, and you have found a powerful one."

"A magic word?" David was horrified. To talk of the most secret name as though it was a stage trick. In Yiddish he asked Velvel, "Is he referring to the . . ."

"The 72nd name of God. Yes."

"It would be of no use to him," David said. "If sages such as the Rebbe and yourself couldn't hear the name, what could this one do?"

The man laughed, obviously understanding, although David had spoken in Yiddish. "*This one* is illuminated," the man said in English. "And there are a great many ways — oh, a very great many ways — open to Illuminated Ones. It would not be the first magic word we have taken from your people. Nor the second. Nor the last." He laughed again.

"Ridiculous," David said. He wrapped his thin arms around himself, suddenly aware of how cold he was. It was still winter down here in the lower basement, and he hadn't bothered with an overcoat on account of the warm spring sun outside. The blond man was dressed only in a T-shirt and pants, yet he seemed unaware of the chill.

"If it's nonsense, tell me the magic word," the man said. "Please. I'll ask nicely. This once." Despite being bound, he managed to put enough menace in his voice that David took a step back without thinking about it.

"No," he said.

"Have it your way," the man said. "There's more than one way to skin a cat. Or a Jew." The man did something with his muscles, and the ropes fell off him. "And there are many, many ways to escape such amateur binding."

He rolled off the bed and stood up in one smooth motion. His hands twitched, and he was holding a knife. "Say the magic word," he urged as he stepped toward David. "Maybe it will save you."

# CHAPTER 10

# DAHLIA

"**W**hat?" Rafe said, and Dahlia realized she had gasped. He leaned in to see the book, his arm brushing Dahlia's elbow. "You just totally zoned out there for a second, and now you look like you just saw a ghost."

Dahlia surprised herself by laughing. "No," she said. "That was this morning."

Rafe laughed too. "No, seriously. What happened?"

"Nothing," Dahlia said. "I just remembered more of this weird dream I had last night. Something about ultra-Orthodox Jews. I think this camp's just a little more Jewish than I'm used to." She glanced at the book in her hand. It had been the translator's name that set her off. How could she have dreamed of him before seeing the book? "Do you recognize this guy's name?"

"David Schank?" Rafe said, and shrugged. "Never heard of him."

Dahlia paged back to the maze that had caught her attention before. "What do you think of this?"

Rafe looked at the maze. "It's sort of dumb, isn't it?" he said. "There's no way to get lost in it — it's just one route."

"It's not dumb. It's called a unicursal labyrinth. The point isn't to get lost." Dahlia was surprised at how irritated Rafe's comment made her. He was right. What was the point of a maze where you couldn't get lost? And how did she even know what it was called? This was the third time something like that had happened today. Her brain felt like a computer full of files that she didn't remember downloading.

"Hey," Rafe interrupted her thoughts. "You want to see the maze your brother found beneath the pool? This is my fourth year, and I didn't even know it was there until Tom —"

"Can you not talk about my brother all the time?" Dahlia snapped.

He edged away from her. "I just thought you might want to see the maze. If you're into mazes, I mean." He waved his hand in front of his face, keeping a small cloud of gnats at bay. "What's your problem with your brother, anyway?"

"It's just annoying how everyone always goes on about him. He's not that great."

Rafe ripped a stem and some leaves off the nearby tree, using the leaves as a makeshift fan to fend off the gnats. "You should meet one of my brothers sometime. You have it easy." He shook his head. "So. You want to see the maze?"

Dahlia looked back at the maze sketched in the book, then glanced up at the sky. Not a cloud in sight. She stuck a leaf in the book to mark her place and hopped off the tree bench. "Why not? Let's go."

Rafe led Dahlia around the cabin toward the woods.

"Isn't the maze the other direction?" she said.

He kept walking. "The other way you go right past the swimming pool, and there are always people around. It's easier to sneak in here."

"Why do we have to sneak?" Dahlia asked.

"Campers aren't supposed to go into the woods without a counselor." Dahlia stopped following him for a moment, and Rafe shot her a quick smile. "You can just say you didn't know."

After a moment, Dahlia shrugged and walked after him. He veered right, leading her past a few bushes and into a concrete clearing. "The old tennis courts," he said. There were no nets, and if there had ever been any painted lines on the concrete, they had long since worn off.

"Try not to brush against any branches in the woods," Rafe said casually. He was already pushing into a tiny path at the back corner of the tennis court. "There are ticks. The big ones are bad enough, but the little ones'll give you Lyme disease. My cousin got Lyme disease last year and had to go home. He could barely move for, like, three weeks."

Dahlia flinched as a plant's leaf brushed her calf.

"We come down here every day in lumberjacks," Rafe said. He glanced back in time to see Dahlia try to avoid a branch whipping toward her. " 'Course, we have to wear long pants when we go in the woods."

Once in the woods, there were more trees and fewer bushes. In the distance, Dahlia could see a fence and an open field beyond. Rafe gestured ahead of them. "There's a big trail that goes around the whole camp up there." He picked up a large branch and broke it in two. "Perfect for the bonfire," he said, and threw the two pieces toward the bigger path. "I'll get it tomorrow. I switched to the lumberjack work group when Barry made your brother . . ." He looked at Dahlia and stopped himself. "Anyway. Here's the trail."

They'd been on the path for about twenty minutes, tracing a loose circle through the woods, when Rafe suddenly said, "Shh!"

"I wasn't talking," Dahlia whispered.

Rafe shook his head and ran ahead a few yards.

Dahlia walked after him. He had paused just before a place where their path cut across a small dirt road. "This is where the CITs — the counselors in training — live," Rafe whispered, pointing to the right. Dahlia saw the tops of a few large tents through the trees. "They get really mad when they see campers back here." He crept toward the dirt road, then dashed across.

Dahlia crossed more slowly. It was hard to run in flip-flops, and besides, she was curious. She looked toward the tents and saw an older kid sitting on a milk crate, playing guitar. He was facing away from her, toward the entrance of the tents. Dahlia stopped for a moment to try to make out the song he was singing. Rafe grabbed her wrist and dragged her forward.

"What?" she said. "What are they going to do? I mean really."

"My brother's a CIT," Rafe whispered.

"So?"

Rafe just shook his head and kept walking.

Dahlia let him lead her for a few more paces. "Okay. You can let go of my wrist now."

"Oh. Sorry."

The path went downhill, and soon Dahlia could hear the creek to the left. Peering through the trees, she caught a few glimpses of sun on water. A moment or two later, she heard the distant pealing of the camp's bell.

"How far is the maze?" Dahlia wasn't quite as hungry as she'd been after that weird flash in the gazebo, but she was still hungry, and getting thirsty too.

"It's close now," Rafe promised. "Maybe five more minutes. Anyway, the bell just means the end of clubs. We're not missing anything — there's a half-hour break before flag lowering."

"We're missing a break," Dahlia said. "So far, those are my favorite activities."

They walked for another minute. "There." Rafe pointed in front of them and to the right. All she could see was a slightly denser patch of green. "That's the back part of the maze, so we'll have to walk around it to get to the entrance."

Dahlia quickened her pace as best she could. Every few steps a little stone would get into her flip-flop, and she would have to pause to kick it out. As they got closer, she couldn't see much more of the maze, just a lot of evergreen bushes.

"Juniper," Rafe said.

"What?"

"They're juniper bushes. Your brother said they were the traditional way to make an English hedge maze."

"He's so smart," Dahlia said. "Thank God he knew they were juniper instead of — I don't know — cedar or something. Yay, Tom!"

Rafe eyed her but didn't say anything. They finally rounded the side of the maze and came in sight of the entrance, which stood in a small clearing.

The maze was beautiful, Dahlia abruptly thought. Not that there was anything so different about the juniper bushes. They looked exactly like the evergreen shrubs that Dahlia's father used to hedge their backyard. It was more the maze as a whole. It looked exactly the way it should. There was something exciting about finding it here, like rediscovering a childhood toy and finding it just as fun as she remembered.

Which was ridiculous, since Dahlia was positive she had never seen any hedge maze before, let alone this one. Still . . .

She opened the book and glanced at the sketched maze that had caught her attention. "This is it," she said. "It's the same maze."

Rafe laughed. "Yeah, right."

"No, I'm serious."

He stopped laughing and gave her a sidelong glance. "Wait. Really? I have no idea when you're joking." He looked at the maze. "Anyway, how could you tell from here?"

It was a good question. Dahlia looked at the maze, then back at the book. "You can see the path goes to the right from the entrance, then turns left," she finally said. "Just like the maze in the book."

Rafe looked over her shoulder and nodded hesitantly. "So the first turn is the same. That doesn't mean anything."

Dahlia stepped closer to the entrance. "It's the same maze," she said. The brambles of a blackberry bush scratched her shins, but she hardly noticed. After the shaded woods, the entrance seemed to glow in the afternoon sunlight.

There were a couple rolls of fencing off to one side. It looked like someone planned to fence off the maze — Barry, probably. She was still a few steps away from the entrance when a growling black shadow burst out of the underbrush.

# CHAPTER 11

The huge black dog ran toward Dahlia, fangs bared.

"Hold 'em, Tramp," a cold, thin voice called, and the dog skidded to a halt inches from her feet. Even on all fours, the dog's head was above her waist. He growled angrily at her. "Sit," the voice commanded. The dog sat back on its haunches, still growling a low and ominous rumble.

Dahlia squinted into the sun, looking for the person who had set the dog on her. Shading her eyes, she made out a man's silhouette moving toward them.

Behind her, Rafe muttered, "Uh-oh." And in a louder, obviously fake-cheerful voice, "Hi, Barry! Say, what kind of dog is Tramp? Is he a black Lab?"

A few more rustling steps through the underbrush, and the caretaker came into view. His hat and sunglasses covered most of his face, but from what Dahlia could see of his mouth, he was angry. "What are you doin' down here?"

"I wanted to see the maze," Dahlia said. Out of the corner of her eye, she noticed Rafe wincing.

"I figured you would." Barry regarded her for a few moments. At least Dahlia *thought* he was looking at her. It was hard to tell with the sunglasses and baseball cap. "You put the tall feller up to cleaning the thing out, didn't you?"

"No," Dahlia said.

The caretaker examined her impassively. "He was with you last night too, when y'all were bothering Tramp."

"So what?" Dahlia snapped, her momentary panic turning to anger. She couldn't even get in trouble without Tom coming up.

The man took a step closer to her — close enough that Dahlia could see her image distorted in the lenses of his sunglasses. He looked like he was about to say something, then he gave his head a quick shake, like he was trying to shake off the gnats. Which made Dahlia notice that the cloud of gnats that surrounded her and Rafe didn't seem to touch Barry at all. Weird.

"This area ain't safe for campers," he said abruptly. He snapped his fingers, and the dog bounded away from Dahlia. "Stay away from the maze." He looked at Rafe. "And I'd stay away from the girl if I were you. She has a way of getting people into trouble."

"No, I d —"

"Shhh!" Rafe hissed. He seized her arm and pulled her up the hill. "Thanks, Barry!" he said in the same obviously fake-cheerful voice. "See you soon."

He led her the opposite direction from the way they had come. A few moments later she saw the blue water of the pool glimmering through the trees.

Rafe didn't say anything else until they were walking around the pool's concrete deck. He sounded awed when he said, "I can't believe the way you talked to Barry. And with Tramp right there."

"What was he talking about? I never get anyone in trouble."

"Who knows? What was he doing there, anyway? I never see him anywhere else in the woods. But he stopped your bro — he stopped the maze work group this morning too."

"And he's fencing off the maze," Dahlia said. "Why's he bothering? It's in the middle of nowhere."

Rafe kept walking. The pool was down a steep hill from the rest of the camp, and he took the cement stairs up two at time. "I'm just glad Barry doesn't talk to the counselors, or I'd be in some serious trouble, what with the Jell-O this morning and all." His voice became a little less subdued. "Although, really, getting in trouble twice on the first day of camp would have to be some kind of record."

The first day of camp. Weird to think how much had happened since she arrived. She'd seen the little girls walk through the cabin walls twice. She'd imagined — no, she'd had a vision — of sketching mazes in a book she was sure she'd never seen before, and a few minutes later the book had been handed to her. She'd had that weirdly vivid dream about black-hat Jews in New York. And she'd understood Hebrew. She thought for a moment, trying to remember if anything else strange had happened.

"Like that's not enough for one day," she muttered to herself.

"What?" Rafe said as they came to the top of the hill. A handful of campers were already hanging out around the flagpole, waiting for flag lowering, and some kids were throwing a Frisbee around. "What did you say? What's so funny?"

Dahlia abruptly realized she was chuckling to herself. Maybe she was going crazy after all. She shook her head. "Just thinking that it seems like I've been at camp a lot longer than one day."

"Yeah. It's always like that for me too."

"Hey! Professor!" One of the CITs, a short boy with a shaved head and glasses, called to Rafe as Dahlia and he emerged from behind the bunks. "Professor! C'mere. I hope you weren't messing with the pool. I swear to God, Mom will kill me if you get kicked out before they're back from Europe."

Beside Dahlia, Rafe sighed apologetically. "My older brother," he told Dahlia.

"I'm John," Rafe's brother said. "Who are you?"

"Dahlia."

He nodded and snapped his fingers. "Right, right — you're Tom Sherman's sister. What were you guys doing by the pool?" He raised his hands before they could respond. "Don't bother telling me." He winked at Dahlia. "I don't believe a word the Professor says."

"We were doing stuff for a club." Rafe gestured at the book Dahlia was holding.

"You're full of crap," John said. "But whatever."

"We were looking at the maze," Dahlia said firmly. "Or trying to."

"Is that what you call it these days?"

She scowled at him. Rafe was right. His brother was more annoying than Tom.

Blushing a little, Rafe said, "Come on, Dahlia." They walked off toward their bunks. When they were out of earshot, he said, "Sorry. My brother's a jerk."

"Why'd he call you 'Professor'?"

His blush deepened. "Because he and Todd — our older brother — used to say I was so full of crap. It was their joke, that I was a professor of making stuff up. Everyone at camp used to call me Professor, but this summer I'm trying to lose the nickname."

They crossed the road and neared Dahlia's bunk. The other girls were all spilling out of the bunk. Dahlia paused. "Well. See you at flag lowering." She held up the book. Her fingers felt cramped from holding it for so long. "You want this?"

"Sure!" Rafe said. "You sure? You seemed really into it."

Dahlia handed him the book. "Nah," she said. For some reason, the book — especially the mazes sketched inside it — seemed creepier than the girls she'd seen go through the walls. They were just little girls, but the maze was something else.

Just the name of the translator creeped her out. David Schank — the same initials as her. She had dreamed about him, brilliant and scared, hours before she'd seen his name inside the book.

# CHAPTER 12

# DAVID

The man moved toward David with the knife. David took another step backward and tripped on the base of the steps. He caught himself on one arm, and the room seemed to explode. Suddenly, the man was lying on the floor a few feet from David, shaking as bullets pounded his body.

And then it was over. Velvel was standing next to David holding a large revolver. He knelt and picked up the flashlight from where he'd dropped it, then thrust the flashlight toward David. "Hold this," he said.

David took the flashlight in fingers that felt numb and clumsy. He watched as Velvel walked down the stairs to where the man had fallen, placed the gun at the man's forehead, and fired another three times, until the gun clicked on an empty chamber.

David stared at what had been a man, the holiest of God's creatures. Then he dropped the flashlight and vomited in the darkness. When he looked up, Velvel had retrieved the flashlight and was at the top of the stairs. "Come on," he said, opening the door.

David followed Velvel back into the middle basement, his stomach still heaving. After the darkness of the cell, the single lightbulb seemed blindingly bright. Velvel reached under one of the benches and pulled out a small duffel bag. He handed it to David.

"What's this?" David said.

"Clothes. Put them on." Behind his full brown beard, Velvel's face was paler than usual. He sat on the bench while David opened the duffel bag and pulled out the contents. Brown wool pants, a blue work shirt, a tweed jacket.

"These are secular clothes," David said.

"You're no longer a Yebavner." Velvel's voice was as gentle as David had ever heard it. "Effective now. The Rebbe's last orders to you are to get as far away from here as you can."

"What?" David felt like he had fallen into some kind of bad dream. "You murdered a man, and I'm the one the Rebbe excommunicates?"

"Don't be stupid." Velvel's voice resumed its customary impatience. "The sages clearly distinguish between murder and defending an innocent. Do you doubt that I was defending you?"

"But that requires a court judgment," David said. His voice sounded strange to his own ears. They were arguing legal details while a dead man lay in a puddle of blood a few yards away.

"Put on the clothes." Velvel looked at him with an odd expression — pity mixed with something else. It took David a moment to recognize the something else: fear. Velvel had just shot a man, and yet he was afraid of David. "Find somewhere to hide. The farther the better. Don't come back here and don't go back to your lodgings."

"Wh-wh-why?" David said.

Velvel nodded down the stairs to where the dead man lay.

"He's dead," David said. "Why can't I stay here?"

"There are more like him. If you stay, you put the whole community in danger."

"But —"

"The Rebbe has decided." Velvel's tone was firm. "Now change your clothes."

David dutifully started to move. He took off his black coat and vest — his nicest ones, worn specially on account of seeing the Rebbe. After a moment, he started to unbutton his white dress shirt too. Velvel glanced up the stairs leading to the rest of the house. "Hurry up," he said. He stood and walked back into the lower basement. When he returned, he was holding the pistol. He offered it to David. "There's more ammunition in the bag."

David glanced at the gun and felt his stomach about to revolt again. He clamped his lips shut and shook his head until Velvel put the gun back in his pocket. After a moment, the urge to vomit passed, and he pulled the blue work shirt on. "Why is the Rebbe sending me away?"

"Have you heard of the Zielonan Chasids?"

"Sure. Of course." David began buttoning the work shirt. It felt strange and coarse against his skin. "Famous weather workers, right?"

"Right," Velvel said. "People from all over used to go to Zielona to ask for their Rebbe's help. They broke droughts, shortened winters, and all the rest."

"I know the stories," David said. They were tales to lull children to sleep.

"Do you know the ending? One day the Zielonan Rebbe and his top scholars stopped leaving their school. A few days later, the smell got so bad, someone broke into their building and found them all dead. Throats cut, bodies beginning to rot. Some of them had been tortured. This was back in World War I, when the Germans were occupying that part of Poland, so there are good records of all this.

"Later that year, the Illuminated Ones had a new leader, the previous one having been killed when a lightning bolt destroyed his home. It seems the new leader had somehow acquired the secret of working the weather, at just about the same time as all the Zielonans were murdered."

"The Illuminated Ones?" David looked down the stairs to where the dead man lay. "Like him?"

"Exactly like him." Velvel took the Rebbe's book from the bench where David had placed it. He pulled out the sheaf of papers that the Rebbe had folded into the book. "Our Rebbe started having visions of the Zielonan Chasids around the time you came to the yeshiva. He hired a shamus in London to find out more about the people who murdered them. This is what the detective sent us." He folded the sheaf of papers back into the book. "Read it when you have time."

David's hands were shaking so much, he was having trouble buttoning his shirt. He thought of the 72nd name, and the shaking diminished, then stopped altogether. His voice was steady when he said, "A whole school murdered, and I never heard about it?"

Velvel looked David over as he fastened his suspenders and drew on the sports jacket. "The jacket's too big, and the trousers are too short, but they'll do." He reached up and plucked off David's black fedora. After a moment he took the slender, black yarmulke off David's head as well. "You didn't hear about it, because the Illuminated Ones didn't want you to. They collect secrets like a rich man collects dollars. Speaking of which . . ."

Velvel drew a slim envelope from his jacket's inner breast pocket and laid it on top of the book. "Money," he said. "Use it to get out of the city. And get a haircut and a shave at the nearest barber you can find."

David touched his beard. "Just because I'm not a Yebavner doesn't mean I'm not Jewish. I refuse —"

Velvel cut him off. "You'll do exactly as the Rebbe orders. A shave and a haircut and maybe you don't end up like that."

David glanced down the stairs where the shadows covered the corpse. He quickly averted his eyes, muttering the prayer for the dead.

"Save your prayers for yourself," Velvel said. "That traifnyak momzer got what he deserved." He thrust the book and the papers into David's arms and pulled him back toward the stairs. "Move," he said. "And keep moving. Try not to think of the 72nd name — it will draw them to you."

"But it will be —"

"Walk." Velvel prodded him until David began walking up the stairs.

"It will be another seventy-two years — at least — before the name can be so easily learned," David said. He walked through the storeroom with Velvel close on his heels, then paused at the door to the street. "Think about it, Rav Velvel. The barriers between the worlds are as weak as they will be for —"

"The Rebbe has thought about it," Velvel said softly. "He has put the safety of the community first." He gave David a firm push, and finally, reluctantly, David stepped into the alleyway. "Good luck. The Rebbe's blessings go with you."

He turned to face Velvel, and found the door closed in his face. He heard the bolt shooting home. "Go!" Velvel said from the other side. After a moment, David heard his footsteps receding up the stairs within.

The Rebbe's blessings and an envelope of money. That was it? Now that it was over, he felt hot with anger. How dare they abandon him for discovering the 72nd name of God? He would stay there and batter at the door. Demand that they let him in and shield him as best they could.

He raised his hand, then hesitated. He could bang on the door all day, and Velvel wouldn't come. No Yebavner would come if the Rebbe said no. David would be the madman standing in the alleyway, drawing looks from everyone who walked past. The madman with the sidelocks and downy beard of a Jewish yeshiva student, wearing badly fitting workman's clothes. If there were really more Illuminated Ones looking for him, they'd find him without even trying.

He lowered his hand and walked a few blocks until he found an Italian barber shop. He didn't want some Jewish barber fussing as he cut off David's sidelocks. David didn't look at the mirror as his locks fell to the ground and his beard was shaved.

"Is much better," the barber said in heavily accented English. "You look like American."

David glanced in the mirror, then quickly looked away. He looked like a kid, a baby too young to grow a beard. He paid the barber and stepped outside. The day had gotten cooler as the sun dipped below the skyline, and with his bare face, he felt doubly cold.

He shoved his hands in his pockets and hurried east on Grand Street toward the apartment he shared with three other students at the Yebavner yeshiva. He didn't care that Velvel had forbade it. They'd laughed, studied, drank, and eaten together for years. At least he could say good-bye and pick up his overcoat.

On the street, a half-dozen kids were huddled around a little fire that they were using to melt the lead glazing off a large steel milk can. Farther down the block, a Ukrainian Jew was selling baked potatoes out of steel trays packed with hot coals. The smell reminded David he hadn't eaten all day. He bought a potato from the vendor and kept walking. Could the Rebbe really be expecting him to leave all this? Where would he go? What would he eat? The Rebbe's money wouldn't last more than a few days.

As he approached his building, finishing off the last of the potato, he noticed two strangers sitting on his stoop. Two men in black suits, clean shaven and bareheaded in the Jewish part of town. They appeared to be idly watching people pass by.

David was too close to turn around now without attracting their attention. He returned his eyes to the street in front of him and brought the last of the potato to his mouth, keeping his face partially covered as he walked past the men. He could feel their eyes following him.

*Don't look back. Walk quickly like you have somewhere to go. You're late for a meeting. Chew the potato. Think about how delicious it is.*

One block. He crossed the street. *Don't look back.* Two blocks.

At three blocks, he let himself turn around. He seemed to have left the strangers behind. The street was empty except for a few Chasids chatting across the street, and a Jewish woman carrying a child on her hip half a block behind him. He took a deep breath and let it out.

He was just nervous. The strangers had probably been newcomers to the block. There were more of them every day, with all the immigrants fleeing the war in Europe. Again the name arose in his mind. Why should he be scared when he was a master of the holiest name of God? The name bubbled up within him, wanting to spread blessings on the street, to protect him, to hallow the world for anyone who heard it. The first syllable had almost made it through his lips when he somehow felt the strangers perking up a few blocks behind him. One of them stood and beckoned for the other to follow.

He clamped his lips shut and walked faster. Sweat trickled down his torso, soaking the heavy workman's shirt Velvel had given him. He tried to force the name out of his mind, but the more he tried not to think about it, the more he felt it crystallizing. Behind him, the two men were now trotting. He could feel them getting closer, could picture their nostrils flaring as they scanned the street in front of them.

*Take a breath*, he thought. *Slow down. Consider the problem.* He couldn't simply command himself not to think about something. He had to choose something else to think about.

*The Rebbe.* No. That would lead straight back to the name. So would any prayers. There had to be something else to think about. His friends, lost to him forever because of the — no. Something else. Street signs. Buildings. The holidays.

"Sukkot," David said out loud. "What are the allowable materials for building the required tabernacle for Sukkot? Corn husks, but only if they are dead. Grapevines, but not if they are bearing fruit. Long grasses, if inedible."

Slowly, the name receded. David turned left on Orchard Street and walked uptown as fast as he could without running. He felt the men behind him. They were walking slower now. They'd lost his scent, but they hadn't given up. He could feel them. Sniffing. Sniffing. David knew they would keep trying.

He kept walking.

# CHAPTER 13

# DAHLIA

**D**ahlia would have fallen back asleep after the first set of wake-up announcements, but she was too hungry. Instead she lay in bed, thinking about breakfast and her latest dream. Why was she suddenly so obsessed with black-hat Jews? Still, she wished she could go back to sleep and see how it ended.

By the time she got to the bathrooms, there was a ten-minute wait, and the showers had no hot water. She stood under the freezing dribbling from the showerhead for a few moments before giving up and washing her face in the sink. The water from the sink was just as cold, but at least it came out with more pressure.

Hungry and still cold from her brief attempt at a shower, she wandered over to the flagpole to bask in the early-morning sun. Other campers slowly straggled up until most of the camp was standing in a ragged circle around the flagpole. The boys in her age group arrived en masse, moments before flag raising started. Their counselors — Ofer and Brad — arrived immediately behind them, with Rafe's friend Benjy slung between them. They dumped him in the dirt in front of the rest of the group. "Next time, you're going in the showers first," Brad said.

"Showers," Ofer said brightly, dusting off his hands. "In Hebrew, that's *miklachot*."

Benjy lay there, pretending to sleep, until Aaron actually started the flag-raising ceremony. To Dahlia's relief, after the songs and announcements, the camp immediately went to breakfast.

Rafe and Benjy fell in with her as they walked toward the dining hall. "That book is pretty cool," Rafe said. "I was reading the translation last night, and it's like a Jewish-themed RPG." Dahlia must have looked puzzled, because he quickly added, "Role-playing game."

Benjy grimaced as he brushed dirt from his hair. "That sounds terrible. Like one of those crappy games they make you play in Hebrew school." In a mock deep voice, he said, " 'You are Samson fighting the Philistines. Write an essay about your feelings.' "

"No, I mean it's all stories about the magic that the rabbis used to do. Calling down lightning. Bringing a golem to life by writing a magic word on its forehead after you shape it from clay." Rafe looked doubtful. "It actually says to make it from mud, but I think the original must have said clay, right?"

"What's the magic word?" Benjy asked.

"It doesn't say," Rafe said. "You have to use these special names of God to make the magic work. I think you're supposed to already know what they are. It's also not real specific about why you'd want to bring a mud person to life."

"Right. Sounds lame."

"It's the coolest Jewish book I've ever read," Rafe said firmly. "It talks about, like, seven different kinds of dead people."

"That sounds like my grandmother's old-age home," Benjy said. Rafe laughed.

Dahlia was thinking about breakfast again, so it took a moment before Rafe's comment caught her attention. "Seven different kinds of dead people?" she said. "Like ghosts, or what?"

Rafe shrugged. "I don't know. I just skimmed it. But I don't think he uses the word *ghost*. It's all, like, dybbuks and gilguls and that kind of thing."

"Let me see it when you're done," Dahlia said. She'd have to read that part herself. She wasn't about to remind Rafe and Benjy of her interest in people walking through walls.

Breakfast was waffles, just as undercooked and gross and delicious as the pancakes the day before had been. Afterward, they broke into work groups. Alyssa had the paints and rollers and brushes waiting on the dining hall porch. It took a few minutes just to carry everything over to the barn. After distributing the rollers and pouring the paint into pans, they had only about ten minutes to actually paint before Alyssa announced it was time to clean up.

Back at the bunk afterward, Dahlia found the kabbala book on her bed. She took it out to the tree bench in front of her bunk to read. The day was warming up, but a mild breeze kept it pleasantly cool in the tree's shade. Shadows trembled on the pages of the book as the wind rustled through leaves above her.

It turned out the book didn't have much about ghosts, at least not in the parts that had been translated. There was a lot about the different kinds of restless spirits who possessed people, and some stuff about demons with supernatural powers. Dahlia found herself reading the bits about possession again and again, thinking about her visions of David whatever-his-name-was. The book's translator.

"Hey." Rafe sat down on the tree bench next to her. His shirt and jeans were covered with dirt and sawdust. "Did you go into my bunk to get the book back?"

"I didn't go into your bunk," Dahlia said. "It was on my bed."

"Whatever," Rafe said. "It's fine — it doesn't belong to me."

"I didn't take it," she said, irritated that he wouldn't believe her.

He held up his hands. "Fine. Someone else took it from my cubby and dropped it on your bed. Anyway. It's a pretty cool book, right?"

"It's okay." Dahlia looked back at the book. It was the kind of thing she'd never have looked at before she came to this dumb camp — completely unscientific, superstitious, and not particularly well written. And now, here she was, frustrated because it didn't have anything about the kind of ghosts that walked through walls. "Not really my kind of thing."

"That possession stuff is great," Rafe said, glancing at what she was reading. "All the different kind of spirits. I'm pretty sure I'm possessed by something or other."

"Yeah? Me too." Dahlia thought again about the book's translator. She could remember the feel of the razor moving across his face as he had his beard shaved in her dream. Why would she dream something like that?

"I'm probably possessed by one of those evil dybbuks that tempt you to do bad things." Rafe grinned. "Although in this case it happens to be a dybbuk with an awesome sense of humor, which is probably how I came up with the Jell-O idea. Which, by the way, was *my* idea, not Benjy's. What about you?"

"I had nothing to do with the Jell-O trick."

"No. I mean, who's possessing you?"

She opened to the book's title page and tapped the translator's name. It felt good to be honest, even if Rafe thought she was just playing along. "This guy. David Schank. His spirit."

"The book's translator?" Rafe laughed. "That would be, like, the most boring possession ever." He leaned back lazily to lie flat on the tree bench. After a minute, he took the book from her and flipped back to the section on spirits. "I figure Schank's spirit would definitely be an ibur. They're the boring kind of do-gooder spirits."

"Let me see." Dahlia grabbed the book back. The author was mostly concerned with how to get rid of the nasty kind of spirits, but Rafe was right. There was a passing mention of iburs, which were described as "the spirits of the virtuous dead. An ibur will help the living complete those righteous tasks that the ibur began when it was still alive."

She looked back at Rafe. "How could you tell if you've got a good spirit or a bad spirit?"

"I figure it would be obvious. If it's, like, telling you to kill people, probably a sign it's a bad spirit." He yawned. "If it's telling you to go to synagogue and give money to charity or something, probably an ibur. I love how specific the guy is — how male spirits will always find a female host."

"What? Why?"

Rafe shrugged. "What, is this crap supposed to make sense?" He looked over Dahlia's shoulder, flipped a few pages, and pointed to a paragraph in the translation. "Look. He says it's because 'female and male energies balance and nourish one another, like a flower and a honeybee.'" Rafe laughed. "Well, that clears it up, right?"

Dahlia smiled, then abruptly realized that this was the time of day that she'd seen the ghosts in the bunk. Hopping off the tree bench, she walked toward her cabin. "See you later," she said.

"Where you going?" Rafe said, pulling himself up on his elbows.

"Back to my cabin."

"Can I have the book back?"

Dahlia was surprised to find she was still holding the book. She hadn't intended to take it with her.

"I mean, since you allegedly don't like it."

"Sure." Dahlia walked back to him and dropped the book on his stomach.

"Oof," he said. And then, to her retreating back, "Thanks."

The only thing that Dahlia found in the cabin was how much hotter it was inside, away from the breeze. She lingered there hopefully for the rest of the washing-up period, but she saw nothing more of the little blonde girls.

# CHAPTER 14

**B**y Thursday, Dahlia had settled into the camp routine. In the morning she leapt out of bed as soon as the loudspeaker went off and, along with Sarah and Hayley, she raced to the bathroom to shower while there was still hot water.

On the way to breakfast, she saw dark gray storm clouds gathering on the horizon. "Looks like rain," she said to Sarah. She automatically checked the dining hall roof for a lightning rod.

"Yay!" Sarah said. "I love rainy days at camp. If it really pours we'll get to watch movies in the rec center."

"Hmm," Dahlia said. "Sounds nice."

It did sound nice. She wasn't liking camp, exactly, but it wasn't terrible either. Most of the other girls in her bunk were nice enough, and Chelsea and Lisa had pretty much settled down to ignoring her. Anyway, there were only three more days left before she could call her parents and go home.

She hadn't seen the little blonde girls since Monday. She still wasn't sure what to make of them. A trick? A sign that she was going crazy? Real ghosts? She figured all she could do was keep her eyes open. She hadn't had any more dreams about David

Schank either, which wasn't really surprising. The weird dreams had probably just been her way of getting used to Jewish summer camp.

After breakfast, Dahlia saw a dark smudge on the horizon where the rain was already falling. By the time work groups were over, the smudge had spread across the horizon. She hurried back to her cabin.

She walked in to find Ofer and Alyssa mustering the girls. "Today, we're going to do the ropes course," Ofer said. "*Hayom na'aseh et maslul ha-chavalim.* We're going into the woods — *la ya'ar* — so everyone dress like me." Ofer was wearing tight black jeans, a tight black T-shirt, and a cheap-looking Yankees cap.

"What — like we're going to play baseball at a nightclub?" Chelsea said. A wave of laughter swept through the kids.

"Closed shoes, long pants, and a hat," Alyssa interjected before Ofer could answer. She waved her hand at him. "Go on out — let them change."

The other girls scurried around the cabin, putting on long pants and shoes and, in the case of Chelsea and Lisa, combing their hair out. Dahlia sat on her bed staring outside. The whole sky was gray now, with the blackish storm clouds rapidly moving closer.

"Let's go, Dahlia," Alyssa said, coming over to her bed. Dahlia looked around and realized all the other girls had already left the cabin.

"It looks like a storm," she said.

Alyssa followed her gaze. "Yep, probably after lunch. You get these summer showers —"

"I know," Dahlia interrupted. "But don't you think it's stupid to go into the woods when a thunderstorm is on the way?"

Alyssa wrinkled her forehead. "Um, I think we have a few hours. Look — if it starts raining, we'll come right back. Worse comes to worst, we'll get a little wet."

Up until now, Alyssa hadn't seemed stupid. Dahlia glanced outside, where the other kids were straggling toward the entrance to the woods. "Not the rain. The lightning. The trees will draw lightning. It's not safe."

"I think we have plenty of time before the storm really hits," Alyssa said. "I really don't want you to miss the ropes course."

Dahlia followed Alyssa to the front door of the bunk. Near the dark gray horizon she saw a bolt of lightning. "Look."

Alyssa turned just in time to see another bolt brighten the horizon. "That's just heat lightning. You can tell because there's no thunder."

"There's no such thing as heat lightning. It's just regular lightning that's too far off for you to hear the thunder."

"Really? Are you sure?"

"I'm sure." Dahlia shook her head and walked back to her bed. "I'm not going into the woods just before a lightning storm."

Alyssa looked closely at her. "You're really worried about the lightning, huh?"

Dahlia nodded. Of course she was worried about the lightning. She wasn't scared of heights or insects or anything stupid like that. But lightning was different. It killed people.

Alyssa sighed. "Okay. You can stay here this time. Hopefully, you'll get another chance to do the ropes course."

Dahlia stood by the window and watched as the group went into the woods. *Stupid*, she thought. Why was she the only one who took lightning seriously?

She stared out the window, watching as the storm grew closer. Out of the corner of her eye, she caught sight of something moving. She yanked her attention back to the cabin's interior.

The girl ghosts — or whatever they were — were back in the bunk, standing a few feet away from her. They were both wearing the same outfits they had on last time. The older girl kept glancing around the cabin, obviously nervous.

"Hi," Dahlia said.

The younger one waved at her, but this time neither of them smiled.

"What are you looking for?" Dahlia said to the older girl.

She didn't answer, but the younger girl tapped her own ears and shook her head. Right. They couldn't hear her any better than she could hear them.

Dahlia grabbed a pen and a notebook from next to her bed. She flipped the notebook open and wrote. "What are you looking for?"

She held the pen and notebook toward the girls. The older girl's brow furrowed and her mouth moved as she looked at the notebook, obviously sounding out the words. She looked up at Dahlia and mouthed one word. "Him."

"Who?"

"The M —" A few more words, or one very long word beginning with an *M*. Outside, the storm was now close enough to hear the low rumble of thunder in the distance.

"The man who was here the other day?" Dahlia guessed, gesturing to where she'd glimpsed the man's silhouette on Monday.

The older girl nodded. Her sister looked intently at Dahlia and said something.

"What?" Dahlia offered the girl the notebook and pen. "Here."

The little girl shook her head impatiently and passed her hand through the bed next to her. Of course. She couldn't write a note, because her hand wasn't solid.

Dahlia looked around carefully. Magicians had been creating this effect for centuries using mirrors. You just put one mirror behind the magician and another mirror across the room, behind the object with which you wanted to create the effect. When the magician reached for the object (which was really across the room), the mirrors made it look like the magician's hand was passing through it. An easy trick.

Except there was nowhere in the cabin for the mirrors to be concealed. And the truth was, Dahlia didn't really think this was a magic trick anymore. The little girls were either ghosts or something else that she had no idea how to explain. She took a deep breath and let it out. Ghosts. Dead girls. How could she be seeing dead girls?

The younger girl slowly mouthed two words. "Be . . . careful."

"Of that guy?" *No kidding.* Be careful of a semitransparent man who stalks little girl ghosts. Like she needed to be told that.

The little girl nodded and launched into a longer speech.

"Whoa." Dahlia raised her hands in what she hoped was a calming gesture. "Slow down."

111

The little girl stamped her feet. She was a cute little thing —
a little dirty, a little bedraggled, but with a face so expressive
Dahlia didn't need to hear her words to understand her frustration
and see how hard she was trying. The little girl bit her lip, then
held up her hands. She left all her fingers widespread on her left
hand, while extending the forefinger and middle finger on her
right hand.

"Seven?" Dahlia said.

The girl nodded. She was staring at Dahlia's lips so intently
that Dahlia suspected she couldn't hear Dahlia any better than
Dahlia could hear her. Next to the little girl, her older sister had
started pacing back and forth, looking increasingly nervous.

"Seven words?" Did she want to play charades?

The little girl emphatically shook her head. She held up seven
fingers again, then closed her left hand, leaving the first two fingers of her right hand extended.

"Seven and two," Dahlia said. "Nine?" Maybe the little girl
didn't know her numbers past seven.

The girl shook her head and clearly mouthed, "Seventy-two
years."

"You've been here for seventy-two years?"

The little girl nodded. "Seventy-two," she mouthed again,
staring earnestly at Dahlia, as if there was great significance
to the number. "Seventy-two years . . . means . . . things . . .
open." She mimed opening a book. "He . . . wants . . . more . . .
children."

"He wants to have more children?" Dahlia said, feeling increasingly stupid.

The girl hesitated. "Not *have*. Capture . . . catch . . . trap." She mimed catching an insect in her hands. "Soon."

A bolt of lightning arced across the field outside. The thunder was definitely getting closer.

The older sister stiffened and turned toward the back of the cabin. If not for her, Dahlia wouldn't have noticed the man arrive. He was suddenly standing just in front of Irit's bed, a few feet from the girls. At least she thought he was. He was a little more visible than he'd been on Monday, but he still looked less like a person than a slight concentration in the shadows. The hint of a tall man's silhouette. Dahlia stared so hard she started to get a headache.

The older girl grabbed her sister's hand and walked toward the front of the cabin, dragging her sister with her. The younger girl twisted around to look at Dahlia. "Don't . . . let . . . him," she mouthed. And then, for the third time, the girls disappeared through the cabin's wall.

With the girls gone, Dahlia abruptly realized how close she was to the man. He was maybe two steps away from her, but she could still barely see him. She kept blinking and thinking the fuzziness around him would disappear. But it didn't.

"Don't let you what?" Dahlia tried to say to him. It came out as a whisper, her throat suddenly so dry she could barely speak.

She wished there were other campers around. Someone else to see what she was seeing. *There is no reason to be scared*, she told herself. If he was a ghost, he would just go through her, right? He certainly didn't look solid enough to hurt her. And anyway, this was her chance to try touching a ghost.

She fought back the urge to run out of the cabin. Instead, she reached toward the man's shadowy outline, hand trembling as she stepped toward him. The man raised his hand to meet her. For a split second, their hands touched.

"Ouch!" She jerked her hand away. She'd felt a small, unmistakable electric shock when they touched. Not so painful, really, but it had surprised her.

Outside the cabin, there was another flash of lightning, followed by a loud, short roar of thunder. Dahlia's gaze jerked outside. The lightning had to be very close for the thunder to follow so quickly.

When she turned back, the man was gone.

A few seconds later, rain began to patter against the cabin's roof. Dahlia walked around the cabin, looking for the guy. She wasn't surprised when she didn't find him. She could barely see him when she knew where he was.

She gingerly tapped her fingers to her face. Her fingertips still tingled where she had touched the man. *Don't let him . . .* Don't let him what? Don't let him get more kids? Don't let him drag me through the walls again? Don't let him give you a static electricity shock? The little girl could have been about to say anything.

A minute or two after the rain started, the other kids started getting back. Chelsea was the first through the door. "Very smart," she said, nodding at Dahlia. She had run back fast enough that her hair was barely damp. "How'd Alyssa miss you?"

The other girls were right behind Chelsea, each one a little wetter than the one before. Alyssa was the last one back, and she was soaked. Still, she grinned at Dahlia. "Okay. Maybe it was a bad time to go into the woods."

Within a few minutes, the cabin was full of drying clothes and campers. Dahlia sat on her bed, staring at the wall the little girls had walked through. How was she supposed to be careful of someone she could barely see? And what was the big deal about seventy-two years? There had been something in her David Schank dreams about seventy-two years too, but she couldn't quite remember what it was.

She belatedly realized that Rafe was standing next to her bed and had asked her something a few times. "What?"

"We need a fourth for euchre," Rafe said. He nodded to the corner where Hayley and Sarah were sitting. "Do you want to play?"

"Do you know how to play?" Hayley said. She smiled a little apologetically at Dahlia. "No offense, but euchre is a pretty complicated card game."

Dahlia was suddenly eager to do something — anything — with people who had voices and didn't walk through walls. She swung down from her bunk. "I'll play," she said. She stepped off the bottom bunk and sat down next to Sarah.

"Okay," said Sarah. "It's kind of like hearts. Do you know how to play hearts?"

"Sure," said Dahlia. "And bridge. Euchre is basically a dumbed-down version of bridge, right?"

"Um, I guess." Sarah shrugged, then smiled. "I'll be on your team!" Sarah moved so she was sitting on the floor across from Dahlia, and Hayley and Rafe were sitting across from each other. She handed Dahlia the cards. "You can deal first."

Dahlia shuffled. Just for practice, she used a blind shuffle, where she kept the top half of the deck in the same order. When she was done, she passed the cards to Rafe to cut. He cut them behind his back, as though that would have stopped Dahlia from stacking the deck. If she had been trying to cheat, which she wasn't. The game seemed boring enough without knowing exactly where all the cards were. Still, she considered palming a few cards next time she dealt, just to see if she could.

"Hey," Rafe said. "So you're, like, totally scared of lightning?"

"No." Dahlia dealt out the cards as she spoke. "I'm appropriately cautious. Lightning is dangerous."

"Two summers ago we got caught in a thunderstorm on our big hike," Sarah said. "Something went wrong with the buses that were meant to pick us up, so we ended up stuck in a big field with no shelter around and tons of lightning."

Dahlia's stomach turned. "That sounds terrible."

Sarah giggled. "It was really fun. We huddled under these big tarps and ate all the marshmallows cold."

Dahlia finished the deal and turned over the top card of the remaining pile. "That's really dangerous." Once again, she resolved to get sent home as soon as she could. Definitely before the big hike, which she was pretty sure was second session, anyway.

Chelsea and Lisa were sitting on Chelsea's bed, hidden by the sheet Chelsea had hung from the top bunk. Chelsea called from behind the sheet, "Hey, Squirt. Are you, like, a total freak at your school too?"

"Shut up, Chelsea," Lisa said with a laugh.

"No, I'm serious," Chelsea protested. "I mean, at school she can probably sort of disguise this stuff. Maybe she doesn't care about lightning when she's in a big school building."

Dahlia scowled. "Last year, two hundred and seven people in the United States alone were struck by lightning," she said. "Forty-eight of them died."

"That's for the whole United States," Chelsea said. "How many people died in a car accident last year? Probably like ten times that."

Dahlia didn't say anything. She'd had the same arguments with her father. But lightning was different than a car accident. She couldn't say why. Ever since visiting the camp three years before, she could picture exactly what it felt like to be struck by lightning: the rain, the thunder, the instant of searing pain. . . . It scared her in a way that a car accident didn't.

Rafe looked up from scrutinizing his cards. "Why don't you just — I don't know — put on rubber boots and a rubber jacket when you go outside in the rain?"

"You think a lightning bolt that can go through half a mile of air is going to be stopped by a few inches of rubber?"

He looked back at his cards. "Um. Yeah?"

"You can't stop that kind of power. All you can do is redirect it. A lightning rod doesn't stop lightning. It just guides it into the ground."

Rafe looked thoughtful, but before he could respond, Hayley interrupted, "C'mon, Rafe. Pass or play."

The game was just as simple as Dahlia had thought, but it was fun too, and it distracted her from the lightning storm raging outside. Not to mention the little girl ghosts. Still, when the announcement came for lunch, she was thinking about the younger girl's warning. *Be careful. He wants more children.*

 CHAPTER **15**

# TOM

Tom walked toward his cabin, watching his kids play soccer in the late afternoon sunlight. The sky had cleared after the thunderstorm earlier, and it had turned into a beautiful afternoon. As soon as he was in earshot, he clapped his hands. "All right, guys," he said. "Next score ties. Time for flag lowering." He kept walking. One of the nice parts of working with younger kids was that he didn't have to take the soccer ball or make threats. He knew they'd be on their way by the time he came out of his bunk.

As he approached the cabin, he saw Jaden and Mitchell scurrying around the back, both of them holding a handful of wildflowers.

"Jaden and Mitchell," he called as he walked into the cabin. "That means you too." No answer from Jaden or Mitchell. The cabin itself was empty of campers. After four days, it had taken on the strong smell of unwashed laundry and barely washed ten-year-olds.

Outside he heard Nat Larson shouting, "Game over. I'm bringing the ball back to the sports shed." *God bless Nat Larson*, Tom thought. The camp should be paying him instead of Tom's alleged co-counselors.

He went into the counselors' room and found Kalish asleep on his bunk. Tom tossed Yoni's pillow at him. Kalish muttered something and rolled over. Tom briefly considered his sleeping form for a moment. How could a guy do so little and yet need so much sleep?

Tom slipped his foot from his sandal and nudged Kalish's gut.

"Leave me alone, bro," Kalish said, pulling the pillow over his head. "I have my free period during clubs."

"So do I," Tom said. "Clubs are over."

Kalish groaned and rubbed his eyes, but after a minute, he sat up. "Hey. You know the British guy — what's-his-name — Johnny? He was totally all over Nicole last night. A few of us were down by the creek, and —"

Tom slipped on his sneakers. "Shut up, Kalish."

"What? I'm just saying . . ."

Tom went back to the main part of the cabin and closed the door on Kalish. Like he needed to know who Nicole was hanging out with. He heard Jaden's voice behind the cabin and walked toward the nearest window.

He popped the screen out from the frame and poked his head out. Below, Jaden and Mitchell were huddled over something on the ground.

"All right, guys," Tom said. "I already told you once. It's flag lowering in five minutes."

Neither of the kids looked up. So much for younger kids being easier. Tom raised his voice. "Don't make me come down there."

Jaden muttered something that Tom couldn't hear. Tom shaded his eyes. It was hard to make out in the shadow of the cabin, but it looked like they were putting flowers on something. "Guys," he said.

Mitchell finally looked up, shaking his head and frowning. "Sorry, Counselor Tom. We weren't ignoring you on purpose; we were simply entranced by our task."

Tom tried and failed not to laugh. Such a little weirdo. "And what's your task?"

"We were having a funeral," Mitchell said brightly.

Tom leaned farther out, trying to see what they were huddled over. "Yeah? For who?"

"The dead man," Jaden yelled, looking up for the first time. His plump cheeks were red.

"Let me see," Tom ordered, but the kids were back to piling flowers over whatever it was they had found.

Tom pushed the screen back into place, then walked out the cabin's door and circled around to the back. He hoped they hadn't discovered a dead bird or something.

He found Jaden and Mitchell still gathered around the pile of flowers. Tom stuck the toe of his sneaker into the flowers. There was no dead anything there, just a slight mound in the grass, probably where the sewage lines had been put in when they ran plumbing into the cabin. "Is this your dead man?"

As usual, Mitchell's eyeballs were vibrating slightly from side to side. "We don't know where he is. But we wanted to have a funeral for him."

Jaden pushed the flowers back into the pile that Tom had disturbed. "We don't like mazes," he yelled at the pile of flowers. "Leave us alone."

"The maze work group is over," Tom said. Weird that Jaden would bring it up three days later. "It's time for flag lowering."

He looked down at the pile of flowers. It was actually pretty impressive. They must have skipped their clubs and spent the last hour or two gathering all the wildflowers they could find. They'd covered the whole mound — about half the size of a single bed — with blossoms. Mostly dandelions and clovers, but they'd also found some bluebells and a few slim orange flowers whose name he didn't know.

Even for a camp that celebrated weirdness, this was weird.

"Come on," Tom repeated. "We have flag lowering and then dinner."

Mitchell threw one more handful of flowers on the pile. Jaden grabbed Mitchell's arm. "What's for dinner?"

"Lasagna," Mitchell said. "That's what the menu outside the kitchen said."

"White pasta!" Jaden bellowed. He pulled Mitchell's arm and the two of them raced off. Jaden lagged a bit behind as he paused every few seconds to shout, "White pasta!"

Tom was about to follow them when he glanced back at their handiwork. They'd put a large gray stone, about the size of Tom's sneaker, on top of the mound. Tom brushed off the flowers to get a better look, and saw they had written four Hebrew letters on the stone in magic marker. "*Malkat*," Tom sounded out. "*Milket. Mall cat?*" Forget it. His Hebrew wasn't good enough. He'd ask Yoni what it meant, if and when the Israeli counselor stopped smoking long enough to actually come to their cabin.

Tom pushed the stone aside to make sure there wasn't anything gross beneath it. Just grass.

He rounded the cabin as Kalish walked out the door. Great.

"What was all that about?" Kalish said, eyeing Mitchell and Jaden running across the field in the distance.

"White pasta," Tom said shortly. He started walking after the kids toward the flagpole.

"Little fattie." Kalish snorted and settled his sunglasses more firmly on his face as he hurried after Tom. "Anyway. It was weird to see Nicole with this other dude. I mean she's always been your girlfriend, right? Even when the two of you were broken up, it was always 'Tom and Nicole, Nicole and Tom.'"

Tom lengthened his stride, but Kalish didn't seem to have any problem keeping up. "I was thinking you should go for what's-her-name — the lifeguard. Amy. She's got an awesome —"

"Shut up, Kalish. Seriously."

Kalish raised his hands. "Just looking out for you, bro."

Tom couldn't stop himself from looking for Nicole in the flag-lowering circle. There she was, laughing at something one of her campers was saying. She was wearing a tight yellow tank top, and it looked like she had just showered, with her hair still wet where it hung to her shoulders.

Tom forced himself to look away. Where was Dahlia, anyway? He found his sister standing between Sarah Kutler and Alyssa. As usual, she looked bored and annoyed. She was staring down the slope toward the pool, ignoring the people singing around her. Alyssa noticed him looking and nudged Dahlia.

Dahlia swung her gaze toward him and, to Tom's surprise, her face brightened. She backed out of the circle and made her way toward him. Tom thought about telling her that she was supposed to stand with her age group, but decided against it. It was the first time she'd seemed happy to see him since she came to camp.

He stepped behind his campers to meet her. "Hey, Dahl."

"Hey. Do you know anything about anyone dying in the camp? Maybe some girls younger than me, and a man too?"

"What?" Tom glanced over at Jaden and Mitchell, who were enthusiastically singing the flag-lowering song. What was with all the morbid campers? "Of course not."

"Are you sure?"

Around them the song ended, and the camp slowly surged toward the dining hall. "Yeah. I'm sure. Come on." Tom started walking toward the dining hall, watching his campers sprinting ahead of them. He heard Jaden shouting, "White pasta! White pasta!"

Beside him, Dahlia kept her voice low. "I'm not talking in the last few years, but a long time ago. Anyway, Rafe said that you used to tell them stories about some girls who went missing."

"What?" Tom hesitated. "You mean those McMasters stories? Was the Professor telling you McMasters stories?" He looked around for the little schmuck but didn't see him.

"Don't call him 'Professor,'" Dahlia said. "And no, Rafe didn't say anything about McMasters." She paused. "I think I heard the name somewhere, though. Who was he?"

"No one. Some guy all the CITs tell stupid stories about. He's supposed to steal a few campers every summer. I told the stories to campers when I was a CIT, just because that's part of being a CIT. But it's obviously ridiculous, right?" They had reached the dining hall, and Tom shrugged apologetically. "I gotta go inside so they can let the campers in. There has to be —"

"I know. One counselor for each table or we can't come inside," Dahlia finished. "No telling what we would do without a counselor at our table. Look. How are you so sure that no girls ever died around here? Or maybe just went missing?"

"Are you serious? Of course we would know. The camp probably would have closed. I mean, it's not the kind of thing a summer camp can just shrug off, like 'Whoops. Sorry. We lost your kids.'"

"But a really long time ago? Like in the 1940s or something."

Tom had forgotten how stubborn Dahlia could be. There was no point in arguing with her when she got like this. "Who knows what happened that long ago? I don't think the camp was even open back then." He squeezed her shoulder. "I gotta go." He slowly made his way through the massed campers into the dining hall, taking the table next to the one where Alyssa was sitting.

"That was so sweet," she said. "The Sherman kids bonding."

"She wanted to know if anyone ever died in this camp," Tom said. "That's why she was talking to me. Purely to gather information."

Alyssa giggled. "I love your sister."

# CHAPTER 16

# DAHLIA

**D**ahlia lay in her bed and waited for the other girls to fall asleep. She figured the easiest time to sneak into the computer room was bound to be after lights-out. There'd be fewer people around, and in the darkness she'd be less likely to be spotted approaching the office, which was off-limits to campers. Once she was in the computer room, she'd just have to hope no counselor came in until she was done.

She was sure Tom was wrong about whether any kids had gone missing. He thought he knew everything about the camp just because he'd been here for a few years.

It seemed to take the other girls a long time to go to sleep. Every couple minutes Dahlia caught herself on the verge of drifting off. Finally, though, the cabin was quiet — or not quiet so much as filled with the soft sounds of girls breathing and fans whirring.

Dahlia slowly climbed off her bed, careful not to touch Michal as she stepped on the edges of the lower bunk. The door to the counselors' room was closed, but their light was still on. Dahlia bunched up her blankets so it wouldn't be too obvious that her bed was empty, then tiptoed out of the cabin, carrying her sneakers in her hand. She paused on the stairs to quickly pull her sneakers over her bare feet, then darted into the darkness of the sports field.

The field hummed with the chorus of crickets. She saw a few counselors on the other side of the field, briefly visible as they walked past the porch lights of a distant cabin. She skirted the lights around the basketball court and paused as she approached the office. The lights in the front room were on, but it looked like no one was inside. Still, as soon as she walked onto the porch, she'd be visible to anyone walking past.

She took a deep breath, then paced toward the office's door as though she belonged there. She flung the door open and scanned the wall for the light switch. There. She quickly turned the lights off. In the sudden darkness she exhaled. So far, so good.

The front room was now pitch black except for the thin line of light at the bottom of the door to the computer room. She quietly felt her way across the cluttered office until she stood in front of the door. For a moment she just listened. No one talking, no clatter of keyboard keys. Nothing.

She rotated the doorknob and opened the door. A gust of cool, cigarette-tinged air-conditioning washed over her. No one was in the room.

She stepped in and pulled the door closed behind her. After the balmy summer night outside, the computer room was cold and smelled gross. Despite several NO SMOKING signs tacked to the wall, an overwhelming odor of stale cigarette smoke hung over the room. A half-eaten plate of food sat next to one of the old iMacs on the front table, a few feet from a bowl full of cigarette butts. There were half a dozen computers in various states of disrepair, all of them surrounded and in one case almost completely covered by stacks of binders and notebooks and copy paper.

Dahlia turned on what looked to be the newest computer — a Dell laptop that *might* have been no more than one or two years old. While she waited for it to boot up, she nervously paged through some of the binders lying nearby. Blah blah blah. A role play about Israel and the Palestinians. A version of Capture the Flag where the kids had to speak Hebrew sentences to capture each other.

It took another minute or two, but finally she got the Internet browser open. Okay. The nearest real town to the camp was Doylestown. She Googled DOYLESTOWN MURDERS and waited for a few seconds.

A long list of links came up. The first half dozen or so linked to local meet-ups to play a murder mystery game, several of which apparently featured a Michael Jackson imitator. She scrolled down. There were a handful of links to bookstores with regard to a mystery novel that was set in the area. She clicked on one of those links, but the book looked like a sort of romantic mystery. Nothing to do with kids at a summer camp. She got back to the main search page and scrolled further down. A few more links for Doylestown law firms, and that was it.

She heard a burst of laughter from just outside the office and froze, heart racing. Oh man. She really didn't want to get caught in here. It would be embarrassing, plus, if she got in lots of trouble, her parents might use it as an excuse to renege on their deal.

She walked to the computer room door, listening. The front room had two doors and the lights were off, so maybe she could sneak out one door if people came in the other.

After a moment, though, the voices faded into the distance. Dahlia went back to the computer and sat down. She thought for a minute and started a new search, typing DOYLESTOWN DISAPPEARANCES into the search box.

This time the first few links featured the disappearance of historic Doylestown. After that, the results got more random. A scientific article about the disappearance of a certain breed of fruit bat. Something about real estate development and the disappearance of farmland in eastern Pennsylvania.

Dahlia rubbed her eyes with the heel of her hands. All this sneaking around for nothing. She was about to close the browser when a few lines of text below one of the lower links caught her eye. The link's title was DOYLESTOWN MYSTERY, and she had assumed it was just one more site about the mystery novel set in Doylestown. The text, however, was about another topic entirely. ". . . while the disappearance of the girls was never conclusively linked to the Mafia . . . indisputable that during that same year or two, New York Jewish mobsters made real estate investments in the Doylestown area as part of a money-laundering . . ." *What?*

Behind her, outside the computer room, the door to the outer office banged open. Dahlia whirled to face the door. Shoot. She was going to get thrown out just as she found something interesting. She heard a man's voice cursing as someone crashed into the furniture cluttering the darkened office outside. Dahlia turned back to the screen, feverishly clicking the link. Nothing happened.

She heard the computer room door open behind her. She half turned to see one of the Israeli counselors step into the room, pulling a box of cigarettes from his back pocket. Dahlia didn't know his name, but she was pretty sure he worked with the same age group as Tom. Great. So Tom couldn't avoid hearing about this.

Dahlia stared at the screen desperately, wishing it would at least give her a hint of what the link was referring to before she got thrown out.

"Eh," the Israeli said, more hesitantly than she was expecting. "You are allowed to be in here?"

Dahlia turned around as though she was just noticing him. "Yes," she said.

The Israeli fished a cigarette and a lighter out of his pack. He glanced at Dahlia as he lit it. There was something tentative in the way he inhaled, and Dahlia's eyes fell on the NO SMOKING sign.

"Hey. You're not supposed to smoke in here," she said. She made her tone as accusatory as she could.

He frowned apologetically. "I just smoke one cigarette and go. The smoking area is too far."

Dahlia narrowed her eyes and turned back to the computer. For a few seconds, she stared blankly at the screen, waiting for him to throw her out of the office. Instead, the guy slouched into a chair in front of one of the old iMacs and turned it on.

Dahlia blinked at her screen as cigarette smoke filled the office. The browser window now said: THIS WEB PAGE IS NO LONGER AVAILABLE. PLEASE CHECK THE URL AND TRY AGAIN. Dahlia quickly backtracked to the search list, but there were no cached versions available either. She opened a new browser window and tried a few more searches, but didn't find anything else remotely related to Doylestown and the Mafia or girls disappearing.

A few seats away, the Israeli guy had Facebook open. The little computer room was full of smoke now, and Dahlia's eyes were starting to water.

She clicked back to the earlier search list and read the blurb beneath the DOYLESTOWN MYSTERY link again. ". . . while the disappearance of the girls was never conclusively linked to the mafia . . ." It was probably nothing. Probably a few sentences taken out of context.

She shot a quick glance at the Israeli counselor. He had his back to her while he furtively lit another cigarette.

She clicked back to the search bar and quickly typed DAVID SCHANK. A ton of links came up. Not surprising, really, with such a common name. There were five David Schanks on Facebook alone. She scrolled down the list of links and found nothing that seemed remotely connected to the David Schank in her dreams.

She was about ready to give up when she thought of the rabbi David had loved so much. The author of the kabbala book, Reb Isaac Ben Yisachar.

*Keep smoking*, she silently directed the Israeli. *Nothing to see here.*

Typing as fast as she could, she typed the rabbi's name in the search box and hit ENTER. Finally, a successful search. The screen filled with links about Reb Isaac. Dahlia sifted through a few stupid websites devoted to how wonderful the guy was before she came across the Wikipedia entry.

Before she even started reading the entry, she caught her

breath. There was a picture at the top of the page of an old, ultra-Orthodox man. His appearance was nothing out of the ordinary: black hat, black coat, full white beard. But his face — the parts you could see between the beard and the hat — she knew his face. It was the rabbi David had talked to in her dream.

Excerpted from http://en.wikipedia.org/wiki/third_Yebavner_Rebbe

## Grand Rabbi Isaac Ben Yisachar (the third Yebavner Rebbe)

Grand Rabbi Isaac Ben Yisachar, better known as the third Yebavner Rebbe, is most famous for relocating the Yebavner community from the Polish city of Yebavneh to the United States. At the Rebbe's instigation, almost every Jew living in or around Yebavneh immigrated to the United States during the spring of 1921. The means by which the Rebbe was able to gain their admission into the United States remains unknown, given the strict quota system that faced would-be immigrants to the United States at the time. The quota system was particularly geared toward limiting Eastern European immigrants, and even more particularly, toward limiting Jewish Eastern European immigrants. Thus, the effective relocation of tens of thousands of Yebavner Jews, including thousands of uneducated and impoverished peasants, was viewed as miraculous by the Rebbe's followers, while it attracted a great deal of suspicion from the larger community.

In the immediate aftermath of the move, there were widespread allegations of bribery, and the famously anti-Semitic J. Edgar Hoover was rumored to be launching an investigation from the fledgling Bureau of Investigation [citation needed]. Despite these undercurrents, due to their numbers, the Yebavner community almost immediately became the dominant Chasidic community on the Lower East Side of Manhattan. As Nazi power grew in Europe, the Rebbe's relocation of the Yebavners became widely viewed as evidence of his uncanny foresight and prophetic talents.

Reb Isaac's fame as a seer grew through the 1920s and 1930s. By the start of World War II in the late 1930s, he was consulted regularly both by New York's Mayor Fiorello LaGuardia and President Franklin Roosevelt [citation needed] until the Rebbe's death in 1944.

In recent decades, like most New York Chasidic communities, the Yebavners have relocated to Crown Heights, Brooklyn. The current Yebavner Rebbe is Reb Chaim Ben Velvel, the grandson of Reb Isaac.

# References:

1. Levine and Dashefsky (2002). "A History of Jewish Immigration to the United States," in *From Mosaic to Melting Pot:*

*Perspectives on Immigration in the 20th Century.* Edited by Balthazar and Mohan. New York: Basic Books.

2. Rosenberg (2004). "Tales of the Chasidim: Take 2." *Annals of American Jewry* (2:14), p. 204–218.

## External Links:

- <u>Yebavner Homepage</u>
- <u>Yearly Jewish Studies conference (Jewish Studies@Cornell)</u>
- <u>Rebbe Isaac's Transcribed Lectures</u>

Dahlia read the page three times. Aside from the picture, nothing really confirmed or denied anything she had dreamed. And after staring at the picture for a few minutes, she couldn't be sure if she'd truly recognized the Rebbe from her dream or not. How different did one old ultra-Orthodox man look from another?

She was still staring at the screen when she realized the Israeli counselor had just glanced over at her for the second time in half a minute. Time to go. She shut down her computer and walked to the door. The counselor furrowed his brow as she went past him, maybe realizing for the first time just how young she looked.

"Good night," Dahlia said, opening the door to the delightfully balmy, smoke-free night.

"*Lilah tov,*" he said, turning back to his computer.

# CHAPTER 17

**D**ahlia was deep asleep when she heard the man's low, assured voice.

"Come on. I know you're awake, David. Stop pretending."

She put her arm over her face. Why wouldn't he just shut up and let her sleep?

"Have it your way." The man was speaking softly, but his voice was so deep it was impossible to ignore. "I just wanted to ask: What is death like for *you*?"

Dahlia was still trying to go back to sleep when his words penetrated. She sat up in a panic, heart hammering. It was the middle of the night. The cabin was dark and quiet. Except for the voice of the man looming over her bed. She had the feeling he'd been talking to her for some time before she woke up.

He went on in the same smooth tones, as though not noticing that she had sat up. "You've been gone a long time. I'm guessing the seventy-two-year cycle makes it easier for you to come back too. Still, I get the feeling you're barely here sometimes. Like sometimes you're front and center in this kid, and other times you're like a passing daydream. You doing that on purpose?"

"Barry?" Dahlia said. She had meant to speak loudly — show that she wasn't scared. Instead, it came out barely a whisper.

"Shut up," the man said casually. She couldn't tell if his voice sounded like Barry's or not. It wasn't like she'd had many conversations with the caretaker. "I'm not talking to *you*. Anyway, David, did you think I wouldn't notice you? Slinking into this child's body? Drawing *my* girls to you?"

Something in Dahlia stirred. She found her mouth opening and a man's voice came out. "Get away," the voice said. "This child is under my protection."

She clenched her teeth shut, panic like electricity in her veins.

"Your protection?" The silhouetted figure laughed, a low, easy laugh. "We know what that's worth, don't we? How did you choose her, anyway? I can't believe it was just her initials. There had to be something —"

Dahlia's mouth opened again, and a long word came out of it.

That's when she screamed. She didn't scream because of the man standing next to her, nor because she recognized the long word as being the magic name from her dreams. She screamed because she again heard someone else's voice coming out of her mouth, and she hated the feeling. She screamed to show that her mouth was still under her control. That this was still her body. Hers.

For a moment everything was still. Then, around the bunk, she heard rustlings as the other girls sat up. A few flashlights flipped on.

"What the . . ." Chelsea said blearily from the next bed over. There were two thumps as she swung her legs off her bed and stood to look at Dahlia. "Did you just scream?"

"There's a . . ." Dahlia rubbed her eyes. No one was standing next to her bed except for Chelsea. "There was a man in the cabin."

A few more flashlights came on, all of them playing around Dahlia's bed. She could clearly see that there was no man anywhere near her bed.

Alyssa appeared in the doorway to the counselors' area. "What's going on?" she said.

"Squirt screamed," Chelsea said. "She thought there was a man in the bunk, so she screamed. Just like anyone would. If they were crazy."

Alyssa crossed the bunk in a few paces. "Are you okay, Dahlia?"

"What about the rest of us?" Chelsea said. "Getting woken up by a screaming crazy woman. She should have to sleep outside."

"Go back to sleep, Chelsea," Alyssa said.

"A guy was in here talking to me," Dahlia said. "He must have run out when I screamed." She glanced at her watch, glowing softly in the dark. 3:45 a.m. She hadn't gotten back to the bunk from the computer room until after midnight, so she'd only slept for about three hours before the guy woke her up.

Chelsea went back to her bed and sat down. "A guy talks to you, and that makes you scream? What, did you think the world was ending? Was he cute?"

"Shhh," Lisa said from the bunk above Chelsea.

"Me? I'm not the one —"

"Seriously, Chels, shut up," Lisa muttered drowsily.

Chelsea sighed, but she lay down.

Alyssa stepped next to Dahlia's bed. "It must have been a dream," she said quietly. "If he ran away when you screamed, we would have heard the door open. It's impossible to open that door quietly. And look." She swept her flashlight around the room and crouched down to look beneath the beds. "There's no man in here, Dahlia."

Dahlia shook her head. "I guess not," she said. "Sorry to get you up."

"Don't worry about it," Alyssa said. "You feel okay now?" Dahlia nodded. Alyssa looked at her for a few more moments, then squeezed her arm before turning away.

Lying in the darkness, Dahlia listened as her heart gradually slowed. What had the guy called her? David. Like in her dreams about David Schank. This place was making her crazy. She took a deep breath. It didn't make any sense. Even if she was possessed — and she didn't believe in possession — why would a man's voice come out of her mouth? They would still be her vocal cords, right? So even if she was possessed, the words should come out in her voice. Maybe it *had* just been a bad dream.

But she couldn't stop thinking about the sound of the man's voice. *The truth was* . . . if you were possessed, you might hear a man's voice even if you were speaking in your usual voice. You might hear a man's voice, because the spirit possessing you was a man when he was alive, and he expected his voice to sound the same when he spoke. *The truth was* . . . if he possessed your mouth, why not your ears? Why not your eyes too? Why not everything?

She was still awake when light started to bleed into the sky outside.

# CHAPTER 18

**D**ahlia was so tired that it took her forever to get up. With the morning sun glinting off the bed frames, it felt ridiculous that she had made such a big deal of a dream. By the time she made it to the showers, there was a long line, so she just washed her face and brushed her teeth. She was almost back to the cabin when Chelsea and Lisa stumbled out the door, bleary-eyed.

Chelsea shook her head when she saw Dahlia. "Watch out," she said to Dahlia as they passed. "There might be some horrible . . . *man* around here. Get ready to scream." Lisa giggled.

Dahlia walked up the cabin stairs so quickly that she tripped and barked her shin on the top step. Chelsea's and Lisa's laughter followed her inside.

Most of the other girls took it for granted that she'd been having a bad dream. On the way to flag raising, Sarah told Dahlia about a recurring dream she had where she was drowning in a huge swimming pool surrounded by people swimming laps, and Hayley offered a dream she'd had a few nights before about one of the Israeli counselors kissing a man. "Who did the guy in your dream look like?" Hayley asked Dahlia.

Dahlia thought for a minute, then shook her head. "I have no idea. It was too dark. All I could see was his silhouette looming over my bed."

Hayley shivered. "I would have screamed, too."

"Thanks, Hayley," Dahlia said, oddly touched.

After breakfast, there were the usual songs and announcements: A little girl from the animal care work group plaintively asked that someone return a missing hamster cage, and one of the counselors in training announced that the lumberjacks work group would meet at the fire pit. Then the deputy camp director — a little woman with spiky hair called Yasmin — announced that about half of the work groups were assigned to spend that day's work period cleaning the kitchen and dining hall. She read off a list of the groups that had been assigned kitchen duty, including Dahlia's painting group. When Yasmin was done, the rest of the work groups cheered themselves as they left the dining hall, shouting, "We do real work! We do real work!"

Dahlia yawned as she watched them leave, then joined the other campers where the counselors were gathering them in the corner of the dining hall. The head of the kitchen, a burly Russian man with a couple days of stubble, stood on a bench. He talked for about five minutes in a low, heavily accented voice.

"What's he saying?" Eileen asked. She and Dahlia were standing near the back of the group.

Dahlia shook her head. "No idea."

Finally, he finished talking. Dahlia and Eileen stood there for a moment. Around them the other kids all seemed to know what to do, picking up the benches and tables and carrying them onto the dining hall's balcony.

"Come on, Eileen," Dahlia said. She picked up one end of the nearest table. It was lighter than she had thought it would be.

Eileen looked at her suspiciously, not moving. "That's not funny."

"What?"

"I hate that song," Eileen said. " 'C'mon, Eileen. Whoa, c'mon, Eileen.' That joke was old when I was, like, eight."

Dahlia looked at her blankly, then shrugged. She started dragging the table toward the door by herself. It wasn't that heavy.

"Stop that!" the head of the kitchen roared. He ran over, grabbed her wrist, and pulled her away from the table. "Idiot! Do not you understand English? Scratches it the floor when drag you tables!"

Suddenly, Tom was there too. He put his hand on the man's shoulder and steered him back toward the kitchen. "All right, Natan," he said. "Sorry 'bout that. I'll take it from here."

Tom waited until Natan was out of sight, then shook his head. "We are so going to get sued if they don't fire that guy." He picked up the other end of Dahlia's table and, after a moment, she picked up her end too. They started carrying the table toward the side door of the dining hall. "They just refinished the floor of the dining hall, and I think he's really worried about it getting scratched up."

"You think?" Dahlia said.

Tom laughed. "You having a better time, Dahl?"

Dahlia hesitated. They took the table outside, and Tom maneuvered it around a few of the benches that were already stacked.

"Sort of," she said.

"Yeah?" Tom put his end of the table down and dragged the benches out of the way. Then he went back to the table and pushed it closer to the wall. "Why just sort of?"

"I've, um . . . I don't know. I've been having these weird dreams and . . ." She tapped her finger on the table, then absently began to pick at one corner where the table's laminated cover had started to peel back. "Remember how I asked you yesterday if any girls had ever died around here?"

Tom nodded. He stood next to another table. "Give me a hand. I want to flip this and put it on top of the other one. We're going to run out of room otherwise."

Dahlia obligingly picked up the other side of the table. This one was made of thicker wood and was heavier than the first one they'd moved. She managed to shuffle a few steps with it until Tom could rest one side of the tabletop on the other table, and flip the first table onto the second one.

"Dahlia," he said. "I'm telling you. Don't let the Professor bother you with those McMasters stories."

"And I'm telling you," Dahlia snapped, "stop calling him the Professor."

Tom gave the table another push, stacking it more neatly, and then turned back to Dahlia. "All right, all right. Whatever. Rafe. Don't let him bother you with McMasters."

"Unlike you, Rafe has never even mentioned McMasters. All Rafe wants to talk about is the stupid book of kabbala."

"The stupid book of what?"

"Kabba — never mind." Dahlia refused to be distracted. "I just want to know if anyone ever died at this camp."

"No one ever died at this camp." Tom started stacking the benches on top of one another and, after a moment, Dahlia helped him. Two little kids brought a bench out between them, and Tom took it. "Thanks, Nat. Great job, Eric." The kids scurried back inside, and Tom stacked their bench on top of the pile he had created. He turned to follow the kids.

Dahlia took his arm. "Are you sure? I mean. No one's *ever* died or disappeared around here? Have you checked?"

Tom turned to look down at her, a half smile on his lips. "Wait. Is this like a setup for a magic trick?"

"I'm serious, Tom. I really think some girls died around here a long time ago. Maybe even before the camp was here. Like," she hesitated. The little girls had said seventy-two years, but she didn't want to tell Tom about the little girls. He'd just think she was crazy. "In the 1940s or something. Can you just try to find out for me?"

"Fine. I'll Google —"

Dahlia interrupted. "Not just that. The web doesn't have anything useful."

"What?! How do you know?"

*Whoops.* "I just do, okay?"

"Did you bring your phone to camp? Campers aren't supposed to have —"

"I didn't bring my phone." Dahlia scowled at Tom and dropped his arm. "I have to spend a week at your crappy camp. Can't you do me this one little favor?"

Tom looked around, probably worried that one of his counselor friends might think he wasn't the world's best counselor.

"Dahlia. Come on. Relax." She held his gaze. After a few seconds, he held up his hands in mock surrender. "Fine. I'm going into town tomorrow to buy some things for Yasmin. I'll go by the Doylestown library and do a little research." He paused. "But I'll only do it if you promise not to call Mom and Dad on Sunday. If you're going home on Sunday, you can do your own research."

Finally, reluctantly, Dahlia nodded. The truth was, she really should stay if she hadn't figured out the ghosts before then. Camp wasn't that bad, and she could be the first person ever to show that ghosts were real. "Okay. But I mean good research."

"Hey, Tom!" Alyssa called through the screen window. "Can you help me with this table?"

"Good research," Tom said to Dahlia. "Like a stinking term paper." Then, louder, to Alyssa, "Sure, I *can* help you. Why do you ask?"

Alyssa giggled far more than Tom's bad, old joke had deserved. Dahlia sighed and followed him back into the dining hall.

# CHAPTER 19

"**T**wenty minutes to lights-out," Selena called. "Wash up now if you haven't already."

Lying on her bed, Dahlia watched the other girls dutifully file out, carrying their toiletries and towels. She turned back to the kabbala book. She'd found it back on her bed after dinner, and she wanted to see if she could find out anything else about ghosts. Thus far, there was nothing in the translation, though there might have been more in the original Hebrew. She stared at the Hebrew intently, wondering if it would just suddenly make sense to her like the announcements had the other day.

After a few moments, she gave up and started flipping through the sketches of the mazes. She was pretty sure that most of the mazes were just doodles. After a while, the translator — or whoever had drawn the mazes — seemed to get bored with the mazes too. For the last quarter or so of the book, the pages left blank for the translation were still empty. She turned through the blank pages, feeling her eyelids getting heavier and heavier.

Then something caught her eye. On one of the last pages of the book, the translator had written a single sentence. The Hebrew side of the text was jammed with print, but the translated side read only, *The gematria for maze is 68.*

Dahlia yawned. *Gematria.* Where had she heard that word?

The screen door rattled, and Rafe called, "Is everybody decent?"

Rafe's voice reminded her: Peter had said something about gematria when he'd been saying how you could convert Hebrew words into numbers. How kabbala assigned each Hebrew letter a number, so you could add up the value of any word, and words with the same values were supposed to be somehow connected. She still thought that was dumb — to say a maze was like something else just because their letters added up to the same thing.

"I'll take that as a yes," Rafe said, and the door slowly opened. He made a beeline for her bed. "Oh, hey," he said. "Just wanted to make sure you had the book. I thought I'd lost it. I was looking everywhere for it."

"Didn't you give it back?"

Rafe shook his head. "No."

Dahlia hesitated. "Wait. You're joking, right?"

"What kind of joke would that be?" Rafe said. "I mean, how is that funny?"

"Well, I didn't take it back. I don't even like it."

"So why are you reading it?"

"Um. Because. It . . ." Dahlia shrugged helplessly. She was reading it because it kept turning up on her bed, and she'd been having dreams about the translator, and most of all, she kept hoping it would help her make sense of all the stuff that had been happening since camp started. None of which meant she liked it.

Rafe lowered his voice. "You know — I looked it up on Amazon and it's not listed?"

"What? How'd you check Amazon? Did you go into the computer room?" Dahlia was embarrassed that she hadn't even thought of looking up the book on Amazon.

He cast a furtive glance around the cabin. "Smart phone. It's pretty fast even without a wireless connection. Anyway, I couldn't find the book online. And that guy whose name is on the title page, Rabbi whoever? He was like a celebrity rabbi, but there's nothing on the Internet about him writing any books."

"Why were you checking all this?"

Rafe shrugged. "I wanted another copy, because you keep taking it back from me before I'm done."

"I haven't taken it back once."

He rapped his knuckles against the bunk bed's steel frame. "Right. Whatever. The point is, I couldn't find anything about this book online, and I looked for, like, twenty minutes."

"Why don't you ask Peter where he got it?"

"That moron? He already told us — he found it in the camp library. Probably while he was hiding in there to burn incense and give Wanda Sorkin more 'massages.'"

Dahlia glanced down at the book. *The gematria for maze is 68.* She flipped through the translated parts of the book, looking for more passages about numbers. The closest she saw was a section where the author gave a lengthy explanation of how to interpret the square root of God's name. Who cared? She held the book toward Rafe. "You want it back?"

"Sure," Rafe said. He reached for the book. Dahlia intended to hand it to him, she really did, but for some reason, when it came down to it, she didn't quite release her grip. Rafe tugged on the book for a moment just as Dahlia tightened her hold on the spine. Then they both let go at the same time, and the book fell on the bed. A folded piece of paper tumbled onto Dahlia's blanket.

Rafe quickly took the book. "Anyway — see you tomorrow." He was out the door in seconds, probably worried that Dahlia might change her mind. "Thanks again," he called as he clomped down the stairs.

Dahlia picked up the single piece of paper that had fallen out of the book. It had been folded four times, and was so old that it ripped in two as she unfolded it. She had to hold it up to the overhead fluorescent lights to make out the faded typewritten letters. Someone had written a brief note in handwritten Hebrew below the man's signature, but the rest of it was typed in English.

*22 Blenbridge St.*                                *26 February 1927*
*London, UK*

*To Rabbi Velvel Ben Eliezer:*

*I wish to God I had thrown your man out the morning he came into my office to hire me. No fewer than three of my detectives have disappeared in the course of this investigation. And for what? You never deigned to tell me why you commissioned this research, so I can only hope that it was in the service of some urgent, commendable goal.*

*Attached you will find an invoice, with the outstanding balance payable upon receipt. You will also find a full summary of the research you commissioned into the group of mystics, criminals, and* stage magicians, known variously as the broken Jesuits, dark templars, the shacholim gidolim, or — as they call themselves — the Illuminated Ones.

As instructed, I have covered the margins of the attached document with the symbols you sent me, although I have real doubts about how effective these — or any other devices — will be for ensuring their gaze does not fall upon it. After reading this report, I would ask you to destroy it, along with all invoices, receipts, and personal correspondence linking this report to me. Do not try to contact me again. I will be taking my family on an extended journey to one of the few places where the Illuminated Ones have not been able to establish a foothold.

The Illuminated Ones are old — far older than I realized when I accepted this assignment. I came across references to them in third-century texts from the Roman empire, and these referred to even older mentions in scrolls that have long since been lost. The sect has tended to alternate between periods of intense activity and virtual hibernation. Right now, we are in the midst of an active period, due largely to the dynamism of the current head of the organization.

As with all of their leaders, their current leader is known only as the Most Illuminated One. Despite my best (and most perilous) efforts, I was unable to determine the background of this individual, nor even his race nor country of origin. There are certain indications that he was at one time a student in a Catholic seminary in Ireland, as well as a popular stage magician in London, but neither of these could be verified.

The Illuminated Ones are not just secretive; they are obsessed with finding and keeping secrets. Gathering knowledge is their one and only task, particularly knowledge that has to do with the nature of life and death. It is not clear to me if they desire this knowledge for its own sake, in order to extend their own lives, or perhaps to pursue some other goal entirely. I will leave the speculation to you.

There is a joke they tell, a kind of warning to new members. The punch line is: "An Illuminated One can share a secret with a non—Illuminated One, as long as the non—Illuminated One is dead." Perhaps you will see the humor. I do not.

Do not contact me again.

Sincerely yours,

Mr. Harvey S. Rutledge, esq.

Dahlia read the letter three times before the counselors turned out the lights. Then she lay in the darkness thinking about it. She imagined David Schank sitting in a café seventy-two years ago, reading and rereading the letter and wondering if the Illuminated Ones were going to find him. Wondering *when* the Illuminated Ones were going to find him.

She fell asleep with the taste of coffee on her lips.

# CHAPTER 20

# DAVID

**D**avid sat in a café and did not think about his hunger. He read and translated the rabbi's book and did not think about his hunger. He spent so much energy not thinking about his hunger that he barely had to try not to think about the 72nd name, or the Illuminated Ones waiting for him at every train station in the city, or about the way the Rebbe had abandoned him.

Every time he felt tempted to use the name, he reread Rutledge's letter. Below the man's signature, someone had written in a fine Yiddish hand, *Mr. Rutledge and family were on the HMS* Sophia *en route to Calcutta when it was lost in a sudden squall on October 14, 1927. Their memories be blessed.*

*One more man the Rebbe had used and abandoned to his fate*, David thought bitterly.

After wandering Manhattan for four days, feeling the net of Illuminated Ones tightening around him, David had spent the last of his money three hours ago on a cup of coffee. The waiter had long since given up on refilling his cup, but he at least showed no signs of throwing him out. Yet.

Outside the sun was shining on the cracked cement sidewalk,

and the midtown streets were filled with businessmen stripped down to shirtsleeves. It was nice to be sitting down.

He delayed thinking about his next step as long as he could. Despite his best attempts to concentrate on translating the Rebbe's book, his efforts kept foundering. Instead, too hungry and scared to focus, he filled the pages with sketches — mazes, mostly. Faces and buildings too, but mostly mazes.

It was an old habit of his, and it was the best way he knew to avoid thinking about the 72nd name. And it was crucial that he didn't think about it, because every time he did, the Illuminated Ones got closer.

Still, he had to do something more. His money was gone, and he needed help. He would use the name to summon the most fearless person he knew. If he was lucky, the person would get there before the Illuminated Ones.

The café was quiet in the morning lull after breakfast. There were two younger men speaking Romanian in the corner, which David didn't understand, and a much older man muttering to himself in Yiddish. This man was sitting at the narrow linoleum bar next to the kitchen, repeating again and again, "It's not so bad. It's not so bad." At first it had annoyed David, but after hearing it some thirty times, he was finding it vaguely reassuring.

"It's not so bad," he said to himself in English. Before he could lose courage, then, he said the name. Holding it in his head, he pictured the one he wanted to draw to him.

Elsewhere in the city, he could feel the Illuminated Ones twitching, sniffing, trying to sense him. He released the name from his mind, brought out the Rebbe's text, and submerged himself once again in translation. When his attention began to wander, he started to sketch mazes across the empty pages. The Illuminated Ones circled closer. He would need to leave this place soon.

Twenty-three minutes later, Samuel Ackerman, more commonly known as "Sammy the Pick," walked through the door. "Sammy," David said. It had been a long time.

Sammy was wearing a pin-striped linen suit that looked like it had been tailored just for him. His thick, brown hair was greased back with not a strand out of place. Still, he carried himself like the bruiser David remembered from when they were kids running errands for the neighborhood toughs.

Sammy scanned the restaurant carefully before he seated himself across from David, his back to the wall. He narrowed his eyes when he looked at David. "Funny story," he said. "Just now I'm sleeping, and I get a call from my mother. She tells me Davey Schank needs my help, and he was always a good kid, not like me, and I should find him in a dive just east of Astor Place. She hangs up. I'm rolling over, thinking she's crazy — you wouldn't catch Davey dead in a non-kosher place — and I'm just about asleep, when it occurs to me that my mother died five years ago. And anyway, she never — but never — figured out how to use the phone."

He beckoned to the server. "So I get one of my guys to drive me across town, and I find you here looking like a goy hobo. What happened to you? The great rabbi-to-be loses his beard and black hat? A brisket sandwich," he said to the waiter. He glanced at David and said, "Make that two."

"This place isn't kosher," David said. Still, he found his mouth full of saliva.

"From the looks of it, neither are you, Rav," Sammy said. He waved the waiter to the kitchen. "Speaking of which, what are you doing in a non-kosher restaurant?"

"Avoiding . . . people who'd be looking for me at a kosher place."

"Right." Sammy leaned back in his seat and regarded David. "What's going on? Must have happened in the last few days, because I can still see the tan line where your beard used to be." He ran his hand over his own pomaded hair, lips twisting into a half grin. "What — you get into a fight with your rebbe about the best way to butter your toast?"

"Nothing like that."

"Good," Sammy said. "God help you if you didn't have a good reason for disturbing my mother, her memory be blessed."

The server returned and set a sandwich in front of each of them. The brisket was piled several inches high on top of the black bread, topped with a solid dollop of sauerkraut and mustard. David sighed and picked up the sandwich. "Some water too, please," he said to the server.

The sandwich tasted as good as it looked. The juices from the brisket ran down David's chin, and he wiped his face with the sleeve of his shirt. He waited until the server was back in the kitchen to continue talking. "I'm in trouble."

Sammy motioned impatiently. "I figured. What kind of trouble?"

"I need to get out of the city. Go somewhere no one is looking for me. You know people."

"Kid, I *am* people. When do you need out by?"

David looked around and spread his hands. "Now. Yesterday."

Sammy took a bite of his sandwich, his eyes not leaving David's face. "Tell me what happened."

David didn't say anything. Sammy took a few seconds to chew, then, mouth still full, said, "You gotta tell me more. Me and my associates are in the middle of some — ah — delicate negotiations with the Italians right now. There are some people I can't afford to cross." He waved the sandwich at David. "Come on. Spill."

David spilled. He was describing his meeting with the Illuminated One in the Rebbe's basement when Sammy interrupted. "So what's the magic word?" he said, leaning close. "Tell it to me, and let the shaygetz momzers come."

David said the word for the second time that morning. If Sammy helped him, he'd be gone before the Illuminated Ones found him. If Sammy didn't help, they'd find him sooner or later, anyway.

Sammy looked at him blankly. "What? Say it again." He motioned toward the open window across the room. "Must have been the construction on Second Avenue — I couldn't hear it."

Knowing better, David said it again.

This time Sammy started out of his seat, spinning toward the door, hand reaching beneath his jacket. He stayed in that position, hand beneath his jacket, staring at the door for several seconds. Then, cautiously, he moved toward the door and peered out.

David stood. "You didn't hear whatever you think you did."

"Crap," Sammy muttered. "I heard bullets firing." Still, his hand came out from under his jacket, and he straightened the jacket so it fell away from the bulge beneath his left arm.

"Only sages can hear the name of God." David sat back down, and after a minute, so did Sammy.

Sammy ran his hand through his hair, rearranging a few strands that had fallen out of place. "So. If only true believers can hear it, why are these traifnyak momzers so hot for you?"

Saying the name twice had definitely gotten the Illuminated Ones' attention. David could feel them getting closer, sniffing the ether, triangulating amongst themselves to figure out from where the emanations had come. He looked out the door nervously. "It *should* be impossible to misuse any part of the most holy name. It *should* be only the most blessed sages who can hear it, let alone use it."

"But it's not," Sammy finished. "Who are they?"

David shrugged. "They call themselves the Illuminated Ones. They collect secrets. I don't know a whole lot more."

"Crappy name for a gang." Sammy started picking his teeth with the toothpick that had held the sandwich together. "So you up and leave yeshiva, cut your hair and the rest, all on account of they put a scare in you?"

"I was pushed," David said reluctantly. "The Rebbe forbade me to come back."

"And that," Sammy said, "is the kind of yellow thinking that is why our people have been getting slaughtered by the goys for two thousand years." He leaned forward, toothpick still clenched between his teeth. "If the name's so powerful — use it. Wipe the momzers out."

David looked at the table, considering. "You spend a lot of time making odds, right, Sammy?"

"Sure."

"Let's say you give me a gun. Then you send one of your — um — *friends* after me with a knife. Now a gun's better than a knife, right?" He looked up, meeting Sammy's eyes. "Still, what kind of odds you give me?"

Sammy stopped picking his teeth. "Right. Let's get you out of town." He glanced down at the doodles that David had been sketching. "Nice mazes."

Sammy was fast. Twenty minutes after he left the restaurant, he came back. He caught David's eyes and beckoned impatiently.

A black sedan was idling in the alley around the corner. A thickset man in a black suit leaned on the car, next to its open trunk. "Monty's going to get you to the Newark train station," Sammy said. He put a train ticket in David's hands. "I'm the only one in the city who knows where you're going. One of my local guys from the area — a legit guy, doesn't know crap about my operation, but a good guy — will pick you up at the station. I got a little side project to keep you busy while you're up there." He indicated the car trunk. "Now go on."

There were a couple of pillows in the trunk, and a flashlight. David looked up and down the alley. All clear. He stepped up to the car and climbed into the trunk. Sammy's man slowly closed the trunk's lid. "There are breathing holes in the grille," he said, his voice clearly audible. "Once we're outta the city, I'll stop and let you sit up front like a human."

The car trunk smelled like strong tobacco and sweat. David obviously wasn't the first person Sammy had spirited out of town. The car started and he turned onto his side, trying to get comfortable in the cramped trunk. As they rolled away, he realized he had never thanked Sammy.

# CHAPTER 21

# DAHLIA

**D**ahlia woke up when someone dropped something heavy on her arm. She blinked and blearily rubbed her eyes. The cabin was already filled with midmorning sun, but most of her cabin-mates were still asleep. Abby Simkin was walking away from Dahlia's bed.

"Hey," Dahlia objected sleepily. "Why'd you do that?"

Abby turned around, looking puzzled. She was a plump, pleasant girl, who spent most of her time on the other side of the cabin. "What?" she said.

Dahlia sat up and found the kabbala book resting on her arm. "You dropped this on me."

From the next bed over, Lisa muttered, "Shut up!" without opening her eyes.

Abby came back toward Dahlia. "Hey," she whispered. "Sorry if that woke you. I — uh — just happened to pick that up when I was in the boys' cabin last night. It's yours, right?" Her eyes were wide and innocent.

Dahlia looked down at the book. "Um. Not really. But okay. Don't worry about it."

Shoot. Was that the big mystery of how the book had been get-ting back to her? Abby being helpful? Or was it that other people "just happened" to bring it back too? One more question to add to the pile.

She eased back down to a lying position. Everything started later on Saturdays, so she still had a few minutes to sleep. She was just beginning to feel drowsy when her eyes fell upon the letter that had slipped out of the book the night before. She had dreamed about David reading the letter, hadn't she? He'd read the letter, and then he'd got himself smuggled out of the city, trying to get away from the Illuminated Ones.

Looking at the letter, a thought struck her like a kick to the stomach. She rolled off her bed, feeling sick. The investigators had been killed for asking questions about the Illuminated Ones. What if the girls' disappearances had had something to do with the Illuminated Ones? She'd started dreaming about David the same day that she'd first seen the girls. The girls had disappeared seventy-two years ago, the same year that David had discovered the 72nd name. Now that she thought about it, what was the chance that the girls and David *weren't* connected?

So she'd basically sent Tom out to ask questions about the Illuminated Ones. Exactly what the investigator had been killed for.

She was hurriedly pulling on her sneakers when Hayley came through the cabin door. "You going to breakfast?" Hayley whis-pered, tossing her toiletry kit onto her bed. "On Saturdays it's a buffet, with donuts and everything."

"I have to find my brother." Dahlia walked toward the cabin door.

"I'll walk with you." Hayley fell into step with her. "His cabin's on the way."

As Dahlia hurried across the field, the bell rang.

"Last call for breakfast," Hayley said, jogging a little to keep up with Dahlia. "There's no point in rushing. By this time the good donuts are long gone. The little kids wake up at eight and get in line for the chocolate ones."

Dahlia didn't say anything. Her heart sank as they approached Tom's cabin. Tom had probably left ages ago. It looked like his campers had been up for hours. A full-field soccer game was going on, and Justin Bieber was blasting from the girls' cabin. When Dahlia and Hayley got near the boys' cabin, a little boy with a crew cut left the soccer game and ran toward them.

"Hey," he said. "Don't make noise. Kalish said if anyone wakes him up, none of us will get ice cream tonight."

"He can't do that, Nat," Hayley said. "And anyway, they've already rung the wake-up bell."

Dahlia knocked on the front door. "Everyone decent?" she called. No answer.

She opened the door and stepped into the cabin. It smelled like dirty laundry and toothpaste. She knocked on the door to the counselors' room, Hayley still by her side.

"HEY!" A man's voice bellowed from within. "I told you — no noise in the cabin!"

Dahlia opened the door. The tiny room was packed full, with one bunk bed, a single bed, and a couple of freestanding shelving units. The single bed and the top bunk bed were both empty. Tom's friend, Jacob Kalish, was sprawled on the bottom bunk bed, his arm thrown over his face.

"Hey, Kalish," Dahlia said.

Kalish rubbed his eyes and squinted at her. "Oh. Hey, Dahlia. You looking for your bro?"

"Yeah. Do you know where he is?"

"Running errands for Yasmin. Because he's, like, so friggin' trustworthy, you know."

Dahlia figured Kalish was trying to sound sarcastic, but it came off as purely jealous. "Do you know when he's supposed to be back?"

He sat up and yawned. "What, am I his secretary?"

"Do you know or not?"

Kalish got off his bed and sniffed his armpits. "He said he'd be back by dinner at the latest. Which sucks if you ask me. Leaving me alone with the kids all day."

Dahlia turned and walked out of the cabin. Okay. Tom would be back by dinner. "No big deal," she said out loud, trying to believe it. The Illuminated Ones had killed the investigators almost a century ago. There was no way they were still around. And even if they were, they wouldn't be hanging around a community library in middle-of-nowhere Pennsylvania. Right?

The day passed slowly. They had special clubs on Saturday, which lots of people skipped, but Dahlia went to all of them, just to have something to do. She went to one club where she learned how to make grass bracelets and another where a counselor took them on a long walk through the woods. She played cards for hours with Sarah and Hayley and Eileen. Still, she found herself on the dining hall porch half an hour before dinner, just waiting for Tom. She watched as, one by one, the counselors picked their way through the crowd of kids waiting by the front doors. Every table had a counselor, and still Tom wasn't there.

Dahlia shouldered her way through the crowd of campers and slipped into the dining hall. One of the kids on serving duty said, "Hey. You can't come in yet."

Dahlia ignored him, making a beeline for Alyssa. "Alyssa," she said. "Do you know if Tom's back yet?"

"I didn't know he was gone," Alyssa said. Then she pointed. "But he's right there."

Dahlia turned to see Tom walk in the side door. She waved him over, and he headed in their direction just as the other campers started to spill into the dining hall.

Dahlia sat down across from Alyssa. Tom just stood there for a second, looking around.

"It's okay," Alyssa said. "All the tables have a counselor — you can sit here."

Tom slid in next to Dahlia. "Cool," he said. "It's probably the only way Dahlia will ever sit at my table."

"I'm the one who waved you over," Dahlia said. Then, before he could answer, "Did you find anything? Did any girls go missing?"

Tom hesitated. He glanced around before saying anything. "Yeah. Two little girls went missing. Sisters. But it was a long time ago. I only found the newspaper articles because the librarian helped me."

"Articles? Did you make copies?"

Tom shook his head slowly, still looking disturbed. "They were on microfiche, and I was running late. The librarian promised to fax them to me."

"But who were the girls? Did you at least get their names?"

Before he could answer, Rafe and Benjy sat down across the table from them. Tom shook his head again. "I'll get the articles for you after dinner, and you can see for yourself."

"Articles about what?" Rafe asked.

"About two girls who went missing," Dahlia said.

"What?" Rafe said. "Where?"

A handful of Tom's little campers took the remaining seats at their table.

"Dahlia's just kidding," Tom said. "I just found her some how-to articles about a magic trick."

"Oh." Rafe met Dahlia's eyes, and she very slightly shook her head.

"Later," she mouthed. She didn't want to get Tom mad when she was this close to finding out who the little girls were. The thought caught her. *Girls.* Seventy-two years ago, they hadn't been ghosts.

# CHAPTER 22

After dinner, Dahlia and Tom walked over to the office together. She waited outside as Tom went in to check the fax machine. *A fax machine*, she thought. *Who uses a fax machine?* Next, Tom would be sending messages by carrier pigeon.

He came out holding a thin stack of papers. "Please don't show these to anyone else," he said.

"Why not? It was seventy-two years ago. Who's crazy enough to care? I mean, aside from me." Dahlia reached for the papers, but Tom didn't release his grip.

"Trust me. Kids will freak out about this. Can you please keep it to yourself?" He let Dahlia take the articles, but he stared at her until she answered.

"I already pretty much told Rafe."

Tom frowned, then surprised her by laughing. "Fine. If you want, you can show them to Rafe. No one believes anything *he* says, anyway."

"That's real nice, Tom." Dahlia started to turn, then paused. "Um. Thanks for this," she said.

"No problem." Now it was Tom's turn to pause. "Dahlia. Just now — how did you know it had been seventy-two years? I didn't tell you that. And yesterday, how did you know to guess that they'd disappeared in the 1940s?"

Dahlia met Tom's eyes. She supposed if she really wanted to go home, she could just tell Tom the truth. *Because the ghost of one of the girls told me.* Her parents would be up there so fast, she wouldn't have time to pack. "Huh — was it really seventy-two years? Lucky guess."

Tom narrowed his eyes. "You brought your phone to camp and did an Internet search, didn't you? That's how you knew girls really had disappeared, and that's how you knew when it happened. Right?"

Dahlia shrugged. Probably better for him to believe that. "Thanks," she said again. She turned and started back toward her bunk.

"See you at the bonfire," Tom called after her.

She waved absently, head bent to read the articles in the fading evening light. When she got to the pictures, though, she stopped walking. It was too dark to make out more than a general outline of the girls' faces. She walked over to the basketball court and held the articles up to the floodlights.

Two photographs, smudged by the fax, or maybe by the age of the originals. She didn't get much more than the impression of big eyes and fake smiles. Still, the pictures were good enough that Dahlia was sure they were the same girls she'd seen in her bunk.

*Amelia and Claudia Owens.* Those were their names. Two sisters who went missing one August morning in the summer of 1941.

The first article was written right after the girls disappeared. They had apparently got caught out in the woods in a sudden summer thunderstorm. Their family had flooded the woods with dogs and searchers, and the police had gone house to house in the area looking for them. But the thunderstorm had washed away their tracks, and the police hadn't come up with anything. The article quoted a policeman saying that the girls must have fallen into one of the overflowing rivers in the area. There was nowhere else they could have gone.

The second article was dated a few days later. This one was longer, with a couple paragraphs about the girls' parents and their five older siblings. The bodies still hadn't turned up, and this was odd, because the rivers all emptied into the same lake. Also, one of their older brothers claimed he had heard his sisters' voices in the woods a few days after they had disappeared.

"That's it?" Dahlia said out loud after finishing the second article. What had happened next? There had to be something else, or why were their ghosts still hanging around more than seventy years later?

She went into her cabin and tossed the articles on her bed. She should have been happy. The articles confirmed that she had seen ghosts. She wasn't going crazy. She was seeing some genuine supernatural phenomena. She should be thinking about ways to prove it and get famous.

Instead, all she could think about was the two little girls. Amelia and Claudia. For reasons she couldn't explain, she felt deeply, personally guilty. And worried. They'd been trying to warn her about something. Something that might happen to other kids, like it had happened to them.

She stared at the wall of her bunk. She hoped the ghosts came again. She hoped she never saw them again.

Her gaze fell on the kabbala book, still lying on her bunk. *David Schank,* she thought. He had fled to the countryside, and then the girls had disappeared. Something had happened. *Had Schank hurt the girls?* In her memories of Schank, he was a little crazy and always frightened. But dangerous? Never dangerous.

She lay on her bed, brooding. She wished she hadn't promised Tom she would stay at camp. She wanted to go home. She wanted her biggest problem to be figuring out how to palm something bigger than a quarter.

The screen door banged open, and Sarah and Hayley burst into the bunk. "Hey, Dahlia!" Hayley said, bustling past Dahlia toward her own bed.

"Hey," Dahlia said, sitting up. She was surprised at how relieved she was to see Hayley and Sarah. They were both so *normal.*

"C'mon." Hayley grabbed her sleeping bag from her bed. "They're about to ring the bell, and we have to get good seats."

"For what?"

"The bonfire!" Sarah said. She climbed onto her bed and grabbed her flashlight. "Bring your sleeping bag and flashlight."

Dahlia stood and glanced at her trunk. Her mother must have packed a sleeping bag, right? "I'm not sure where my sleeping bag is," she said.

Hayley took her arm and gave it a tug. "We can all share mine. Come on."

Dahlia imagined jamming into a sleeping bag with the two of them. "We don't sleep down there, do we?"

Sarah giggled. "No. We just sit on the sleeping bags to watch the show. Come on. You'll see."

Dahlia let them draw her out of the cabin. Anything was better than sitting around rereading the newspaper articles.

As they walked toward the woods, the bell rang behind them, and they joined a stream of campers and counselors going down the hill. After a few minutes in the forest, they emerged in a clearing where a huge fire — taller than Dahlia — was burning. A few dozen kids had already laid out their sleeping bags in front of it, and a counselor was standing nearby, playing guitar.

"Hey, Dahlia. Up here." Dahlia saw Rafe's silhouette a few yards from the fire. He walked toward them and pointed, a little smugly, to his sleeping bag spread right at the very front.

"Great!" Sarah said. "Thanks, Rafe!"

Dahlia, Sarah, and Hayley picked their way through the seated campers. By the time they had settled on Rafe's sleeping bag, the entire camp seemed to be trying to jam itself into the clearing.

"We're going to improvise a skit," Sarah told Dahlia. "Like we do in improv club."

"Oh yeah?" Dahlia said.

"If you want," Hayley said, "you could do a magic trick as part of it." The firelight glittered off her glasses as she looked at Dahlia. "Do you want to?"

Dahlia picked up a stray piece of wood about the size of her fist. She passed her right hand over her left hand and tried to palm the piece of wood, but it slipped onto the sleeping bag. Hayley didn't seem to notice that she had bungled the trick.

"That's great!" Hayley said. "We could totally work that into whatever we end up doing."

"Um. Maybe next week," Dahlia said. She leaned back and watched the sparks spiral off the fire into the darkness.

After a while, a trio of counselors in training started calling up the campers who had signed up to perform. One little girl sang a song called "Castle in the Cloud," to widespread whispers of "She's so cute!" An older girl played guitar and sang a song that Dahlia didn't know. Two of Tom's campers did a skit about a man trying to order dinner. Dahlia wasn't totally sure what was happening in the skit, but she couldn't help laughing every time the skinny kid — Mitchell, she thought, although maybe the skinny one was Jaden and the plump one was Mitchell — burst into laughter at one of his own jokes. With the fire burning, and the noise of the other campers all around her, it was hard to imagine that anything sinister had ever happened in these woods.

After the bonfire, she found herself walking up the hill next to Rafe and Benjy, who were deep into a spirited argument about whether the bonfire had been the biggest one they had ever seen (Benjy's position) or if there had been another one a little bit bigger the summer before (Rafe's position). When they got to the top of the hill, Benjy stopped by the bathrooms as Rafe and Dahlia continued on to their cabins.

"Hey," Rafe said casually. "What were you and your brother talking about at dinner tonight? You know — you said something about some missing girls, and Tom said you were joking?"

Dahlia hesitated, then shrugged. "Tom found some newspaper articles for me about two little girls who went missing around here. A long time ago. Like in the 1940s."

"What? Seriously? That happened?"

"You want to see the articles?"

Rafe's eyes widened. "Definitely."

They walked into her cabin together. A counselor in training brushed by as they went inside. Another counselor in training — a redheaded girl in a tight University of Pennsylvania T-shirt — sat on Eileen's bed tuning a guitar. She glanced at Rafe. "Hey, Professor."

"Oh. Hi, Lianne," Rafe said, blushing slightly. "Um, actually could you call me Rafe?"

"Sure. No problem. I'm Lianne," she told Dahlia.

"So I hear. I'm Dahlia." Dahlia handed Rafe the articles, feeling irritated. Lianne wasn't that pretty. She was just sixteen and had boobs.

Rafe sat on Michal's bed and glanced down at the articles. "Huh," he said in a low voice. "Claudia and Amelia Owens."

Just the sound of their names made Dahlia feel guilty. Rafe shook his head as he read. "I can't believe it. Kids actually did go missing."

"You don't have to sound so happy about it," Dahlia said. "Two little girls died."

He looked back at the pages. "Maybe. It sounds like they never found them."

"Seventy-two years later — what do you think, they just lost track of time?"

He didn't answer. He turned the first page over and read the rest of the article. His eyes widened and he held the paper out toward Dahlia. "Did you see? It mentions McMasters."

Dahlia took the article from Rafe and looked where he was pointing. It was a single mention on the second page of the first article. He read out loud over her shoulder, " 'Ned McMasters, foreman of a local construction site, reported seeing the Owens girls walk into the woods just before sunset on August twenty-fifth.' " He shook his head. "That is so crazy."

"What's so crazy about it? What's the big deal about McMasters?"

"You know — the *McMasters* story."

"No, I *don't* know. Everyone keeps mentioning it, but no one has told me the story."

Rafe shook his head again, looking bewildered. "It's the dumb story they tell little campers to scare them. You know . . ." He started talking in a low, ominous voice. "Old Man McMasters was never seen again, but every summer one kid goes missing on —" He paused and in his normal voice asked, "What's the date today?"

"July sixth," Dahlia supplied.

Back in the low, whispery voice: "Every July sixth, one child goes missing from the camp."

"Will you get out of here, Professor?" Chelsea had come in without Dahlia noticing. Her voice was disdainful. "You can whisper to Dahlia later. I have to get changed."

"Okay," Rafe said. "I was just —"

"Leaving," Chelsea finished. "Right now."

The door was still swinging shut behind him when Chelsea said, "That guy is such a dork. Don't let him bother you with his dumb stories."

"Whose dumb stories?" Lisa said, walking in with Michal as Chelsea was speaking.

"Who do you think?" Chelsea said. "The Professor."

"I asked him to tell me," Dahlia said. "I wanted to hear the McMasters story."

Michal giggled.

"You asked the right person," Chelsea said. "No wonder he likes you."

"Hey," Lisa said warningly. "I like the McMasters story too. 'My wife, my kids!'"

Lianne looked up from her guitar and played a chord. Apparently, she was done tuning it, but it still sounded off to Dahlia. "Five minutes to lights-out," she said. "If you haven't washed up yet, now is the time."

"Aren't you going to brush your teeth?" Chelsea asked Dahlia. "You'll want fresh breath if he comes back to say good night." She winked.

Dahlia got up from her bed. "Grow up," she said.

Chelsea burst into laughter. "'Grow up'? That's the best you can do? Aren't you supposed to be smart?"

"Shh," Lisa said. "You saw what she did to the saltshaker. She'll turn you into a frog."

Their laughter followed Dahlia into the night. She tried to ignore it. Then she tried to forget about it as she entered the bathroom. She stopped at the front sink, wetting her toothbrush and scowling at her reflection in the mirror. Here she was, about to document a real ghost manifestation — what did she care what Chelsea said about Rafe? It was just stupid and immature and . . .

Ow. She had been brushing her teeth so furiously she'd scratched her gums.

A few older campers brushed past her on their way to the showers. One of them muttered something. Dahlia couldn't hear the whole thing, but she clearly heard the word *professor*. The others broke into laughter. Dahlia wished she were at home, where at least she could brush her teeth in privacy. Again she regretted promising Tom that she'd stick it out. She should have just gone home and done the research herself. Or better still, forgotten about the ghosts altogether.

She came back to the bunk to find the lights out and the other girls in their beds. She made her way through the darkness. Someone shone a flashlight in her eyes, and Lianne said, "You're late."

The other CIT handed her flashlight to Dahlia. "Here. You can use my flashlight to get changed. I'm Becky."

"Thanks," Dahlia said. Once the light was out of her eyes, she saw that Lianne was still sitting on Eileen's bed with her guitar on her lap. "Um. Where are Alyssa and Selena?" Dahlia took Becky's flashlight and started to pull on her sleeping sweats.

"It's Saturday night," Becky said. "So the counselors have their big meeting and the CITs put all the campers to bed."

"Speaking of which." Lianne strummed her guitar. "What songs do you guys want tonight?"

"Elliott Smith," Eileen said.

"No song," Lisa said. "We want an SOS."

"What's an SOS?" Eileen asked, and several voices shouted, "Session on sex! Session on sex!"

Alison Bilt said, "Last year, Nadine used to tell us stories."

By now everyone was talking and the bunk was louder than it had been before the lights were turned off.

"Okay," Becky said. She paced around the bunk, speaking so quietly that people had to be quieter to hear what she was saying. "No SOS. We aren't allowed —"

"It's 'cause last year Jay Granstein told the girls in Tsofim about how he and his girlfriend —" Chelsea interrupted.

"The point is," Becky said firmly, "no SOSes this year. You can vote between a song and a story."

The vote went eight to seven for a story, with two girls not voting, Dahlia supposed. There was a moment of silence afterward, and she saw her chance. "Could it be about McMasters?"

A few people groaned, but Lisa quickly said, "Yeah, tell us the McMasters story!"

Lianne sounded disgruntled as she put her guitar away. "Fine. Becky will tell you the McMasters story."

"Sure." Becky paused for a few seconds. When she started talking again, her voice was low and serious. "You guys have probably heard some version of the story of Ned McMasters. Now, a lot of the stories are totally made up. But there really was a guy called Ned McMasters who used to live here — before the camp was here, I mean. His farm was pretty much exactly where the camp is today. He grew corn mostly, but he also had a little apple orchard, some chickens, and a few cows. In those days, farmers grew a lot of stuff for themselves to eat, as well as the stuff they sold to the market."

"I thought he was the caretaker before Barry," Lisa said.

"This is my story," Becky said.

"Is this a true story?" Eileen asked.

"You decide," Becky said quietly.

"She means no," Chelsea said.

"Shhh!" Lisa said. "I love this story."

"So McMasters lived here for years. He inherited the place from his father, and he had a wife and three children. He was a fine father. Not great. You know, every once in a while he would slap his kids, things like that.

"He worked hard and saved as much money as he could. But every Friday night, McMasters would go out drinking with his friends. They would have a few beers at the local bars. One particular Friday night, McMasters's wife — Mrs. McMasters, I guess — asked him to stay in. Their youngest kid had been up the whole night before with the flu, and she was exhausted. But McMasters said no.

"That night, he was driving home — not too late, maybe just around ten forty on a Saturday night." Dahlia looked at her watch, gently glowing in the dark. 10:41 p.m. "It was a warm summer night, so he was driving with his window down. And he smelled smoke.

"He kept driving and the smell got stronger and stronger. In those days there were a lot more fields around here, so he could see his house from a long way off. His house was covered in flames."

" 'My wife, my kids!' " Lisa said.

Becky coughed, in what sounded to Dahlia like an attempt to smother a laugh.

"That's right. His wife and children were dead, his house was gone. And McMasters went crazy. He never built another house. Before long, the bank owned his old farm, but people weren't sure if McMasters even knew. He just kept on living in the woods. No one around here wanted to buy the farm, so the people who started this camp got a good deal on the land."

"That part's true," Sarah said. "Benjy's grandfather was on the committee that bought the land, and they got a really good deal on it."

"Yeah, but Benjy said that was because a Jewish gangster sold it cheap because he needed money for lawyers," Hayley said.

"Benjy just made that up," Chelsea said. "As if there was a Jewish Mafia in Doylest —"

"Shhh!" Becky said. "The point is, the bank sold McMasters's farm to the summer camp. The problem was, no one told McMasters. Most of the time he just sleeps out there in the woods. But every once in a while, on a nice summer evening, he creeps back toward where his house used to be. And then a camper or two might go missing."

No one said anything for a few seconds after Becky stopped talking. Finally, Eileen said, "That's the dumbest horror story I've ever heard. He couldn't live in the woods during the winter."

Someone else said, "They couldn't keep the camp open if kids really disappeared."

"Do you know the story about the guy with a hook hand?" Hayley asked.

"Now *that* is the dumbest horror story," Chelsea said. "It would be impossible to open a car door with a hook."

"He'd just use his other hand," Lisa put in.

"Exactly," Chelsea said triumphantly. "So why would the hook be in the car door handle? What, is he, like, just now figuring out that you can't open a car door with a hook?"

"Okay," Becky said. "That's enough. You had your story. Now no more talking."

By then, Becky was sitting on the floor, her back to the wall, her flashlight turned off. Dahlia heard people shifting on their bunks. The cabin grew quiet enough that you could hear the crickets outside. Someone in the nearest corner — she couldn't tell if it was Hayley or Sarah — started snoring.

A few minutes later, Dahlia heard the door creak quietly. She watched Becky step outside, and then sit down again on the steps of the bunk. She supposed that she was making sure that everyone stayed quiet.

The story sounded like Becky had made it up on the spot. But the newspaper article had quoted McMasters. He had been a real person. She wondered if he'd ever met David Schank. She had a feeling that the answer was yes.

For some reason, Dahlia had a clear idea of what McMasters had looked like. Tall, sun-bleached brown hair, piercing blue eyes. No wife and kids, despite the story.

The Doylestown train station was little more than a raised platform and a handful of benches. Most of the platform was taken up with half a dozen stalls where people were selling huge boxes of lettuce and asparagus and other vegetables that David didn't even recognize. He stepped off the train, feeling more alien than ever. Farmers and shoppers thronged the platform, but he was the only Jew in sight. Not that he looked like a Jew anymore.

A tall, pale man made his way through the crowd. "Mr. Schank?" he said, extending his hand.

"That's right." David took the man's hand, examining him cautiously. Bright blue eyes under the brim of a baseball cap; a strong American handshake.

"Man, are you young to be a rabbi! I figured it had to be you, but then I reckoned you were too young."

"I'm not a rabbi," David said. "I was studying to be a rabbi, but . . ." He took a deep breath. "I'm not anymore."

"But Mr. Ackerman told me you were a rabbi."

"Mr. Ackerman will have his jokes," David said, wishing for a moment that Sammy had come too. "And you are . . ."

The man's fair face darkened. "Oh — yeah. Sorry. I'm Ned McMasters. Mr. Ackerman asked me to pick you up. I'm looking after the resort site for Mr. Ackerman. Just until construction starts, you understand." His forehead creased. "Which might not be for a while, I guess. I hear Mr. Ackerman ran into some trouble with his investors."

David looked around at what he supposed was the main street of Doylestown. What business did Sammy have here? There was a little strip of stores on the other side of the train tracks, including a bank and a newsstand and a small hardware store. Beyond them, he saw a sprinkling of houses. The other direction, though, there was nothing. Empty grassy fields with cows — actual cows — grazing, a stone's throw away, right up to the fencing that kept them off the platform. They were the first live cows David had ever seen. They looked different than he'd expected, bigger and darker. He could smell their heavy animal scent from yards away, overlaid with the strong odor of their manure, and the still-lingering exhaust from the train's engine.

McMasters glanced around the platform. "No bags?" he said. David shook his head. They went down the stairs to the street. "As long as you have your landscaping plans, I guess."

"What landscaping plans?"

McMasters chuckled. "Mr. Ackerman said you had a sense of humor. Anyhow, the resort construction is on hold, but Mr. Ackerman said not to worry, you could work on the hedge maze as soon as the seedlings arrive." He shook his head wonderingly. "He must feel real strong about that hedge maze to ship you all the way here to build it. Plus, he paid the nursery extra to send the seed-lings just as fast as they could get them to us. I suppose you've got the maze all designed and ready to go. . . ."

McMasters ended with a little uplift in his voice. After a min-ute, David realized he was expecting an answer. "Ah. Excuse me?" he said.

"Your designs," McMasters said. "For the maze. Are they ready?"

"Ready?" David shook his head. "I wouldn't say that, no."

"You don't have the designs prepared?" He stopped walking. "Mr. Schank, the seedlings are arriving later this week. We'll have to start getting them in the ground right away."

He looked so alarmed that David took pity on him. "Don't worry," he said. "I'll draw you a maze."

The "site," as McMasters insisted on calling it, was a handful of muddy fields, bare except for a sparse cover of weeds and a few remnants of scrub forest in the valley and hilltops, which David supposed had been too much trouble to clear. There were two buildings in the center of the site: an old, crumbling barn where the construction crews were meant to stay, and a small farmhouse where McMasters had set up camp. David couldn't believe Sammy really intended to build a resort this far from the Catskills. More likely, it was some kind of money-laundering scheme. He figured Sammy had bought the property with dirty money, maybe from one of his illegal gambling operations. He'd sell it in a few years and be left with a tidy sum of clean money.

McMasters gave David the front room of the farmhouse — a sunny space, empty except for a bedroll and an ancient rocking chair. McMasters slept a few yards away in the open living room. The living room was just as empty as David's bedroom, separated from the kitchen only by a round-bellied wood-burning stove.

The whole house smelled strongly of mildew and the pigs that McMasters kept in a small enclosure on the side of the barn. David took a deep breath and winced. Disgusting, unclean animals. As though he wasn't debased enough. The 72nd name flashed into his mind, and he pushed it away for fear of attracting the Illuminated Ones' attention.

Only then did he realize that the pressure of the Illuminated Ones looking for him was gone. He let the name fill his mind deliberately. Nothing. No one was looking for him. He was sure of it. Their attention must have gradually slipped off him as he was driven out of New York and took the train to Doylestown. He took another deep breath, this one more appreciative. *Who*, he thought, *would look for a Yebavner Jew in the shadow of a pigsty?*

He sat down on the rocking chair — more comfortable than it looked — and took out the Rebbe's book. Perhaps the Illuminated Ones had given up. Perhaps he was simply too far from the city for them to sense. Whatever the reason, he relaxed for the first time since Velvel called him into the Rebbe's study.

# CHAPTER 24

# DAHLIA

**D**ahlia perched on the edge of the dining hall porch and stared at Barry's front door. She watched kids walking up the road, returning from their work groups, and she tried to relax. So what if she got caught breaking into Barry's house? The worst thing they could do was send her home.

Yeah, right. The worst thing they could do. She thought of the little girls and found herself shivering, despite the sun. No one had sent *them* home.

Somehow knowing the girls' names made the whole thing less fun. Amelia and Claudia Owens. They had been real people, and something bad had happened to them. Dahlia didn't care anymore about being the first person to prove that ghosts were real. She just wanted to know what had happened to the little girls and why their ghosts were still hanging around.

Which was why she was standing across the road from Barry's house. If her dreams meant anything at all, she was sure that Schank was connected to whatever had happened to the girls. In last night's dream, David Schank was not only living in this area, but staying in a little farmhouse that looked exactly like Barry's house. The house in her dreams was painted blue, and it didn't have a patio in the back, but otherwise it was a perfect match.

She'd seen the outside of Barry's house in real life, so it was possible that her subconscious had put the house in her dreams. But she'd never seen the inside of his house. Getting inside the house was the only way she could think of to check if there was some truth in what she'd been dreaming. She was sick of not being sure.

Dahlia kicked her heels against the side of the porch and glanced down the hill. Barry's tractor was still parked next to the barn. Every day around this time, he drove up the hill to collect the tools and timber that various work groups used in their projects. *Any minute now . . .*

She pulled her little notebook out of her pocket and flipped it open. She'd written down everything she could remember about the house in her dreams. If she got inside and recognized things, she wanted to be sure it wasn't just her mind playing tricks on her. She'd listed seven items:

*A wood-paneled kitchen that smelled of cedar*
*A threadbare throw rug in the living room*
*A potbellied Franklin stove between the kitchen and living room*
*Narrow wooden stairs leading up to an attic bedroom*
*A canvas sleeping bag that smelled of mothballs*
*An old rocking chair*
*Peeling white paint in the bedroom*

She hesitated. Even if her dreams were real memories, the paint would probably long since be gone. Same with the rocking chair, sleeping bag, and throw rug. That left her with only three things to check: the kitchen, the stove, and the stairs.

She was gnawing on her pen cap, trying to think of things to add to her list, when Barry's tractor finally put-putted past her, his big, black dog perched in the trailer. Taking a deep breath, Dahlia hopped off the dining hall's porch and started walking toward Barry's house. She had her hand on the gate when a voice interrupted her.

"Hey, Dahlia!"

Dahlia started, then turned. "Oh. Hi, Sarah."

Sarah's eyes were wide. "Are you looking for Barry? I think I just saw him drive up the hill. I wouldn't go in his yard. He gets really mad when people go in his yard — even counselors." Behind Sarah, a few more campers had come up and were looking at Dahlia curiously.

"What? No. I was, um, just going back to the barn." Dahlia turned and started walking down the hill. "I forgot my sweatshirt." She quickened her pace before Sarah could offer to come with her. There was no way she wanted to get Sarah involved in something that might be dangerous and was definitely against the rules. Unlike her, Sarah would care if she got sent home from camp. "See you back in the cabin."

"See ya!" Sarah called after her.

As soon as Sarah was out of sight, Dahlia veered off the path to circle around to the back of Barry's house. She should have known the front yard was too exposed. The best way would be to approach the house from behind.

She rounded the corner and frowned. She hadn't realized the

camp directors' trailer was quite so close to Barry's house. One of the directors — the short woman with spiky hair, Yasmin — was sitting on the trailer's porch talking on a cell phone, maybe twenty yards from Barry's back door. She saw Dahlia looking at her and raised her hand distractedly, probably figuring Dahlia was walking toward the storage shed behind the barn.

Dahlia awkwardly returned her wave. Shoot. This camp was just too crowded.

The camp director turned away, still talking on her cell phone. Dahlia froze for a moment. This might be the best chance she was going to get. She hopped over the low, wooden fence surrounding Barry's backyard and crouched down, so the fence was between her and the camp directors' trailer. She waited for someone to shout after her.

A few seconds passed. Silence except for the low murmur of Yasmin's voice on the phone.

Dahlia glanced at Barry's back door. The main door was open, with just the screen door between her and the inside of the house. To get there, though, she'd have to cross his little yard in full view of the camp director.

Dahlia peeked over the fence. Yasmin was looking straight at Barry's back door. Dahlia immediately ducked back into a sitting position, her back against the fence. Shoot. She had to do something. Anyone who walked past the other side of the yard couldn't help seeing her.

As if to prove her wrong, a counselor stalked past Barry's yard, clutching a sheet of paper in his hand. Dahlia held herself perfectly still as she watched him pass a few feet from her. He didn't glance to his left or right, just glared straight ahead of him at the camp director.

"Yasmin," he said. He stormed up to Yasmin, brandishing the piece of paper. "This is totally unfair. I just had kitchen duty yesterday and you put me back on —"

The camp director turned to face him, and Dahlia made a break for it. Three steps to get to the little wooden deck, two more to get to Barry's back door. The screen door turned out to be locked, but one hard yank opened it, and Dahlia darted inside. The door slammed loudly behind her.

Dahlia flattened herself against the interior wall of the living room, heart hammering. The camp director's voice floated after her. "If you don't like it, trade with someone. It's not my problem. . . ."

Dahlia looked around the room she'd entered. It felt a bit anticlimactic. A few feet to her right, a tall fan pushed warm air around the living room. The far corner of the room was devoted to a surprisingly new computer workstation, with the remainder occupied by an orange sofa covered in dog hair, a television, and a black easy chair.

She stepped through the room, running down her list. *The kitchen, the Franklin stove, and the narrow wooden stairs.* Now that she was here, the whole idea that seeing the inside of the house would settle anything seemed kind of stupid. Seventy-two years was a long time. It would be hard to find anything conclusive after that long.

And then she saw it. The Franklin stove, just where she remembered it.

She raced around the couch to get a better look. The stove was a little potbellied iron thing, about waist high on Dahlia, attached to a metal stovepipe that extended through the room's ceiling. A small pile of wood was stacked next to it, along with a little basket full of old newspaper. Both the stovepipe and stove were a little cleaner than she remembered them, but there was no mistaking them. She'd seen them in her dreams.

She quickly moved on to the kitchen. It looked totally different. In her dreams, McMasters got water from a well behind the barn. Now a small sink faced the window, flanked by a plastic electric teakettle. The wood paneling was gone, replaced by faded yellow wallpaper.

Even without the wood paneling, though, she smelled the faint scent of cedar — maybe from the wooden cupboards. She opened one of the cupboards and took a deep breath. The smell was exactly the same as she remembered it from her dreams.

She blinked as she realized something else — the cupboard was completely empty. She opened the cupboard next to it. Nothing. She opened the cupboard beneath the sink. Two large bags of dog food and a dustpan.

Quicker now, she opened the rest of the cupboards. A few plates in one cupboard and an unopened box of gourmet black tea in another. Aside from the dog food, there was nothing edible in the whole kitchen. How much did they pay Barry? Couldn't he afford to eat? She was turning to open the refrigerator when she heard the tractor pulling up outside, behind Barry's house.

Okay. No reason to panic. Barry would park the tractor in front of his workshop. She had plenty of time to get out of here.

She was still a few yards from the front door when she heard the back screen door creaking open. Whoa. How had he moved so fast? She quickened her pace, tiptoeing as quickly as she could.

"Stay, Tramp," Barry muttered. She heard him slowly, inexorably, walking toward the front of his house. For such a big man, he walked very softly — she could barely hear his steps on the creaky floorboards.

She paused with her hand on the screen door's handle. *Crap. Crap. Crap.* How did you unlock the stupid screen door? No way Barry wouldn't hear her if she broke this one the way she'd broken the back door. She felt around the little latch, hands moist with sweat.

The road outside Barry's house was empty, all the other campers back at their cabins. She wondered if anyone would hear her if she screamed.

Barry paused in the kitchen. She heard the cupboard doors slam shut one after another. *Slam. Slam. Slam.*

"David?" Barry said softly.

# CHAPTER 25

*D*avid?

Dahlia shoved the screen door open with all her strength, no longer caring about a quiet exit. It turned out it hadn't been locked. The door flew open, crashing against the front of the house like a cymbal. She sprinted down Barry's front walkway, leaping over the fence.

She ran. Not because she was scared of Barry. Or not *just* because she was scared of Barry. But because she was suddenly and finally sure she was possessed. More sure than when she had spoken in that man's voice. That could have been a dream. More than when the book had seemed so familiar — that could have been déjà vu. But this time, there was no denying it. The woodstove and the smell of the kitchen had been exactly as she'd remembered them. And Barry had called her "David."

That was the creepiest part. She was possessed, and Barry knew it. Had probably known it since that first night of camp when he'd glared at her and said, "What are you doing back here?"

Up to now, she hadn't considered that Barry could have been personally involved with whatever had happened to David Schank and the girls. That had happened seventy-two years ago, and whatever else she thought about Barry, she hadn't thought he could be more than seventy-two years old. Now she wasn't so sure. If he knew David, couldn't he have known the girls too? Or maybe he was working for the same "Illuminated Ones" who'd been chasing David. But why would they leave a person at a summer camp all these years after David had been here?

She was about fifty yards from Barry's house, still running, when she realized he wasn't following her. Some of the little kids were meeting with their counselors on the rec center's porch, and a few of them glanced at her curiously as she sprinted toward them, running like someone possessed.

What a dumb expression. As though you could run away from being possessed.

She slowed to a walk and glanced back toward Barry's house. He was standing in front of his door, looking at her. His expression was unreadable as usual, face hidden beneath his sunglasses and the brim of his baseball cap.

She turned around and kept walking. Oh man. First ghosts and now possession. Didn't anyone ever just stay dead?

She waited all day to get in trouble. For Barry to find her at her cabin. For *something* to change now that she knew she was possessed. But nothing happened. She went to lunch and clubs and dinner and the evening activity, and that was her second Tuesday at camp.

The next day, the rain came back. It started out just a little cloudy, but the clouds built throughout the morning, and by noon the sky was a dark gray and you could see the lightning in the distance. At lunch, one of the counselors announced that all afternoon activities were canceled on account of the rain. Instead, they'd be showing movies in the rec center, starting in half an hour.

By the time Dahlia got back to her cabin, it was full of campers. The temperature had dropped with the rain's approach, and for once it wasn't stifling hot in the bunk. Dahlia was glad there were other kids around, and not just because of Barry. She didn't feel like seeing the ghosts again either. She just wanted to be a normal camper for a while.

Eileen was writing a letter, and Dahlia borrowed a few sheets of her stationery. Dahlia's grandma lived alone in Cleveland, and Dahlia had promised to write her from camp.

She sat on Eileen's bed and wrote *Dear Grandma*. Then she paused. What could she write? *Dear Grandma. I'm possessed by the spirit of a dead yeshiva boy. There are two girl ghosts who have warned me about a man — or maybe the ghost of a man — who wants to trap more kids. How are you?* Not exactly the kind of letter to send your eighty-year-old grandmother. Or anyone else.

She put the pen down for a second and pulled a deck of cards from her pocket. She idly started riffling it back and forth and watched, a little jealously, as Eileen steadily continued with her letter.

After a few minutes, Eileen signed the letter with a flourish and put it in an envelope. She stood. "You coming to the movie?"

Over Eileen's shoulder, Dahlia saw lightning flash over the field in front of the bunk. She glanced around the cabin. Most of the girls had already left, but Chelsea, Lisa, and Michal were sitting on Michal's bed.

"Not right now," Dahlia said. "I'm writing my grandma a letter." She put the cards down and picked up the paper and pen.

"All right." Eileen walked toward the door, slinging her rain coat over her arm. "I'll save you a place to sit. I want to get there before it starts pouring."

Dahlia turned back to the letter. *Dear Grandma, Camp is very . . .* She paused. *. . . Jewish. You would like it. They make blessings on Friday night and all announcements are in Hebrew. The girls here are nice.* She glanced over at Chelsea and Lisa and wrote, *At least most of them are.*

Chelsea pulled on a red wool sweater and walked over to the wall mirror. "Come on, Chels." Lisa stood and grabbed her raincoat from a hook in the wall. "Do you have to try on every sweater in the bunk?"

"What, you really need to see *Up* or whatever stupid kid movie they're showing today?" Chelsea glanced at herself in the mirror and took off Michal's sweater. "Don't you have anything *tight*, Michal?"

"Are you seriously looking through Michal's clothes for something that's tight on *you*?" Lisa took Michal's arm and pulled her toward the door. "Good luck. We'll see you there."

They walked out the door, leaving just Chelsea and Dahlia in the cabin. Chelsea turned back to Michal's clothes, and Dahlia looked down at her letter.

Thunder boomed outside, and Dahlia jumped a little. The rain finally started to really come down.

This time Dahlia could feel it before the ghosts arrived — that particular feeling, like electricity building. She looked up to find the girls standing in front of Eileen's bed, a few feet away from her. They weren't happy. The older one was glaring furiously at Dahlia, and both girls looked like they'd been crying.

And behind them — still less clear than the girls, but definitely easier to see than he'd been before — Dahlia made out the silhouette of the man. He was pointing at Dahlia.

The older girl, Claudia, moved her lips. "Why?" A single angry question.

Dahlia glanced over at Chelsea. She had headphones on, listening to her MP3 player, and was facing Michal's shelves.

"Why what?" Dahlia said quietly.

Furiously mouthing each word and stabbing at Dahlia with her forefinger, Claudia said, "Why . . . did . . . you . . . do . . . this . . . to . . . us?"

"I didn't do anything." Despite her words, Dahlia felt a flush of guilt.

Before Claudia could respond, her little sister — Amelia — spoke. She didn't look nearly as angry as Claudia. "He . . . told . . . us."

"He told you what?" Dahlia mouthed.

The man abruptly stepped toward the girls, his silhouette stretching longer and darker. The older girl, Claudia, didn't hesitate. She ran toward the front of the cabin, glaring at Dahlia as she passed through the wall. Amelia, though, stayed there, her lips still moving as she tried to tell Dahlia . . . something. The cabin was quiet except for the sound of rain hitting the cabin roof.

The man seized Amelia's arm in his dark, barely-there hand.

"Leave her alone," Dahlia said, forgetting to mouth her words this time. She dropped the pen and letter on Eileen's trunk and stood.

"What?" Chelsea had taken off her headphones as she pulled a sweater over her head. "Michal doesn't mind if I borrow her sweater."

"Not you." Dahlia stepped toward Amelia.

Chelsea's head popped through the top of her sweater. "Um. Then who?"

Dahlia could see Amelia clearly, right down to the tears welling in her eyes. She was shaking her head and crying. The man looked at Dahlia and seemed to bow mockingly from the waist. Dahlia felt a flush of anger.

While he was bowing, Amelia managed to pull free. She ran toward Dahlia, and the man moved to grab her again.

Dahlia stepped in his way. His hand touched her arm, and it tingled for an instant, a tiny electric shock. The man quickly drew his hand back. Dahlia took another step, putting herself squarely between the man and Amelia. "Go away," she told the man quietly.

"What?" Chelsea said. "This is my cabin too."

"I wasn't talking to you." Dahlia kept her gaze focused on the man. "I'm — uh — practicing for a bonfire sketch I'm doing with Hayley. Go away," she hissed at the man.

He shook his head. She couldn't make out his face, but she had the impression he was smiling.

Inside her head, Dahlia felt something stirring inside her. Shoot. She might as well admit it, at least to herself. She felt David Schank stirring. He was in her brain, showing Dahlia how he had sent the man away the other night. A series of Hebrew letters rose up in her mind. "Go away," she told the silhouetted man, this time holding the letters in her mind. "Go away."

And the man was gone. She could feel him lingering outside somewhere, furiously feeding off the storm's power, but he couldn't get back into the cabin.

"That's your bonfire sketch?" Chelsea said. "Standing there and saying, 'Go away'?"

Dahlia ignored her. Amelia stood a few feet away, looking red-eyed and tiny. Dahlia felt her own eyes burning. Why should she feel so guilty? She hadn't done anything to Amelia. And based on her memories of David's life, she couldn't imagine that David had deliberately hurt the girls either.

She turned her back to Chelsea and mouthed slowly to Amelia, "What did he tell you about me?"

The little girl shook her head, impatiently dismissing Dahlia's question. "No time." She held up seven fingers.

Dahlia interrupted. "I know. Seventy-two years have passed. What do you want me to do?"

"What?" Chelsea said from across the cabin. "Who practices for a bonfire act on Wednesday, anyway?"

Dahlia blushed but didn't look away from Amelia. It wasn't like Chelsea could think any less of her than she already did.

"Lead . . . us . . . out." The little girl paused. Outside the cabin, the man's fury surged. Another bolt of lightning split the sky. "And . . . no . . . more . . ."

Amelia started sliding toward the front wall, pulled by some invisible force — like the floor had tilted and she couldn't stop herself from falling toward the front of the cabin. Her lips were still moving, but Dahlia had no idea what she was saying. She grasped for Amelia's arm, and her hand passed through the little girl's elbow without even the tiny shock that occurred when she touched the man. It felt like she was grabbing air.

Dahlia tried to open herself up to David's possession, willing

David to do something, anything. "Stop him!" she said out loud. "Make him leave her alone! Come on!" But nothing happened, and Amelia kept sliding toward the cabin's front, eyes turned beseechingly toward Dahlia, still talking — right up until she disappeared through the wall.

"Stop who?" Chelsea was staring at Dahlia from Michal's bed. "What's wrong?"

Dahlia realized her face was wet with tears. Great. On top of everything else, she'd given Chelsea something else to ridicule her about. She hastily wiped her eyes and turned away. "Nothing."

Chelsea hesitated. When she spoke again, her voice was gentler. "It's the ghosts, right?" she said. "It's depressing when they cry."

Dahlia spun back toward her. "You can see the ghosts?"

Chelsea's eyes narrowed. "No one can see ghosts, Squirt."

"Oh." Dahlia's heart fell. Somehow Chelsea had heard about what she saw and was making fun of her. She racked her brain. Who had she told about the ghosts? Tom and Rafe both knew about the girls disappearing seventy-two years ago, but Dahlia could have sworn she hadn't told either of them about seeing the little girls.

"I hear them," Chelsea finished reluctantly.

"You hear them?" Dahlia stared at her. No wonder the ghosts tended to appear when Chelsea was around. They probably heard her, just like they saw Dahlia.

"Didn't I just say that?" Chelsea wrapped her arms around herself, then walked to her bunk bed. "Sometimes I hear them. Like just now I heard a little girl crying. I thought that's what was bothering you."

"What was she saying? Can you tell me what she was saying?"

Chelsea shook her head. "I don't . . . I try to ignore them. Usually, they're just crying, or there are a bunch of voices and I can't make out what any of them are saying." She pulled a green rain jacket from a shelf.

"But . . . I mean . . . how do you hear them?"

Chelsea zipped up her raincoat and pulled the hood over her head. She glanced in the mirror. "I don't know. I don't even know if they're really ghosts. Lisa thinks I can just hear people's cell phone signals in my brain or something."

"Do you hear them at home too?"

Chelsea flung the door open. She stood there staring out at the rain. "Not at home, but once in a while in other places. Mostly just here, though." She stepped through the door.

"Wait," Dahlia said, following her to the doorway.

"What?"

"I can see them. The ghosts, I mean."

Chelsea stepped back inside the cabin, letting the door slam behind her. "Is this, like, your idea of a joke? Maybe something you and Professor Andorkson came up with?"

Dahlia shook her head. "The one you heard crying is a little blonde girl. She's always wearing the same dress — a long-sleeved orange dress. It's nice but a little ragged, like she's been playing in the woods or something. She's been trying to tell me something. Something important, I think, but I can't hear her."

Chelsea glanced around the bunk. "Is she still here?"

"No. She left." Dahlia felt an overwhelming relief that someone else could perceive the ghosts. She wasn't just crazy. "Do other people hear them?"

Chelsea started to shake her head, then paused. "When I started camp, there were a few of us who could hear them. All girls. The others all left after the first year or two."

Dahlia stared at her. "You mean you could always hear ghosts here? And you still came back?"

Chelsea shrugged. "What's the big deal? I usually hear them two, maybe three, times a summer. This summer it's more, but so what? This is where my friends go. What, am I going to go to Camp Bimah and spend all summer praying?"

"But you said it depresses you when they cry."

"Sure. And it depresses me when it rains, or when I pass a homeless person on the street. But it's not like I'm going to stay in my bedroom and sob all the time." She looked at Dahlia. "Sorry. I didn't mean — you. It must be weird to see . . ."

"What about the man — do you hear him too?"

Chelsea hesitated. "I'm not sure. There's always — there's usually — another voice when the girls talk, talking over them. I'm not sure if it's a man or woman talking."

"There's a man," Dahlia said. "He's the reason Amelia was crying." She glanced back at where the ghost had been. Where did they go when they weren't here?

"Amelia? How do you know her name if you can't hear her?"

Dahlia told her about the articles Tom had found. Chelsea shook her head. All she said, though, was, "Gross." Dahlia didn't say anything, and after a second Chelsea turned to go back outside.

"Wait. What language do they speak?"

Chelsea paused, without turning. "The girls speak English. The other voice talks Hebrew, I think."

"I thought you said you didn't understand the girls."

"Not because of language. Because the other voice talks over them, repeating a few Hebrew words again and again and again."

"What words?"

Chelsea shrugged. "It says 'Malkoot' a lot. Even Michal didn't know what that means, so I'm not sure it's really Hebrew."

"You mean *Malchut*, right?" Dahlia let the "ch" sound roll out of the back of her throat.

"That's what I said. And how do you know the word if you can't hear the ghosts?"

Dahlia decided not to mention David Schank. "From Kabbala Club," she said. "Malchut is the tenth sefira." She turned to her bed. "I should show you the kabbala book."

"No. You really shouldn't." Chelsea opened the door again. "I'll see you later."

Dahlia followed her to the door. "Why are you so anxious to get to the movie all of a sudden? I was thinking that maybe if we hang out in the cabin some more, the ghosts might come back. With you there, I could finally hear what they're telling me."

Chelsea abruptly turned to face her straight on. "Look. Just because we have this thing in common . . . This doesn't, like, suddenly make us best friends. I didn't come to camp to sit in an empty cabin with you."

199

"There are ghosts talking to you!" Dahlia said. "Aren't you curious? Why don't they come when there are more people around? Why can I see them and not you? Why can you hear them, and I can't? I mean, we know how vision works, right? Why can my eyes perceive —"

"Enough," Chelsea said. "Do you have to try to be such a nerd?"

"God! Do you have to try to be so nasty?"

To her surprise, Chelsea giggled. "Not so much. It sort of comes naturally."

"I think the girls need help," Dahlia said. "Don't you want to know what's going on?"

"Sure." Chelsea looked out at the rain. A little canopy sheltered the entrance to the cabin, but the rain was heavy enough that Dahlia could still feel the spray, even from behind Chelsea. "Not really. The whole thing just creeps me out. And you said the girls disappeared, like, seventy years ago. Seventy years. I think they're pretty much beyond help."

"But don't you want to *know*?"

Chelsea turned to look at her. "My first year at camp I spent days with Lori Nelson, this other girl who could hear the ghosts. We'd sit around the steps of the cabin, trying to figure out what they were saying. What it all meant."

"What happened to her?" Dahlia asked in a low voice.

Chelsea rolled her eyes. "Nothing. She stopped coming to camp. She had no friends except me. And it turned out I didn't want to spend all my time hanging out with a girl who scratched her scabs until they bled and wore the same T-shirt every day for three weeks."

"I just want to talk to them once. Please."

For a moment, Chelsea didn't say anything. Then she took a deep breath and sighed. "Fine. Tell you what. You get your brother to bring in a few magazines for me, and I'll give the ghosts a few chances. Um. Three magazines for three chances. One hour each time."

"Magazines? Like what?"

"*Us. People*! I'm not fussy."

"You'll read those stupid gossip magazines, but not a book —"

"Of kabbala," Chelsea interrupted. "Exactly. Deal or no deal?"

"I'll ask. But I don't know how often he leaves camp. And I think we have to do something fast. They keep saying —"

"He'll have a night off tonight or tomorrow," Chelsea interrupted again.

"How do you know?"

"Counselors get one night off a week. Now that your brother and Nicole are broken up, Tom's bound to take his night out with Brad, and Brad was with us last night and the night before. So they're going to have their night out tonight or tomorrow, because no one likes to miss Friday or Saturday night in camp. So. Deal or no deal?"

Dahlia blinked. Chelsea wasn't nearly as stupid as she pretended to be. "Deal," she said.

# CHAPTER 26

# TOM

**T**om put the entertainment magazines on top of the beer at the convenience store. The clerk darted a look at his face, but didn't ask to see his ID, which was a relief — he'd borrowed Yoni's passport, but he really didn't look much like the guy.

"What's with the magazines?" Brad nodded toward the counter. "You thinking of becoming a girl?"

Tom shrugged. "They're actually for your mother. I'm trying to teach her to read."

The clerk laughed, but Brad regarded Tom seriously. "That's really mean," he said softly, and shook his head.

They got into Alyssa's car, which they'd borrowed for the night, and drove back toward the camp. Tom idly paged through the magazines as Brad drove.

"Seriously," Brad said. "What's with the magazines?"

Tom shrugged. "No idea. Dahlia wanted them."

"Dahlia? No way. Making out with boys, reading gossip magazines. What's next?"

"Wait. Making out with boys?" Tom said. He looked at Brad. "Are you serious?"

"Um. Yeah. She didn't tell you about her and the Professor?"

"She told me not to call him that." Tom imitated Dahlia's voice, " 'His name is Rafe.' So I figured maybe . . ." He shook his head. "But Dahlia . . . Are they . . . *dating?*"

"Unclear. I mean, the Professor has definitely been saying they are, but he's the Professor. It's not like you can take his word for it." Brad shifted gears as he turned off the highway. There was a grinding sound from the gearbox and another as he turned into the parking lot. "I'm glad we're drinking here. I would not want to drive stick shift after a few drinks."

"You couldn't get any worse." Tom walked around the car and took the case of beer from the trunk, while Brad grabbed his guitar and a flashlight.

"C'mon." Brad turned on the flashlight and started walking through the parking lot. It was a balmy night with a breeze and an almost full moon, and Tom suddenly realized where Brad was going. There were a few huge, water-smoothed rocks in the creek, not far from where the creek ran past the parking lot. When Brad and he were CITs, they hung out down there all the time.

"No way," Tom said. "We aren't going down there."

Brad put his guitar down. "Where do you have in mind?"

Tom looked around. "This way." He walked over the little bridge, out of the camp's parking lot. After a moment, Brad followed him. They crossed the quiet country road, and Tom put the beer down in the small, grassy field next to a neighbor's long, gravel driveway. "Here," he said. "Now we're not drinking on camp property."

"Right," Brad said. "The camp committee would be much happier knowing that we're drinking *and* trespassing." Still, he put his guitar case down and sat next to Tom. "What's the big deal? We used to drink over there all the time."

"That was different," Tom said. "We were CITs then. Now we're real counselors."

"Uh-huh." Brad opened a beer and took his guitar out of its case. He strummed a chord and half said, half sang, "Stop brooding about Nicole. You're gonna have to let it go."

"I wasn't thinking about her," Tom lied.

"Right," Brad said. "You just suddenly started caring about drinking on camp property. It had nothing to do with the fact that you and Nicole used to hang out down there. So what were you thinking about?"

Tom searched his mind for something that wasn't Nicole. "You know those two kids Mitchell and Jaden?"

Brad nodded. "Sure — the cute, little weird kids. They remind me of you at age ten."

"They've gotten really morbid lately," Tom said. He told Brad about the "funeral" the kids had staged.

Brad opened another beer and handed it to Tom. "So what? When we were that age, we were spending hours playing *Dungeons & Dragons*."

"You were," Tom said. "I was playing basketball."

"Yeah, right. As I recall, you and Kalish once got in a fistfight when he told you your dwarven ranger was dead. I remember you running out of the bunk sobbing. Besides, what are you going to do — punish them for putting flowers on a stone?"

"No one's talking about punishing them," Tom said. He stared absently at the parking lot across the street. Beyond the fireflies, he saw something move out of the woods, dimly illuminated by the moon overhead. "What's that?" he said.

"Hmm?" Brad had been absently plucking a melody on the guitar. "I don't know. Just something I'm . . ."

"No." Tom pointed. "There. I think it's a deer."

Brad put the guitar on its case and squinted where Tom indicated. "Too tall. Maybe a camper cutting the night activity?"

"Maybe." Tom rose to his feet, peering where he thought he'd seen the movement. "Yeah. Someone sneaking down to the parking lot for a smoke." He could make out an orange glow around face level. He took a step toward the road. "Let's bust them."

"Dude." Brad put his beer down and stood. "You're going to bust a camper with a beer in your hand?"

"Oh. Right." Tom put his beer on the ground next to the guitar before following Brad across the road.

Tom expected the camper to turn and run back into the woods when he or she realized they had been spotted, but whoever it was continued walking toward them. The figure grew more clear as it left the woods for the full light of the moon. It was a tallish person, probably not a camper after all. Tom thought it was a man by the way he walked.

The person seemed to see Tom and Brad for the first time and brought his hand to his head. The orange light Tom had seen vanished. *Probably hiding his cigarette*, Tom thought.

"Hi there," Brad called pleasantly. The figure half raised his arm in a sort of indifferent salute and kept moving toward them, neither quickening nor slowing his pace.

Brad and Tom passed the cars in the parking lot and were just a few yards away when Tom recognized the figure. *Oh.* He stopped walking. "Hi, Barry," he said.

The caretaker took a drag of his cigarette by way of response. Then, almost too low for them to hear, he said, "Hello. Wondering who was drinking in the parking lot."

"Actually, we're drinking across the road," Brad said.

Another slow drag of the cigarette. "Uh-huh. Neighbors'll love that." He walked past them and trudged slowly up the hill toward his house, not looking back.

Neither Brad nor Tom said anything. They watched Barry walk away until his silhouette vanished in the larger shadows. Finally, figuring he was out of earshot, Tom said softly, "You saw that too, right? He was wearing sunglasses?"

"Yeah. And his Mets hat. What else is new?" Brad turned back toward where they'd been sitting. "Dude is one weird hombre. Why wouldn't he wear sunglasses when he's walking through the woods at night? Probably wears them to bed too."

Tom followed Brad as he started walking. "Did you see that glow when we first saw him?"

"Sure. His cigarette."

"It couldn't be. The glow I saw went out before we got there, and he was still smoking his cigarette when we passed him." He paused. It was too weird. "I think the glow was coming from something on his forehead, and he put his hat over it."

Brad put his hand on Tom's shoulder as they crossed the street. "My man, you need to get a girlfriend. You are getting strange."

"You sound like Kalish. I'm just saying what I saw."

"Right," Brad said. "Maybe Barry's been killing handfuls of fireflies and smearing their glowing crap on his forehead. Maybe you can ask your little weirdoes to have a séance for the fireflies and ask their tiny dead spirits what happened."

Tom laughed despite himself and picked up his beer.

"And by the way," Brad added, "I will kick your butt if you ever even think of comparing me to Kalish again. I mean it. I will kick your butt if the thought even crosses your mind."

"How would you know if the thought crosses my mind?"

"Oh, I'll know."

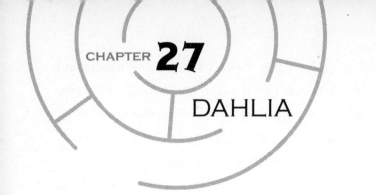

It was so hot on Friday that Dahlia almost wished for a thunderstorm to cool things down. Almost.

After lunch, she sat on her bed sweating, despite the fan pointed directly at her and the wet washcloth slung around her neck. The cabin hummed with the noise of clip-on fans, drowning out the music someone was playing on the other side of the bunk.

Dahlia heard Tom's voice outside and paused in the card shuffle she was practicing. A few seconds later, she saw his silhouette at the screen door. "Everyone decent?" he called.

"Come in," Eileen sang out. She was sitting on her bed knotting a friendship bracelet.

Tom stepped inside. "Dahl," he said, holding up a handful of magazines. "I got your magazines." He glanced around the bunk. It was empty except for Dahlia, Eileen, and Irit. "Um. Can I talk to you outside for a minute?"

Dahlia swung down from her bunk bed. "Sure," she said, feeling grateful that he had gotten the stupid magazines so quickly. She really wanted to know what the ghosts were saying. She kept thinking of Amelia telling her there was no time.

Following Tom outside, she squinted against the sunshine and the heat.

Tom handed her the magazines and then looked oddly abashed for a moment. "Listen," he finally said. "Are you and Rafe, ah . . ."

"Going out?" Dahlia finished. "No."

" 'Cause I heard —"

Dahlia cut him off. "It's none of your business, but no."

"Okay." Tom just stood there for a second.

"What?"

"So you haven't . . ." He paused. "Um . . ."

"No!" Dahlia shook her head. "Not once. Not ever."

"Well. Um. That's what I said when Brad told me. That it was just a dumb rumor. But Brad said that the kids in his bunk were talking about it. And — um — Rafe was talking too."

"Really?" Dahlia felt herself flushing. Stupid fair skin. "What did he say?"

"No idea," Tom said immediately. "Not the kind of thing I want to hear about my sister. I mean, what you do is your business. Like you said, it's not my business. At all."

"I didn't *do* anything." Dahlia scanned the sports field. A bunch of kids were playing soccer in the field next to her bunk. She didn't see Rafe, but Benjy was a few dozen yards away.

"Hey, Benjy," she shouted, waving at him. "Come over here for a second."

He shot her a quick look, then looked back toward the game. Jake Konigsberg was running toward him, dribbling the ball. Benjy darted at him, managing to cut off his break toward the goal, but

Jake passed the ball back toward the center. Benjy sprinted after it, too late to stop Joey Susskind from scoring.

"Benjy!" Dahlia called again.

"Water break," Benjy shouted. He walked toward Dahlia, red-faced and covered with sweat. "What's up?"

Dahlia took a few steps away from Tom. "Is Rafe saying that we're going out?" she asked, keeping her voice low.

Benjy hesitated, eyes widening. "You and me? Definitely not."

"You know what I mean," Dahlia said. "Me and him."

"I don't know if I've heard him actually *say* that."

"Did you think we were going out?" Dahlia was humiliated to even be asking the question. This was the kind of conversation morons had — the kind of girls who had fourteen shades of lipstick and nine shades of fingernail polish. Not her.

Benjy looked upward and waggled his head. "A little."

"We aren't. We were never going out." Dahlia made herself keep her voice calm. Bad enough that she was blushing. "We never even kissed or anything."

"Okay," Benjy said. "You know, no one believes Rafe on this kind of stuff, anyway."

That didn't make Dahlia feel better. She had thought Rafe was her friend. He had been the only one she could really talk to about the kabbala stuff. "If you see Rafe, tell him I'm looking for him."

"Sure," Benjy said. "I'll tell him."

Tom was still waiting by the door of her cabin. Dahlia didn't slow down as she walked past him. "Don't say a word. I don't want to talk about it."

Tom followed her into the bunk, still holding the magazines he had bought for Chelsea. "It's no big deal. Camp is always full of stupid rumors." He handed the magazines to Dahlia.

"But he lied about me," she said. "Why would he lie?"

Chelsea and Lisa walked in through the door after them. "Ha," Chelsea said triumphantly. "I told you Rafe was lying."

Lisa nodded sourly, trudged over to the shelves next to her bunk, and pulled a pack of peanut M&M's from underneath her clothes. She tossed them to Chelsea.

"Girls," Tom said. "You can't have food in the bunks."

Chelsea threw the M&M's to Dahlia. "They're for your sister."

Dahlia shifted the magazines to her left hand and caught the M&M's in her right. She pretended to move them to her left hand, and tried to palm them, but she was too mad to focus on it and her hands were too full. The candy fell onto the wood floor with a loud clunk.

Tom sighed. "Just eat them quickly, okay?"

Dahlia bent to pick up the candy. As though it wasn't bad enough about Rafe, she wasn't getting any better at sleight of hand. If anything, she was getting worse.

"Look. Do you want me to talk to him?" Tom said. "I —"

"No!" Dahlia cringed. "Definitely. Not a word."

"All right." Tom patted her shoulder and stood there for a second. "Hang in there."

"I'm fine," she said. "You can go."

"Um. Right. If you want to talk, you know where my cabin . . . You do know where my cabin is, right?"

"The camp's not that big, Tom."

"Right." Tom turned and left. The screen door slammed behind him.

Dahlia looked at the other girls. "You all heard about me and Rafe?"

"Sure we did. I knew it was a lie," Chelsea said, still triumphant. "You're dorky but not stupid."

"What's the big deal?" Eileen said, not looking up from her friendship bracelet. "So what if people thought you were going out? Oh. And can I have some of the M&M's?"

"But why would he tell such a stupid lie? I mean, he had to know I was going to find out."

Chelsea rolled her eyes. "He's a jerk. And I speak as someone who's gone to camp with him for four years."

Dahlia looked down at the magazines. She handed them to Chelsea. "Here. We have a deal, ri —"

"We have a deal," Chelsea said hurriedly, before Dahlia could say more.

"Soon."

"Sure."

Dahlia tossed the M&M's to Eileen and stomped out the door to find Rafe.

There were a handful of different sports going on, all optional because of the heat. Rafe wasn't playing basketball, baseball, soccer, or volleyball. She doubled back and tried his cabin. No luck. He was probably hiding in the woods, the coward.

When she got back to her cabin, she found the Schank book back on her bed. Most of the other girls had fled the heat, but Eileen was still working on the friendship bracelet.

"Who put this here?" Dahlia demanded. Rafe had taken the book to his cabin again after clubs the day before. "Did Rafe come in here while I was gone?"

"Rafe didn't come in here." Eileen shook her head, then wiped her face with her elbow. "I think it was Hayley, actually. She stopped by on her way to the pool."

That afternoon, Rafe didn't show up at her cabin like he usually did during clubs. She ended up reading the book on the tree bench by herself. It was even more boring without him. Who cared what the equivalencies of the number sixty-eight were? Who cared if the "good name" could be used to get rid of spirits, if the book didn't tell you what the good name was?

Every few minutes she found herself looking around for Rafe. He wasn't at the gazebo where their club used to meet, and he wasn't playing ultimate Frisbee with the sports club either. Fine. It wasn't like he could avoid her forever.

He finally showed up during flag lowering. He came late, but after it was over, Dahlia walked over to him before he could escape. "What did you tell people about us?" she said. "What exactly did you say?"

"Nothing," he said. He blushed and turned away. "Hey, Ben. Wait up."

"Nothing?" Dahlia said to his back. "Then why do all your friends think something else?"

"Look." Rafe turned back to her. "It's not my problem if some people got the wrong idea that I was willing to go out with you."

"That you were *what*?" Dahlia felt so mad, no words came out.

"It's not *my* problem," he repeated.

Dahlia spun and walked off to dinner.

Behind her she heard Chelsea say, "You are *such* a loser, Rafe."

She went directly to Tom's table that night. She ended up sitting with a bunch of the little kids, but she figured Rafe wouldn't dare sit with her brother after saying that stuff about her. Whatever it was that he had said.

Back at the bunk afterward, Dahlia tossed the book in her trunk and locked it. She didn't feel like reading it, but she didn't want Rafe reading it either.

She got to bed early that night. There were still a few minutes until lights-out, but she was tired. She leaned back on her pillow and heard paper rustle beneath it. As she turned to see what was underneath her pillow, she felt a sharp pain on her right calf. "Ow!" she said. She instinctively rubbed the sore spot with her left foot and felt a new sharp pain in the bottom of that foot. "Ow! Ouch!" Something had bit her.

She pulled the sheets off her body and swung off her bed. Whatever it was bit her again, and then again. Once just above her knee, and once on her arm.

Alyssa came out of the counselors' room. "What's wrong?"

Sarah grabbed a large book off the top of her cubby. "Wasps!" she said, pointing with her book. She hopped down from her bed and swung at a large, black-and-yellow wasp hovering above Dahlia's bed, crushing the wasp to the sheets. "Oh. Um. Darn." Sarah picked the book up and examined the black mess. "Sorry."

Dahlia looked down at the rising welts on her legs.

"You're not allergic, are you?" Alyssa asked.

"No." She stood on her right foot and looked at the bottom of her left. Ow. Ow. Ow. That really hurt.

"Thank God," Alyssa said. "Still, walking is going to hurt for a few days."

Dahlia flinched as another two wasps sleepily struggled out of her bedsheets.

"Wow. Three wasps in your sheets," Sarah said. She swung her book again. It was a large hardcover book — probably summer reading for school — and she got both wasps with one stroke.

Alyssa shook out Dahlia's sheets, discovering one more wasp — this one already dead. Dahlia must have rolled over on it when she was getting into or out of bed.

"Okay. Four wasp stings," Alyssa said. "You're going to the infirmary for some anti-bite stuff."

Sarah was scraping dead wasp off her book into the trash. "Sorry about your sheets," she said. "You can borrow my extra ones if you want."

"Thanks, Sarah," Dahlia said. Four wasps in her sheets. She wondered if Rafe would think that was a funny prank.

"There are tons of wasps around this year," Sarah said. "I saw Barry spraying the woods in back of our bunk this afternoon. He said he's never seen so many nests."

"When did you see him?"

Sarah paused. "Um. Just before dinner. Hayley and I came back after flag lowering to drop off her camera."

"C'mon," Alyssa said.

Dahlia took a step. Tears flooded her eyes, and she gasped. It felt like she had a spike through her left foot.

"It really hurts, huh?" Alyssa's brow furrowed. "Okay. Just sit down for a minute. I'll be right back." She walked out of the bunk and came back a few minutes later with Peter and Ofer.

"I'm telling you," Peter was saying. "I could carry her myself."

"Yeah, yeah," Alyssa said. "Just do it like I said."

The two counselors knelt and laced their hands together.

"Y'allah," Ofer said. "Come on."

Dahlia put her arms around their shoulders and they picked her up. It was actually a pretty comfortable way to be carried, which was good, as the infirmary was at the other end of camp. The nurse was smoking on the porch when they arrived. "Hey, handsome," she said to Peter. "What's the problem?"

"Bee stings," Peter said.

"Wasps," Dahlia corrected. They hurt much worse than bee stings. And wasps didn't make honey.

The nurse stubbed out her cigarette and led them inside. They went through a small hallway with benches on either side and entered a fluorescent-lit, white-tiled room lined with cabinets. The place smelled strongly of antiseptic cleaner. "Hop up here," the nurse said, indicating one of the cabinets with a medical examination table on top.

With Peter's help, Dahlia hoisted herself up on the exam table. "Weird," the nurse said. "Mud wasps are everywhere in the woods this year, but they don't usually come inside. And by this time of the day, they should be snuggled back into their hives." She opened a small refrigerator beneath the exam table and pulled out a few ice packs. "Let's try some ice, and then some hydrocortisone."

Between the ice and the medication, Dahlia was feeling better after a few minutes. The stings still throbbed, but not too badly. Ofer had already gone back to his bunk, and Dahlia half hopped, half hobbled back to her cabin, leaning on Peter only as much as she had to.

Her bunk was dark and quiet when she got back, the other girls already asleep. She had forgotten about the paper she'd heard rustling under her pillow until she lay back on her bed and heard it rustle again. Someone — Sarah probably — had changed her sheets, but her pillowcase hadn't been changed, and the paper must have been stuck inside. She started to reach in, then pulled her hand back, thinking of wasps. She turned on her flashlight and gingerly shook her pillow out of its case. No wasps fluttered out with the pillow, just a piece of folded notebook paper.

She unfolded the paper. Three words in large, hand-printed letters.

## GO HOME SCHANK

Dahlia stared at it. It could have been Rafe. They had joked about her being possessed by the translator's spirit. She eased back down in her bed, trying to convince herself it was Rafe. She didn't believe it. Rafe was a jerk, but he wasn't a jerk like that.

Besides, Sarah had told her that Barry had been by their cabin, poisoning the wasps during dinner. When he knew there'd be no campers around. Two days after she'd snuck into his house and he had called her "David."

Dahlia lay awake for a long time. It was hard to get comfortable with the wasp stings rubbing against the sheets. And every time she started to drift off, she'd think of Barry putting the wasps in her bed. He knew she'd been in his house, knew she was getting closer to whatever his secret was. What else would he do to make her leave the camp?

When she finally went to sleep, her dreams were full of confused images of Barry throttling McMasters. Barry had one hand wrapped around McMasters's throat and was holding him off the ground as easily as Dahlia would hold a can of soda. McMasters's face was turning purple, and he seemed to be trying to tell Dahlia something. She was just about to figure out what McMasters was saying when her dream changed.

The morning he met the little girls for the first time, David woke up early. His little room was still dark, with the color just beginning to bleed into the sky outside. He walked into the living room and found McMasters already up, standing over the woodstove. McMasters winked. "There he is! Just in time for breakfast." He ladled a few scoops of porridge into a bowl and handed it to David. "How's the maze coming?"

David took the bowl gratefully. His years at the yeshiva hadn't prepared him to cook much of anything. Two months into his stay, he still appreciated McMasters's food. "Fine, thank you. How's the construction?"

McMasters shrugged. "I got to tell you, I'm not sure your buddy is ever going to build his resort. It's like he's waiting for it to build itself."

David didn't say anything. He figured it was much more likely that Sammy was waiting for a few years to pass before he sold the property. He wasn't sure why Sammy was even bothering with the maze. Maybe to make the whole thing look more legitimate. Maybe just to give him, David, something to do.

"Still," McMasters said. "He told me I could plant corn if I felt like it, so I'm happy."

David shoveled the porridge into his mouth and stood up.

"Never a minute wasted," McMasters said. "Man, are you dedicated."

"I guess so," David said. He liked spending as much time as possible planting the seedlings. Planting the labyrinth was the best way he had found to empty his mind of the 72nd name. He couldn't feel the Illuminated Ones chasing him anymore, but that didn't mean they weren't still out there.

"Thanks for breakfast," he told McMasters. He walked out the back door of the farmhouse, heading straight for the clearing where he was planting the maze. This early in the morning, the light was still dim in the forest, with the rising sun not yet high enough to penetrate the trees. Still, he had been down the path so often in the last two months, he didn't miss a step, even in the semidarkness.

The light was better in the clearing around the maze. It was his favorite place on the property, on the border between the scrub forest and the old, overgrown cornfields. David picked up one of the seedlings he hadn't planted yet, idly holding it for a moment before looking around for his trowel. He had long since discarded the work gloves McMasters found for him. He preferred to feel the dirt. At first, his hands had gotten dry and cracked, with the dirt leaching out the moisture, but after two months of work, they'd turned hard.

Carrying the seedling, he walked the first circuit of the labyrinth, the bushes still so low he could see over them. He found the trowel where he'd left off planting the night before and took a deep breath of the clean piney smell of juniper, before kneeling to resume his work.

This early in the morning, every shovel of dirt had a handful of worms squirming away from the light. A blue jay fluttered to the ground a few feet from David and placidly plucked a worm from the earth that he'd discarded. When the hole was big enough, David gently placed a seedling within, and patted the dirt down around its roots. He rocked back on his heels, brushed the sharp needles from his forearm, and moved on to the next one. After a lifetime in the city, mostly spent in the study house, David was still surprised by how much he liked working outside. His arms and face had grown so dark that his old friends wouldn't recognize him, especially without his whiskers and sidelocks.

He had been working for a few hours when a girl's high voice startled him. "What are you doing?"

It was a little blonde girl who couldn't have been any older than ten. She was wearing a long-sleeved green dress and a wide-brimmed green hat. She'd evidently walked through the creek, as the bottom of her dress was a little wet.

"Er. Hello. I'm planting a labyrinth," David said. She looked at him blankly, and he added, "It's a kind of maze. The bushes will be the walls of the maze, and when it's done you can walk through it."

Behind the girl, another, even smaller, girl appeared among the trees. She was wearing a dress too, but hers was so covered with mud that he couldn't be sure what color it was. David smiled at her, and she shrank behind her sister.

"Amelia doesn't like new people," the older girl said. "She only came up here with me because she's not allowed to play at the creek by herself." The littler girl — Amelia — said something that David couldn't make out, and the older girl said, "She wants to know if it will be a hard maze to find your way through."

"Very easy," David said. "It will only have one path."

The older girl looked scornful. "That's stupid. What's the point of a maze with only one path?"

"The joy of walking through it," David said. "In Europe, Christians have used this kind of labyrinth for hundreds of years to help them pray. The pilgrims kneel and —"

"Why do you talk funny?" the girl interrupted.

"I grew up speaking a different language," David said. "To me, it sounds like *you* talk funny."

The older girl scowled.

He wiped his hands on his pants. "Do you girls want to plant a tree?" he asked.

"Why would we plant a tree?" The girl looked at him suspiciously. "There are enough trees around here."

David nodded and turned back to the seedlings. "True enough," he said.

When he looked up again, the older girl was out of sight, but the smaller girl was bending over one of his shrubs and sniffing it.

"Amelia," her sister called from somewhere down the hill. "I found some tadpoles!"

The little girl gave David a furtive glance, then darted back into the woods.

He turned back to his work. In the following weeks, he sometimes saw the girls wandering through the woods in the distance, but he didn't give them much thought. Not until it was too late.

## CHAPTER 29

# DAHLIA

**D**ahlia was pretty sure Rafe was avoiding her. She wasn't positive, as she refused to look at him or acknowledge his existence in any way. But she was finding this very easy, as Rafe seemed to be skipping most of the activities they had together.

More annoyingly, Chelsea was avoiding Dahlia too. Well, as much as she could avoid someone whose bed was a couple of feet away from hers. Three nights in a row, Chelsea came back to the bunk seconds before lights-out, and it seemed like she was never in the cabin during breaks. They were both in the painting work group, but there were always other people around during work period, and Chelsea refused to talk about the ghosts if anyone else might hear.

On Tuesday morning, though, Dahlia saw her chance. Their work group was painting the outside of the rec center, and Chelsea spilled half a jar of paint over her pants. Alyssa let her go back to the cabin to change into clean clothes. A few minutes later, Dahlia left the work group and headed toward their bunk as well.

"Where are you going, Dahlia?" Alyssa called after her.

"Bathroom," Dahlia said.

"They're cleaning the bathroom now."

Dahlia pretended not to hear. She saw Chelsea walking into the cabin ahead of her and she broke into a jog. Despite Chelsea's usual slowness in changing her clothes, Dahlia had a feeling she would be very quick if she saw Dahlia headed toward the bunk.

Sure enough, by the time Dahlia walked in, Chelsea was already wearing clean pants and putting on her shoes to go back to their work group.

"Hey," Dahlia said. "So, when are we going to wait for the ghosts?"

Chelsea finished tying her shoes and virtually leapt off her bed toward the door. "Don't know."

"We have a deal, right?" Dahlia said. "It's important, Chelsea. I think the ghosts need our help."

"Have you seen them lately?" Chelsea asked. "I mean, if they need our help so badly, they're probably always in here asking for help, right?"

Dahlia frowned. As it happened, she hadn't seen the ghosts since the previous Wednesday. "We have a deal, right?" she said again.

"Sure. Definitely. Just not right now."

"When, then?"

"I told Alyssa I'd hurry." Chelsea opened the door and stepped outside. "Not all of us are Tom's sister."

"What? What does that mean?"

"Unlike you, when I skip an activity, I get in trouble."

"So do I. Alyssa makes me go to things all the time."

Chelsea paused long enough to roll her eyes elaborately. "Sure.

If she happens to see you moping around the bunk, she *might* make you go. Anyone else gets in trouble for not being there."

Dahlia followed Chelsea down the stairs. "Whatever. You've obviously been avoiding me."

"No, I haven't."

"You're never around the bunk. You came in just before lights-out, like, the last three nights."

Chelsea looked at her for a moment and shook her head. "So, to you, that means I'm avoiding you. Do you really not know that I'm dating Joey?"

"Oh," Dahlia said. "No. I mean — yes. I really didn't know that. So when are you going to wait for the ghosts with me?"

Chelsea turned away from Dahlia. "You're obsessed." She didn't walk away, though. "Let me think for a second."

Dahlia looked past her. A single white cloud lingered on the horizon, but aside from that the sky was perfectly blue.

"Clubs," Chelsea finally said. "We'll do it during clubs. No one is in the bunk, and the counselors don't really check about people skipping clubs." She started to walk back toward the rec center, then stopped in mid-step. "One more thing. If you tell anyone what we're doing, I'm done. I won't help you."

"That wasn't part of the deal."

Chelsea shrugged. "It is now." She lengthened her pace so she was walking a few steps ahead of Dahlia by the time they got back to the work group.

"Did they let you in?" Alyssa said to Dahlia.

"Who?"

"The bathroom cleaners. Sometimes they don't let campers in when the bathroom floors are wet."

"Oh," Dahlia said. "Yeah. It was fine."

Chelsea was good to her word. That afternoon, at the start of clubs, she and Dahlia lingered in the cabin. They sat quietly on Chelsea's bed, concealed behind the sheet Chelsea had hung off the top bunk, and watched as the other campers filed out. Chelsea paged through one of the magazines Tom had brought in for her, while Dahlia impatiently waited for Alyssa to leave the cabin. She was pretty sure the ghosts wouldn't come while Alyssa was there. And even if the ghosts did come, Chelsea wouldn't be able to tell her what they were saying without attracting Alyssa's attention.

Dahlia lifted the edge of the sheet that concealed them. She watched as Alyssa sat on her bed, writing in her notebook. "Probably writing love poems about your brother," Chelsea whispered.

"Shhh," Dahlia hissed. After a few minutes, Alyssa got out her guitar and strummed a few chords. Finally, she walked outside, still holding her guitar. Dahlia immediately pulled the sheet to one side and surveyed the cabin. No ghosts.

"She's just going to come back," Chelsea said.

From outside, they heard Alyssa begin to sing along with her guitar. "Not for a while," Dahlia said.

Alyssa didn't come back. But neither did the ghosts.

Dahlia got the kabbala book out of her trunk for the first time in days. She flipped to the section Rafe had found about dybbuks, iburs, and all the other kinds of spirits. There was nothing about how to make ghosts appear. Except, of course, that the most holy name could summon spirits and anything else you wanted. If you knew how to use it.

She thought of her dream where David Schank had used the 72nd name to summon his friend. She could *almost* remember the letters he'd put in her mind the other day, when the man was standing by her bed, but she didn't know how to do anything with them. If his spirit expected her to take care of some unfinished business, it was going to have to be more forthcoming.

Whatever. She was tired of trying to figure it out on her own. She wanted to talk to the ghosts and just ask them. What had happened to them? What did they want with her? Who was the man?

But no ghosts came that day. As soon as the bell marking the end of clubs rang, Chelsea was out of the cabin like a shot.

The next day, it was exactly the same. Chelsea relaxed on her bed reading a magazine as Dahlia sat and watched the cabin for any sign of the ghosts. Nothing. They weren't showing themselves to Dahlia. Maybe the man was keeping them away. She wondered again why he had brought them there the other day when he so clearly didn't want them talking to her.

Chelsea didn't bother pretending she was sorry the ghosts hadn't come. Or, rather, she didn't bother pretending very hard.

"Sorry 'bout that," she said at the end of the hour, grinning. "Oh well. One more chance tomorrow." And she was gone, off to meet Joey or Lisa or whoever.

# CHAPTER 30

That night, Dahlia again woke up to find a shadowy figure looming over her. This time the figure was more solid, though — she could feel its hand clutching her shoulder. She wrenched herself away from its grasp and sat up, fists clenched. She recognized Chelsea's voice just in time to stifle her shriek.

"Can you see them? I heard someone talking, but I don't see anyone there."

Dahlia rubbed her eyes. Chelsea was standing on Michal's bed, her head peering over the edge of Dahlia's bunk. "What?" Dahlia said. "What are you talking about?"

"The ghosts," Chelsea whispered. "I hear girls' voices coming from over there, but I don't see anything."

"They never come when other people are in the bunk."

"Yeah? Maybe someone forgot to tell them that."

Dahlia looked where Chelsea was pointing. For a moment, she didn't see anything, just shadows and the odd glint of moonlight off a bunk bed. Wait. Had those shadows moved? She stared into the corner and waited for her eyes to adjust.

There they were. The little girl was clutching the older girl's hand, and they were both staring at Dahlia, looking anxious. The older one — Claudia — shook her head at Dahlia. "Claudia is shaking her head," Dahlia said. "Wait. Now the little one — Amelia — is beckoning and saying something. What's she saying?"

Chelsea paused, listening. After a moment, she furrowed her brow. "Stop who?"

The ghost girl narrowed her eyes, looked around, then back at Dahlia, like she was playing some kind of trick. "I think she can hear you but only see me," Dahlia said.

"Sad for her," Chelsea said.

Dahlia didn't look away from the ghosts. Amelia was still looking at her and talking seriously. In the darkness, she could barely see the little girl's mouth, let alone make out what she was saying. "What's she saying?" she asked Chelsea again.

Chelsea listened intently and shook her head. "I *think* she's saying something about not letting someone into the maze. But that I should go to the maze. Or you should, I guess. Some other voice keeps speaking Hebrew over her. Now she's saying something about how seventy-two years have gone by, and the maze is reopening so we have to be quick." Chelsea cursed softly. "The stupid other voice is making it really hard to hear the girl."

Hayley rolled over in her sleep and muttered, "Shut up."

"What's the other voice saying?" Dahlia whispered. "Is it the other girl?"

Chelsea shook her head. "It's a man. He just keeps saying the same two Hebrew words again and again. . . . Wait. The girls are both saying the same thing now." She listened for a moment. "Follow you?"

Amelia beckoned urgently to Dahlia.

"The girls want us to —" Chelsea began.

"Follow them," Dahlia said, pushing her sheets off her. "I get it."

"Right now."

Dahlia jumped off her bed, spurring a sleepy whine from Michal as Dahlia's foot brushed her shoulder on the way down. Dahlia hurried toward the cabin door as the ghosts slipped through the wall.

She stood on the stairs in front of the bunk for a moment, scanning the area for the girls. It only took her a few seconds. It was lighter outside than inside the bunk, with a half moon and tons of stars illuminating the night. The stars were much brighter at camp, she'd noticed.

The girls were walking toward the road. Every few steps Amelia turned around, obviously looking for Dahlia. Dahlia waved and hastened down the stairs after them.

Behind her, the door to the bunk softly closed again. "Where are they?" Chelsea asked.

"You're coming?" Dahlia whispered. The grass was wet with dew, and she shivered a little in the night air.

"No, I just happen to be taking a walk in the middle of the night. Where are they?"

Dahlia pointed ahead of her, following the ghosts across the road.

Chelsea came up beside her. "Ow. Ow. Ow," she said as they crossed the gravel road. "Why didn't I bring my freaking flip-flops?"

Above them, bats swooped and fluttered in the night. The crickets and cicadas were croaking at full throttle, joined by frogs in the woods a few yards away. There were more trees around the flagpole, blocking the moonlight, and making it harder to see the ghosts. Still, Dahlia saw a flicker of movement between the bunks and led Chelsea that way.

"Where are they?" Chelsea asked again.

"Somewhere over there," Dahlia whispered, pointing again. "They don't glow in the dark." Still, once the ghosts were past the bunks, it was easy to make them out as they walked down the open, grassy slope to the pool.

"Guess we're lucky they're not going through the woods," Chelsea said. "It'd be impossible to follow them."

"Yeah, lucky," Dahlia muttered. Every few steps, Amelia looked over her shoulder and beckoned for her to hurry up. "They're doing it on purpose. They want us to stay with them."

"Well, great." Chelsea said. "They're friendly gho . . ." Her voice trailed off as they saw a flashlight click on below them, by the pool's deck. At the same instant, the ghosts disappeared.

Chelsea and Dahlia were halfway down the slope, so there was nowhere to hide.

"Hey. You kids," Barry's voice called from down by the pool. A dog barked nearby.

Dahlia froze. The wasps had been a warning, and she'd ignored them. Now, without anyone around, he'd kill her just like he'd killed the man in her dreams. His thick fingers around her throat.

The flashlight played over the ground, coming closer to them.

# CHAPTER 31

"**C**ome on!" Chelsea seized her arm and yanked Dahlia up the hill. Dahlia resisted for a moment. What was the point? The dog could run faster than they could. She looked around for a stick or something. At least she could put up a fight.

"Come on — he doesn't see us," Chelsea hissed.

Dahlia squinted into the flashlight's glare and saw that she was right. Another person — no, two people — had been walking down the hill below them. That's who Barry was talking to. Probably kids sneaking down to skinny-dip in the pool. They said something, but Dahlia couldn't make out their words.

Again, Chelsea pulled on Dahlia's arm. This time, Dahlia let herself be drawn back toward the top of the hill.

Behind them, Barry gave a short, humorless laugh. "Sleep-walking? I'll bet. With your flashlight? And a friend?"

Chelsea ducked into the sheltering branches of one of the willow trees that grew near the top of the hill. Dahlia lingered in front of the tree and peered down the grassy slope.

She could just make out a high voice talking to Barry. A girl, or a really little boy. The hair on Dahlia's forearms prickled with tension. She was sure something important was happening down there. This was why the ghosts had woken them — so they could see this, or maybe so they could rescue the kids from whatever Barry planned to do to them. Maybe he planned to lure the kids farther into the woods, out of earshot of the rest of the camp.

She felt almost disappointed when Barry finally said, "Get on back to your bunks. Sleepwalk somewhere else next time."

The flashlight turned and started bobbing its way back up the slope. Another flashlight turned on below them and shone at the figures walking up the hill.

Dahlia reluctantly stepped farther into the shelter of the willow's branches, still trying to see who the other kids were. All she could make out were vague silhouettes. The flashlight behind them distorted their shadows so much, she couldn't even tell how big the campers were.

She'd follow them, she decided, and see what they were doing. She was slipping out of the willow when she heard Barry say softly, "C'mere," much closer than he had been.

She stopped moving. A dog's collar jingled behind her. "Good boy," Barry muttered.

Dahlia turned, very slowly, and saw that Barry was walking up the steps after the campers. Still moving very slowly, she stepped around the willow tree, putting as much of it as possible between her and the stairs.

She and Chelsea waited for what felt like an eternity until Barry and his dog passed them. When his flashlight had finally been swallowed back into the summer night, Chelsea's teeth flashed in a moonlit smile. She beckoned to Dahlia and started back to their bunk. After a minute, Dahlia followed her. The other campers were long gone by now, anyway.

They stayed in the darker shadows on their way back, skirting the woods behind the cabins. As they approached the bathrooms, though, Chelsea laughed quietly. "That was awesome. Barry was, like, ten feet away." She giggled and imitated Barry's bass. "Sleep-walk somewhere else."

"We got lucky," Dahlia said.

"No kidding. If the other kids hadn't been there, we would have been nailed for sure." Chelsea paused. "Wait. Do you think the ghosts were setting us up? Just for fun or something?"

"And the other kids just happened to be there first?" Dahlia shook her head. "That'd be too weird of a coincidence."

"Yeah," Chelsea said. "Because none of the rest of this is weird."

"I don't think they were trying to get us in trouble." Dahlia said. "I don't think they really get that there are rules and stuff."

The bathroom lights were still on, making the woods to their right seem even darker. Dahlia heard an owl hooting, but she couldn't see a flicker of movement.

Just as they were walking up the stairs to their bunk, another thought struck Dahlia. It was quiet and dark inside the cabin, and she kept her voice soft. "Maybe they wanted us to make sure that Barry didn't hurt those other campers."

Chelsea looked at her and shrugged. "Like we could have done anything if Barry had wanted to hurt them. Maybe they just wanted you to meet some other weirdos."

"You're the one they woke up," Dahlia said.

Chelsea laughed. "On that note. I'm going back to sleep. Good night."

They tiptoed through the cabin, and Dahlia climbed onto her bed, thinking she'd never fall back asleep.

It seemed like seconds later when the first announcement woke her up. Hayley and Sarah were already out of their beds, towels in hand. Early morning sun filled the cabin. "You coming?" Hayley whispered to Dahlia.

Dahlia shook her head. She was too tired to move. "You guys go on."

Hayley gave her a little wave as she and Sarah walked out the door.

For a while, Dahlia just lay there, thinking about the ghosts and what they wanted. What did you want when you were dead? They looked like such average little girls, it was hard to imagine that they were trying to do something evil. The truth was, it was still hard to believe that they *were* ghosts instead of someone's little sisters dressed up in old-fashioned dresses. Just thinking about them being dead, really dead, made Dahlia teary.

Which was stupid. People died all the time. Why cry about two girls who had died seventy-two years ago? But somehow, seeing the ghosts, and the way they had laughed at her little magic trick . . . They still seemed like such real little girls.

She wished that Chelsea had been able to understand more of what the ghosts were saying last night. Which reminded her — what were the Hebrew words that Chelsea kept hearing instead?

Most of the bunk was awake by now. The loudspeakers announced ten minutes to flag raising, and Alyssa bustled through

235

on her way back from the shower. "Let's go, girls," she said, walking into her room. "I want everyone up by the time I leave this room. If you're too tired to get up, we'll move lights-out earlier."

There was a general flurry of movement around the bunk. Dahlia sat up and wiped her eyes. No point in going to the showers now, with only freezing-cold water left. She glanced down, and saw Chelsea was still in bed too.

"Hey, Chelsea," she said.

Chelsea flung an arm over her eyes and rolled over.

Lisa stood next to the bunk bed she shared with Chelsea, gathering her toiletries. She squinted up at Dahlia, bleary-eyed. "I'd leave her alone, if I were you," she said. "The girl doesn't wake up well."

"I want to talk to her."

Lisa pushed a hand through her hair. "Whatever," she said, stumbling off toward the bathroom.

Dahlia hopped off her bed and picked up her own toothbrush and towel. She walked over to Chelsea's bed and pushed her mattress. "Chelsea," she said.

"Leave me alone!" She pulled her pillow over her head. "I'm sleeping."

"No you're not. You're talking to me," Dahlia said reasonably. "I want to know what the other voice was saying last night."

Chelsea's hand emerged from beneath her pillow, middle finger extended.

"Thanks. Real original." Why couldn't it have been someone a little nicer who heard the ghosts? "Look. I figured you wouldn't want to talk about it when there other people around. That leaves now."

"Jesus!" Chelsea flung her sheets off her and hopped out of bed. "I wake you up to see the ghosts. I even follow them with you. Can't you wait until I'm awake to talk about this? They're ghosts. They're not going anywhere." She grabbed her towel and toiletries and walked outside.

Dahlia followed her out the door. "Just tell me the words the guy's voice said."

Chelsea paused on the stairs and squinted against the bright early morning sun. "I don't know. He just said the same two words over and over again. *Mafok* and *malkut*. That's all."

"Wait? *Mavoch* and *Malchut*?"

"That's what I said." Chelsea started walking to the bathroom.

Dahlia followed behind her. "*Malchut* is something in kabbala, and I *think* mavoch means 'maze.' I'm not sure, though." She shook her head. Thanks to David Schank's stupid translation, she was sure that the numerical equivalent of the Hebrew word for maze was sixty-eight, but she didn't know the actual word.

Ahead of them, their Israeli counselor Ofer walked out of the bathroom, wearing a towel. "Hey, Ofer," Chelsea called. "How do you say 'maze' in Hebrew?"

Ofer hesitated. "Eh, maze — like" — he sketched a pattern in the air — "like a laverinth?"

"Labyrinth," Chelsea corrected. "Yeah. Like that."

He beamed at her. "*Mavoch*," he said. "*B'ivrit* it is *mavoch*."

"Thanks," Chelsea said, continuing to walk toward the bathroom.

"*B'vakashah*," Ofer said. "You're welcome."

Dahlia followed Chelsea into the bathroom. "Such a dork," Chelsea said. "But sort of good-looking."

"What?" Lisa looked up from the sink where she was washing her face and looked out the bathroom door. "Ofer? Are you blind?"

Chelsea took her toothbrush from the bucket she used for her toiletries. "He's got good hair and big muscles."

"He's got slimy hair and oddly large muscles."

Dahlia stood there for a moment. *Mavoch and Malchut. Mavoch and Malchut. Mavoch* meant "maze," and Malchut was the tenth sefira, which was like, what — the lowest door to God, or something? She had no idea what the two of them together meant.

"Just those two words?" she said.

Lisa glanced at Chelsea. "Don't respond. You're rewarding bad behavior."

Chelsea shrugged and answered Dahlia. "He might have said more, but that's all I remember."

The bell rang again for flag raising. They walked out the bathroom door just in time to be intercepted by Alyssa. "Let's go, girls," she said.

"Sure," Lisa said brightly. "We'll just drop off our towels and run over."

Alyssa shook her head. "Nope. Bring 'em with you. Let's go."

The three of them walked directly to the flagpole, carrying their towels and toiletries. They got there just as announcements were ending (the twelve-year-olds were going on their hiking trip that day; the animal work group was still missing the gerbil cage, and the gardening work group was missing a few of their rakes). When the ceremony was over, Dahlia began walking back to the bunk to drop off her towel. A few feet in front of her, Chelsea, Lisa, and Michal were doing the same.

Lisa stopped walking. "Okay," she said to Dahlia. "No offense, but can you stop following us around?"

Chelsea looked a little apologetic but didn't say anything.

"I'm putting my towel back in the bunk. Just like you," Dahlia said.

"I didn't mean, like, right now," Lisa said. "I just meant in general."

Dahlia quickened her pace. Michal walked so slow it wasn't hard to outdistance the other three girls. She dropped her towel and toiletries on her bed and left the bunk again, passing the others without a word on her way to breakfast.

By the time she got to breakfast, the only seats left were with the little kids. She ended up sitting with seven ten-year-olds and Jacob Kalish. Kalish spent the entire meal asking her what boys she liked. She hated this camp.

# CHAPTER 32

# DAVID

**D**avid planted the last seedling by the light of the moon. He'd been working on the maze for twenty hours straight by then, but he simply couldn't make himself stop. Not until he was done. He felt a wave of exhaustion as he patted the dirt down. He stood and looked around, but it was too dark to get any more than a dim impression of the knee-high seedlings spread out around him. David made his way back to the house in almost pitch darkness, walking slowly, and feeling his way up the familiar path.

The next day, he slept through the morning and much of the afternoon. When he woke, the sun was already nearing the horizon. McMasters had left some kindling prepared in the wooden stove, and David lit a fire before eating a sandwich and drawing some water from the well to wash himself.

Then he prayed — the first time he said his afternoon prayers since the Rebbe cast him off. At first, there'd been no time, what with his headlong flight from the Illuminated Ones. Then, in earshot of the pigpen, the Rebbe's rejection still fresh in his mind, David had had no desire to pray. Now, though . . . He covered his head with his work hat and laid his still-moist bath towel around his shoulders as a makeshift prayer shawl.

He didn't pray for long. A few minutes after beginning, he felt an odd sensation. A throb, a feeling of power coming from the woods behind the house. He stopped in mid-prayer and walked outside, following the sensation. It led him down the path toward the labyrinth, becoming stronger as he walked.

Still, the truth didn't strike him until he stepped out of the trees and saw the labyrinth. It was the first time he'd looked at the finished maze from above. He felt a lurch in his stomach.

What an idiot he'd been. To believe the labyrinth was a way of *not* thinking about the 72nd name. From above, now that the maze was complete, it was obvious. The first circuit of the maze traced the first letter of the name. The second circuit sketched both the second and the third letters. In ten circuits, the labyrinth twisted perfectly through the eighteen letters of the 72nd name. David had somehow taken the name and compressed it into a single elaborate pattern — a pattern that anyone could walk through.

He walked to the labyrinth's entrance and sank to a sitting position, where he couldn't see the shape of the maze. It didn't help. Now that his eyes had been opened, looking at the roots and branches was no better than looking at the maze as a whole. Just gardening with the name in his mind had been too much. Every shrub in the maze had the name in its every curve. The Illuminated Ones wouldn't need to find him to learn the 72nd name. They'd just walk through the maze, and the name would be obvious to them.

David wasn't sure how long he sat there, but at some point he realized the sun had dipped below the horizon. He stared at the brilliant oranges and reds filling the sky, then forced himself to his feet. He grimly walked through the maze. Every twist in every branch described multiple Hebrew letters, the holy name visible in everything from the smallest wrinkles of the bark to the overall shape of the labyrinth.

And not only in this dimension. David's fear mingled with pride. Somehow *his* maze linked this world to the higher realities. Walking through the maze, he could feel himself moving through the upper dimensions of existence as well. He saw the trees that supported the universe, and they were framing the paths *he* had traced with his little maze of juniper seedlings.

He had never read — never even imagined — that such a thing was possible. His labyrinth had made it impossible for the most secret name of God to hide. No meditation necessary, no spiritual awakening. Just one step ahead of the other for fifteen, twenty minutes, and the divine name would emerge to anyone with even a hint of spiritual awareness.

There was nothing to do but destroy it. The thought of the Illuminated Ones finding the name so easily was beyond bearing. David knelt and grasped the nearest seedling. It had somehow already grown from knee height to thigh height, and it was strongly rooted. He had to dig up a good portion of the roots, but eventually he managed to get the little tree free from the ground. The remaining roots came up with a soft, moist plop, and he threw the seedling out of the maze. Then he turned to the next one.

It was slow work. Digging up the roots with his hands was difficult, and he couldn't find the trowel or the bigger shovel in the twilight. He managed to uproot only a half dozen or so seedlings before it was too dark to continue. He would have to come back tomorrow, he decided. He'd bring McMasters's ax to make the job easier.

# CHAPTER 33

# DAHLIA

That Friday was the hottest day of the summer so far. The dining hall was so sweltering that they had to move lunch to the little grove of trees next to the building. Ordinary afternoon activities were canceled, and the pool was open for free swim all afternoon.

Dahlia didn't usually go to free swim. Because the pool was at the bottom of a hill and surrounded by tall trees, it was always freezing. It was always dirty, too, since every time it rained, dirt washed down the hill. Still, after an hour of sweltering in the thick air, Dahlia put on her bathing suit and headed to the pool.

As she walked down the stairs, she thought of the maze, no more than a few hundred yards away. In her dream, David had wanted to pull up the maze. She wondered what had happened afterward. Had he changed his mind? Had something stopped him? If she walked the maze now, would she find herself knowing the supersecret name of God? She tried to sense David, to tease out the answer to some of her questions, but she felt nothing. It was hard to believe in spirits or possession on a scorchingly sunny afternoon like this one.

The whole camp seemed to be at the pool — two hundred kids and counselors trying to cram themselves into a not-very-large swimming pool at exactly the same time. Campers were only allowed to use the deck on one side of the pool, with the other side reserved for the lifeguard and the counselors on swimming-pool duty. By the time Dahlia got to the pool, the camper side of the deck was jam-packed with campers getting into the water, waiting to get into the water, and getting out of the water. Finally, Dahlia was able to push her way to the edge. For a moment, she perched there and dangled her legs in the water. Even with the heat, the pool felt electrifyingly cold. She kicked her legs, and it felt like there was ice flowing through her veins. She wondered if she even wanted to go the rest of the way in. There was pretty much no room to actually swim.

A few yards away, a girl shrieked. Dahlia turned and saw that one of the CITs had pushed her into the water. The lifeguard — a plump British girl named Amy — blew her whistle. "Oy," she shouted from across the pool, pointing at the guy who had done the pushing. "Out of here, Jeremy. You're banned for the next week."

"What? Come on, Amy!" the kid sputtered. The lifeguard had already returned her gaze to the pool. Without looking at him, she kept pointing up the hill.

Somebody touched Dahlia's shoulder. She turned to see Rafe squeezing himself in beside her.

"Can I talk to you?" Rafe looked even skinnier in his bathing suit.

"No." Dahlia looked behind her. No escape that way. The cement platform was jammed with kids.

"C'mon!" A little kid standing a few inches behind her motioned impatiently. "Get in or get out!"

"I have something to show —" Rafe started.

Dahlia dived into the pool. A moment later, she heard a splash as Rafe jumped in beside her. She stroked away from him, swimming around a cluster of kids who had paired up to wrestle from one another's shoulders.

She surfaced on the other side of the pool. Selena and one of the other counselors were standing there, holding long poles as they surveyed the water. "Here he comes," Selena told Dahlia.

Dahlia turned to see Rafe gracelessly dog-paddling after her. He saw her looking. "Wait." He was struggling to keep his head above water as he swam. "I just want —"

Dahlia went back under the water, pushed herself off the side of the pool with her legs, and stroked past him the other way. She wasn't an especially fast swimmer, but he was *slow*. He was only halfway across when she pulled herself out and headed toward her towel.

She was walking up the concrete stairs when he came after her, still dripping. "Come on," he started.

Dahlia was about to keep going when a smiling older kid put his hand on Rafe's shoulder. It took her a second to recognize him as Rafe's older brother, Jake or John or something. "Learn to take a hint, Professor," he said, grinning widely. "She probably has something more fun to do than talk to you. Like, say, walk over burning coals or something."

Rafe looked up at her beseechingly, and Dahlia sighed. His brother really did make Tom look great. "Hurry up, Rafe," she called, as though all along she'd intended for him to follow her.

Rafe's face lit up, and he pushed past his brother. Dahlia wrapped her towel around her waist and kept walking.

"Thanks," Rafe said as he caught up. Then, under his breath, "Ow. Ow. Ow. These stairs are hot."

She glanced down at his bare feet. "Get your flip-flops, idiot."

"You'll wait?"

She motioned impatiently, and Rafe gingerly made his way down the stairs. He pushed through the crowd, grabbed his towel and flip-flops, and jogged back up to her.

Dahlia didn't look at him as they climbed the stairs. "I'm still not talking to you," she said. "I just felt sorry for you."

"Right. Thanks." Rafe walked next to her in silence until they got to the top of the hill. "Thing is — I have something to show you." He turned to the left, away from their cabin and the showers. "It'll be quick."

"I'm not going anywhere with you."

"I made something for you."

She hesitated. "What?"

He shook his head. "Come on. I'll show you. Please."

"Okay. Walk."

Rafe started toward the rec center. After a few seconds, Dahlia followed, keeping about ten feet between them, too far to talk without shouting. He paused to let her catch up, but she paused too. After a few seconds, he started walking again. He tried again to let her catch up as they passed the office. Finally, as they went past the dining hall, he stopped and called back, "Are you going to stay behind me the whole way?"

"I don't want to give anyone the impression that you'd be willing to date me."

"Are you still mad about that?"

"I just don't want to confuse anyone." Dahlia turned and started walking back to her bunk. Rafe jogged after her.

"Wait. Hey. Come on. I'm sorry I said that. Okay?"

"No." Still, she let him catch up to her.

He kept his gaze on the ground between them. "I didn't lie, you know. I just didn't say anything when . . . Look. Seriously, I'm sorry. The thing I want to show you — it's something I made as, um, a way of apologizing."

"Yeah? What is it?"

Unexpectedly, Rafe grinned. "Hard to describe. Come on."

Dahlia rolled her eyes. "Fine." They walked together past the dining hall.

As they approached the barn, they heard voices. Dahlia looked in the doorway and saw Tom's friend Kalish, shirtless and gleaming with sweat, talking to a cluster of his campers.

"Practicing for tonight's play," Rafe said, seeing where she was looking. He led her around the corner of the barn and down the hill toward the parking lot beyond.

Dahlia didn't say anything, and after a moment Rafe kept talking. "Um. Did you hear that Benjy's grandfather visited a few nights ago? He was at camp, like, a million years ago, just after it opened, and he was saying that the caretaker used to be a guy named McMasters."

Dahlia still didn't say anything, unwilling to admit interest.

"McMasters!" Rafe said. "So the last person who saw the girls alive ended up being the caretaker of *this* camp. Oh. And he said — Benjy's grandfather, I mean — he said that Barry is, like, McMasters's nephew or something. Is that not freaky? Barry's the bogeyman's nephew."

Rafe was a few paces ahead of Dahlia, but now he froze, staring back at the barn. Dahlia caught up with him and followed his gaze. Barry stood in his little workshop below the barn, bent over his workbench, doing something noisy with a power saw.

"He couldn't hear me, right?" Rafe whispered. "Right? I mean, that saw has got to be loud."

Dahlia shrugged, and Rafe kept walking, shoulders hunched a little. He led her toward the goat pen below the barn.

She hadn't been all the way down to the parking lot since she'd driven into the camp three weeks before. Three weeks. Strange to think that first session was already almost over. If she didn't figure out the ghosts in the next two days, it would be another year before she got another chance. The thought made her feel a little panicky, like she couldn't possibly leave until she had done *something* for the ghosts.

There were two goats in the pen. The white one ran toward them and butted his head against the gate. Rafe walked around the pen and into the woods. "This way. Come on."

A few yards into the woods, he brushed some leaves off a thick tarp and picked it up. It had been covering a few pieces of scrap metal and an old plastic cart someone had stolen from the kitchen. Rafe extended the tarp to Dahlia. "Here it is."

"What do I want with a tarp?"

"No, no. Look." Rafe reached out and grabbed a piece of the scrap metal. He heaved it into an upright position. "I made this for you."

Dahlia just looked at the thing for a moment. It wasn't scrap metal after all. For some reason Rafe had duct-taped a long metal rod to the corner of the cart. He'd mounted the rod vertically, so one end touched the ground while the other stuck straight up in the air, going a bit higher than Dahlia's head. He'd then used a thick, rusty chain to hang a metal cage from the top of the rod. This cage dangled precariously at around shoulder height on Dahlia.

"What is it?" she asked.

"It's a lightning guard," Rafe said. "Because you're scared of lightning."

"I'm not scared," Dahlia said automatically. "I'm appropriately cautious."

"Right. Just take this with you and you'd be fine in the middle of a lightning storm. The old gerbil cage would go over your head. You'd push the cart around with you to keep the cage centered over your head."

Dahlia reached out and touched the plastic cart, moist with dew and mold. "That's . . ." Rafe smiled, and she felt a small twinge. Still, it was the dumbest thing she'd ever seen. Well. One of them. "Totally stupid. If you're pushing the cart, the lightning would go right through you."

"No." He shook his head. "The cart's plastic. If lightning hit the cage, it would run through one iron rod, then into the other." Rafe leaned down and showed her how the lower end of the long rod brushed the ground. "Then it would run into the ground."

"And into anyone around the cart. Plastic doesn't conduct electricity well, but that close to the lightning, you'd still fry."

Rafe looked at the cart. After a few seconds he coughed. "But it's the thought that counts, right?"

She pulled the cart toward her. "I don't know if this counts as thought."

He laughed tentatively. "That was a joke, right?"

"Yeah." Dahlia had to give the cart a hard yank before it came free of the shrubs and undergrowth. It actually moved pretty well once it was out. She gently tugged the cage. "That girl in the animal care work group is going to be so happy. She's made, like, a hundred announcements about this stupid gerbil cage."

"They should buy a new one," Rafe said. "Who has an iron cage? It's a million pounds and it rusts."

Dahlia let go of the cart, and it slowly rolled back down the slope until it ran into the bushes a few feet below. "Okay," she said. "I want you to swear that if you ever hear anyone say anything about us going out, you'll tell them it's not true."

"Unless it is, right?" Dahlia scowled, and Rafe quickly raised his hands. "Just kidding. Mostly, I mean. Anyway, I swear. If I hear anyone say anything about us, I'll make sure they know we're not together."

"And that I have no interest in dating you."

"And that you have no interest in dating me. Okay?"

The truth was, it would be a pleasure to talk to someone about the ghosts who wasn't so . . . so whatever Chelsea was. Sarah and Hayley were nice, but Dahlia couldn't imagine talking to them about the ghosts or David Schank. Still . . . "One more thing. If you told anyone that I wanted to go out with you and you rejected me, you have to go back and tell them the truth."

Rafe winced. "Including my brother?"

Dahlia shrugged. She didn't care what his brother thought. "Anyone aside from your brother."

"Deal," he said immediately. He stuck out his hand, and Dahlia shook it. They were silent for a moment.

"So. Last night, Chelsea and I came this close" — she held up her forefinger and thumb, half an inch apart — "to Barry catching us sneaking around the pool after midnight. We were on the way to the maze. I think."

"Chelsea?" Rafe said. They walked back to the animal enclosure, leaving the "lightning guard" in the bushes below. "What were you doing sneaking around with *Chelsea*?"

"She hears ghosts." Dahlia ripped off a handful of grass and fed it to the goats.

*"What?"*

Dahlia took a deep breath and told Rafe about the ghosts, then all the rest, as they stood there feeding the goats. It took her longer than she expected to get through her memories of David Schank and the maze. Rafe didn't say much until she got to the failed attempt to follow the ghosts to the maze.

"You went down the main stairs?" He made a face. "No kidding he caught you."

"It was two in the morning. We didn't figure Barry lives down there."

Rafe glanced up at Barry's workshop. "Of course he was there," he said. "Haven't you noticed? He's always there when people go near the maze."

Without talking about it, they started walking back toward the camp, this time going around the front of the barn so as not to pass Barry's workshop.

"The thing is," Rafe said. "I don't know. It sounds like a joke.

251

A caretaker with the magical power to know when kids are going out of bounds."

"Yeah. It's hysterical."

"Still, when you eliminate the impossible, what's left — no matter how improbable — must be the truth."

"I saw the *Star Trek* movie too," Dahlia snapped.

"Actually, it's Sherlock Holmes," Rafe said. "I mean originally. The *Star Trek* mov —"

"The point is, how do you eliminate the impossible? Ghosts are impossible. So is possession. But I'm possessed by a guy who put the 72nd name of God into our camp's juniper maze."

"Whoa," Rafe said. "What?"

He stopped walking, and Dahlia stopped too. They were standing in front of the open barn door. Inside, the little kids were practicing a song to the tune of the *Sesame Street* theme song. For a moment, the only sound was the little kids singing, "*Saaaturday. Nobody works today.*"

"So . . ." Dahlia finally said. "Remember how I told you I was possessed by David Schank?"

"I remember you joking about —"

"I was serious. Anyway, last night I dreamed that Schank accidentally put the 72nd name of God into the maze."

"What? How is that even possible?" Rafe's lips twitched. "I hope that you're possessed. Because otherwise, I'd be seriously freaked out by how weird you are."

"What, because possession wouldn't freak you out?" She started up the hill again, and he followed her. "Everything comes back to that stupid maze. I have to get inside it."

"No problem." Rafe waved some gnats away from his face. "Tell you what. I distract Barry, and you and Chelsea sneak down there."

"You can't distract Barry," Dahlia said. "He ignores you when you're right in front of him."

"Fair point," he admitted. They walked past Barry's house and the dining hall in silence. "What if I set his house on fire?" Rafe said.

"Idiot. We aren't starting a fire in the middle of the camp."

"Just a small fire."

"Rafe. It's the hottest day of the summer."

"Okay. Okay. What about Tom? Your brother."

"I know who Tom is," Dahlia said.

"I mean, you should get him to distract Barry. He's a counselor. Barry can't just ignore him."

"Maybe," Dahlia said doubtfully. She thought of Barry's big hands around McMasters's neck. "Barry's dangerous. We need a better plan than just sending Tom to distract him with a question about tree benches or something."

Sarah and Hayley were sitting on the rec center porch. Hayley was playing guitar, but she stopped when she saw Dahlia and waved her over.

"Hey, Dahlia," Hayley called. "Come here for a sec. I have a question."

"We're not going out," Rafe said loudly. "Dahlia has no interest in dating me."

"Oh my God!" Sarah said. "Did you just ask her out?"

Rafe eyed Dahlia and she shook her head. "No," he said. "I'm just saying."

"Anyway," Hayley said. "We're doing an act for the bonfire tomorrow. Dahlia, I was thinking, do you want to do some magic tricks as part of it?"

*Magic tricks*, Dahlia thought. They were all about misdirection. It wasn't enough to distract Barry. They needed to specifically misdirect his attention.

"There's no bonfire tomorrow," Rafe told Hayley. "The woods are too dry with all the heat."

"Whatever," Hayley said. "They'll just have the acts without the fire."

"You can't do that," he said indignantly.

"Sure you can!" Sarah chirped. "Like when we have it indoors when it's raining."

"But you still have a fire when it's ind —"

"Come on, Rafe," Dahlia interrupted. She smiled apologetically at Hayley. "Sorry. Maybe next week."

"Oh my God! You're going to be here next week?" Sarah asked. "You're staying second session?"

Dahlia hesitated.

"She's thinking about it," Rafe said brightly. "That's what we were just talking about."

Sarah screamed, "Yay! That's awesome!"

Dahlia felt mildly guilty. "I'm still not sure. Anyway. Thanks for the invitation. See you guys."

As she walked away, she heard Hayley whisper to Sarah, "They're totally back together."

Dahlia kept walking.

# CHAPTER 34

Dahlia and Rafe didn't get a chance to talk to Chelsea until after the play that night. Every Friday, a different age group put on a play. This week's play was being put on by Tom's little campers and had something to do with *Sesame Street*. Dahlia wasn't sure exactly what the play was about, as most of the kids muttered their lines, and anyway, she spent the bulk of the performance scanning the overcrowded barn for Chelsea. She finally spotted her sitting near the back next to Joey Susskind.

As soon as the lights came on, Rafe and Dahlia made their way through the crowd to Chelsea. "I have to talk to you," Dahlia said.

Chelsea shook her head. "No way. We're done."

"Look. I'm going to talk to you," Dahlia said. "Do you want me to talk here, or do you want to come with me and talk in private?"

Chelsea looked around, but there was a solid press of campers between them and the door, and there was nowhere for her to go. She set her chin. "Right now is fine. The answer is no."

"I want you to listen to the ghosts for me one more time," Dahlia said.

Chelsea cast a quick sidelong glance at Joey, who was standing behind her chatting with Michal. "I have no idea what you're talking about."

This got Joey's attention. He gave Dahlia a friendly grin. "What?" he said. "What'd she say?"

"I have a plan to distract Barry while we get to the maze," Dahlia said quietly. "But I'm going to need your help once we're there."

"What did she say?" Joey said again. "Man, it's loud in here." To Chelsea, he said, "I'm going to cut out of Israeli dancing. Probably play b-ball for a while. You wanna hang out after?"

"Sure," Chelsea said.

"Great," Dahlia said sweetly. "So you're free now."

The crowd in front of them started pouring out the door. "No," Chelsea said. "I'm going to Israeli dancing. It's mandatory this year."

"You never go to Israeli dancing," Rafe said.

"Sure she does," Lisa said, overhearing Rafe. "We *love* Israeli dancing."

"Okay, name the first three dances," Rafe said. "Or any three dances."

"There's the one with the clapping," Lisa said.

Chelsea drew Dahlia aside while Lisa and Rafe walked out of the barn. "You're just going to harass me until I agree, aren't you?"

"Um." Dahlia considered. She really needed someone who could hear the ghosts, and she didn't know anyone else who could. "Yeah."

"I think you're, like, borderline autistic, you know that?"

"Oh my God, really?" Dahlia said. "I'm totally going to get that checked out."

Chelsea sighed and led Dahlia out of the barn. "I'll catch up to you guys later," she told Lisa and Michal. "I'm hanging out with the dorks for a few minutes."

She turned back to Dahlia and Rafe, and the three of them started walking back toward the cabins. Chelsea glanced at Rafe. "Wait. Since when are you talking to him again?"

"Since about three this afternoon," Rafe said brightly.

Chelsea shook her head. "Great. Like this wasn't dorky enough."

"What's dorky about talking to ghosts?" he said.

"Not the ghosts. You."

"Shut up," Dahlia said before Rafe could respond. "Both of you. Here's the deal." She told Chelsea about David Schank and what she proposed to do.

"So let me get this straight," Chelsea said. "You think Barry is going to be distracted by your brother waving some letters in his face?"

"Yeah," Dahlia said with more certainty than she felt. "They're not just any letters. They're a kind of magic word. I think Barry was sent by the Illuminated Ones, so I think the 72nd name will definitely distract him for the two minutes it will take for us to get into the maze."

"But why would he have stayed here for seventy years if the Illuminated Ones sent him?" Rafe said. "That part still makes no sense to me."

Dahlia shot Rafe a betrayed look, but his objection seemed to make it easier for Chelsea to agree with Dahlia. "Oh — and the rest of this makes sense?" she snapped at Rafe. "Moron."

They came to the girls' cabin. The lights were on, and they saw someone's silhouette moving around inside. Rafe sat down on the tree bench. "Fair point," he said mildly. "The part about none of this making sense, I mean."

Dahlia sat down next to him. "Anyway, I know a group was after this word, and I think they killed David Schank."

"Who went on to possess you?" Chelsea stayed standing, facing them from a few feet away.

Dahlia nodded.

"Well, so much for the whole 'you only live once' thing," Rafe said. Neither Dahlia nor Chelsea said anything, and he continued, "You know, like *You Only Live Twice*?"

"Could you please shut up?" Chelsea said.

"I was making a reference to an old James Bond movie," Rafe said.

Chelsea looked at him. "And I was making a reference to you shutting up." To Dahlia, she said, "I liked it better when you were mad at him. Anyway, you want me to come to the maze with you, so I can tell you what the ghosts are saying? Fine. This is the last time, though. Okay?"

"Okay."

"You promise. Whatever happens down there. No more harassing me about this stuff. Not another mention of ghosts ever."

"I said okay," Dahlia said.

"When are we going to do it?"

"We could do it Tuesday," Rafe said. "The CITs are planning their big —"

"Tomorrow," Dahlia interrupted. "We're doing it tomorrow. First session ends Sunday, and I'm leaving."

Rafe frowned. "You're still planning on leaving after first session?"

To her surprise, Dahlia felt a little pang at the thought herself. "Yep," she said. "Anyway, better to get this over with." *Before Chelsea can change her mind*, she thought. "I'll talk to Tom tomorrow morning, and we'll do it in the afternoon."

"All right," Chelsea said. "Tomorrow afternoon."

"During swimming," Rafe said. "It'll give us a reason to be down there. We'll synchronize our watches with Tom so we get the timing just right."

Chelsea groaned. "'Synchronize our watches.' This is just like a fantasy come true for you, isn't it?" She started walking away.

"Not at all," Rafe said. "In my fantasies you're a little nicer. Or you go to a different camp."

Chelsea held up her middle finger as she continued walking.

"Well." Rafe turned to Dahlia. "I think that went well, don't you?"

"Yeah," Dahlia said. "Actually, I do."

# CHAPTER 35

**D**ahlia held the piece of notebook paper out to Tom until he took it. If Schank hadn't spent months brooding on the name, she didn't think she could have done it, and even with his memories in her head, writing the unfamiliar Hebrew letters had been hard. It had taken her a dozen or so tries. Still, she was pretty sure she had finally gotten it right.

Funny to think there had been so much fuss over eighteen letters. At first glance, they didn't look special — just black ink on a piece of paper that she'd torn out of her little pocket notebook. Still, Dahlia was confident that they would work. After she'd finished writing the letters, her cheeks had felt flushed, her lips dry, like she was sitting too close to a fire. When she looked at them for more than a second or two, she had to concentrate on *not* understanding them. On *not* feeling their power. Tom didn't seem to notice anything special about what she'd written. He looked at the paper and glanced up. "You want me to show this to Barry — that's it?"

"Yeah," Dahlia said. "At exactly three this afternoon. We'll synchronize our watches."

"And why am I doing this?"

She hesitated. Chelsea and Rafe had both wanted to make up some story, but she didn't think that would work. Tom wasn't an idiot, and anyway, he was her brother. He should help them because it was the right thing to do. She'd decided that she would tell Tom the truth. Just not the whole truth.

"It'll distract him while we go to the maze."

"Riiight." Tom drew out the word. "Because it's a magic word, and you think Barry is some kind of magician."

"Yeah. It's the 72nd name of God. I'm almost positive it will distract him, at least for a few minutes."

"Wait — God has seventy-two names? What are the other seventy-one?"

Dahlia shrugged uncomfortably. "I don't know any of the others. Just that the kabbalists believe there are seventy-two names of God hidden in the Torah, and according to kabbala, this is the most important one."

"Kabbala." He shook his head. "You mean like what Madonna does?"

"Yeah. Like Madonna does. It used to be Jewish."

Tom looked out his window. Dahlia waited for him to remind her that she was supposed to be with one of the special clubs that met on Saturday afternoons. There were a few groups visible from the window, sitting in circles or playing games in the sports field next to the cabin.

He surprised her by saying, "Look, Dahl, Peter's a nice guy, but you can't take him too seriously."

"Peter? You think I'm learning this from Peter? He didn't . . . he didn't —" She was laughing too hard to even finish her sentence for a few seconds. "He didn't want to do anything in his club except chant *om* and do massages. I don't think there's anyone even in his stupid club anymore except for him and Wanda Sorkin. And I doubt those two are actually talking about Jewish mysticism, if you know what I mean."

Tom blinked. "Okay. So, if it's not Peter, where's all this stuff coming from? The Prof — I mean . . . is this coming from Rafe?"

"This is coming from me," Dahlia said. "And a book Peter found in the camp's library."

"And you figure this" — Tom waved the piece of paper — "will distract Barry while you infiltrate the maze? Tell me again — why do you even want to get in there?"

Dahlia chose her words carefully. "I think there may be something in the maze. Something that Barry doesn't want anyone to find."

He rubbed his eyes. "There's *nothing* in the maze, Dahlia. There's hardly even a maze. There's just a few feet of cleared path in a bunch of overgrown juniper bushes. It took us an hour to do that much."

"So no harm in us going down there, right?"

Tom leaned back on the wall next to his bed. "It just freaks me out to see you so obsessed with this."

The words burst from Dahlia. "It freaks you out? It freaks me out. I've been *dreaming* about Barry killing someone. Strangling them."

"Who? Those girls who disappeared?"

Dahlia shook her head. "A man. But I'm sure Barry had something to do with the missing girls."

"Right. Even though they went missing seventy years ago."

"Yeah. That's right."

"Even if Barry — or his uncle or grandfather or something — was involved in the girls disappearing, what would it help you to get into the maze? You think Barry keeps a journal down there or something?" He made his voice slow and drawling. " 'Dear world. My grandpappy killed those kids that Dahlia is obsessed with. Love, Barry.' "

Dahlia didn't say anything.

"Seriously, Dahl, what do you expect?"

"All I know is, every time anyone tries to get into the maze, Barry stops them. You've said yourself how he stopped you from clearing it out. There has to be something there."

"Yeah," Tom said. "Copperheads."

One of the groups had built a small fire and was cooking some kind of bread on it. The smell wafted in and made Dahlia's stomach grumble. "You believe that?"

Tom thought for a moment and slowly shook his head. "No. But I believe it more than anything you've said."

Dahlia sighed again. "So don't believe me. If it makes you feel better, tell yourself it's just a game that Rafe and Chelsea and I are playing. What's the worse that can happen? Barry will look at the Hebrew letters, grunt something, and go off to mow the lawn."

He stared out the window toward the campers gathered around the campfire. "You're going with Chelsea and Rafe, right?"

"Yeah."

He looked down at the letters.

"Please, Tom."

"Fine," he said. "Three p.m. today. You got it. Not because I believe any of this. Just because you're my sister."

"Finally," Dahlia said. "I knew there had to be an advantage to that sometime."

Tom looked a little hurt, then laughed. "Be careful down there. Maybe there really are snakes."

Dahlia stood to leave. "Thanks," she said. "Really."

CHAPTER **36**

**C**helsea wrapped her towel around her waist. "Okay," she said. "Let's get this little dork-u-drama over with."

She and Dahlia walked out of the cabin. Rafe was waiting on the tree bench, wearing his bathing suit, towel slung over his shoulder. Instead of flip-flops, though, he was wearing hiking boots.

"Hiking boots?" Chelsea looked at Rafe accusingly.

"I'm not wearing flip-flops into a blackberry bramble." Rafe hopped off the tree bench and led them behind the bathrooms. A small path ran down the hill toward the fire pit and the maze.

"I thought the bathing suits were your idea." Chelsea followed behind Rafe, with Dahlia bringing up the rear.

"Just the suits. Not the flip-flops. That way if we get caught, we can say we were going to the swimming pool by another path," Rafe said.

"Right. And why would you be wearing hiking boots to the swimming pool?" Chelsea didn't give Rafe a chance to answer. Dahlia figured she was talking mostly as a way to hide being nervous. "If I get Lyme disease, I'm going to kill you. And stop looking at my breasts."

"What?" Rafe glanced back at Chelsea and then quickly back in front of him. "I'm walking five steps ahead of you and don't have eyes on the back of my head. How could I be looking at your breasts? Or lack thereof."

"What?!" Chelsea said. "What did you just say?"

Dahlia glanced at her watch. 2:50. "C'mon," she said. "We have eleven minutes to get there."

She didn't know how Barry always knew when someone was approaching the maze, but she figured their best bet was to reach it a minute or so after Tom knocked on his door. Which meant they'd better hurry. She was leaving tomorrow morning, so she had to get into the maze today if she wanted to figure out what had happened to the girls. Not to mention what had happened to David Schank. Obviously he had died, but how? Had Barry murdered him, too?

She picked up her pace until she was jogging down the hill, passing the others and leading them toward the creek.

The sounds of the camp became more distant as they made their way into the woods, until all they could hear was the occasional shriek from the swimming pool. Once the swimming-pool sounds were above them, Dahlia veered left, deeper into the forest.

"Great," Chelsea muttered as they picked their way through the underbrush. "Poison ivy everywhere down here."

"Keep your voice down," Rafe hissed. A moment later, he said in a low voice, "We're going to check out ghosts, and you're worried about poison ivy?"

"Yeah," Chelsea said. "Two years ago I got poison ivy so bad I needed to get steroid shots every day for three weeks. The ghosts never hurt —"

"Hey!" A shout from the woods above them, where the larger path headed toward the pool. "Who's down there?"

Dahlia froze, then glanced at her watch. 2:56. They had five minutes to reach the maze.

# CHAPTER 37

# TOM

**T**om glanced at his watch. 2:56 p.m. He'd been hovering on the dining hall's porch for five minutes to make sure he got to Barry's house at exactly 3:00. He wondered again why he was doing this. It wasn't too late. He could just walk away.

He could imagine what Nicole would say. *You're getting just as weird as your freaky little sister.* He almost turned around then. But he had told Dahlia he would do this. Screw it. Screw Nicole, anyway. Dahlia was his sister, and he was going to wave the stupid paper in Barry's face, even if it was totally, irredeemably crazy.

He stared down the hill, tapping his fingers on the porch's wooden rail, then glanced at his watch again. 2:58 p.m.

Down the dirt road, he saw two small figures walking across the parking lot. He squinted after them. The plump blond one had to be Jaden. Tom sighed. He'd told them a dozen times they weren't allowed into the woods without a counselor.

He glanced at his watch. 2:59. He'd have to talk to Jaden and Mitchell later. Tom walked down the stairs and headed toward Barry's house.

"Hey, man!"

He spun around. Natan hurried down the dining hall stairs after him. "Hey there. You want something to eat?"

"Thanks, but no," Tom said. He wasn't sure why Natan liked him so much, but for some reason he was one of a handful of counselors that the head of the kitchen had taken a shine to. "Actually, I gotta go."

"C'mon, man. I got muffins just coming out of the oven for the afternoon snack. Good stuff."

Twenty yards ahead of them, Tom saw Barry's front door open. Barry stood there, looking around, almost like he was sniffing the air.

"Sorry," Tom said. He jogged toward the handyman's house, digging the scrap of paper out of his pocket. "Barry," he called. *Distract him before he catches their scent*, he thought, then he shook his head. Man, craziness was contagious.

He opened the gate to Barry's yard. The big black dog started barking and lunged out of his shaded corner.

Barry snapped his fingers, and the dog immediately bounded to his side. "Yeah?" Barry said.

Tom held up the sheet of paper. He didn't say anything, just walked across the yard and handed it to Barry. Barry took the paper and looked down at it.

He expected Barry to say something like, "What is this crap?" Instead, he took a deep breath and then relaxed. Tom had never registered the unnatural stiffness with which Barry held his shoulders until it was gone.

"You better come inside," Barry said.

# CHAPTER 38

# DAHLIA

**F**or a few seconds, the three of them just stood there. Dahlia nourished a faint hope that the counselor would keep going if they didn't say anything.

"Get up here!" the woman's voice called. "Don't make me come after you."

"All right, all right," Rafe said loudly. He glanced at Dahlia and Chelsea. "Keep going," he mouthed, and waved them on their way.

Rafe began picking his way through the bushes above them. "I'm coming," he called. "I just took a shortcut to get to the pool."

A few moments later, he became visible to the counselor above them. "Of course." The woman sounded disgusted. "Professor."

Moving as quietly as they could, Dahlia and Chelsea continued working their way deeper into the woods.

"Please don't call me that," Rafe said. "I was on my way to the pool."

"Why are you wearing hiking boots?"

"Ticks. Poison ivy . . ." Rafe's voice grew fainter as Chelsea and Dahlia kept walking. They cut directly down the hill until they came upon the large path that circled the boundaries of the camp's property. 2:59. They started jogging again. Dahlia could make out the darker bulk of the maze in the woods above them.

3:01. Perfect.

They came out in the small clearing around the maze's entrance. Since the last time she'd been down there, the maze had been completely surrounded by orange safety fencing, like the kind she'd sometimes seen around construction sites.

As she was looking for an opening, a movement within the maze caught Dahlia's eye. She walked closer to the fence and peered into the shadowed entrance.

"Ghost?" Chelsea said.

Dahlia shook her head uncertainly. She was almost sure she'd seen something, but whatever it was, it was gone now.

The woods were silent except for the drone of insects and the distant sounds of kids shouting and cannonballing into the swimming pool above them. It suddenly seemed ridiculous that they were looking for ghosts in the middle of a sunlit afternoon. There was just the bright orange fencing; the juniper hedges, grown twice as tall as she was; and the scrub weeds that the maze work group hadn't gotten to clearing.

"Look." Chelsea pointed to where a raccoon or something had dug a small hole beneath the fence, in the process pulling some of the fencing loose. She gave the fence a tug, making the opening a little bigger.

"Huh," Dahlia said. She put her hands next to Chelsea's and threw her weight back. She may as well not have bothered. The rest of the fence was firmly anchored. She knelt down. Between the hole in the ground and the gap in the fence, there was just about enough room for a small person to squeeze through. "I think I could —"

"Go on," Chelsea said.

Dahlia crouched before the hole. Houdini had squirmed through way smaller openings, even bound hand and foot. She lay down and wriggled through on her stomach, hands first, then her feet.

"It's not *that* small of an opening," Chelsea said. She crawled through after Dahlia on her hands and knees. "Ow!" Dahlia glanced back to see that Chelsea had scratched her calf on the ragged tip of the fence. A thin bead of blood appeared on her leg.

"You okay?"

Chelsea rose, rubbing her calf. "I'm fine. Come on."

Dahlia stepped toward the maze's entrance. Dried juniper needles crunched beneath her flip-flops and pricked the tips of her toes.

Side by side, she and Chelsea walked into the maze.

When Dahlia was ten, her parents had taken her hiking in a small park a few miles from their house. One portion of the hike had run parallel to a huge power line, with a dozen thick metal wires running over the trail. Her father had said it was a major relay in the East Coast power grid. The power line had been flanked on either side by huge fields of wildflowers, but the main thing that Dahlia remembered was the hum that the lines gave off. The energy was so concentrated that you could *hear* the power running through the thick wires.

Stepping into the maze, Dahlia experienced the same feeling. She didn't hear anything, but she felt it — a deep thrum of power running through the labyrinth.

They rounded the first turn of the maze and confronted the tangled undergrowth that Tom's work group hadn't cleared. "*Malchut*," a voice said. It took Dahlia a moment to realize that it was her own voice . . . that she was the one talking. She could feel David Schank coming to the front of her mind, feel him visualizing the roots of a tree, the foundation of a huge golden castle. The golden castle had ten towers laid out in a perfect circle around the castle's perimeter, and . . .

Dahlia blinked. The tangled bushes and undergrowth were gone. The maze before them was perfectly manicured, the juniper bushes trimmed neatly around a lush, grassy path, shimmering in the late afternoon sun.

"Wow," Chelsea said. "Did you do that?"

Dahlia hesitated. "Um. Define *you*."

The feeling of power was even stronger now. It felt like the energy was streaming right in through the top of her head, flooding her whole body.

"Feels good, right?" a man's voice asked companionably. Dahlia and Chelsea whirled to see a tall man standing behind them. He wasn't transparent, or warped, or throbbing. He looked as solid as Chelsea did to Dahlia. More solid even, as he seemed somehow filled with the maze's power. "Welcome to my maze!"

Even without David inside her head, Dahlia would have recognized him from the visions. "McMasters," she said.

He was wearing a faded baseball hat, but that was where the resemblance to Barry ended. McMasters had a much thinner, much more expressive face. Handsome, even, with piercing blue eyes and a flawless, pale complexion. He inclined his head, winked brightly at her. "The original version. Accept no imitations!"

She glanced at Chelsea. "Do you —"

"I see him," Chelsea said, her eyes not leaving McMasters. "You're McMasters. McMasters. With the daughters and wife and . . ." Her voice trailed off.

He briskly shook his head, chuckling. "Aw, no. Actually, never married. Can't blame the kids for embellishing a story. I mean, a maze is pretty boring, for Pete's sake."

His neck was bruised a deep purple.

"You were David's helper, and Barry killed you, didn't he?" Dahlia said. "Then he stole your identity."

McMasters's face went so still it was hard to imagine he had ever smiled. "Something like that," he said. "Not quite the way you're thinking."

Dahlia belatedly became aware that the David part of her was somewhere between extremely excited and extremely angry. "What?" she said. "What happened? I remember lots about you, but I never quite remember the stuff at the end."

"That's natural enough. Death can be traumatic. Makes remembering harder." McMasters smiled, the same "aw-shucks" smile he'd had a moment before. "To be honest, I did what I could to slow Schank's memories down. Didn't want them to distract you. Guess no reason to worry now."

And like that, the memories flooded back.

# CHAPTER 39

# DAVID

**D**avid had intended to wake up early to continue uprooting the maze, but after spending the darkest hours of the night awake in his bed, picturing the Illuminated Ones getting closer, he slept in. The late-morning sunlight was streaming through the window when he woke. He immediately sensed the completed maze on the hillside below the house. It felt *more* powerful today, despite the handful of seedlings he'd uprooted.

As he sat up, he realized why the maze felt more powerful. Two girls. Terrified and lost. Probably the same little girls he'd seen playing in the woods throughout the summer. They must have wandered into the maze just before he woke up. And now, for some reason, they couldn't get themselves out. He could feel their spirits bleeding into the maze, giving it more power even as the girls grew weaker.

He dressed quickly and rushed out of the house, shoelaces flapping. He buckled his belt as he jogged down the hill. High above, he felt a storm gathering.

"David. Your maze looks fantastic." McMasters was sitting on the stump outside the barn where he split logs for kindling. There was a pile of chopped wood next to him.

David didn't pause as he ran past him. "McMasters. Come with me. Bring your ax."

McMasters fell in next to him, whistling a tuneless melody. "Where are we going? It looks sunny now, but the clouds are rolling in fast. Let me tell you, mister, summer storms are no time to get caught in the woods."

David glanced to his left and saw the horizon was already dark, illuminated by occasional flashes of heat lightning. "It doesn't matter," he said. "Come on."

"You say that now," McMasters said, jogging after David. "Just wait until the lightning is all around you."

David shook his head and quickened his pace, desperate to get to the maze. What the devil was keeping the girls inside the thing? Something to do with the 72nd name, but what? The spiritually unaware should have passed through the maze without pause, without even realizing how close they were to the divine. And they were only children.

A minute or two later, he saw the labyrinth through the trees. He froze. The seedlings were gone. In their place was a labyrinth of full-grown juniper bushes. Each one was half again his height, if not more.

Beside him, McMasters exhaled. "Whoa. I didn't think even juniper grew *that* fast."

David stared at the juniper bushes. The spiritual energy the girls had bled into the maze had somehow quickened the plants' growth. Once he rescued the girls, he'd need McMasters's ax to even begin clearing the trees. "C'mon," he said.

By the time they got to the maze's entrance, the sky was deep gray overhead. The rain hadn't reached them yet, but David could hear the drops approaching in the woods around them. He hesitated for a moment, trying to feel the girls. Ah. There they were. Their spirits were weakening fast, but they were still alive, trapped in one of the higher dimensions. He stepped up to the entrance. "I need to put something right with the maze," he said to McMasters. "While I'm in there, I want you to start chopping down the juniper bushes."

"Whoa," McMasters said. "You lost me. Weren't you the one dead set to finish the ding-dang thing?"

"I made a mistake. Two little girls got trapped in there."

"What? Trapped?" McMasters said. "Two little girls?" He didn't sound surprised.

"Yeah. I'm going to go in there, carry them out, and then we're going to have to chop —" He paused, half turned toward McMasters, then closed his eyes for a moment. *In drerd arayn. The earth should swallow him.* He'd been a fool. "You knew they were there."

"Sure did," McMasters said brightly. "I helped them into it. Didn't take much — a little nudge here, a push there. Little girls are curious as cats, ain't they?"

"What have you done?"

"Me? Not much. Just, ah, encouraged them to step into the entrance. See, I had this hunch. The way I figure it is, kids — even without any spiritual training — they got something that makes them receptive to the higher dimensions. Problem is, without the training, they can only make it so far. Then, well, shoot . . . mazes are always easier to get into than out of, ain't they? Turns

277

out that once you get into the higher dimensions of your labyrinth, it's real hard to turn around. You either go all the way through it . . . or you don't."

David tried to enter the maze, but McMasters's arm was in his way, as broad and strong as a tree trunk. "'Fraid I can't let you in there, David."

"You're him. It. The Most Illuminated One," David said. "How did you find me?"

McMasters shrugged. "Finding you was easy. You kept thinking about the name, wandering around the city like some little lost sheep. I figured the real challenge would be getting you to teach it to me. It wasn't some secret we could just torture out of you, know what I mean?"

The rain started to patter around them. McMasters didn't look away from David. "Anywho . . . When your buddy sent you out this way, I got here a few hours earlier. I figured I'd earn your trust, get you to teach me the name. Then I saw what you were doing, and . . ." He glanced at the maze and shrugged again. ". . . here we are."

David didn't say anything, and after a second or two, McMasters kept talking. "Funny thing is, the maze really *was* your buddy's idea — his little joke, I guess. When I killed his guy up here, this crazy hermit who'd been living in the house when your buddy bought the place, I figured it couldn't hurt to go along with it. Just a stroke of luck the way things worked out. You didn't have to teach me nothing. I walked through the maze last night, and here we are."

All David could think of was the little girls wandering in the maze, getting weaker. "So you have the name now," he said. "Let the girls go."

"Can't do it, friend." McMasters's teeth glinted through the rain when he smiled. "Turns out that the maze with those girls in it is better, much better, than the name by itself. It's a living medallion. It's a spell made out of earth and blood and wood. It's a —"

"Prayer," David said. He looked up at the sky. The distant lightning was closer now, and he had some dim hope that God would strike the man down. Surely that wasn't too much to ask.

"You say potato, I say patahta. The point is, it's more power from that magic word of yours than you'd get from a lifetime of meditating on it."

"The point isn't power —"

"You're right. The point isn't power. Although the power is nice. Real nice." McMasters casually raised one arm, and lightning turned the sky white. A few seconds later, thunder roared overhead. "The point is eternal life. And that, my friend, is what this power is going to give me. An eternity to spend hunting down every secret this world has hidden away."

"Please. The 72nd name will open other routes to power." David's voice sounded tinny with his ears still ringing with the thunder. "You can still just let the girls go."

The man shook his head briskly. "Their life force along with the maze makes things so . . . easy. All I need is to get some boys in there, balance out the energies, and I won't need to wait for a storm to do *this*."

He lifted his arms again, and again the lightning crashed, the thunder pealed.

"A few more kids after that, and I won't need to wait for anything ever again. Mind you, I won't take any more kids than are useful. A few dozen. A few hundred. No more than necessary."

David could feel McMasters throbbing with the power of the maze. The pupils of his eyes were dilated like the eyes of drug addicts David had seen in the city. McMasters turned his face toward the sky, and David seized his chance.

Or tried to. He dodged around McMasters and started to run toward the maze's entrance, but McMasters effortlessly hooked his rear leg with the blunt edge of the ax. David tumbled down the slight hill, coming to a stop a few feet from the entrance. McMasters — even now David had a hard time thinking of him as the Most Illuminated One — crouched beside him.

"I'm afraid I can't let you in the maze again, guy." His tone sounded honest, regretful. So very American. No wonder David hadn't suspected him. "You have no idea how long I've been looking — how many useless secrets I've waded through, on my way to . . . this." McMasters patted David's shoulder, then stood. "Don't blame yourself. You weren't cut out to keep secrets. The good news is, that's not going to be a problem for you anymore." He tilted his head back to face the sky and spread his arms. The thunder roared overhead, even louder.

David didn't bother climbing to his feet. He blinked the rain out of his face, thinking furiously. There was one chance. One chance to save the girls. Or at least to stop McMasters from taking more children. He used his forefinger to trace the figure of a man in the dirt beneath him. The figure's outline immediately filled with rain water.

David glanced up at McMasters, wondering how he had ever thought the man had a soft face. His face was hard and angular and driven. The one thing that David had seen right were his eyes — just as penetrating and blue as David had always thought. He had them open now, staring straight up at the sky, gathering more power from the storm overhead, barely paying attention to David.

David turned back to the figure he'd sketched in the earth. He retraced the head, tearing the fingernail of his index finger as he did so. He kept redrawing the figure anyway, digging deeper, letting his blood trickle into the watery outline. The blood would help.

"Don't be a sore loser, David," McMasters said in between two claps of thunder. His voice sounded deeper, stronger. The lightning flashed closer overhead. "Nothing you can draw could possibly rival the maze for power."

He was right, of course, but David wasn't trying a big undertaking like the maze. He wasn't attempting anything that hadn't been done many times before. There. The figure was done. The head, the arms, the legs. He leaned down and sketched a few lines on the figure's forehead. The lightning flashed closer, and the earth below him surged. "Protect them," he whispered. "Stop him. Don't let any more children in there."

He glanced toward the maze, wishing he had the chance to walk it just one more time.

Then the lightning was no longer close, but upon him.

# CHAPTER 40

**D**avid didn't hurt. There had been a moment of searing pain, but that was over now. Everything was over now.

Only his guilt, his desire to make things right, kept his spirit tethered to his body. The girls were still trapped in the maze. *His* maze. He hovered above his corpse, watching as the golem he had summoned rose from the earth. In seconds, it expanded from the little figure he'd traced into the mud to become taller than David. Stockier too. The holy name glowed like fire on its forehead, and there was a soft hiss as the rain pattered against the fiery letters.

The golem stood there frowning for a moment before heavily walking a few paces to where the lightning had thrown David's body. He crouched and placed his thick fingers on David's neck.

Behind the golem, McMasters pronounced the 72nd name of God. Then, in a ringing voice, he said, "I am your master!" His voice was clear and confident. He took a few steps closer to the golem. "Do you understand me?"

The golem nodded slowly. Around them, the rain kept pattering through the trees, the shadows growing longer in the dust. David looked down at his corpse and tried to imagine the feel of the cooling raindrops on his seared skin. He felt nothing.

"I am your master," McMasters repeated to the golem. "Your first task is to dispose of this man's body. There's a pigpen up the road. Take the body there." He pointed up the hill, and the golem slowly turned to look that direction.

Even dead, David felt a stab of revulsion. Eaten by those unclean creatures? Was there no mercy in this world?

"Then find two boys for me and bring them to the maze."

The golem didn't move, still staring up the hill.

"Go," McMasters said.

The golem slowly turned back toward McMasters. For a moment, he simply stared at him. The eyes were the most human part of the golem, large and brown, strangely naked, with no eyelashes or eyebrows to conceal them.

McMasters said the 72nd name of God once more. David felt the world shiver, become a bit more attuned to McMasters. "By the name you wear on your forehead, I command you!"

The golem moved so fast, David barely registered his movement: One moment the golem was staring at McMasters, the next he was clutching the man's neck with his right hand. He lifted McMasters off the ground and held him at arm's length.

"I was summoned," the golem said slowly, "to protect children."

McMasters kicked once, twice, and went still, his face a purplish blue. The golem slowly eased McMasters's body to the ground.

"And you," he said to David's corpse. "Idiot. Building your cursed maze, then summoning me when it's too late to keep the girls out of it."

*It's not too late*, David tried to say. *They're still alive.*

He wasn't sure if the golem heard him, but after a moment the creature stepped toward the labyrinth's entrance and began to walk through it. David could see the girls clearly now, sobbing in one of the maze's higher dimensions, but the golem strode past them, moving right through the older one. He seemed to have no sense of the higher dimensions at all. The golem didn't pause until he reached the center of the labyrinth. He looked around and sighed. Then he glanced directly at David's spirit. "You still there?"

*Yes.* David tried to say. *Yes. Yes. I'm here. The girls are here. Free them. Please. Show them the way out. The maze's number is sixty-eight.*

The golem hesitated, then started walking out of the labyrinth. "You made me from mud, rabbi. I'm no mystic. I can barely sense you, and you're the guy who made me." It was full night by then, but the golem paced through the maze quickly and certainly. He emerged and slung McMasters's body over his shoulder. "Those girls are out of my reach." He trudged up the hill without a backward glance.

Being dead, David couldn't scream. He couldn't curse. He could only watch the girls grow weaker with hunger and thirst. Watch them die, still trapped in his maze. Watch their dead spirits awaken, still trapped in the maze. There were no remnants of the girls for searchers to find when they showed up later that day — just an empty hedge maze looking forlorn among the untended fields and scrub forest.

The next morning, a few men from the Philadelphia burial society — the closest Jewish community — came and took his body for burial. The golem, dressed in McMasters's clothes, introduced himself as Ned McMasters and helped them carry David's body across the river.

And that, for almost seventy-two years, was that.

**R**emembering was fast. Faster than fast. It took no time at all. Dahlia was still standing with Chelsea and McMasters in the maze. Chelsea was talking to McMasters.

"It's — ah — too bad about being dead and all." Chelsea's voice had regained its usual edge of impatience. "But we're here for the girls. Where are they?"

McMasters shrugged, made a vague gesture. "They're around. Without a solid electric storm, it's tough for me to keep track of them. Least it used to be. That'll change soon enough." He winked at Dahlia. "Thanks to you."

Dahlia felt a flash of anger and guilt from David's spirit that was so intense she gasped. Only then did she put it all together. She remembered the little hole in the fence, and the movement from within the maze that she'd seen when she and Chelsea got here.

"Oh no," she said. It had seemed like such a good idea to have Tom distract Barry.

"What?" Chelsea said.

"It was a trick," Dahlia said. "You remember those kids Barry caught the other night? He was keeping them safe. Keeping them out of the maze. For seventy-two years, Barry kept kids out of the maze. And we were the suckers who distracted him long enough for McMasters to get what he wanted. A couple of little boys to suck dry." She took a step backward, suddenly worried that the maze's exit would have disappeared. But around the turn, she could still see the fence. She could even still hear the kids at the pool, although the surrounding greenery dampened the sounds somewhat. "Get out of here, Chelsea."

McMasters laughed, a relaxed, easy laugh. "Don't you want to see my new guests?"

David's anger surged, overwhelming her. "I'll free them," David said, Dahlia's voice sounding hoarse and manlike. "And I'll send you to Gehenna where you belong."

"Oh, David," McMasters said softly. "Always trying so hard, and always so, so late." He flicked his fingers nonchalantly at Dahlia. "Go away. Leave the girl alone."

And like that, David Schank was gone from Dahlia's head. It felt terrifying. It felt wonderful. It felt like she'd taken off a heavy winter jacket she'd been wearing all summer.

"That's better, right?" McMasters said. "I tried to help you before, to get him out of your mind, but I was too weak. Now I'm stronger." He smiled again, the same simple, happy smile. "It's the least I could do after you distracted the golem for me."

Dahlia didn't say anything.

"Don't feel too bad about that. Schank's guilt would have made it hard for anyone to think straight."

"That's why you brought the girls to the cabin that last time, isn't it?" Dahlia said. "Just to push Schank into doing something.

You wanted to get him — us — focused on getting into the maze. So we'd have to distract Barry." She was disgusted at herself for falling for it. Basic misdirection.

McMasters grinned. "You're sharp as a tack, aren't you? Remind me of myself at your age."

Chelsea backed toward the entrance. "Come on, Dahlia."

"Don't expect your friend to understand," he said to Dahlia mildly. "She's not like us."

"I'm nothing like you," Dahlia said.

"Aren't you? You like knowledge. Especially secrets. You don't really like other people. You're closer to *me* than you are to that poor old spirit I just sent home." McMasters shook his head in what seemed like genuine sadness. "Smart guy, but so blinded by super-stition. I couldn't teach him a thing." He took a step closer to Dahlia. "You — you, I could teach. I could show you real magic. You like magic, don't you?"

Dahlia hesitated. He wasn't lying. She could feel it. There was power here that she could learn to use however she wanted. She could figure out the way the world *really* worked. She could . . .

She remembered the way Amelia and Claudia had laughed at her magic trick. Claudia's sad little face when McMasters dragged her through the cabin wall.

"Let the kids go," she said.

# CHAPTER 42

# TOM

The inside of Barry's house was strangely normal. Tom followed Barry down the front hallway to a small, neat living room with a hardwood floor, a threadbare sofa against one wall and a television perched against another. A fan spun in the back corner. The dog walked over to a pile of cushions to one side of the back door, lay down, and began worrying a small rubber bone, paying no further attention to Tom.

Barry took off his hat and sunglasses and looked at Tom. "So," he said. He ran his fingers through his fine white hair. "What are we going to do about this?"

Tom couldn't believe he had never noticed how strange looking Barry was. His face looked unfinished, like a sculptor had roughed out a human head and then walked away without bothering to add the eyelashes, the eyebrows, and the other details that make a face look real. And his forehead . . . There was this weird yellowish tattoo on his forehead. It was hardly visible when the sunlight hit him straight on, but every time Barry moved his head, Tom caught a glimpse of what looked like Hebrew letters. This on a man who had always acted like he didn't speak a word of Hebrew.

"What do you mean?" Tom said.

Barry held up the paper. "This makes for a bit of a situation, know what I'm sayin'? You having the 72nd name, what with the maze so active these days." He shook his head and met Tom's eyes. "But if you know anything at all, you wouldn't have shown me the name if you were here to use the maze. So what do you want?"

"What if I *was* here to use the maze?"

Barry regarded him for a moment. "Now that depends," he said. "If you were . . . ah, 'illuminated,' I reckon I'd kill you."

Despite his threatening words, Barry's voice was far softer than usual. For some reason, Tom found this *more* scary rather than less. He wished he had gotten one of the Israeli counselors to come with him — one of the ones who had been a commando in the army.

Barry shook his head. "You don't smell like that, though. I reckon you're here to clean up the mess. Those two little girls still trapped in the maze, along with that nasty old ghost. That right? So what do you want from me?"

Tom hesitated. What he really wanted was to get out of the little room and get back to the real world where things made sense. But he had promised Dahlia to keep the guy distracted. "Who are you?" he said.

"Me?" Barry shrugged. It was an awkward shrug — not because he was so old, as Tom had always thought, but because his shoulders moved more than they should. "I'm just the guy who's been stuck here for seventy-two years, making sure no more kids walk into the maze."

If it had been anyone else, Tom would have laughed. Even now, for a split second he wondered if Barry and Dahlia had cooked this whole thing up just as a joke. But it was all too . . . weird.

"Why would you . . ." Tom caught himself just before he asked about the maze. He was supposed to be distracting the guy from the maze, not reminding him of it. Instead, he said. "Seventy-two years? There was no camp here seventy-two years ago."

"No," Barry said. "But there was a construction site. Not that any construction ever happened on it. A site with a caretaker called Ned McMasters." His lips quirked. "A few of them, actually. The final Ned McMasters ended up being me. When the mobster who owned the place sold it, I didn't find out the buyers planned to set up a summer camp here until it was too late. By then, the best I could do was convince them to hire me as the new camp's caretaker."

"But . . ." Tom said. It was hard to keep talking with his skin crawling, and every instinct he had telling him to get out of Barry's house. "You couldn't . . . no one could have been the caretaker for that long. Someone would have noticed."

Barry snorted. "Nobody notices the caretaker. Not so long as the lawns get mowed. Anyway, it's not like I was the same care-taker all that time. In 1972, I let the camp committee know I was sick. Never said what was wrong with me. Just that I was so sick that my nephew, Barry, was going to start helping out around here. After a few months I let them know my uncle had passed on. They hired me later that week."

"But didn't anyone notice that you looked exactly like your —"

"But, but, but," Barry mimicked. He waved his hand dismissively. "Sure people noticed. No one cared. The caretaker looks just like his uncle. So what?"

"What about the neighbors?" Tom asked. "Didn't any of —"

"Enough," Barry interrupted. "You still haven't answered my question. What do you want with me?"

Tom hesitated. It had to have been five minutes by now. It felt like he'd been talking to the guy for hours. "Nothing," he said. "Just to distract you for a few minutes."

Barry wrinkled his forehead. It was a strange, unnatural expression, more like a very bad actor pretending to be puzzled than someone actually being puzzled. Then he sniffed the air. His eyes widened. "You idiot."

He rushed to his front door, thrusting a cigarette between his teeth and jamming his hat on his head as he ran out of the house. It was like a disguise, Tom realized belatedly. You saw so little of his face, you couldn't see how weird he looked.

Tom jogged after the — whatever Barry was. To his surprise, he could barely keep up. Each of Barry's steps was jerky, but they mounted up quickly. He didn't show any signs of being out of breath either. His voice retained its same slow drawl as he pulled away. "Stupid idiot . . . distracting me. Four more kids."

"Four more?" Tom gasped, out of breath. By now he was sprinting flat out. Barry might have answered, but Tom was too far behind to hear him.

CHAPTER **43**

# DAHLIA

"**I** can't let the boys go," McMasters said with transparently false regret. "They're lost in the higher dimensions, and nobody can do anything for them now. On the bright side, at least the girls will have some company."

"I'm going to get them out," Dahlia said. "I'm going to stop you."

"You can't stop me," McMasters said mildly. "It's too late for that. All you can do is stop yourself from reaching your true potential."

"Great. She'll take that option." Chelsea's voice startled Dahlia. She'd almost forgotten the other girl was there. Chelsea seized Dahlia's hand and yanked her back toward the entrance. Whatever it was that had been keeping Dahlia there — curiosity, orneriness, whatever — broke. She turned and ran.

Or tried to run. They seemed to be moving in slow motion. She could feel McMasters walking after them, easily keeping pace. She and Chelsea slowly rounded the corner and slowly continued out of the maze's entrance.

Once she was out of the maze, time seemed to catch up with her. Dahlia threw herself to the ground and squeezed through the gap in the fence, suddenly conscious that she didn't feel the thrum of power anymore. She turned around to help Chelsea.

Chelsea wasn't there.

Dahlia rose and looked through the fence. She didn't see McMasters, but for a moment she saw Chelsea standing just within the entrance of the maze. Her mouth was moving, saying something, but Dahlia heard nothing but the usual forest sounds: insects and birdsong, and the far-off shouts of the campers at the pool.

And then, as she watched, Chelsea grew smaller. It was like watching someone fall down a deep hole in slow motion. Somehow — without walking or even moving her feet — Chelsea was getting farther and farther from Dahlia. In moments, Dahlia couldn't see her at all.

She heard McMasters's voice, little more than a whisper blending in with the drone of a nearby wasp nest. "Bleeding in the maze," he said. "Bad move if you want to leave again."

"Chelsea!" Dahlia screamed.

The next few moments were a blur. Dahlia struggled to get back to the maze, but she couldn't seem to crawl under the fence. Someone had hold of her foot and was pulling her back. Then a tall figure was leaning over her, grasping her shoulder and shouting. Another tall figure had hold of the first figure and was shouting too.

Slowly, meaning penetrated. She was on the ground, and Barry was holding her shoulders, shouting, "Where are they? Where are they?" Tom was standing next to him, futilely trying to drag Barry away from her.

Dahlia pointed into the maze. "In there," she said weakly. "Three kids, I think."

Barry released her. "Idiot! I told you to get out of here. Weren't the wasps enough to get your attention?"

Tom knelt beside her, getting between her and Barry. "Leave her alone," he said. "She's just a kid."

"Just a kid," Barry said. He stared at Dahlia, then reluctantly nodded. "Maybe she is. Now." He turned and grabbed the steel post holding up the orange fence webbing. He bent it like it was made of clay. "Get her back to camp."

Dahlia sat up. "Chelsea's in there. She bled in the maze, so she couldn't leave."

"Huh." Barry stepped through the hole he'd made in the fence. "He's getting stronger. The boys bled in the maze too, but he couldn't keep them in here."

"You knew he was after the boys?" Dahlia said.

"I was there when they got scratched up in this idiot's work group." Barry hooked a thumb at Tom, then turned to face the maze's entrance. "Even with their blood, the ghost couldn't do much to the boys as long I kept them out of the maze. Which I was just doing just fine."

"Until I got Tom to distract you." Dahlia looked down at the scuffed dirt around the fence. McMasters's spirit must have been spying on them the whole time. The minute Tom knocked on Barry's door, McMasters had the boys ready to enter the maze.

Tom made a weird noise, like someone had kicked him in the stomach. "I saw two of my kids headed down to the woods before. Jaden and Mitchell. Is that who you're talking about?"

Dahlia looked at Barry, who was standing in the maze's entrance with his back to them. "You'll get them out, won't you?"

she said to him. He was a golem. Protecting children was what they did, right?

Barry didn't turn around. "If they're trapped in the maze? Probably not. You'd need to be a *rabbi*" — he put a world of loathing into the word — "and a master of the name to do that. The higher dimensions are off-limits to a dumb old mud-man like me." He stepped into the maze without looking back at her.

Tom and Dahlia stood there. It seemed impossible to her that the sun was so bright, that kids were still playing at the pool, when three campers had just been swallowed whole by the maze and the monster who lived there.

"Man," Tom said. "And I thought *I* didn't like synagogue. That guy really doesn't like rabbis." Despite his casual tone, his hands were clenched so tightly into fists that his knuckles were white. After a second, he stepped after Barry, but Dahlia seized his arm before he could pass through the fence.

"I have to take a look," he said. "Maybe I can —"

"Get trapped in there too?" Dahlia shook her head and tightened her grip until Tom winced. "No way. I dragged Chelsea . . . I basically blackmailed her into coming down here with me. This is my fault." She released Tom and moved toward the opening Barry had bent in the fence.

Barry emerged from the maze's entrance before she got there. "They're not there," he said. "Not your friend . . . Not the little boys. There's just the first turn cleared, then the solid brush. They must be trapped in one of the higher dimensions, just like those little girls. Thanks to your idiot rabbi friend."

"David wasn't a rabbi," Dahlia said. "Just a kid."

"He made me. That makes him a rabbi." Barry turned to Tom. "Take her back to her bunk. Tell the head of the camp that you're missing three campers." He sighed. "You can look for them in the woods, but you won't find them."

"They're not in the woods," Dahlia said. "They're in the maze."

Barry looked at her for a moment, no emotion on his face. "Sure they are. You want to tell your friends that? Do you *want* to lead more people into the maze?"

"No. Just me," Dahlia said.

"You're not going back in the maze," Tom said. Then, to Barry, "What can we do?"

"Call the missing kids' parents," Barry said. "Get ready to close this place down. Stupid to have a summer camp so close to the maze, anyway. 'Specially now that he's got more kids in there."

"There must be something else —" Tom said.

"Keep an eye on your sister. Three missing campers are enough. And each one makes McMasters stronger." Barry looked past them into the woods. "It's going to be harder to keep kids out now."

"Let me go back in the maze," Dahlia insisted. "I can help them."

"Yeah?" Barry said. "How you gonna do that?"

She didn't have an answer. Barry stood there, arms folded across his chest. She'd have more luck getting past a bear. "The idiot who made this mess gave me one job," he said. "Stop children from getting into the maze. I failed three times today. That's enough."

"Why didn't you just knock down the maze seventy years ago?" Dahlia said.

Barry stared at her. "You think I didn't try, genius? You notice anything special about the maze? A nasty old guy talking to you, maybe? It's impossible to take down any part of this thing as long as his spirit's tangled up in it."

He didn't say anything more, just glared, until Dahlia finally let Tom lead her up the hill. She felt like she should cry, but she was too dry, too guilty. Chelsea and the two little boys would die in the maze, just like the girls had seventy-two years ago. McMasters would suck up their life force like a rechargeable battery sucking up electric current. Then, if he felt like it — or really, *when* he felt like it — he'd draw more kids to the maze and get more power. Barry would try to stop him, but the more powerful McMasters got, the less Barry could do. And it was her fault. No wonder McMasters had been so keen to teach her.

# CHAPTER 44

The next few hours passed in a blur. Dahlia wasn't sure what exactly Tom told the other counselors, but soon every camper in the camp was called back to their bunk.

A few crisp moments intruded through her misery. Lisa glaring at Dahlia. Sarah saying confidently, "It's a trick. This is the beginning of some kind of special activity. How could they even know three kids were missing this quickly? I mean, Chelsea was here at lunch." Rafe begging her to tell him what happened. Dahlia trying to, but somehow missing the main point: that it was all her fault, that three more kids would die in the maze because of her.

Alyssa told them with transparently false calm that half the counselors were blanketing the woods looking for the missing campers, and that no one should worry, they'd find them soon.

They still hadn't found them by dinner, of course. As if in response to the mood in the camp, the sky outside had rapidly grown overcast, and on the horizon, Dahlia saw black storm clouds moving closer.

After dinner, back at the cabins, there was a flurry of packing. Everyone was being sent home. Second session was canceled.

"Dahlia. Dahlia, you have to pack. Half the bunk is already at the dining hall."

Dahlia blinked and found she was sitting on the bare mattress on Eileen's bed, staring out the window at the rain beginning to mist down. Alyssa was next to her, gently touching her arm. "We're waiting there for the parents."

"Right. Sorry," Dahlia mumbled. She dutifully rose, pulled her clothes from her cubby, and piled them on her bed, stripping her bedsheets as she did so. She pushed the pile into her trunk, but she couldn't get the lid closed.

Heavy footsteps on the front steps. A knock on the door. "Hello?"

"Come in," Alyssa said.

Ofer walked into the room, bringing the smell of the incoming storm with him. He nodded dolefully at the remaining girls. "The boys are all already at the dining hall," he told Alyssa. "I come to help bring the rest of the girls over. Better we get them all there before it's dark."

Alyssa took his arm and steered him back outside. Still, her voice was clearly audible to Dahlia. "Any luck?" she asked.

"Nothing. We walk every inch of woods." Ofer's voice sounded heavy, leaden, his accent more pronounced than ever. "And it looks like it will to rain before the police dogs can scent their trail."

Through the screen, Dahlia saw Alyssa's shoulders slump and heard a sob. After a second, she said, "Most of the girls are done packing — you take them to the dining hall, and I'll bring the rest in a few minutes."

Ofer chaperoned nearly all the girls to the dining hall, leaving only Michal, Lisa, and Dahlia in the cabin to finish their packing. Alyssa waited on the front steps, staring glumly into the distance.

No one had spoken for what felt like hours when Lisa turned to Dahlia. "Why couldn't you just leave Chelsea alone?"

It was almost a relief to have it out in the open — Dahlia had been starting to think that no one else even realized she was responsible. She didn't say anything. What was she going to say? Lisa was right. Dahlia had used Chelsea just like McMasters used people.

"This is all your fault," Lisa said.

To Dahlia's surprise, Michal shushed Lisa. "Hey," she said in a low voice to Dahlia. "Have you seen the ghosts since Chels went missing?"

"She told you about the ghosts?" Dahlia said.

"Of course she told us," Lisa snapped. "We're her best friends."

"Have you seen them since she went missing?" Michal repeated.

Dahlia shook her head. She noticed dully that it had begun to really rain outside. Lightning was visible on the horizon, with the storm clouds sweeping toward the camp.

Michal wiped her eyes with the sleeve of her shirt, but she kept looking at Dahlia. "Can you ask them? I mean, maybe they can help."

This was too much for Lisa. She burst out, "For God's sake, Michal, the ghosts are what lured Chelsea into this to begin with."

"No, they weren't," Michal said. She looked to Dahlia. "Were they?"

Dahlia shook her head again. "I don't think so. I think they were trying to warn us about McMasters."

"McMasters?" Lisa said. "You're saying some crazy old man has been living in the woods for, like, a million years and he took —"

"Not like that," Dahlia said. "He's dead, but —"

"Can you ask the ghosts?" Michal refused to be distracted. "Maybe they can help."

Dahlia sighed. "I guess I could ask them," she said. "But it's not like they come when I want them to. They hardly ever came when there were other people in the bunk either."

Michal stood, looking resolute. "C'mon, Lisa." She pulled Lisa toward the door. Lisa resisted for a moment, then let Michal lead her out the door. Outside, she heard Michal say to Alyssa, "We have to pee. Can you walk us to the bathroom?"

"I can't leave Dahlia alone in the bunk," Alyssa said.

"Selena's on the other side," Michal lied. "She'll be fine."

Alyssa didn't bother checking. Michal spoke so rarely, no one figured she could lie.

Dahlia heard their voices fade as they walked away, leaving her alone in the bunk.

She sank onto the bare mattress left on Michal's bed. The cabin looked naked, all the beds unmade, the cubbies bare. Her eyes finally filled with tears. Lisa was right. Chelsea was dead because Dahlia hadn't been brave enough or smart enough or somehow good enough to save her. She had failed.

She looked around the empty bunk. "Chelsea," she said. If David Schank had still been inside her, he probably could have summoned her spirit with the name. But all Dahlia had were her own memories. No Hebrew, no kabbala, no numerology aside from the scattering of things she remembered on her own.

Okay. Dahlia took a deep breath and thought about the maze. That was where Chelsea was trapped. Still alive. Probably not even that hungry. Yet. She focused on the feeling she'd had when she stepped into the maze, like the top of her head was off and energy was flooding into her body. She held that feeling in her mind and concentrated on Chelsea. She imagined a wire running between Chelsea and her.

And just like that, Chelsea was there, standing in the bunk before her.

For a moment, Dahlia thought she was really back. She was about to scream happily for Michal and Lisa. Then she realized: Chelsea's lips were moving, but no sounds were emerging.

"You can't be dead yet," Dahlia said. Still her tears resumed. Her fault. Chelsea was a ghost, and it was her fault.

Chelsea shook her head, looking annoyed. Dahlia noticed she was wearing the same clothes as when they'd gone into the woods — a towel wrapped over her bathing suit. She didn't seem cold, despite the chill of the incoming thunderstorm.

"I'm sorry," Dahlia whispered, letting the tears roll out of her eyes.

Chelsea curled the index fingers on both hands and pretended to rub her eyes, obviously mocking Dahlia's crying.

"What? So I'm sad," Dahlia said, although the truth was that she was getting a little irritated as well. Even mute, Chelsea was extremely aggravating. "I'm sorry I led you into the maze. It's my fault that you're stuck there, and it's my fault that the boys are —"

Dahlia stopped talking when she saw Chelsea was beckoning impatiently to her.

"What? Where do you want me to come?" Dahlia said. "Barry won't let me back in the maze. Anyway, there's nothing I can do. McMasters said there's nothing anyone can do."

Chelsea's lips moved, and she spread her hands in obvious frustration. Then she cupped her hand at her ear, miming the act of listening.

"I am listening. You know I can't hear ghosts." Dahlia said. Her stomach twisted. "Or whatever you are."

Chelsea pointed to a name graffitied on the wall.

"Hester Grunfield, 1996 to 1999?" Dahlia said out loud. "Can she hear ghosts?"

Chelsea shook her head furiously.

"Oh. I get it. It's a code." Dahlia said. For the first time since she'd entered the maze, she felt a surge of hope. She wrote down *Hester Grunfield*, and was just writing *1996*, when Chelsea waved her hand between the notebook and Dahlia's face. She looked up to see Chelsea tapping the name again. "What?" Dahlia said. "I was just writing down —"

Chelsea shook her head, looking increasingly frantic. Outside, the rain was picking up. In a few moments, no matter what Lisa and Michal did, Alyssa would come back and make them all go to the dining hall.

Chelsea pointed to Hester Grunfield again. Then, in a flurry of activity, she gestured to another four names: *Eddie Onstein (2007–2008), Linda Gomez (Chotrim 1996), Eva Hornick (1999–2003), Sam Green (2002)*.

As she was pointing to the last one, Dahlia heard the other girls returning from the bathroom. Chelsea's mouth was still moving, but as the door opened behind Dahlia, her image simply faded away.

Dahlia didn't look up at Lisa and Michal. She was too busy scribbling down the names. Chelsea had pointed to Linda twice. Had she intended that, or was that just some kind of tic? Did ghosts have tics? Not that Chelsea was a ghost. Dahlia must have summoned her still-living spirit from the maze. She tried hard to believe that.

Michal and Lisa walked into the cabin. They stood on either side of Dahlia.

"Did you see them?" Michal asked.

"I saw her," Dahlia said. "Chelsea, I mean."

"Oh God," Michal said. She bit the palm of her hand. "Is she already —"

"No. No," Dahlia said quickly. "I'm almost positive she's still alive." She looked back toward the wall where Chelsea had been standing, then down at the names she'd jotted. She couldn't imagine Chelsea using some kind of complicated code. Not that quickly, anyway. She showed the pad to them. "Do you recognize any of these names?"

Lisa and Michal looked over her shoulder. Lisa shook her head. Michal pointed to Eddie. "I sorta remember him, but he and Chelsea weren't friends or anything. He was a few years older."

On her other side, Lisa took a few steps away from Dahlia and started crying again.

Dahlia stared at the names furiously. "Hey. If you guys couldn't talk and had to communicate, how would you do it?"

"Sign language," Michal said.

"You know sign language?"

"No, but I —"

"She'd write a message," Lisa interrupted, rubbing her eyes. "That's what anyone would do."

Dahlia looked at the names again. What if Chelsea was just trying to write a message the easiest way possible? The easiest thing to do would be to spell a message using people's first names. The first letters spelled *H-E-L-E-S*. Maybe she was trying to say something about a helix and couldn't find a name starting with an *X*.

H-E-L-E-S. Scrambled, it could be "she le." Maybe Chelsea was going to write "She leaves," but was cut off. But what would that mean?

The door opened again, and Alyssa and Ofer walked in. "Okay, folks," Alyssa said. "We're all going to the dining hall now. If you have more packing to do, you'll have to do it when your parents get here."

"N-no," Dahlia said.

"Yes," Ofer said. "Now. *Acshav.*"

"I know you're sad," Alyssa said, "but everyone has to go to the dining hall."

"*Chodar ochel,*" Ofer said.

Dahlia closed her eyes and tried picturing exactly what Chelsea had done. She had been scanning the room for the names she wanted. And she had paused over Linda Gomez, tapping her name twice. . . .

Dahlia's eyes snapped open and she seized her notebook. Linda twice. If you took the first two letters of Linda you got *L-I*.

*H-E-L-I-E-S. He lies.*

Whatever else Chelsea was, she wasn't stupid. She wanted Dahlia to know that McMasters was still lying. About what? McMasters had told her how sharp she was, how she was just like him. Something about how the kids were lost in the higher dimensions, and nobody could do anything for them.

Dahlia froze. That was the lie. That had to be it. Chelsea was telling her that there was some way that she could help the kids. Some way that Dahlia could help her.

But she couldn't. She didn't have David in the back of her brain anymore. She barely knew any Hebrew. Her eyes welled up. Dahlia thought of Chelsea mocking her tears and pushed the tears away. She'd have time to cry later.

"Um. I have to pee," she said.

Alyssa frowned and glanced outside, where the rain was rapidly turning into a downpour. "Okay. I'll take Lisa and Michal. Ofer will wait for you." She raised her voice. "Selena." No answer. She walked over to the counselors' room, slid the door open, and looked across to the other side of the cabin. "I guess she already left. Come on, girls." Alyssa and the other two girls stepped out into the gathering gloom. A few seconds later, Dahlia could barely make out their silhouettes in the rain.

Dahlia pulled her rain boots on as slowly as she could. Anything to buy some time before she was in the dining hall. Once she was there, it would be impossible to help Chelsea, or the other kids she had doomed.

"*Y'allah*." Ofer pushed Dahlia gently until she stepped out the door into the rain.

Okay. She would wait until after the storm and then go to the maze and do *something*. She would just wait until the lightning passed.

*No*. By the time the storm passed, it would be too late. There'd be too many counselors at the dining hall for her to slip away. Anyway, her parents were planning on picking her up tomorrow morning. The truth was, if she didn't do something now, she never would. And that regret, she knew, would last as long as she was alive. She thought of David Schank. Longer, even.

She walked in front of Ofer to the bathroom. It was weird to see the camp so deserted.

Her gaze fell on the gazebo where the Kabbala Club met — used to meet. She had a sudden memory of her argument with Peter that first day, about how meaningless an alphanumeric code was, and how it couldn't possibly mean something when totally unrelated words added up to the same number. She remembered what she had said, but it was like remembering someone else's words. David Schank making himself felt in the back of her brain even then. She had mentioned a few words specifically. *Life* and *nothingness* and how they both added up to the number sixty-eight. As did *maze*.

"Ofer," she said suddenly as they reached the communal bathrooms, "how do you say 'life' in Hebrew?"

"Life?" Ofer said. "*Chai*."

Standing under the slight overhang at the bathroom door, rain spilling around them, she pulled out her notebook and pen. "Could you write it in Hebrew for me? And the word for 'nothingness' too?"

Ofer looked toward the shadows of the woods. Between the rain and dusk, darkness was already falling between the trees. "When we get to the *chodar ochel*. This is, eh, not the time for an *ivrit* lesson."

"Please. It'll just take a second."

Ofer reluctantly took the pen and notebook and quickly jotted two words in Hebrew. Glancing over his shoulder, Dahlia added up their numbers. She remembered the Hebrew alphabet from preparing for her Bat Mitzvah, and even without David, the calculations were pretty easy once you got the hang of it. The word for *nothingness* added up to sixty-eight, just like she'd said that day at the gazebo. The word for *life*, though, came to only eighteen.

"Is there another word for *life*? A longer word?"

Ofer thought for a moment. *"Chaim,"* he said. He jotted another two letters without her even asking.

Dahlia looked at it. *Sixty-eight.* "Thanks." She slipped the notebook back into her pocket.

Terrific. Now all she needed to do was get away from Ofer, get to the maze before it was pitch black, avoid any lightning summoned by McMasters and . . . what? Scribble the words in the dirt?

She walked into the girls' side of the bathroom. Ofer started to step in after her. "I'll wait outside your stall," he said.

"I'm not going to pee with you waiting outside the stall." Dahlia tried to sound as indignant as possible. She started bringing the door closed on Ofer's foot.

He rolled his eyes. "What? Has your brother never heard you —"

"Just wait here!" Dahlia said. "I'll lock the back door and scream if anyone comes in." She pulled the door firmly shut behind her. Thunder crashed directly overhead, but she didn't have time to hesitate. She raced through the bathroom, out the back door, and into the woods, not letting herself think about how stupid it was to be outside in a lightning storm. Not just outside, but surrounded by trees. They'd draw the lightning, but they'd also splinter and fall on her.

She focused on Chelsea and the two boys. Jaden and . . . She didn't even remember the other one's name. How did you save someone from a maze? Not from an evil spirit. That was the point. It wasn't McMasters who was keeping them there. It was the maze. A bunch of bushes in a pattern that happened to reach into other dimensions.

She had deliberately chosen to go through the woods, in case Ofer tried chasing her, but in the rainy dusk, it was hard to stay on the path. She kept veering into the surrounding bushes and trees, slender wet branches slapping at her face and hands. Water pooled on the lenses of her glasses, making it impossible to see. She took them off and made her way the best she could.

Lightning struck in the woods to her right. She kept going. "Lightning never strikes in the same place twice," she said.

A moment later, another bolt of lightning arced nearby, the

accompanying thunder so loud it felt like her head was exploding. "Almost never," she said.

Her hands were shaking, but she kept moving. She was afraid that if she stopped, she wouldn't be able to make herself start going again. There. The path to the swimming pool where the counselor had caught Rafe that afternoon. Another lightning bolt, and there. Through the rain she could see the fence. And there. The gap Barry had made in the fence.

She started jogging toward the gap. She didn't see the dark silhouette standing next to it until a strong hand closed on her wrist.

"Let me go!" she screamed. With five kids in the maze, McMasters must finally have the power to take a solid shape even outside it. She flailed her hand, knocking off sunglasses and a base-ball cap. Sunglasses in a rainstorm. "Barry," she said.

She squinted up at his face. Without the hat, the glowing letters on his forehead were subtle but unmistakable in the semidarkness. She had the faint memory — or maybe just the memory of a memory — of the feel of the gravelly earth beneath her fingernails as she scrawled the letters into the ground.

"You stupid?" He stepped between her and the maze. "It's not safe for you in there."

"I know," she said. "So what? He told you to keep children out of the maze. I'm not a child. Let me go."

For a moment, Barry just looked at her. Then one side of his lips twitched. He released Dahlia's wrist and eased himself slowly out of her way. "Awright," he said. "About time someone started cleaning up their own mess."

Dahlia stepped through the gap Barry had made in the fence. She froze when she felt the electrical charge building. This was where Schank had died. He'd been fighting to free the children, and McMasters had called down the lightning. Seventy-two years later, it would happen again.

A crack of thunder, deafeningly loud. She felt the lightning come for her.

CHAPTER **45**

**D**ahlia cringed, hands over her head to ward off the unwardable bolt of lightning.

But she felt only a tiny jolt, no worse than a static electricity shock. She waited for more, her ears still ringing with the massive thunderclap, but nothing happened. Slowly, she straightened up.

"Keep moving, you idiot," Barry barked. "Before he does it again."

She looked at Barry and saw something attached to the top of the fence: several feet of red-hot metal, twisted but still recognizable as something that might once have held a hamster. It was steaming in the rain as it cooled. Next to it, a thick wire ran down the fence into the ground.

"Seems to me we get too much lightning 'round the maze," Barry said. "So I mounted your friend's idiot contraption on the fence."

"Thanks," Dahlia said. She spun back toward the maze and stepped inside.

Nothing happened — no surge of power, no miraculously neat hedges. Just mud and rain and the smell of wet pine. She took a few steps forward, rounded the first bend in the path, and confronted the blackberry bramble that hadn't been cleared. She tried pushing past the bushes, but got nothing, for her trouble but a handful of thorns poking through her jeans.

"McMasters!" she shouted. No answer.

She wiped her glasses on her raincoat and put them back on her nose. The walls of the maze blocked the rain a bit, and she could see through the lenses again. Not that there was much to see — just rainwater dripping off the jumble of juniper, blackberry, and whatever other bushes were surrounding her.

She had to be missing something. The last time she walked into the maze, she had still had Schank's spirit inside her. Okay. Schank had said "Malchut" last time, right?

"Malchut," she said out loud. Nothing happened. Crap. What was she missing? Schank hadn't just said the words. An image had flickered across her mind at the same time.

"Malchut," she said again. This time, she visualized the roots of a tree, and felt something shifting. *Almost.* She kept the tree in her mind and put a castle on top of it: the symbol of Malchut, just like Peter had said. She held the castle in her head until she could virtually see its towers and spires and flags and whatever the little crinkles on top of a castle were called.

And suddenly, it was a beautiful sunny evening. The rain was gone. The path in front of her was a wide-open grassy lane, glowing a luminous green in the late evening sun as it stretched into the juniper maze ahead of her. She glanced behind her and saw the golden castle exactly like she'd envisioned it. She instinctively stepped toward it.

"Don't bother." Chelsea was standing next to her. She looked paler than usual. Despite the sudden mildness of the evening, she had her arms wrapped around herself for warmth. "Going back to the castle, I mean. They won't let you in or give you anything to drink." Her voice was hoarse.

"Okay," Dahlia said. "How can I get you out?"

"Oh God. You're seriously asking me?" Chelsea's laugh almost immediately turned into a coughing fit. When she stopped coughing, she looked at Dahlia, eyes watering. "No idea."

"But you told me he was lying. You must have some idea."

Chelsea's voice was even hoarser when she replied, "It was obvious that he was lying. Why else would he kiss up to you like that? There has to be something you can do. Why don't you ask your little spirit friend?"

"He's gone," Dahlia said.

Chelsea winced. "Great. Did you at least bring some water with you?"

Dahlia searched her pockets, knowing full well she didn't have any water. Along with her notebook and pen, there were a few crumpled tissues and that was it. "Sorry," she said. She took off her raincoat and handed it to Chelsea. "You look cold."

Chelsea took the jacket. "Why is your jacket wet?" She wiped the jacket over her face and licked her lips before putting it on.

"It's raining outside the maze." Dahlia glanced at the sunny field behind her. "I mean, in the real world." She stared off at the golden castle for another few moments before turning back to the path. "We have to keep walking. The other kids must be ahead of us."

"Walking," Chelsea said, "is harder than you think."

"Come on." Dahlia took Chelsea's hand and started forward. At first, it was like walking against a gentle summer breeze, but

314

slowly the wind they were walking into grew stronger. After a minute or two, it felt like they were pushing against a gale. Each step was a struggle, and they still didn't seem to be getting anywhere.

There had to be some trick to get through the maze, but without Schank, Dahlia had no idea how to do it. What had Peter said the name of the ninth sefira was? The English translation had been "foundation," she remembered that. "Foundation," she said, and tried visualizing the tree and the castle again. Nothing happened.

She pushed forward against the wind, pulling Chelsea with her. "How did the other kids get farther?"

"It's easier for little kids," a man's low voice answered. "Easier to get to the higher dimensions. Problem is, the higher you get, the harder it is to turn around." Dahlia spun to find McMasters had materialized on her other side and was walking with apparent ease next to her. He smiled at her companionably. "Welcome back."

"Get away from us!" Dahlia snapped.

"I don't think so," McMasters said. "So. You reconsider my offer?"

"I'm going to get them out of here." Dahlia was breathing so heavily her words came out as a pant.

He pretended concern. "You'd better stop playing around then. The boys don't have more than a few hours left. Funny thing, how much weaker boys are than girls. Let me tell you, those girls" — he shook his head ruefully — "they were tough. Amelia lasted almost twenty-four hours. Didn't cry at all after the first few."

"You're a monster," Dahlia said.

"You think?" McMasters said. "Everyone dies. Lightning hits you today or you cough up your lungs in forty years. In the scheme of things, what does it matter? Those girls would have been dead by now anyway. This way their lives meant something. They gave their lives to my search for the truth."

"Your search for power."

"Same thing, sweetheart. It takes power to seek the truth. It takes power to stay alive for long enough to see through the illusions." McMasters shrugged. "What does it matter if a few kids die so we can live forever? So we can figure out what we're really doing here? What does it matter if a *thousand* kids need to die? I mean, really. There are seven billion people on this planet. Who's going to miss a few?"

"It matters because it's wro —"

"Seven billion people," McMasters interrupted her. "And most of them are sheep. The world's no different for them living or dying." He turned to Chelsea and said, "You're tired, aren't you?"

Chelsea slowly lowered herself to sit on the grassy path. "I'm so tired," she said. Her face was alarmingly pale.

Dahlia leaned down to help her up. "Come on. Get up."

"Why bother?" McMasters said.

Chelsea nodded. "Why bother?"

"Leave her alone!" Dahlia said.

"What's it to you?" McMasters looked at Dahlia. He seemed honestly curious. "This girl's done nothing but mock you. Just because you're interested. Just because you want to figure out how the world works. Why do you care what happens to her?"

Despite everything, Dahlia hesitated. Why did she care? It wasn't that she liked Chelsea so much. It was just . . . "What else is there?" she said. "I mean, really? If other people don't matter, what does? What's the point of knowing secrets that you never tell anyone?" She tried again to help Chelsea to her feet. She couldn't even get Chelsea to look at her.

"What's the point?" McMasters repeated incredulously. "Knowledge is the point."

"Not if you don't tell anyone." Dahlia said. "If you don't tell anyone, then knowledge isn't anything." She pulled Chelsea's hand harder, and for a moment it seemed like Chelsea was on the verge of standing up.

Then McMasters snapped, "Close your eyes. Lie down."

Chelsea crumpled to the grass. Dahlia knelt next to her, and glared up at McMasters. "Leave her alone!" she said again.

McMasters smiled at her. "Make me. You did it before."

It took Dahlia a second to remember — memories from outside the maze were increasingly hazy — but then she had it. She'd made him leave the bunk when he was tormenting Amelia. "That was Schank," she said.

"Sweetheart," McMasters said, "before he met you, Schank didn't have the guts to make me do squat."

Dahlia wished McMasters would just shut up. Why was he bothering to taunt her, anyway? There was no mystery about how Schank had made him go away — he'd used the 72nd name. Which Dahlia didn't know.

She froze for a moment, marveling at how stupid she was, then took out her notebook. She still had the pages where she had practiced writing out the name for Tom. In the warm, late-evening sunlight, it was easy to see the letters pressed into the paper.

She let the letters fill her thoughts, trying to remember how it had felt when Schank had used the name. She was close; she knew she was close. She grasped after the memory of being Schank, of always having the name hovering in the back of her mind.

And like that, the name fell into place. The breeze shifted, coming from behind her now. Chelsea looked up, her face suddenly more energetic.

"That's it," Dahlia said. She leaned down and hauled Chelsea to her feet.

"I knew it!" McMasters's smile seemed genuine. He shook his finger at Dahlia. "I knew you were something special."

With the name in her mind, it seemed strange to Dahlia that she'd found McMasters so scary. He wasn't even as solid as the little girl ghosts. Unlike them, he'd died outside the maze. He was just a shadow of the person he'd been — a nasty, violent shadow — but a shadow nonetheless.

She flicked her fingers at him. It took the tiniest push of her will to send him so deep in the maze that she lost track of him. She wondered why he had bothered reappearing. Did he really think she was going to desert the other campers?

"C'mon," she said to Chelsea. She held the 72nd name in her mind as they moved forward.

"That's better," Chelsea muttered. Even the slope of the maze had changed, so they were strolling downhill, a pleasant breeze behind them.

As they walked, the boundaries of the path shifted. Instead of juniper bushes, the way was now bounded by very tall, white-barked trees on either side. The tree branches arced over their heads, so it felt like they were walking through a huge, white cathedral. Dahlia figured they had passed through one or two of the sefirot, and the trees were linked to whatever the new sefira was. How had it gone? Kingdom, foundation . . . splendor. That was the last one she had even let Peter get through before she lost interest.

Unlike the juniper bushes, there were spaces between the trees. Through them, Dahlia could see more of a seemingly endless forest of the white-barked trees. She wondered what would happen if she stepped off the path. She didn't try.

They found the two boys around the next bend. They were sitting next to each other, leaning against the same tree, both still wearing their bathing suits. The skinnier one was shivering, arms wrapped around his knees, staring into nowhere. The other one — Jaden — looked up at them as they rounded the corner. He nudged his friend until the other kid looked up too. "Who are they?" Jaden said. "More ghosts?"

"Th-th-that's Counselor Tom's sister," the skinny one said, his teeth chattering so much he could barely talk. "I am Mitchell and this is Jaden. D-d-do you have any water, Tom's sister?"

"I'm Dahlia," Dahlia said. "This is Chelsea. No water."

Mitchell slumped back against the tree. Dahlia pulled off her sweatshirt and dropped it in his lap. "Come on," she said. "Time to go."

Neither of the boys showed any signs of moving. Dahlia grabbed Mitchell's hand and pulled him to a standing position, then wrapped her sweatshirt around him.

"Come on, Jaden," she said. Jaden sluggishly extended his hand. He was heavier and harder to get up. As she heaved him to his feet, Dahlia worried that she wouldn't be able to make the boys follow her. Once they were up, though, they seemed willing enough to be led. They plodded silently after her, faces dazed and distant.

The trees grew bigger and darker as they took first one turn to the left, then another. Each time the maze turned, Dahlia thought they'd come to its center, but each time an additional fold of the path spiraled before them. She wondered if it would ever end.

After one of these turns, they came upon the older girl, Claudia. Unlike the boys, she was alert and waiting for them. She leapt to her feet the moment Dahlia and the others rounded the corner.

"Amelia said you might come back," she told Dahlia. "She wasn't sure, but she said you might."

"Hey," Jaden said slowly. "You were in our bunk the other night. Girls aren't supposed to come in our bunk without knocking. Noam Spinnaker doesn't wear any clothes at night."

Claudia looked at him scornfully. "We told you not to come down here. Stupid." She had a slight English accent, Dahlia thought. Or maybe that was just how people used to talk. Claudia looked back at Dahlia and Chelsea. "And we told the two of you not to let them."

Chelsea prodded Dahlia. "Come on," she rasped. "Let's go."

Dahlia led them onward.

Time passed. Dahlia wasn't sure if it was minutes or hours, but at some point she began to sense that they were getting closer to the center. She could feel it, the raw power emanating from the heart of the maze. The space beyond the path changed again as they walked. The trees grew squatter, their bark more yellow, until suddenly Dahlia found herself leading the kids down a corridor girded by low stone walls, made of large, yellowish rocks that glinted golden in the setting sun.

There were no trees in sight now; just the endless meandering of the walled labyrinth going into the distance behind them and to the sides as far as she could see. Looking around her, Dahlia couldn't tell if it was all just the twisting of the single path that she was on, or if there were several paths that converged behind her somewhere. They came around another turn, and the path ended in a small, grassy courtyard.

It was anticlimactic, Dahlia thought. After all that way, it just ended like this: a courtyard in the shape of a six-pointed star, carpeted with long grass and empty except for a sprinkling of yellow wildflowers. No magical glow of light, no monsters or angels or gods — just an empty courtyard.

The younger girl, Amelia, was perched on the low wall leading up to the courtyard. At the sight of Dahlia she hopped off. "Careful," she started to say. "Don't —" She broke off, thrusting her hand into her mouth. "Oh!"

Dahlia felt a sudden fierce pain in her left side and clapped her hand to her ribs. McMasters stepped past her, holding a small silver knife. Something wet was seeping through her shirt. Ow. That really hurt. When she looked down, she saw blood oozing through her fingers.

McMasters stood several yards in front of her, holding the knife. His face was stiff with concentration, but he managed to meet Dahlia's gaze with a smile. "Well," he said. "If you can't join 'em, kill 'em, right?"

His outline wavered, then solidified. Dahlia could feel his struggle to maintain the knife's physical manifestation. She applied more pressure to her side, trying not to think about how Chelsea's bleeding had made it impossible for her to leave the maze. She wasn't going to leave without the others, anyway. Again, she used the 72nd name to flick McMasters away. He disappeared, but she still felt him there, on the fringes of the maze, waiting for her attention to waver so he could come back. He was too attached to the maze for her to exorcise him the way he'd driven off poor David Schank.

She stepped into the grassy courtyard and glanced down. The side of her T-shirt was soaked through with blood. She wondered hazily if she'd lost too much blood to stay conscious. Obviously not, if she was wondering that.

Dahlia looked behind her just as Chelsea tried to follow her into the courtyard. There was a giant ringing sound, like an immense bell had been pounded, and Chelsea was thrown several steps backward.

"I'll just wait here," Chelsea said. She slid to a sitting position outside the entrance to the courtyard.

Amelia had vanished, Dahlia noted distractedly. McMasters had snatched her away with him. Okay. Worry about her later. First, figure out how to send them all home. It should be easy. Here she was in the center of the maze, all this power vibrating around her. She brought the 72nd name to her mind.

"Go home," she said. "All of you. Go home."

Nothing happened. After a moment, Chelsea frowned, a pale

imitation of her usual scowl. "That's the best you can do?" she said. "What's next — you want us to click our ruby slippers together?"

Dahlia rubbed her eyes. It was hard to think about anything aside from the feel of the blood — her blood — dripping through her fingers. All this power and no way to use it. What did she even know about kabbala without Schank? Names were important. Numbers too. Wait. Okay. She needed something to write on. Something that was part of the maze.

Her wandering gaze happened upon two small stones among the grass at her feet. She bent to pick them up, then froze as pain exploded from her wounded side. At first, she thought McMasters had stabbed her again, then she realized that bending had reopened the wound. She slowly straightened and took a shallow breath, waiting for the pain to subside.

Then she tried again, more carefully. This time she squatted, keeping her back very straight. She grasped for the stones, unable to look down without hurting her wound. There. One stone. Two. They were smooth, flat stones — the perfect kind for skipping on water. *Great. Real helpful, Dahlia. Now, if only there was a lake nearby and your side wasn't killing you, you could skip a few stones.*

She looked around as she straightened. The kids were all waiting, watching her, except for Amelia. She wondered what Amelia had been about to tell her when McMasters stabbed her.

Dahlia put the stones in her left hand, while continuing to press the base of that hand into her side. With her right hand, she reached into her jeans pocket. For a moment she panicked. Her pocket was empty. She thrust the hand into her left pocket, and there it was. Her pen. A disposable ballpoint she'd picked up somewhere.

She brought the pen to the stone and tried writing. The pen's point scratched over the stone's surface, but no ink came out. Maybe the stone was too rough, or the pen was out of ink. She remembered Schank scrawling in the dirt with his fingernails when he made the golem. His fingernail had torn, and he'd had a fleeting thought about how blood would make his writing more powerful. Fine.

She took a deep breath and gritted her teeth. Then, moving her hand away from her side, she dipped the tip of her pen into the blood oozing from her injury. She tried to avoid touching it to the actual wound, but it grazed close enough that she felt a lancing pain and jerked the pen away. The tip shone with a whitish light where the blood touched it, like it was reflecting the light of the moon, even though there was no moon visible. Above them, the sky was the deep blue of a clear evening twenty minutes before sunset.

She took her left hand off her wound, so she could bring the stones closer to her face. Her side hurt, but the lightheaded feeling wasn't too bad. She'd be fine to finish this. She hesitated. Which was a little too convenient. If McMasters could cut her, he could have killed her.

He must think she was an idiot. It was misdirection, plain and simple. He'd cut her to distract her from whatever Amelia was going to warn her about — probably about doing exactly what she was about to do. Fine. He wasn't the only one who knew about misdirection.

Her wound had begun to bleed again, and she jammed her left elbow and upper arm against it. Okay. Any magic trick needed patter for it to work.

"The thing is," she said to the other kids, trying to keep her voice steady, "there's this thing in *kabbala* where you add up the letters in a Hebrew word to get the word's number. If two words add up to the same number, they're supposed to somehow *be* the same thing."

Chelsea rolled her eyes but didn't say anything, probably because she was too tired to tell Dahlia off.

"'Maze,' for instance, adds up to sixty-eight. So does the Hebrew word for 'nothingness' — *chalal*." Dahlia brought the bloody tip of the pen to one of the stones in her hand and sketched the letters Ofer had shown her earlier. Each letter glowed as she wrote it. Before writing the third and final letter, she looked away. The moment she'd finished, she could feel the nothingness waiting to engulf her. All she had to do was look closely at the word or even think too hard about it and she would slide in. She closed her hand around the stone.

Dahlia took the second stone between her thumb and forefinger. Then she paused. "Bring her back," she said softly. "Or I won't write another letter. And you'll be trapped in the maze forever."

For a moment, nothing happened. Then McMasters and Amelia rematerialized, perched side by side on the wall next to the courtyard.

"He wants you to write 'life,'" Amelia said immediately. "He's trapped here too."

"I know," Dahlia said. "That's why he was so eager for me to remember the name before. I get it." She carefully, painfully, rewet the pen with her blood. Onward with the patter. "Like I was saying, the Hebrew word for 'nothingness' adds up to sixty-eight. Turns out that so does the Hebrew word for 'life.'" She wrote the first letter of *chaim* on the stone.

"Stop," Amelia said. "It will get him back to the real world. All the way back."

"He's dead," Chelsea said softly — so quietly Dahlia wouldn't have heard her, if not for the preternatural silence around them. "What's he going to do — rot on people?"

"He wouldn't be that dead," Amelia whispered.

McMasters looked at Dahlia and yawned. "Your choice, chief. Let me out, or stay here and watch your friends die."

Dahlia hesitated. The little girl was right. McMasters coming back to life would be worse than everything that had happened so far. He'd be free of the maze that had confined his spirit, and he'd still have the power of the 72nd name. She knew he'd have no hesitation about feeding more kids to the maze, or killing anyone who came between him and its power. And she wasn't sure it would be possible to kill him again, not if he got a few more children into the maze.

She looked around at the kids. It was the boys who decided her. They were slumped next to Chelsea and barely seemed to register what was going on. Mitchell had his eyes closed, and Jaden was staring at the grass between his feet. If she didn't do something now, it would be too late.

"All right," Dahlia said to them. "We'll get you home and

worry about McMasters later. Barry killed him once. He can do it again." She finished writing *chaim* on the second stone, closed her hand over it, then held it up, the word facing outward. "This is life."

Dahlia didn't so much see McMasters move as feel him. Feel him think: *At last.*

Feel the split second of rage when he realized his mistake.

Then he was gone. Really gone. Gone so far into nothingness that she didn't think he could ever come back.

Dahlia quickly pulled her hand down before the kids could see the stone she was holding. "Whoops," she said, her mouth dry with relief. The sleight of hand had worked. It had actually worked. "Wrong stone."

She opened her other hand, where she'd palmed the second stone — the one on which she'd written *chaim*. The letters written in her blood glistened in the evening light. "'Life.' This will take you home." She flinched when she looked at Amelia and Claudia. "I mean. Sort of."

It didn't take long. Chelsea elbowed Jaden and Mitchell until the boys roused enough to glance at the stone. In an instant, both boys were gone.

Behind them, Amelia hopped off the wall and stepped toward Dahlia. She smiled and looked at the stone, then she too vanished.

Which left Chelsea and Claudia. Chelsea weakly shook her head at Dahlia. She opened her mouth, but seemed to run out of energy before she spoke. Dahlia rubbed her eyes with her right hand. Her head was starting to hurt almost as much as her side. "Oh, go home," she said to Chelsea. "I know it was dangerous.

I know you might have looked at the nothingness stone when McMasters did."

Despite her words, she was surprised when Chelsea closed her mouth, looked at the stone Dahlia was holding out toward her, and disappeared. *She must really feel crappy*, Dahlia thought.

Claudia kept her eyes averted from the stone. "What happened to Amelia?" ·

"I don't know," Dahlia said honestly.

"I think she's dead now."

"She was dead seventy-two years ago." Dahlia sank to a sitting position. Her side really hurt.

"But *he* could have come back to life if he had looked at the right stone."

"Yeah," Dahlia said. "He thought he could, and I think he was right. He was a master of the name." That must have been how Schank had been able to come back as an ibur, too. Something about the 72nd name strengthening his spirit.

"That's not fair. That he could use it to stay alive and we can't."

"No," Dahlia said. Now that she wasn't so worried about McMasters, the full weight of her fatigue fell on her. Being in the center of the maze was so comfortable and safe, and she was so tired. She could fall asleep here, and when she woke up, she would fix everything. Dahlia blinked once heavily. "It's not fair," she agreed, no longer certain what she was talking about.

Claudia walked into the center of the maze, still keeping her eyes away from the stone Dahlia was holding toward her. She touched Dahlia's shoulder. "That's what I missed the most," she said. "Touching other people."

"I could stay here," Dahlia said, not really listening. McMasters had been right about that, anyway. Even without the kids, there was enormous power in the maze. She could think of plenty to do with it. Like heal her side. At just the thought, the skin and muscles started to knit back together.

Claudia grasped Dahlia's hand where she was holding the stone. "It's not real. What happens here, I mean. Not like what happens out there. I remember that much." She brought Dahlia's hand up until it was at her eye level, a little below Dahlia's shoulders. Dahlia noticed how small Claudia's hand was compared to her own. "Go home while you still can," Claudia said. Her gaze flickered down, and she was gone too.

Dahlia hesitated another moment. She could just go to sleep and decide when she woke up. Then she thought of McMasters, grinning and saying that she reminded him of what he was like when he was young. He would have stayed, she knew. Stayed until he had thoroughly mastered the power of the name and the maze. Returned a different, more powerful, even less human person.

She took a deep breath and let her gaze fall on the stone.

# CHAPTER 46

**B**lackness. Pitch blackness. Nothingness. She'd looked at the wrong stone. Dahlia knew a moment of blistering fear before she realized her eyes were closed.

She opened them.

Pitch black turned to dim light and shadows, glasses lenses blurred with rainwater. It was still drizzling. And warm, despite the water soaking her shirt. She glanced down at herself. Her T-shirt was still torn, and she smelled the coppery scent of blood. She reached down and cautiously probed her side. For a moment she felt an ache, a dim phantom of the pain she'd been in a few moments before. Then her fingers brushed past her ripped shirt and she touched smooth, unmarked skin beneath.

Over the sound of rainfall, she heard Jaden's voice. "Hey, get up, Mitchell! Get up. There's a bigger puddle over here." As her eyes adjusted, she saw the boys a few yards from her, partially obscured by bushes. Mitchell was crouched on his hands and knees, lapping water from a puddle like a dog.

Dahlia squinted through the rain. She and the boys seemed to have emerged in the center of the real-world labyrinth, with the bulk of the juniper bushes looming all around them. She looked around as best she could, but in the darkness and rain she couldn't make out the overgrown path.

Dahlia took a step toward the boys, but the blackberry brambles tore at her arms and she stopped moving. She cursed. After everything she'd been through that night, to be frustrated by a few blackberry bushes . . .

"Dahlia?" Tom's voice calling from a distance. "Dahlia? Is that you?"

"In here!" Dahlia shouted. "I found the other kids too." She wiped the water off her face.

Mitchell made his way through the bushes toward her. He had an impressive knack for getting through the bramble. Behind him, Jaden blundered with more difficulty.

"Chelsea?" Dahlia called.

"Over here." She could barely hear Chelsea's voice, but when she turned around, she saw the other girl was just a few feet away.

"I didn't like that at all," Mitchell said, arriving in the small hollow where Dahlia was standing. He extricated himself from a final bush and tilted his head upward. The rain was still trickling through the branches, though the bulk of the storm seemed to have passed. "No offense, sister of Counselor Tom."

"None taken."

Chelsea pushed through the bushes separating them. Steadying herself on Dahlia's shoulder, she lifted her face to the rain. After a few swallows, she said hoarsely, "What a dorky way to be rescued. Math and letters. It was like some crappy movie they'd show at Hebrew school."

"No need to thank me," Dahlia said. She took off her glasses to wipe the water from the lenses. "Really. It was my pleasure."

She heard Tom's voice again. He sounded farther off than before, probably because he was making his way through the labyrinth. She couldn't understand what he was saying, so she just shouted in reply.

It took about half an hour, although it felt like much longer, before they saw the flashlights approaching them. Tom and Ofer were each holding a machete, while counselors behind them pointed three or four flashlights to light their way.

"My God," Brad said when the group got closer. "How did you guys even get in here?"

No one answered. For a few moments the only sounds were the rain and the slash of the machetes against the bushes. "Great . . . timing . . ." Tom said between strokes. "Getting lost on a rainy night. We couldn't use a chain saw for fear of cutting you guys in the darkness."

"Not to mention ourselves," Brad said.

Ofer paused in his bushwhacking to say, "I am to feel very disappointed that you lied to me, Dahlia."

Dahlia had nursed the halfhearted hope that everything that had happened earlier that day would somehow be forgotten in their triumphant return. "Sorry," she said. "If everyone wasn't leaving tomorrow, you could send me home."

"No one's leaving tomorrow except for you first-session types," Brad said cheerfully. "All campers are hereby accounted for. We already called Aaron, and he's calling your parents back as we speak."

Tom broke through the last of the bushes and grabbed Dahlia's shoulders. For a moment, he just stared at her face. "Okay," he said quietly. "So maybe there was something to what you were saying before."

"I have no idea what you're talking about," Dahlia said.

Tom hugged her, getting her even more wet. "Don't do this again, okay?"

"Yeah. Okay." After a second or two, Dahlia hugged him back.

When Tom released her, Dahlia noticed that Ofer was still looking at her mournfully. She shrugged apologetically at him. "Sorry I ran away from you," she lied. She wasn't sorry at all. "I'm not sure what happened."

That was pretty much all Dahlia said for the next hour or two until people got tired of asking her: "I'm not sure what happened." By the time they got out of the maze, the other three kids seemed to have genuinely forgotten everything that occurred, although Dahlia wasn't sure she believed Chelsea's wide-eyed ignorance any more than her own.

They were all telling the same story. They had gotten lost in the woods, it had rained, the counselors had found them. The amazing thing was that everyone seemed to believe them. Never mind that the counselors had already combed through the woods for hours without finding anyone. Never mind that Dahlia had gone back five hours after the other kids had disappeared and met up with them in a completely impassable section of the maze. Never mind — and as far as Dahlia was concerned, this was clearly the least believable part of the story — never mind that Chelsea was supposed to have been wandering the woods with two much younger boys, when anyone who knew Chelsea knew that she had absolutely no interest in even talking to any of the younger kids, much less two of the most peculiar younger campers. None of it surprised anyone. The only thing that did seem to amaze everyone was the panic that had swept the camp. In hindsight, everyone knew all along that it was no big deal. Just a few campers lost in the woods who were bound to turn up.

As Alyssa said, when the girls were all safely reinstalled in their cabin, beds remade, lights out, the only noise the drip of rainwater from the cabin's gutters, "Just the usual camp drama. There's always something. I'm just sad we didn't get to have the party for the people who are going home tomorrow."

# CHAPTER 47

**O**n her way to the bathroom the next morning, Dahlia heard the far-off sound of machinery down by the maze. She had no urge to investigate.

A half hour or so later, she was walking with Rafe and Benjy from flag raising to breakfast. They passed Barry's house. He was putting out some food for Tramp, but he straightened when he saw Dahlia. He put his fingers on the brim of his hat. "Morning."

"Good morning," Dahlia said.

"Funny thing," he said. "A couple trees fell on the maze last night. Lots of lightning. Pretty dangerous, so I cut it all down." He looked at her meaningfully. "All of it. There's nothing down there you need to worry about anymore. You feel like traipsing around the woods, you go right ahead."

"Great," Dahlia said. She felt a nervous giggle waiting to escape from her throat, but she kept her face still. She was probably the first camper in seventy years to whom Barry had been friendly, and she didn't want to ruin it.

"See you," Barry said. He patted Tramp on the head and walked into his house.

At her side, Benjy was thunderstruck. "Did Barry just — just — *talk to you*? Can you please explain how that happened?"

Rafe shook his head. "That was the weirdest thing I've ever seen at camp."

"He said, like, six sentences in a row." Benjy looked at Barry's front door. "Maybe more."

It was weird what people noticed, Dahlia thought. People hadn't so much forgotten about the campers getting lost the day before as lost interest. A bunch of girls were crying at breakfast, but that was just because the first-session people were leaving. Dahlia was surprised that she was feeling a bit melancholy herself. Probably just the aftereffects of the night before. She rubbed her side, still half expecting to find an open wound there, instead of the scarcely visible scar she'd seen in that morning's shower.

Walking down the dining hall steps after breakfast, Dahlia saw that parents had already started arriving to pick up their kids. Down the road, crowds of campers were milling around outside every cabin, saying good-bye.

"Hey, Dahlia!" She turned to see Rafe jogging after her. "Wait up."

Dahlia relaxed. Rafe was the only person to whom she'd told the truth about the night before. It was nice for there to be one person who knew what had really happened — aside from Chelsea, who seemed determined to put the whole thing behind her as quickly as possible. They walked in companionable silence for a few moments, watching the kids carrying luggage to the cars of the early arrivals. The big-screen television was on in the rec center, showing movies for the campers who were staying for second session.

"So," Dahlia said as they arrived back at her cabin. "I guess this is it." Her parents would be on time, of course, and she wasn't going to run around saying good-bye to every person in the camp.

"Yea-ah." Rafe pronounced the word like it had two syllables. "Um. Maybe. I mean, depending on what you mean by 'it.' "

Dahlia was surprised at how hurt she felt. "I mean I'm leaving today." She extended her hand. "See you at the reunion, I guess." She suddenly wasn't sure she'd go to the reunion.

Rafe took her hand for a second, then dropped it. "Um, sure. You probably won't be mad by then. I mean if you're mad now. Which really you have no reason to be."

"I'm not mad," Dahlia said, then froze. "Wait. Why should I be mad?"

"Who said you should be mad?" he asked.

She looked at him warily. "What did you do?"

Rafe looked away. "Wee-eell."

"Will you stop with the drawl?" Dahlia said.

"Sorry. Nervous tic." He glanced at the road, where a constant stream of cars was driving past them toward the cabins. "So you know how last night they called all the missing kids' parents?"

"Um. No. But okay."

"We-ell."

"Rafe! Just come out and say it."

"Um. Okay. So, Aaron accidentally left the list of kids and phone numbers in the dining hall when we were all waiting there last night. I wrote down your phone number. You know, so we could stay in touch. Or so I could call your parents if — you know — you didn't come back. Then, when you all came back last night, I called your parents. Just spur of the moment, let them know you were fine, make sure they didn't come to get you last night. Then, when it turned out they had never been called in the first place, I had to figure out something to say. And, um, I mean . . . Well, obviously, I was pretending I was Aaron."

"Obviously." Dahlia was torn between wanting to laugh and wanting to throttle Rafe. The last thing she felt like doing was talking to her parents about what had happened in the maze. And she couldn't imagine her mother accepting some hazy "I'm not sure what happened" story.

"Right," Rafe said, clearly encouraged by her acceptance so far. "So there I am, pretending to be Aaron, and your parents are all like, 'Why are you calling us?' I figured you wouldn't want me to tell them about the maze."

"Good," she said. "So you didn't tell them about it?"

"Definitely not. I just told them that you decided to stay at camp for second session."

"Great," Dahlia said. Then the rest of his words registered. "Wait. What? I'm not staying at camp. No way. Uh-uh."

"Actually. Um. Right now you are. Second session is always better. And you'll have more fun without all the ghosts and crap."

"The ghosts were the best part of my summer," Dahlia said. All the warm feelings she'd been having toward Rafe evaporated. "And I have magic camp."

"Don't worry," Rafe said. "Aaron told them to come and get you a week early to get you to magic camp."

"Aaron?"

"I mean me, pretending to be Aaron."

"You're crazy. And you promised —"

"I promised I wouldn't pretend we were going out. I didn't. That would have been gross. The head of a camp and a thirteen-year-old . . ." He saw the look on her face and paused. "Look, I really think you should stay."

"You can't just . . ." Dahlia was fighting against it, but she couldn't help laughing. It was like he half believed he actually *was* the head of the camp. "Okay. Give me your phone. I'm going home today."

Rafe pulled out his cell phone and gave it to Dahlia.

Dahlia looked at it. She would go home and focus on magic and . . .

"Just touch the phone icon," Rafe said helpfully.

"I know how to use a cell phone." Dahlia hesitated, letting him stew for a few seconds. "If I stay here, we're not going out," she said. "Just to be clear."

Rafe raised his hands. "We're just friends."

*Friends*, Dahlia thought. *See, McMasters? I like people. I have friends.* She handed the phone back to Rafe. "Stop smiling," she said. "I was planning on staying anyway. I just wanted to make them drive up first. You know. Get them to take me out for a decent lunch."

"Sure," Rafe said. "Smart thinking. Sorry to mess that up."

"Stop smiling," she said again.

# ACKNOWLEDGMENTS

You can't write a book by yourself. Well, you can, I guess, but I had a lot of help with this one. In particular, I want to thank:

Cheryl Klein, my fantastic editor at Arthur A. Levine, for her supernatural ability to somehow keep 320 pages in her brain at once and understand not only how it all fits together, but how it can be improved. And to communicate this in language that doesn't offend my oh-so-tender sensibilities. Also the rest of the terrific editing team at Arthur A. Levine, including but not limited to Susan Jeffers Casel and Elizabeth Starr Baer.

Lindsay Ribar, my agent at Sanford Greenburger, for her keen and incisive help in making the manuscript better, and for getting the improved manuscript to Cheryl.

Patrick Rothfuss for referring me to Lindsay. Also for writing some great epic fantasy.

My generous and perceptive second and third readers, including Linda Demeulemeester (who has also served as an inspiration in writing middle grade fantasy), Tamar Goelman, Sarah Eisenstein, Ben Rosenbaum, and Samantha (Ling) Liu. Also to the members of the Helix Writing Group, who critiqued various bits of *The Path of Names* over the years.

Dr. Robert Adler Peckarar & Dr. Yael Chaver for help with the Yiddish.

Julie Esris for the incredible job she did on the novel's map.

My family for their support and patience (such as it was) as they waited to read this book. In particular, my uncle Hillel for his information about kabbala, which I proceeded to mangle and distort as I found necessary; my father for his quick ability to calculate the gematria of various Hebrew words; and my great uncle Yak for his stories about growing up in the 1930s Lower East Side.

I also want to call out to my class at Clarion West. This novel originated as a short story I wrote for the fifth week of the Clarion West writing workshop in 2001. I put it aside for about eight years, during which time I lost any record I had of the comments from my colleagues at Clarion. Still, I'm sure some inchoate memory of their wisdom remained when I started turning that little seed of a story into this novel.

I want to thank my babies for their smiles, giggles, and the enormous quantities of drool and other, less savory bodily fluids that they contributed to the revision process.

I want to thank Ellie for her charm, her intelligence, her multiple suggestions as far as the next Dahlia story, and for her constant and general insistence on knowing what happened next.

Finally I want to thank Jessica. You are a star wife, mother, planning visionary, and partner. And a great first reader. Thank you, thank you.

# ABOUT THE AUTHOR

**A**ri Goelman is a proud alumnus of Camp Galil (1983–1997), where he spent years as a camper, counselor, and camp director. Since then, he's earned a PhD at the Massachusetts Institute of Technology and worked as a researcher, teacher, writer, and stay-at-home dad. Ari's short stories have appeared in *Strange Horizons* and *Fantasy Magazine*, among other places. This is his first novel. He lives in Vancouver, British Columbia, with his family. Please visit his website at www.arigoelman.com.

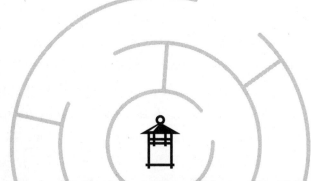

This book was edited by Cheryl Klein and designed by Yaffa Jaskoll. The text was set in Perpetua, with display type set in Copperplate Gothic. This book was printed and bound by R. R. Donnelley in Crawfordsville, Indiana. The manufacturing was supervised by Irene Huang.